NOT DEAD ENOUGH

TYFFANY D. NEIHEISER

VIKING

VIKING

An imprint of Penguin Random House LLC, New York

First published in the United States of America by Viking,
an imprint of Penguin Random House LLC, 2024

Visit us online at PenguinRandomHouse.com.

Library of Congress Cataloging-in-Publication Data is available.

ISBN 9780593205549

1st Printing

Printed in the United States of America

LSCH

Design by Opal Roengchai
Text set in Garamond MT Std

For Rob. Thanks for being the opposite of a dream killer.
This book wouldn't exist without you.

And for Mom and Dad. Thanks for buying eight-year-old me
a typewriter and telling me I could do anything I set my mind to.

SEPTEMBER

CHAPTER 1

I hated being awake at two a.m. It was the loneliest hour, the time when it was hardest to keep my thoughts in check. During the day, it was easier to pretend I wasn't broken. But at night, it was impossible to ignore. Even my cat, Paisley, was curled up asleep somewhere else. She never came into my room anymore.

The house creaked and I flinched. I never used to be like that. But now, everything made me jump.

It was just a settling noise. Probably.

But what if it wasn't?

Were the doors locked? I'd checked them an hour ago, but what if, when I checked them, I'd accidentally unlocked them?

My therapist, Gemma, told me my anxiety lied to me, and I knew she was right. But knowing something and feeling it were two different things. My brain knew the doors were locked. I remembered locking them.

But my anxiety whispered that I couldn't trust what I thought.

I huffed out a breath and got up.

I eased my bedroom door open and tiptoed downstairs, using my phone to light the hallway. I checked the front door, then the kitchen door. They were locked. Of course they were locked. I closed my eyes and sighed.

When I got back to my room, I stopped in the doorway. My room was cold, and it hadn't been a few minutes ago. Weird. I put on a sweatshirt and sat back down.

I thought about texting Lori or Ian, but normal people were asleep.

I'm the only one who'll ever love you, Charlotte. The memory of Jerry's voice echoed in my head.

If Jerry and I were still together, I could text him. He never cared if I woke him up. He'd send me videos of ocean waves and tell me stories of how we'd lie on the beach or build sandcastles. While he talked, I could almost smell the salt and feel the hot sand.

But I couldn't text Jerry anymore. That part of my life was over.

I rubbed my achy eyes. Eventually, I'd be able to sleep.

As I scrolled through my phone, I tapped my foot. I opened Awake All Night, an app for insomniacs like me. I'd never messaged anyone, but I liked knowing other people were awake too.

One of the dots was only a few miles away. I'd looked at his profile before, but never messaged him. *Starry_Nate, 16, Connoisseur of the Weird.* The next closest people were *Twinkletoes, 77, Former Ballroom Dancer*, and *Cogsworth, 43, Collects Talking Clocks.*

Starry_Nate's feed showed an article he'd shared about smart people being messy and staying up late. It was one I'd already read, but I skimmed it again. I hesitated. There was a Nate in a few of my classes. He seemed nice, but I'd never talked to him.

Randomly talking to someone wasn't something I normally did, and if I were less exhausted, maybe I would have been nervous. But I was tired of thinking about the locks and Jerry.

2:03 AM

Sew_What?

Did you actually read the
article before you shared it?

Starry_Nate

Of course. I read anything that
makes me look good. According
to the article, I'm a genius.

Sew_What?

You know it was probably written
by someone who wanted to justify
being messy and sleeping in, right?

Starry_Nate

Obviously. But that
doesn't mean it's wrong.

I smiled. But then the skin on the back of my neck prickled, like someone was watching me. I tried to ignore it. I was alone in the room. The doors were locked. Everything was fine.

2:10 AM

Sew_What?

What does "Connoisseur
of the Weird" mean?

Starry_Nate

Did you know bullfrogs don't sleep?

Okay, who even knew stuff like that? Did he just Google "weird random stuff"?

2:11 AM

Starry_Nate

Or snails have teeth?

I laughed, then covered my face with a pillow to muffle the noise. My parents would freak if they knew I was still up. They liked to pretend my insomnia wasn't happening. My mom always told me "fake it till you make it," meaning that I was supposed to pretend nothing was wrong, even when it was. She was the master of that, saying she was okay when she wasn't and putting on makeup as armor so no one would know she had feelings.

2:12 AM

Sew_What?

Gotcha. Weird random facts.

Starry_Nate

What is up with girls being

obsessed with Pride & Prejudice?

My smile faded. How did he know I loved *Pride and Prejudice*? But then I remembered my profile had a "favorite books" section, and I could breathe again. It didn't mean anything.

2:14 AM

Sew_What?

Does liking something make me obsessed?

It's not like I'm going to change my name to

Elizabeth and start wearing petticoats.

```
Starry_Nate
Changing your name would
be stepping over the crazy line.
```

The crazy line. I flinched and my fingers went still on my phone.

I knew he was joking but still, I hated that word. Sure, I called myself crazy sometimes, but it was different when someone else said it.

Thump.

I jolted and looked toward the sound. My heart sped up.

Everything looked the same as it had a moment ago. Except for the book now lying on the floor. It must have fallen off my nightstand. For no reason. I rubbed my hands up and down my arms, then picked up the book. It was cool to the touch. I hesitated, then put it back.

My laptop sat open on my desk, the screen saver giving my dark bedroom a subtle glow. I couldn't sleep in the dark anymore, so I left my laptop open as a night-light. I lay back down on my bed and scrolled through pictures on my phone. There was ten-year-old Lori and me in a blue kiddie pool in my backyard, our smiles and pink bathing suits matching, Lori's hair dark where mine was light, her skin tanned golden, while mine was pale and luminescent with sunscreen.

Next up was a picture of Ian and me when we were about twelve, grinning at the camera with our arms wrapped around each other, our faces smeared with icing from our annual birthday cake fight. Ian's brown skin had turned a richer shade of sepia from his being outside all summer. Then Ian standing alone in his basketball uniform. A freckled arm slung over his shoulder was the only indication that I'd cropped Jerry out.

My eyes pricked with tears, and I squeezed them shut, trying to remember who I'd been without Jerry. It was like taking the stitches out of leather. You could remove the thread, but the holes would still be there, showing something was missing.

When I was with Jerry, I'd become a version of myself I didn't recognize. Now that he was gone, I wasn't sure who I was or if I liked the person I'd become.

I threw my phone down, not wanting to think about how I used to be. I turned onto my back and stared at the beach poster on my ceiling.

My phone pinged.

2:23 AM

Starry_Nate
You still there?

I deleted the message I'd started writing. I started to delete my chat history, then remembered I didn't have to do that anymore. Jerry wouldn't see me messaging some other guy and get jealous. He couldn't accuse me of hiding things. He couldn't make me feel guilty.

I pushed the thoughts away. There was no point in thinking about any of that.

Because Jerry was dead, and he wasn't coming back.

CHAPTER 2

The next day, at lunch, I half listened to the buzz of conversations around me as I picked up an overcooked chicken nugget and tried to convince myself to take a bite. Lori was scrolling on her phone. Ian was sitting at the same table as us, but facing away.

Everyone around me was talking and laughing, eating their lunches. We were together in the middle of the cafeteria, but I might as well have been on a deserted island.

If Jerry were still here, he'd be the center of attention. He could turn even the most boring story, about turning in some homework late or getting caught using his phone in class, into an adventure. Even when he was talking to someone else, he'd be paying attention to me. He would have picked up my hand and kissed it. Or started thumb wrestling with me. I smiled a little and reached up to touch the locket I used to wear before remembering that it was in a box at home. My smile faded and my shoulders hunched.

Gavin plopped down next to Lori, his tray clattering on the table. "Aren't you two juniors?" he asked, looking back and forth at me and Lori.

I wanted to squirm, but I met his eyes. "Yes."

"So why are you guys at the senior table?" He gestured. "Run along with the other children."

Lori shifted to face him and scowled.

Ian turned toward us. "Leave them alone. They always sit with me and Jer—" Ian cleared his throat. "With me."

Gavin shrugged and turned away, talking to someone else.

Ian slung an arm around my shoulder. "Charlie."

"Ian." I looked at him and raised my eyebrows.

"What's with the gray?" He jerked his head toward my T-shirt.

I looked down at it and fidgeted self-consciously.

"Shut up," Lori said. "What's wrong with her shirt?"

Ian shook his head. "Wrong? Nothing. It's . . . fine, if that's what she's into." He shifted his eyes to me. "But what happened to the rainbow one? Or the one that said 'Stop Slut Shaming'?"

I smiled, remembering. I'd pieced together letters from a bunch of other T-shirts to make the slut shaming one, so it looked like an old-time ransom letter. It had taken weeks to find the right shirts at the thrift store, but it had been worth it.

"It's hidden at the back of my closet," I said. "My mom threw it away after the principal called her, but I rescued it from the trash."

"So why don't you wear them?" Ian asked. "This isn't you."

"I just . . ." Jerry's voice echoed in my head: *Why do you wear that weird shit? You'd be so pretty if you wore something feminine.* My smile faded.

That morning, I'd thought about wearing a tangerine-colored shirt I'd bought over the summer, but I couldn't make myself put it on. The gray shirt didn't feel right either, but I thought it would help me fade into the background. Apparently I was wrong.

"She's in mourning," Lori said. "Stop teasing her."

A headache crept across my temples and I looked down at my lunch.

"Sorry," Ian said. "Wear what you want. Not like you need my permission. I just . . ." Ian shook his head, squeezed me in a one-armed hug, then turned back to his other friends.

Lori leaned across the table toward me and said, in a low voice, "I still can't believe he's really gone."

"Neither can I." I pushed my tray away. "I still feel like any minute, he'll show up, acting like nothing happened."

"I just wish things would go back to the way they were before." Lori leaned her chin on her hands and sighed.

Lori had been through a lot in the last year too. Ever since her parents split up, it seemed like nothing went right for her. "Did your dad pick you up for dinner last night?"

Lori looked down at the table and shook her head. "He canceled. I guess taking his tacky whore to Hawaii must have tired him out."

I flinched a little at *whore* but didn't say anything. She already knew how I felt about words like that, and reminding her would just feel like kicking her while she was down. "I'm sorry." I handed her a slice of orange.

She took it, but didn't eat. "Let's not talk about me. Yes, my life sucks. But Jerry dying is the worst of all."

"Okay, I just . . . You've had an awful year."

"We both have. I just want this year to be over," she said. "Maybe I'll wake up on New Year's Day and find out everything was a bad dream— cheer squad, my parents, and JD."

I rubbed my left wrist. She couldn't blame me for her dad's midlife crisis or her bad breakup, but having to quit cheer might have been on me. "I'm sorry we dropped you—"

Lori grabbed my hand and squeezed it. "It wasn't your fault. Brittany and Angelica never take anything seriously. Coach should never have let them be bases."

I couldn't meet her eyes. My wrist had hurt that day, but I'd gone ahead with practice anyway. I should have sat out, but I didn't want anyone to ask how I hurt it.

"And anyway, who knew my mom would freak out so much over whiplash?" Lori rolled her eyes. "Like, yeah, it's a neck injury, but I'm totally fine." She laughed. "How do you always get me talking about me?"

I shrugged. "I guess I'm just not that interesting."

"Jerry thought you were," she said, sighing. "You two were perfect together."

I forced myself to smile, even while my shoulders tensed. Everyone thought Jerry had been the perfect boyfriend, but it was more complicated than that.

I think I'd be willing to live in any eternity, as long as you were there.

That's what he'd said to me on prom night. I wouldn't think about what happened after that. As long as I didn't think about the rest, it was a good memory.

I knew he loved me. I really did. I tried to focus on that instead of remembering all the times he hurt me. I took a deep breath and changed the subject. "How are things going with Aiden?"

A shadow crossed Lori's face. "Fine. He's cute, I guess." She fiddled with the necklace JD had given her.

I knew Lori still wasn't over JD, but I wasn't sure that them breaking up was a bad thing. Their relationship seemed sketchy. She'd never posted any pictures of him online, saying he was "shy." He went to another school, so I'd never met him. And then he'd broken up with Lori right before prom.

"I don't know." Lori's lips twisted. "I guess I'm not good at getting over things."

"It's not easy," I said quietly.

Lori nodded. "I wish I could be more like you. Nothing ever bothers you."

I laughed, a sharp, unhappy sound. I knew I'd become good at pretending, but I still expected *someone* to see through me. "Trust me, lots of things bother me." My mom always said that half the battle of being okay was just acting like it was true.

Lori shook her head like she was trying to shake off her mood. "Speaking of handling things . . . do you think Jerry's memorial is going to be terrible?"

I crossed my arms over my chest. "I still don't understand why we're having it now. He died months ago."

Lori shook her head. "He died so close to the end of the school year that it didn't make sense then. I'm glad Principal Karsko didn't just forget about him."

A loud laugh broke through the cafeteria noise. Lori and I turned to see Brittany sitting next to Ian, touching his arm. Lori's jaw tightened. "Can you believe her?" she asked in a low voice.

Brittany looked perfect, as usual, with her auburn hair in a perky ponytail and her tawny, flawless skin. She wore a pristine white T-shirt and looked untouchable. "What do you mean?"

Lori wrinkled her nose. "Her boyfriend almost *died*. It's like she doesn't even care. She dumped him, and look at her hanging all over Ian. Gross."

My stomach turned over. The night Jerry died, he and I had been leaving prom when he crashed his car into Brittany and Caleb's. Brittany broke her wrist and had bruises, but Caleb ended up with a traumatic brain injury. He'd been our star quarterback, but I'd heard he'd probably never walk again, let alone play football.

"It's not like they were even together that long," I said.

"Still. If she really loved him, she wouldn't be acting like that. You're not hanging all over any guy who looks at you."

"Jerry and I were together for over a year." My palms went sweaty.

"They weren't even together a month. And why do you care if she's flirting with Ian? Or anyone, really."

"I don't." Lori shrugged. "Have you seen what she's posting online about Jerry?"

I shook my head.

Lori huffed out a breath. "About the accident. And all these memes about drunk driving, like she's so perfect. It's like she doesn't know you aren't supposed to say bad things about someone who's dead. She's such a bitch."

My stomach sank. If Lori thought that was bad, I couldn't imagine what she'd say if I told her the truth about Jerry. But I couldn't. Any opportunity I'd had to tell the truth had died with him.

"You know, she's probably the one whose grip was off." Lori glared at Brittany. "She was always jealous that I beat her out for flyer. I'm not saying she did it on purpose, but sometimes when you really want something, you do it . . . what's the word?"

"Subconsciously?" I asked. "But I don't think she'd do that."

Lori rolled her shoulders. "Well, whatever. Brittany isn't my problem anymore. Field hockey is great. It's a lot of fun, and the other girls have been really great."

"Congrats on winning your first game."

"Yeah, thanks!" she said, but it sounded like she was forcing herself to sound excited. "Though it would be nice if someone came to cheer me on." She shrugged, like it didn't matter. "My mom had to work. Like that's a surprise."

"I'll come to a game," I said, then bit my lip. I didn't ever feel like going anywhere, but I'd force myself to go for Lori.

"Really?" she asked, brightening. "That would be awesome. Maybe we can go to the diner afterward. We haven't been there in forever."

"Yeah." I used my finger to smash one of the tater tots on my tray. "I'll go the next time I have off work."

"Where are you going?" Ian asked, turning toward us.

"Lori's field hockey game," I said.

Ian grabbed an unsquished tater tot off my lunch tray and popped it in his mouth. "I was there. Good game." He grinned at Lori.

Lori rolled her eyes. "Of course you were. Girls running around wearing short skirts."

"Hey, just because I enjoy ladies in hot uniforms doesn't diminish my school spirit." His eyes twinkled.

Lori laughed. "Bring Charlotte to a game. I need a cheering section."

"Your wish, my command." Ian shot Lori a grin.

She shook her head, then took her tray to the trash.

Ian bumped me with his shoulder. "You okay? You look tired."

I avoided Ian's gaze. "I'm fine. Just had a lot of homework last night."

He hesitated, like there was something more he wanted to say, and my heart sped up. When we were younger, he could always tell when I was lying. But I'd had a lot of practice in the last year, and had gotten better at it.

Finally, he said, "You know I'm here for you, right? That's never going to change."

"I know."

He waited for a second, like he was waiting for me to say something else. I knew I could talk to Ian, but I wasn't sure what to say. Then someone called his name, and he turned away.

During history, my eyes kept drifting two rows over to Nate. His brown hair was a little too long and he had dark circles under his eyes. He was pale, like he didn't get enough sun. His glasses were hooked in the front of his shirt. He rested his head on his left hand, and his right hand was curled around a pen like he meant to take notes. His eyes kept closing, which could have been because he was the guy who messaged me last night, or because Mr. Heller was the most boring teacher in existence.

He wore a pewter T-shirt with some kind of print on the front. I tried to see what it said, but it was wrinkled from him being hunched over. His eyes opened and locked on mine. Before I snapped my gaze back to my notebook, I saw a slow smile spread across his face. For the rest of class, I kept my head down and pretended to take notes, doodling in my notebook.

That night, when I was taking a quiz online, a notification from Starry_Nate popped up on my phone.

1:12 AM

Starry_Nate
Hey, are you up?

I grinned. After ghosting him the night before, I wasn't sure he'd message me again.

1:15 AM

Sew_What?

I'm here.

Starry_Nate

Did you know the bees are dying?

Sew_What?

I've heard that. Is that
what you think of in the
middle of the night?

Starry_Nate

Obviously. Doesn't everyone?

I thought of my dead boyfriend. I wasn't sure if thinking of dying bees was more or less depressing.

I was overthinking it. I hated my brain sometimes. He was just trying to keep it light. I could do that. Maybe.

1:20 AM

Sew_What?

I do online quizzes. Apparently
my perfect hair color is fuchsia.

Starry_Nate

I had no idea that
even was a color. Google pause.

Starry_Nate

Why can't they just say pink?

Why would anyone dye their

hair pink, anyway?

Sew_What?

Self-expression, to stand out,

to rebel. And it's not pink anyway.

It's more of a dark purply pink.

Starry_Nate

So what's wrong with

saying dark purply pink?

Sew_What?

Because there's a word for that.

It's fuchsia.

Starry_Nate

Okay, there's a word for it.

But it's a word no one understands.

Wouldn't it be better to

say it in a way everyone gets?

Sew_What?

So you're saying I should dumb

it down because someone

doesn't understand me?

Starry_Nate

Are you saying I'm dumb?

I hoped he was just messing around with me. Jerry had often twisted my words so he could get upset, and I was not doing that again.

1:25 AM

Sew_What?

Well, as long as you

don't say you don't

know what color puce is.

Starry_Nate

I had to look it up. That

one's pink too! Why do all

these awful colors have names?

Sew_What?

You're obviously anti-pink.

My phone flashed a warning that my battery was low, which was weird, since I'd plugged it in when I did my homework. Maybe the cord had been loose. I rolled over on my bed, grabbed the charger, and plugged it back in.

Tap, tap, tap.

I paused, waiting to see if the sound would come again.

Tap, tap, tap.

The sound was coming from the window, like a finger on the glass.

I peered out the window. The night was dark except for the streetlamp on the corner. The tree in front of my window partially blocked the view to the sidewalk. The branches swayed. But I didn't see branches touching the window.

Knock, knock.

I froze, then forced myself to take a breath. The soft knock had come from the door. One of my parents was awake, that was all.

I strode over to the door and opened it, but there was no one in the hallway.

My heart picked up speed. I leaned out my door again, looking left and right. Moonlight streamed through the hallway window, lighting the dark just enough to see I was alone.

Knock, knock.

I almost screamed as I whirled around. There. Someone was there. I saw them out of the corner of my eye.

Jerry.

I froze.

No no no. It couldn't be.

I turned slowly toward him, but he was gone, like he'd never been there. It was just my dresser mirror, throwing my reflection back at me, my eyes too wide and skin bleached of color.

But I'd seen him. Except, of course, I hadn't. I couldn't have. He was dead.

I wiped my clammy hands on my pajamas. My insides trembled with adrenaline.

I tried to make myself think logically. It was probably tree branches hitting the house and just sounded like someone knocking on my door.

I waited for the knocking to come again so I could pinpoint where it came from, but the house was silent now.

I put on headphones and turned the music up. Then I checked my texts.

1:27 AM

Starry_Nate
Not staunchly anti-pink.
But why 10,000 different names
for colors that all look the same?

Starry_Nate
You still there?

1:37 AM

Sew_What?
I'm here.
I just heard
something weird.

Starry_Nate
Like Bigfoot?

Sew_What?
Why would it be Bigfoot?

Starry_Nate
It wouldn't.
He's mostly in the
Pacific Northwest.

                                    Sew_What?
                        Got it. I'll take visiting
                            the Pacific Northwest
                            off my bucket list.

Starry_Nate
What else is on there?

Being able to sleep. Not flinching at loud noises. Not seeing my dead
boyfriend in the mirror. Not checking the locks a million times. But I
couldn't say any of that.
    Light. Keep it light.

                            1:39 AM
                                    Sew_What?
                        Make a dress out of duct tape
                            Time travel to 1980 and ask
                        them about their fashion choices
                        Win a chicken wing—eating contest
                            Re-create all of Taylor Swift's
                        videos using only stuffed animals.
                                        Your turn.

Starry_Nate
I suddenly feel boring. I
want to camp at the base of
the Grand Canyon and buy a
camera I can do star trails with.

His goals sounded real. They were simple things he could probably do, but just getting through each day was about all I could handle.

1:41 AM

Sew_What?
I don't actually have
a bucket list. I used to
have a bunch of things I
wanted to do, but I don't
even know anymore.

Starry_Nate
Why not?

I paused. Could I tell the truth?

1:42 AM

Sew_What?
Some bad things happened
to me and my life has
been weird since then.

It was true, just not the whole truth.

1:44 AM

Starry_Nate
Like you don't even know
who you are anymore?

> Sew_What?
>
> YES!

Starry_Nate

It's like everything is the
same but it's all different.

> Sew_What?
>
> Exactly.

> Sew_What?
>
> I don't even know why
> I'm telling you this.

Starry_Nate

It's scientifically proven
that between midnight and
three a.m. you can say things
that you can't at any other time.

> Sew_What?
>
> Maybe that's why I'm
> always up at this time.
> I have a lot to say.

Starry_Nate

Me too. Like, what will aliens
think of the music on the record

we sent out to space? Is Johnny

B. Goode the pinnacle of our

musical achievements?

We kept talking about random things for a while longer. When I started yawning, I realized that I was grinning. And that I hadn't thought of Jerry in almost an hour.

2:28 AM

Sew_What?

Hey, I'm going to try

to sleep now.

Starry_Nate

Me too. I can't stop yawning.

Sew_What?

Sorry I bored you to sleep.

Starry_Nate

I look forward to being

bored to sleep

tomorrow night.

CHAPTER 3

I half expected Nate to talk to me at school the next day, especially after he caught me staring at him twice in calculus and once in history. He smiled at me, but didn't approach me.

After dinner, I carried Paisley into my room, hoping she'd curl up with me while I did homework. She jumped onto my bed and kneaded the bedspread like she was going to lie down. Then she got stiff, hissed at the closet, and ran out. A chill raced down my spine. Cats could sense things. And my room freaked her out for some reason.

What if someone were hiding in the closet? What if they'd snuck in while I was at school and were waiting for me to fall asleep?

My breath came in little gasps. All I had to do was open the closet door, see that there was no one in there, and I'd be fine.

My heart pounded in my ears, drowning out every other sound. With shaking fingers, I grabbed the chilly knob and flung the door open.

Hangers swayed from the force of the door opening. My shoes were lined up on the floor. But no person. Nothing out of place.

I shivered as I scanned the room. My room had gotten chilly again. I put on a sweatshirt before sitting down to do my homework.

Jerry and I used to do homework together. I'd helped him with English and math, and he helped me with history and science. We'd been such a good team. Most of the time. Sometimes, when he hadn't gotten the grade he wanted on an essay or a test, he'd blamed me.

My phone buzzed, and my stomach jumped.

Jerry.

I shook my head. Even after all this time, I still thought of him first.

It was just a notification from my Word Bombs app, signaling that Gabe had made a move. I played back, and then he texted me.

8:21 PM

Gabe

Hey there! ☺

I closed my eyes and sighed. I didn't mind playing games with him, except that he often used it as an excuse to text me. And I didn't want to talk to him.

I had to, though. During the short time we'd been together, he told me about how the guys on the basketball team were always picking on him. And hanging out with me made him feel like someone actually cared.

But then I'd broken up with him for Jerry. I hadn't meant to hurt him, but it was complicated.

8:22 PM

Me

Hey.

Gabe

What's going on?

Me

Just homework.

Gabe

Are you ever coming back
to Game Club? We want to
play Mystery Room, but we
haven't found a replacement
for you

Gabe

Not that anyone could replace you.
You know what I mean

Me

Haha, yeah.

Gabe

Yeah, you'll come back?!

Gabe

We miss you

Gabe

I miss you

My stomach clenched. I didn't want to be mean, but I didn't want him to think I was flirting with him either. Jerry always said I flirted with other guys too much, but most of the time, I was just trying to be nice.

8:27 PM

                                                Me

                        No, I can't. I'm busy with
                        work and stuff. I just meant
                        that I knew what you meant.

Gabe

Okay, I get it.

I'm not going to

stop asking though. 😉

I straightened my pen and notebook, lining them up with the edge of
the desk. I'd bumped my pen mug, moving it out of place. I straightened
it so that the smiley face on the cupcake faced me.

8:31 PM

Gabe

So maybe I can stop by

Scoops the next time you work

                                                Me

                        My boss gets really mad when
                            people come to hang out.

I imagined Gabe coming into Scoops and forcing me to make polite
conversation with him. I saw him at school, and we had a couple classes
together, but there, the bell would ring or I'd have to be somewhere. If

he came to work, he could hang out as long as he wanted. He could even wait for me after work.

I was breathing too fast, and I tried to slow down.

I didn't know why I was freaking out. It wasn't like Gabe had ever hurt me.

8:32 PM

Gabe

The way you never want to hang out with me makes me think you're cheating on me again. LOL

Me

. . .

My face burned with the memory. Gabe and I had been dating for two weeks, and I'd liked him. I knew, even then, that it wasn't love or anything. But he texted me funny things and we laughed a lot when we hung out at Game Club.

I was supposed to meet him at the dance, but he was late. While I waited for him, Jerry asked me to dance. I'd danced with Jerry before, but that time felt different from the moment he pulled me into his arms.

"So, you and Gabe, huh?" he'd said.

"Yep."

"You know he's a loser, right?"

I'd shoved Jerry away. "I like him!"

Jerry pulled me back toward him and stared down at me. His look was so intense that it made my stomach flutter. "You can do better," he whispered. "He's not good enough for you. No one is." He leaned closer to me. "But I'll try to be."

And then he kissed me. I'd forgotten about Gabe and that we were in the middle of the school gym. All that existed was me and Jerry.

When we broke apart, I saw a horrified Gabe watching us from the side of the gym. I'd hurried after him to explain, to apologize. We'd broken up but tried to stay friends. Except that didn't work either because Gabe didn't actually want to be just friends.

8:39 PM

Gabe

Just kidding! Seriously,
though, when can we hang out?

I threw my phone down. Saying something terrible and then "just kidding" was such a jerk thing to do. But I'd been a jerk to him first, so it didn't seem right for me to call him on it.

My phone chimed again. And again. And again.

My hands started to shake. Jerry used to text me over and over when I didn't answer. Even if I was in the shower or napping, the accusations would start. *Who are you talking to? Why are you ignoring me? Don't you love me anymore?*

And when I'd finally respond, he'd call me names and tell me I was crazy. Or he'd ignore me until I apologized enough.

I couldn't catch my breath. My phone kept chiming.

I wished I could stop myself from thinking about the worst parts of Jerry. It didn't seem fair to remember the bad things now that he was gone. But my mind couldn't help going back there.

I took a breath. Gabe wasn't Jerry. I picked up my phone.

8:49 PM

Gabe

I said I was sorry

Gabe

You know I was just joking, right?

Gabe

It was a stupid joke. Obviously
you can't be cheating on me
because we aren't a couple

Gabe

I shouldn't have said that

Gabe

Okay, you're probably not
actually ignoring me, but I'm
freaking out because I didn't
mean to make you mad

Gabe

I'm really sorry

Me

I have to go. My mom is calling me.

Gabe

Okay! I'll talk to you later! ☺

It didn't matter what I said or how I responded. He just didn't get a clue. Like how he'd kissed me when Jerry and I were together. Jerry and I had gone to a party, but we got into an argument, so Gabe found me standing alone. We'd talked about what they were playing in Game Club. I wanted to go back, but Jerry wouldn't like it.

Then Gabe said, "You always seem so sad. I hate seeing you like this." And he leaned forward to kiss me. I put my hands up to push him away. My protest of "don't" was muffled when his lips connected with mine.

I was trying to push him off me when suddenly, he was airborne. Jerry stood in front of me, jaw clenched, eyes flashing with rage. "Are you okay?" he asked.

I nodded.

He stormed over to Gabe, grabbed him by the shirt, and punched him. Gabe crumpled to the ground, and then Jerry came back over to me. He dragged me out of the party, to his car.

He drove to an empty parking lot.

For a few very long minutes, he sat looking out the windshield, his hands clenched tightly on the steering wheel. Then he turned to me. "I told you. I told you he wasn't your friend. He just wants to get in your pants." His voice was low and choked with emotion. "But did you listen to me? No, of course not. Now everyone will think my girlfriend is a slut, off screwing around with some guy the minute my back's turned."

I shrank backward. "I'm sorry. I didn't—"

Jerry grabbed my arms and slammed me against the car door.

My breath whooshed out of me and my head hit the window so hard I saw stars.

When I got home that night, I'd had a headache. And the bruises on my arms where he'd grabbed me turned purple by the morning.

I thought about telling Jerry I couldn't keep dealing with his temper. But then, at school, he greeted me with a rose and a soft kiss. And he said, "I'm so sorry. I get so crazy sometimes. I just love you so much. More than anything. Please forgive me. I couldn't live with myself if you didn't forgive me."

Gabe had never even apologized. I knew he was lonely, so I didn't want to be mean to him. But ever since he kissed me, I didn't want to be around him. He was always trying to stand too close to me and acted like I owed him something. The problem was, I felt like I did. Like I hadn't quite paid for the mistake I made.

I sent Lori screenshots of the messages.

9:10 PM

Me

Help!

Lori

☺ You need to be like,

"Hey creeper, get a clue.

No one likes you."

                                                  Me
                                    That's really mean.

Lori
Yet effective

                                                  Me
                                Maybe he'll just go away?

Lori
☻ Creepy guys never just
go away. Block him, ghost him,
move to another state

                                                  Me
                                Move to another state?

Lori
It might work. Maybe

CHAPTER 4

Every other Tuesday, one of my parents took off work early to drive me to see my therapist. This week it was my dad. While I sat in Gemma's office, he took his laptop to the coffee shop around the corner.

Before I'd met Gemma the first time, I expected her to be white-haired and wear beige with sensible heels.

Gemma wore ripped jeans and chunky turquoise glasses. Her dusky olive skin was freckled across her cheeks, and her purple hair was pulled into a ponytail.

Her office also wasn't what I'd expected. She had a jungle of plants and a short wooden shelf full of books. We sat across from one another in comfortable armchairs, and she never took notes.

"Sometimes I feel like I'm losing my mind," I blurted out.

"Like when?" She looked at me like my answer really mattered to her. So many people didn't.

"Like when I check the locks over and over, even though I just checked them. Or when I have a panic attack because some guy is texting me."

Gemma nodded. "Tell me more about that. The panic attack about the guy texting you."

"So, there's this guy, Gabe. And we were together for like two weeks. And I . . . well, we broke up when Jerry and I got together. But now he won't stop texting me and he can't take a hint." I rambled on, trying to explain. "But it wasn't really about him texting me. I don't want him to, but I didn't freak out because of that. I—" I stopped, realizing I'd just talked myself into a corner. If I told her the real reason why it made me panic, that it reminded me of Jerry, then she'd want to talk about that. I'd never told anyone about the bad parts of Jerry, and I wasn't going to start now.

After the silence went on too long, Gemma pursed her lips. "I know that there are things you don't want to talk about. In psych terms, I'd call you guarded. You have something that you're protecting, some secret thing you don't want me to know."

"It's not like that. I just . . ." I looked down at my hands. We both knew I was lying.

Gemma just waited for me to stop talking, wearing her ever-patient expression. "It's okay to have secrets," she said, her voice gentle, "but only if the secrets feel good."

"I don't know what that means," I said.

Gemma smiled. "There are lots of great secrets, secrets that feel exciting and happy. What you got someone for their birthday. Maybe a secret crush on someone that you're not hiding but you just aren't ready to share."

"So . . . secrets you keep because you want to, not because you feel like you have to?" I turned it over in my mind. I'd never thought of secrets that way before.

"Exactly." She nodded. "But if you're keeping a secret that hurts you, then you need to talk about it. Otherwise, it's like a wound that never heals. Something you can't move past."

I'd sewed my secrets inside me, but her words snipped one of the threads. I was afraid the whole thing would unravel and spill open before I stitched it back up. "I'm not keeping secrets," I said, too quickly.

She put her hands up in the *calm down* gesture. "I'm here to help you, to support you. I can tell there's something more here. That being said, I won't force you to tell me. But I can only help so much if you won't or can't talk about it. I want to help you feel better, but you're the one who needs to do the actual work. So tell me, Charlotte . . . what is it you really want?"

What did I want? I wanted to feel better. To forget about all the things that made me feel terrible. Focusing on Jerry wouldn't make anything better. I was ready to focus on me, to leave the past behind me. Jerry had already taken too much from me. Every aspect of my life was influenced by him. Even what I wore.

For a long time, I'd worn what he liked. Not because I wanted to, but because my life was easier when I did what he wanted. And because he'd made me worry that the shirts I loved so much really were "weird" and "immature."

If I wanted to feel better, maybe I needed to figure out who I was. Me. Charlotte. Not Charlotte and Jerry.

I didn't know how to find myself. Or who I'd find if I went looking. But maybe I could start off by wearing something I liked. Something that made me feel like more than just Jerry's girlfriend again.

CHAPTER 5

When I got home, I went upstairs to finish my homework. While I was watching videos online, a notification popped up on my phone and I grabbed for it.

10:47 PM

Starry_Nate
Do you think aliens abducted
the people at Roanoke?

I grinned and shook my head.

10:47 PM

Sew_What?
I don't even know what
to say to that. Is that
how they say hello
where you come from?

Starry_Nate
No, that sounds more
like uhrifeo ahirue ahugio.

Sew_What?
That looks like what

happens when my cat walks

over the keyboard.

Starry_Nate

You caught me. I'm from

the Land of Cats.

Sew_What?

Is it nice there? Do you

just knock things off tables

and take naps all day?

My laptop caught my eye, and I froze. It should have been the screen saver, just random colors moving across the screen in a wave.

But instead, my Photos app was open on a picture of Jerry.

My breath caught in my throat as a sharp pain jabbed me in the heart.

The picture was Jerry and me at a school dance. Jerry looked amazing in jeans and a tight black T-shirt that showed off his muscles. He was looking down at me, smiling like I was everything to him. But what I remembered best about that night was feeling trapped, like I couldn't breathe and I'd never get away.

I moved to my computer to close Photos, but the pinwheel of death was rotating on-screen. The app wouldn't close.

Jerry kept smiling at me from the picture.

My hand trembled as I clicked again and again, but the pinwheel kept spinning.

I clicked Force Quit, and the app finally closed.

I rubbed my eyes. What just happened? I checked my laptop, scanning for pictures of Jerry. I didn't find any, which was how it was supposed to be. I'd deleted all the pictures of Jerry off my laptop and phone.

It must have just been a glitch. I didn't know how a glitch would open an app and show a picture that was deleted, but it had.

I closed my eyes. Maybe I was seeing things.

When I looked back at my phone, I had several messages, including a picture of a black Lab holding a chicken toy.

10:52 PM

Starry_Nate
Actually, I have a dog. Galileo.

Starry_Nate
That's not to say I'm just
a dog person. I like pretty
much all animals.

Sew_What?
Me too. Though I'm not
a fan of horses.

Starry_Nate
Horses, right? They're so
big and creepy! You just
know if they wanted to
take over the world,
they could totally do it.
And we couldn't stop them.

We'd be their human servants,
bringing them hay and cleaning
up after them.

                                    Sew_What?
                    Isn't that how horses live now?

Starry_Nate
The horse invasion has begun.

I laughed for a moment, then stopped and sighed. The Nate in
my classes had noticed me looking at him. I needed to know if he was
Starry_Nate or not before things got too weird.

                         10:59 PM

Starry_Nate
Did the horses abduct you?

                                    Sew_What?
                             No. I was just
                    wondering something.

Starry_Nate
What you'd say if you met
an alien tomorrow? Because
I wonder that all the time.

Part of me wished he was the Nate from school, but there was another part of me that hoped he wasn't. It was easier to talk to someone who might be a stranger.

11:01 PM

Sew_What?

Do I know you? I think you're

in a couple of my classes.

After a moment, he sent me a picture of him with the dog from earlier. It was a selfie of the Nate I recognized, with messy hair and wearing a lime-green T-shirt.

I liked knowing for sure that he was a real person and not some creeper old guy, but I didn't send that first message thinking he was someone I'd actually meet. I wasn't sure I could still be myself with him now that I knew him in real life.

But I knew who he was now, so there was no going back. I was not going to snap a selfie. My hair was in two braids, and I was in baggy, mismatched pajamas. I looked through the photos on my phone, but I didn't have any of me since Jerry died. The last ones taken of just me were from almost two years ago, when Jerry and I had first gotten together. I looked so different. I looked happy.

I sent Nate one of my favorites, me with my hair loose and wavy, wearing a funky retro orange and brown top.

11:02 PM

Starry_Nate

I'm pretty sure we've never

talked in person. Have we?

                                              Sew_What?

                            Nope. I would have remembered.

                                      Not many people talk

                                          about Roanoke.

              Starry_Nate

              I know! It's a conspiracy.

              They don't want us to know that

              aliens are abducting entire towns.

                                              Sew_What?

                      There would be panic in the streets.

My Photos app opened again. And there was a selfie of me and Jerry
in the woods. I wiped my clammy palms on my pajamas and moved
slowly to check my laptop.

There were no pictures of Jerry in Photos. Just like it was supposed to be.

What kind of glitch would do that? Was someone messing with me?
Had someone done something to my laptop?

If Jerry had known about computers, he would definitely have messed
with mine to make sure I was paying attention to him. But Jerry was dead,
and no one else would bother.

Could a ghost mess with my computer? I shook my head. That was a crazy
thought, and I didn't believe in ghosts anyway.

I shivered, then snuck out of my room to check the locks.

It was a lot warmer in the hallway. I'd have to tell my dad that the heat
in my room wasn't working.

My phone vibrated, and I glanced at it on my way down the stairs.

11:04 PM

Starry_Nate

So, what do you like to do

when you're staying up half

the night and not sleeping?

I typed as I walked.

11:05 PM

Sew_What?

Other than online quizzes?

Worry about things I

can't change, think about

how amazing sleep is,

watch cat videos.

Starry_Nate

I ponder the mysteries of the universe.

I stumbled over Paisley on the steps, making more noise than I intended. I froze, listening, but there was no sound from my parents' bedroom. After a moment, I started moving again. The doors were still locked.

11:06 PM

Sew_What?

No mysteries for me.

I like answers.

```
Starry_Nate
Yeah, answers are great,
but how often do people think
something's true when it's not?
```

That made me think of Jerry, how people thought they knew him just because he smiled and was a good student. Because he was a basketball star and made people feel good just by being around him. I thought I'd known him too because we'd been friends since we were kids. He'd rescued me from bullies and taught me how to ride a bike. How Jerry could be so sweet and caring but also sometimes hurt me was a mystery I didn't think I'd ever solve. Part of me didn't really want to solve it, because if I did, I might find out that I'd been the problem all along, like he always said.

```
                         11:08 PM

                                    Sew_What?
                    That's why I stick to online
                        quizzes. At least knowing
                           that my dream vacation
                        spot is Aruba makes sense.
                    I don't want anything more
                           complicated than that.


Starry_Nate
I wish everything were that easy.
```

CHAPTER 6

Jerry and I were hurtling straight for Caleb's car. I threw my hands up to protect my head—

The roar of my neighbor's loud engine startled me awake. I swallowed a scream and kicked at the blankets trapping my legs. I was in my room. The accident had happened already. I willed my heart to slow as I choked down lungsful of air.

Dawn broke, spilling milky light through my window. My laptop was still sitting open, casting light around my room.

Nothing can come between us.

You were made for me.

The song echoed in my head. I clapped my hands over my ears to block it out. The image of the broken windshield and my bloody prom dress flashed into my mind. I twisted facedown on my bed and wept into my pillow, wanting to escape.

Reliving that final moment was my punishment. I was being punished because I hadn't stopped Jerry from dying.

With shaking hands, I grabbed my journal and pen from my nightstand. Gemma said to dump my thoughts out on paper, so that's what I'd do. *Last night I dreamed about the accident again.*

As I wrote it down, it was like it was happening all over again.

The ballroom at Stokesay Castle was crowded with dancing couples. Dim lighting from the hanging chandeliers made it seem like a dream. It was prom night, and we were dancing to our song. Jerry sang the words to me as we swayed. "'Nothing can come between us. You were made for me. I'll never let you go. You're all that I can see.'"

He kissed me gently and smiled. "Have I told you how beautiful you look tonight?"

My stomach swooped as I smiled up at him. "Maybe a dozen times."

"Not nearly enough. You look amazing. How did I get so lucky?"

"Let's freeze this moment, never leave prom." I caressed his face. "What do you think?"

"I think I'd be willing to live in any eternity, as long as you were there."

I melted. He stroked my hair. I closed my eyes and leaned into his palm.

When the song ended, we left the dance floor. He wanted to get some punch, and I floated after him. Some guys from the basketball team were hanging out by the punch bowl. Jerry got himself a drink and started talking to them.

Ian came up and nudged me with his elbow. "You look great."

"You do too." I smiled.

"So when are you going to honor me with a dance, milady?" Ian asked.

My smile dimmed. Jerry was in a good mood, but probably not that good of a mood. I didn't want to insult Ian, though, so I just said, "Perhaps later, kind sir." I hoped my smile seemed playful instead of strained.

I checked where Jerry was, hoping he wouldn't be upset that Ian and I were talking, but he was looking at his phone, frowning and texting.

When he caught me watching him, his jaw tightened for a second before he relaxed into his normal public Jerry face.

Jerry came back over and clapped Ian on the back. "Are you flirting with my girl, bro?"

"Nah. Just keeping her company until you got back."

Jerry leaned over to kiss me, and I tasted liquor. He was drinking. My stomach plummeted. He offered me his cup. "Want some?"

"No, I'm okay," I said.

"Aren't you thirsty?" Jerry asked. "We've been dancing all night."

"I'll get my own cup," I said.

Ian grabbed a cup and handed it to me. "Here you go."

Jerry's eyes narrowed, and my stomach twisted. I shot Ian a small smile of thanks. Maybe he wouldn't notice that his nice gesture had pissed Jerry off. "Let's dance some more," I said, hoping to recapture Jerry's good mood.

Jerry grabbed my arm, and his fingers dug into my skin. I tried not to wince. "Let's take a walk," he said with a tight smile.

"Sure." Maybe once we got outside, he'd feel better. "See you later," I said to Ian.

Jerry dragged me through the crowd, and I tried to keep up, even though my heels made me unsteady. "You're hurting me," I finally whispered. "Slow down."

We got outside, and some other couples were clustered near the fountain in front of the castle. It had three tiers and was all lit up. No one paid any attention to us. Jerry pulled me around the corner, to where he was parked. We were alone. He shoved me, and I stumbled back several steps, trying to get my balance.

"I'm hurting you?" Jerry asked. "I'd never hurt you. What about all the times you hurt me?"

I rubbed my arm where he'd grabbed me.

He shook his head in disgust. "You're so fucking dramatic."

I tightened my lips so that I wouldn't argue with him. It only made him madder when I argued.

"You can't let me have one good night, can you?" He raked his hands through his hair. "Do you know what I had to go through to be here? My dad didn't want me wasting money on all this, but here I am, because you wanted to come."

"It's been wonderful." I took a step toward him.

He shook his head and put his hands up so I wouldn't touch him. "So why are you flirting with Ian?"

"I wasn't. I'd never . . ."

"I see the way you look at each other. I'm not blind."

"We're just friends."

He tugged his bow tie loose. "Perfect Ian with his perfect grades and perfect family. You think I'm trash, don't you? That's why you keep trying to throw me away."

I touched his arm. "I love you."

"Do the two of you laugh at poor Jerry with the drunk parents who can't even keep the lights on?"

I blinked back tears so I wouldn't ruin my makeup. "No! We'd never laugh at you."

"You're such a liar!" He threw his hand out in a sharp gesture.

I paused. My hands were shaking too much for me to hold the pen. I squeezed my eyes shut, trying not to think about what happened next. I couldn't tell anyone about it. Ever. If I could erase it from my memory, I'd do it.

I wish I could forget all of it. I wish I could forget Jer— Something cold grabbed my hand. My pen jerked, leaving a black scribble on the page. I shoved the journal away from me and threw down the pen. I jumped out of bed, slamming my hip on my nightstand so hard the lamp rattled.

Fingers. Cold fingers had grabbed my hand.

The pages of my journal fluttered, like a breeze had touched them. My muscles were bunched up, braced for a shove. I did a slow turn and tried to catch my breath.

There must have been a blast of cold air from somewhere. But my window and door were both closed. The heater wasn't blowing.

What if it's a ghost? My heart sounded loud in my ears. *If Jerry were haunting me . . .*

No. I would not think that. I'd been thinking of Jerry, and that made me imagine that he grabbed me.

I leaned down to smooth the pages of my journal. I forced myself to breathe slowly. There was nothing to freak out about.

I grabbed my pen and wrote in block letters: THERE'S NO SUCH THING AS GHOSTS.

I went to my closet to get dressed. I reached for another drab T-shirt but stopped. Half my closet was bright and cheerful, with T-shirts I'd made and clothes I'd altered. The other side had what Jerry had liked. Blouses in muted pastels like lavender or blush with classic lines and feminine details like ruffles or lace.

I never felt comfortable when I wore what he liked. And I barely felt like anyone at all in the gray and navy I wore lately.

I reached for an orange shirt with clashing geometric designs. I put it on, braided my hair, and did my makeup. When I looked at myself in the mirror, I smiled. I looked like someone I remembered.

Mom was in the kitchen drinking coffee and frowning at a PowerPoint slide on her laptop. She was wearing a white button-down and a black pencil skirt. I fed Paisley before her starved meows woke the neighbors.

Mom stood. "How do I look?" She twisted left and right. "The buttons aren't pulling, are they?"

"No, you look good," I said. "How come you're still home?"

"My boss scheduled a late meeting tonight," she said.

"Tonight? But tonight's the memorial." It wasn't even so much that I wanted her to go. But I didn't want to deal with it alone.

She sighed. "I know. I'm sorry."

"Couldn't you tell your boss that you were going to a memorial?"

Mom approached me and tried to draw me into a hug, but I moved away. "I already took off for his funeral back in May," she said. "He was family to us, but that doesn't matter to a company. When Grandma died, I only got three days off. Three days!"

I turned away to fix myself a to-go cup with a packet of hot chocolate, coffee, and lots of cream. I grabbed a granola bar from the pantry.

"Dad will go," Mom said.

"Yeah, right." He was allergic to people crying. There was no way he'd go.

"Charlotte, don't be rude."

"Sorry." I set my cup on the counter harder than necessary and turned back toward her.

Mom grimaced as she seemed to notice my outfit. "You're wearing that?"

My face burst into flames. "What's wrong with it?" I asked.

"I hoped you were past the 'look at me' phase."

If it wasn't a neutral, my mom didn't wear it. She hated that matching wasn't part of my religion. Though she hadn't complained about the pastels Jerry had liked.

I shrugged, hoping it wasn't obvious that she'd made me feel ugly. Even though I felt awkward now, I wasn't going to go back up to change.

"Just don't wear that to the memorial, okay? It's a solemn occasion. Wear the black dress we got you."

Like I didn't know that. "Fine."

On the bus, I felt like everyone was watching me, judging me. I tugged at the shirt, wishing I'd worn something a little less conspicuous.

When I got to history, I spotted Nate right away. He was wearing jeans and a black T-shirt with a print of an astronaut pushing a lawn mower on the moon. I wasn't sure if I should smile as I walked past him or keep my eyes on Lori. I sat down and Lori leaned toward me.

Nate came over, sat on the edge of my desk, and said, "I think I'd say, 'Don't kill me.' But after that, I'd definitely ask what they think of country music."

"What?" I asked, confused.

"What I'd say if I met an alien. I ponder it. My answer changes, though. If you ask me tomorrow, it'll be different."

I burst out laughing. Heads turned in my direction, and I went quiet. I glanced at Lori out of the corner of my eye. She was frowning.

Nate had been smiling, but when my expression went serious, his did too. He looked around the room, and people turned away, trying not to get caught staring. A couple of whispering girls put their heads together and giggled.

Nate stood up and rapped his knuckles lightly against my desk. "I'll talk to you later, right?" he asked quietly. He hesitated, waiting for me to respond.

"Definitely," I said.

Lori leaned toward me again. "What was that?"

But the bell rang before I could answer.

CHAPTER 7

After school, I got dressed for the memorial as slowly as possible. Maybe I could pretend to be sick. My stomach was upset, not that that was unusual.

Jerry's funeral had been terrible. It had felt like a bad dream, like I'd wake up and Jerry would still be there.

My parents had kept their arms around me, as if I'd fall without their support. Jerry's parents had glared at me during the burial, and when he was lowered into the ground, his mom fell on her knees and wailed. His sister, Sandy, had kept her head down and shoulders hunched like the weight of it all would crush her.

A text message dinged.

6:37 PM

Gabe

I'm not coming to the
memorial tonight but text me
if you need anything, ok?

I stared at his text. What did that even mean? And why would I *ever* text him instead of Lori or Ian?

6:38 PM

Gabe

I'll be thinking of you

I wrinkled my nose. Was that supposed to be comforting?

6:41 PM

Me

Okay, thanks.

When I got downstairs, my dad was on the phone. He held up a finger to signal for me to wait, then kept talking to whoever was on the line. It sounded like one of his employees.

"Hang on a second," he said, then pressed mute on his phone and looked at me. "Honey, I'm so sorry, but I have an emergency. I really wanted to go with you."

Surprise, surprise.

"I wish we could be there for you, but . . . work."

"It's okay," I said, knowing what was expected of me.

I thought he'd go right back to his call, but he pulled me into a hug. "You know how much Jerry meant to us. He was . . ." My dad shook his head. "He was such a good, polite kid. Hard worker, treated you like a princess. What happened to him was a damned shame."

"Yeah . . . it was," I said quietly.

"You're such a strong girl."

But I wasn't strong. And Jerry hadn't always treated me like a princess. My parents only saw what they wanted to.

I flushed. I shouldn't think about Jerry that way. It wasn't fair to him.

"It's fine," I said. "I'll text Ian."

Dad hesitated a moment, looking at me as if he were trying to decide if I was really okay. Then he looked at the phone in his hand, like he'd forgotten it. "Thanks." Dad kissed me on the top of my head. "Sorry."

He put the phone back to his ear as he started walking away. "Thanks for waiting. So the . . ."

I stood for a moment in the now silent kitchen, tempted to go back upstairs and pretend I'd forgotten about the memorial. Instead, I texted Ian.

He showed up a few minutes later, and I got in the front seat next to him. I buckled my seat belt, then closed my eyes and concentrated on breathing. Cars reminded me too much of the before and after. The before: me screaming and bracing myself in the second before we'd hit Caleb's car. And the after: the broken windshield, the blood streaming down my face, and how everything, inside and outside, had hurt.

"You okay?" Ian asked, patting my hand.

"Cars freak me out," I said, my voice tight.

"Yeah, of course they do. Is there anything I can do?"

I shook my head. "Distract me, maybe. Your parents aren't going?" It surprised me. Mr. and Mrs. Williamson were always there to support him.

Ian nodded. "My mom is driving separately. Dad's staying home with my sisters."

"She didn't want to drive with you?"

Ian shrugged. "She's not staying that long. She wanted to come, pay her respects, but she felt like it's for us. She didn't want to intrude."

Her thoughtfulness made tears spring to my eyes.

When we pulled up at the memorial, Ian cut the engine but didn't get out right away. He kept looking through the windshield, like he had to steel himself too. "Are you going to say anything?" Ian asked. "I'm giving a speech, and I think Lori's reading a poem."

"No, I . . ." There was both too much to say and not enough. "I can't."

Ian nodded. "I'm just hoping I make it all the way through without embarrassing myself."

We got out of the car and crossed to the football field, where everything was set up. Shanice, from the spirit squad, handed Ian and me unlit candles. Her face was set in serious lines. "I'm sorry about Jerry," she said.

"Thanks." I said.

"He was so funny!" she said, a smile lighting her face. "And he was always nice to me. When I found out he died, I cried for days."

He told me you never shut up. That if your mouth was open, gossip was falling out.

"Anyway, it's good to see you!"

"You too," I mumbled.

"Ian, can I just talk to you for one second?" Shanice asked.

He turned toward her and I took several steps away from them. I was already tired of it, and it hadn't even really started.

About two hundred people were gathered in the football field. The sun had set not long ago, and the field was turning to purple in the twilight. There was a table decorated with bouquets of flowers and photos of Jerry. Several people stood in front of the table, looking at the pictures and talking in low voices.

I spotted Brittany and her best friend Angelica, standing off to the side. Their heads were together like they were caught up in an intense conversation. Then Brittany looked at me and met my eyes. She glared, pressed her lips into a flat line, and looked away.

Why was she mad at me? I hadn't even talked to her in . . . I tried to remember. Probably not since before the accident, when we were both on the cheerleading squad. She'd texted me over the summer, and I'd never answered, but we were only friends at cheer. If it weren't for the squad, we would have never hung out.

Kyle, from the basketball team, approached me. "Hey, um . . . how are you?"

"Fine."

Kyle shuffled his feet. "Yeah. Um. I just wanted to say, you know, that Jerry was super cool. I mean, we worked together at the garden center last summer, and he kept me laughing. It was hot as balls, but it didn't suck going to work."

He said you were a slacker and you never stopped complaining. "Yeah, he was funny."

"So I'm, um . . . I'm sorry for your loss."

"Thanks." I turned away, forgetting that I was waiting for Ian.

Someone else stopped me. I wasn't sure, but I thought Jerry had had some classes with him. "I'm sorry about Jerry. He was a good guy. Rescued me one time when my car battery died."

As I moved through the crowd, more people stopped me. The names and faces blurred together.

"I was going to get dropped from the basketball team because I suck at chemistry, but Jerry helped me out."

"He was a good listener, you know? You could always count on him."

He told me how dumb you were, that you were too slow to be on the team, that you flirted with him and he thought you were ugly.

Listening to everyone talk about how funny Jerry was, how helpful, how dependable, made it feel like I'd made up the other side of Jerry. But I hadn't. I had the scars to prove it. I rubbed my finger along the one on my head.

Because I'd kept his secrets, none of these people knew what he was really like.

Something shifted inside me. It was like those hidden 3D pictures. You couldn't see the whole picture unless you looked at it in a certain way.

Just because no one had seen that side of him didn't mean it wasn't real. It just depended on how you looked at him.

I thought I was supposed to keep his secrets, that that's what you did for someone you loved.

Gemma said not to keep a secret that made me feel bad. Which sounded easy enough, except that I wasn't sure telling the truth would make me feel any better. No matter what, I ended up feeling terrible.

Ian came up beside me. "There you are. I've been looking for you."

"Oh . . . yeah. Everyone has been talking to me about Jerry."

"Yeah, me too." He blew out a breath. "Sandy's here. We should go say hi." He took my hand and led me over to her.

I didn't want to talk to Sandy. It wasn't that I didn't like her. It's just, what was I supposed to say to my dead boyfriend's sister? We'd always gotten along but it wasn't like we were close.

She was a plain-looking thirteen-year-old with sallow skin, piercing dark brown eyes, dirty-blond hair, and oversize glasses that covered half her face.

Tonight she was wearing dark eyeliner and wine-colored lipstick. She was probably trying to look older, but the makeup didn't suit her. She was with two high school girls. One of them was wearing a jean jacket, and the other had a mass of curly brown hair. Sandy was crying, and jean-jacket girl had an arm wrapped around her shoulders.

Ian stopped in front of the girls. "Hey, sweetie," he said softly.

Sandy looked up at him and then lurched into his arms. "This sucks so much." She sobbed while the rest of us stood around awkwardly.

When she started sniffling, Ian released her and took a pack of tissues out of his pocket. He handed one to Sandy. "My mom made me bring these."

Sandy laughed a little and blew her nose loudly. "My parents said they were going to come but . . . you know."

Ian nodded. We both knew what she meant. By this time of night, they were probably both too drunk to go anywhere.

Ian nodded at the girls. "Hi, Penny."

The curly-haired one nodded.

"Renee."

Jean-jacket girl said, "Hey."

"Are you going to say anything?" Ian asked, turning back to Sandy.

Sandy shook her head. "No, I just wanted to be here. I wanted to listen to people talk about him." She looked over at me. "Are you going to say anything?"

"No."

She frowned. "Why not?"

I looked past her, to the groups of people milling about. "I don't . . . know what to say."

"How about how much you loved him? How about that he was your whole world?" As she spoke, her voice kept rising. "If he were still around and you were dead, that's what he'd say about you."

"Sandy," Ian said softly, disapproval in his voice.

"No, if she were the one who died, he'd be miserable." Sandy gestured past me. "Those girls over there seem sadder than she is!"

I glanced around. A group of girls with tears running down their faces was watching us.

There was a time when I would have grieved and it wouldn't have been complicated. It wouldn't have been this messy knot of confusion tangling in my stomach. I had cried when I was alone in my room. But most of my tears had been used up while Jerry was still alive.

Sandy's whole body seemed to sag. "It hurts so much. I miss him so much."

"I miss him too," Ian said.

Sandy looked toward me, like she wanted me to say I missed him. Of course I missed him, but it wasn't that simple. I didn't miss making up stories about why I had bruises or worrying that I'd get in trouble any time I talked to a guy.

I must have paused too long, because Sandy looked furious. "Why did you even come?" she asked.

Because I'm supposed to. But of course, I couldn't say that.

"Sandy, come on," Ian said. "You know why she's here."

"He was right," Sandy said, like she was talking to herself. "I didn't want to believe him, but it was true."

My stomach sank.

"What's true?" Ian asked.

"The two of you." Sandy's lip curled. "You're together now, aren't you?" Her face was blotchy red and furious, but her lips were trembling and I could see she was close to tears again.

"What? No." Ian's tone was as if Sandy had asked him to eat live spiders.

"We're just friends," I said softly. "That's all we've ever been." Jerry had talked trash about other people to me, and I realized, for the first time, that Sandy was the one he'd talked to about me.

Sandy jabbed her finger in my direction. "You broke his heart!"

I went cold all over. How did she know about that? She couldn't know about that. No one knew. "What . . . what do you mean?"

Sandy started crying again, her hands covering her face as her shoulders shook. Renee put an arm around her. "Just go," Renee said to me.

"This is hard enough without her having to deal with you."

I wished there was something I could say to help, but anything I said would probably just make it worse. So I turned and walked away, leaving Ian standing there with Sandy and her friends.

I wanted a few seconds of quiet, but Lori threaded her way through the crowd to me. I closed my eyes, willing myself not to cry.

Lori grabbed my free hand. "When did you get here? I've been looking for you."

"Not long ago."

Lori's eyes were red and puffy. "I keep expecting him to walk into the middle of this and be like, 'Just kidding! I'm not really dead!'"

I shivered and thought of the cold fingers that had touched my hand.

"How are you holding up?" she asked.

I fidgeted with the buttons on my dress. "It's really hard to be here." That, at least, was true.

Lori sniffled. "I miss him so much."

Principal Karsko tapped a microphone. "Hello, everyone."

"We have to get closer," Lori whispered. I didn't move for a moment, wishing I could hide somewhere. But then I let Lori pull me through the crowd.

"Thanks for coming. Jerry Stone was a fine young man, a good student, and an excellent basketball player. He's been greatly missed since the tragic accident that took him from us. Please bow your heads for a moment of silence."

Lori and I stopped. People did as he said, but I peeked under my lashes. I heard quiet crying, saw several girls clustered together, holding on to one another.

"Thank you," Principal Karsko said. "I'd like to start lighting the candles now, and while we do that, one of Jerry's friends will read a poem."

We were at the front of the crowd now, and Lori squeezed my hand before she let it go, then moved beside Principal Karsko. Ian joined them. Sandy was off to the side, as far from me as she could get and still be in the front. Penny had her arm wrapped around Sandy's shoulders.

Principal Karsko lit his candle, then tapped it to Lori's. She lit Ian's and he walked to me and lit my candle. I had no idea who was standing beside me, but I lit their candle, then so on. As the candles started dotting the field, Lori recited.

> "Are the dead really gone
> If they live on in your heart?"

Tears glimmered in Lori's eyes, but her voice was strong. I tuned her out as she kept reading. Despite myself, I could easily imagine what Jerry would say about all this. *It's ridiculous, right? All these people, devastated by my death.* He'd put his arm around me and pull me tight against his side. *This doesn't have anything to do with me. They should be blasting Lyrical Lobotomy's latest album, serving pizza, and telling jokes while we all laugh our asses off.*

Lori finished the poem, and there was a light smattering of applause.

Ian stepped up to the mic. "Hey, everyone." He cleared his throat as several people said "hey" back. "I met Jerry in first grade. We got into a dispute over a kickball game and ended up punching each other until teachers broke it up. But we were brothers from that day.

"Charlotte moved down the street from me when I was nine, and the three of us did everything together from then on. When we were kids, we used to play this game. Charlotte came up with it, I think. She read all the time, and we'd pretend to be people from the stories. We were orphans or witches and wizards. But our favorite one was when we pretended to be aliens."

I closed my eyes, wishing that would block out the sound of Ian's voice. But as he talked, I remembered the way we looked as kids. Me in my blond pigtails, Jerry with his freckled sunburned skin, and Ian, awkward with the gangly limbs he hadn't yet grown into.

"We'd walk around the neighborhood or explore the woods and act like we didn't know what anything was. We'd hide behind bushes and trees, trying not to get spotted by 'the locals.' Jerry was the best at it. He'd be like, 'Why do the locals stare at these strange devices? Are they hypnotized by the tiny rectangle?'" Ian chuckled, and so did several other people.

Tears tried to escape from my closed eyes, but I wouldn't let them. I blinked them back and sucked in a deep breath, trapping the pain back inside where it belonged. Even on days he'd hurt me, on days he made me feel worthless, if he tried, Jerry could make me laugh.

"The day Jerry died, a piece of me died too. Every day, I wake up, and it hits me all over again that he's gone. Of course, if he were here, listening to this, he'd say 'Suck it up, buttercup,' or one of his other really insightful sayings."

That got a laugh out of the crowd.

"This is what I know about Jerry. He was funny and kind. He was loyal, and loved by anyone who ever met him. The two people he loved the most were his sister, Sandy, and his girlfriend, Charlotte. And I will miss him every day of my life." He cleared his throat again. "Anyway, thanks for listening." Ian stepped away from the mic, and got much more enthusiastic applause than Lori had. She was still standing there, her head bowed and crying.

Principal Karsko took the mic again. "Thanks, everyone. There's a poster on the back table where students can write messages to Jerry. It will be on display in the trophy case for the remainder of the school year. We'll now open up the mic for anyone who'd like to share a story or memory about Jerry."

Someone bumped into me. I looked around, and there were so many people, so many faces that they went blurry. Sweat broke out on my body. They were standing too close. I couldn't move. Couldn't breathe. My heart started to pound as the panic attack crept in.

I searched for Ian, but my vision was a narrow tunnel. I was going to lose it in the middle of the crowd. Everyone would see how crazy I was. Maybe Sandy would say I was faking it. Or maybe I really was dying this time.

I fumbled through the crowd, bumping into people.

Someone grabbed my arm. "Charlotte? Are you okay?"

My vision was too narrow to see who it was, but I thought I recognized the voice.

The person led me somewhere, and I stumbled after them, trying not to collapse into a blubbering mess.

"I'll get you some water. Stay here."

I sank to the ground and gathered my dress fabric in my hands. I ran my fingers over the bumpy stitches along the hem.

My vision started to open back up and my breathing slowed down a little. Gemma always told me that even though I felt like I was dying, panic attacks wouldn't kill me.

I finally noticed my surroundings. Whoever had helped me had led me under the bleachers. Some light reached through the seats in stripes, but it was mostly dark and quiet. No one could see me here. No one would come up to me to talk about Jerry.

I stood, leaned against a metal post, and kept concentrating on the material of my dress.

Lori appeared, holding a bottle of water. "Here," she said, handing it over. "Drink it slowly."

The cold water tasted good, washing the stale dryness out of my mouth. "Thanks for rescuing me."

"Anytime. It's what we do, right?"

I smiled. "Yeah, like the time I saved you from flashing your Wonder Woman underwear everywhere."

Lori laughed. "Seriously."

Her dress had ripped, and I'd walked behind her, hiding the tear until I could fix it.

She shook her head. "You were the only fifth grader who'd carry a sewing kit in her backpack."

"Hey, you never know when you'll need it," I said.

She cocked her head. "You look a little better. Are you okay?"

"I don't know." I ran a shaky hand over my face. "I'm so confused."

"About what?"

"I . . . Listening to everyone talk about Jerry . . . it just feels like no one else really knew him."

"I know what you mean," Lori said.

"And it's just . . . sometimes he said awful things about people. He could be so mean. And sometimes he was . . . mean to me." I watched Lori closely, unsure how she'd react.

"*Mean* to you? Mean how?" Lori's face went blank.

I couldn't hold my secrets in anymore. They were straining at the seams, ready to burst out. "He was mad at me all the time. He wanted me to dress the way he told me and wear my hair the way he said. I wasn't allowed to talk to other guys, and he demanded all my passwords so he could check up on me."

Lori's face cleared. "He just wanted you all to himself. Because he loved you so much." She half smiled and her eyes shone with tears.

"That's not all. He . . ." My heart pounded so loudly in my ears, I could barely hear my own voice. "He shoved me sometimes. He'd grab me and leave bruises. I was afraid of him."

"What?" Lori blinked a few times.

I had to look away from her. "He'd grab me and leave bruises," I repeated, my voice getting quieter. "I was afraid of him."

"Sometimes? Like more than once?"

"Lots of times. I covered them up with makeup or long sleeves. Sometimes I said the marks were from cheerleading or whatever."

Lori's eyes lost focus, like she was trying to remember seeing the bruises. "Did he ever hit you?"

"Well, no . . . he didn't *hit* me." My stomach knotted. Shoving, grabbing, and hair pulling weren't hitting, exactly.

"Wow," she said. "I just . . . Wow."

We were silent for several moments, and doubt crept into the silence. Jerry always told me I made a big deal of nothing when I tried to talk to him about it.

"I guess I can't . . . I mean, it's hard for me to imagine. Didn't he always take care of you?" Lori cocked her head. "Like that time you twisted your ankle, and he made you keep your foot up and brought you ice packs."

"He wouldn't let me get up and do anything," I said, remembering how sweet he'd been. "He kept making me hot chocolate."

"And at school, he got permission to leave early to help you to every class."

Jerry could charm anyone, even the people in the school office.

"And he was always doing romantic things for you," Lori continued. "He gave you presents and cards, bought you clothes. He brushed your hair and painted your nails."

Lots of girls told me how jealous they were of all the nice things he did for me.

"That's true," I said. It should have made me feel better, but that sick, twisted feeling in my stomach lingered.

Lori hugged me. "Nobody's perfect! Yeah, he talked about people behind their backs, but isn't how he treated them what really matters?"

"I . . . guess so."

"We all get mad sometimes. I've done stuff I regret. But he wasn't like that all the time."

"No," I said. "Just . . . sometimes." Enough that I was afraid of him, never knowing which Jerry would show up.

"This is one of the worst nights ever," Lori said. "We all feel like crap. I know what it's like to be lonely, to just want someone around, even if they can't compare to who you really want. But don't change who he was in your head to make room for someone else."

"I don't want anyone else," I said.

"Don't you?" Lori asked, peering at me closely. "What about . . . ?"

"What about what?"

She shook her head. "Nothing." She looked like she was trying not to say anything else, but then continued, "Do you think he meant to hurt you?"

I'd wondered that a lot, and I didn't have an answer. I wasn't sure if it mattered if he meant to or not because he had hurt me, not just once, but over and over. "I don't know. Sometimes I felt like I didn't really understand him. Like there was some hidden part of him."

"People hurt you sometimes. It doesn't mean they're bad people."

"I didn't say he was a bad person." It wasn't that simple. He was a good brother. He worked hard and would have cut off his own hand before stealing a dollar from anyone. But he also had a temper that scared me.

"Come on, let's go find Ian," Lori said, walking out from under the bleachers.

Everything Lori said was true, but it felt like there should be something between *not perfect* and *scary when mad*. Lori had said it wasn't a big deal that Jerry talked trash about people because the way he treated them was what mattered. But what about how he'd treated *me*?

CHAPTER 8

Lori was out sick the next day, so when I got home from school, I baked her a batch of chocolate chip cookies. I'd always loved it when I was home sick and Jerry showed up bearing donuts.

I dressed in my work uniform for Scoops, a bubblegum-pink polo shirt with black pants. Scoops was a retro-style ice cream shop, and usually a fun place to work. Before I went to work, I headed to Lori's house. My bike tires crunched through fallen leaves. It was the kind of perfect weather that made me wish winter didn't have to come.

As I was leaving my neighborhood, I spotted Gabe running. He didn't live in my neighborhood, so I didn't know why he was exercising there. He waved at me, trying to get my attention, but I kept pedaling, pretending I didn't see him.

When I got to Lori's, I texted her and she answered the door. Her face was pale, her hair a tangled mess. She had dark circles under her eyes, and they looked puffy, like she'd been crying.

"I didn't mean to wake you," I said. "I brought you cookies." I held the container out to her.

"Chocolate chip?" she asked, smiling, but it looked forced.

"Obviously."

"I've been dying for chocolate!" She stepped back from the door. "Can you hang out for a few minutes? I'm tired of myself."

I nodded and followed her inside.

The house was dark and stuffy. We went to her bedroom and she plopped on her bed. I sat at her desk and noticed a notebook page with her mom's signature scrawled over and over. "What's this?" I held up the paper.

"I'm practicing. My mom wouldn't have let me stay home because I don't have a fever. I feel like crap, so I wrote my own note."

I'd be afraid to get caught, but Lori didn't worry about things like that.

"Did anything interesting happen today?" she asked, choosing a cookie.

"Melissa finally broke up with Tyler. It was insane."

"Shut up! And I missed it?"

"He forgot her birthday. She freaked out, and then he said, 'Calm down, it's not that big of a deal.'"

"No he didn't!"

"She went ballistic, screaming about how he's a lousy kisser."

Lori leaned forward, her eyes alight. "Please tell me someone got video."

"Duh," I said. "It's probably already online."

Lori laughed. "I can't believe I missed it!" She stared into space for a moment, then narrowed her eyes at me. "Is something going on with you and Nate?"

I flinched and averted my eyes, staring at the pictures tacked up on her wall. There was a roller-coaster selfie from a day we went to Dorney Park; another of us, much younger, on skates at the local rink. Then pictures of us in cheerleading uniforms, pictures of Jerry and Ian in basketball uniforms. There was one of the four of us at a game. Another of all of us at Sunrise Diner after a game.

I looked away, not wanting to see Jerry grinning at me, but I felt the weight of his gaze. They were just pictures, but I didn't want to talk about Nate with Jerry watching me. "No, nothing."

She rolled her eyes. "Oh, come on! You've been staring at him for days now. And yesterday, he sat on your desk like you're friends."

Was it really that obvious that I'd been watching him? My cheeks got warm. "We've just been texting. It's not a big deal."

"It kind of is," she said. "Isn't he the first guy you've, you know, texted? Since Jerry died?"

"Yeah," I said softly.

Lori shook her head. "It feels so sudden. The memorial was only last night."

"We're just texting."

"But you like him."

"I barely know him." I didn't want to talk about this. "What about you and Aiden?"

Lori made a face. "I don't know. He's fine. He likes me, I guess. But he's kind of boring. He's not . . ."

"Not JD," I finished for her.

Lori sighed. "Am I wrong to want passion and drama and romance?"

"Why would you want drama?"

Lori laughed. "It can be fun! And exciting and sexy. There's nothing like driving a guy so crazy that he can't control himself."

That had been Jerry's excuse, that I made him lose control. I looked down at my lap. There was a small hole on the hem of my shirt. I needed to fix it before it got bigger. "You . . . wanted JD to lose control?"

Lori made an irritated sound. "You know what I mean. There was this one time we got into a fight because he was talking to another girl. I tried to walk out on him, but he wouldn't let me. I made him so crazy! It was scary for a minute, but in a sexy way, you know? He was so intense."

I frowned. Scary in a sexy way? "I don't think scary is ever sexy." But maybe that was because I knew Jerry might hurt me.

Lori shook her head impatiently. "I don't know, it just made me feel like I was important to him, you know?"

There was so much I wanted to say to Lori, but I wasn't exactly an expert on good relationships. If Lori didn't think it had been a big deal, maybe it wasn't. "And Aiden isn't like that, so you're not interested?"

Lori toyed with her necklace. "He just doesn't make me feel anything. It's like there's this huge hollow spot where my heart used to be." She sighed. "What happened with JD was my fault and I'd do anything to fix it. To take back everything I did wrong. I just . . . want him back." Her voice cracked.

I rubbed my wrist. When Jerry and I first got together, it had all been exciting. At first, his jealousy felt like love. But after a while, it had felt like something else. It had been scary, and not in a sexy way. "Just be careful. It feels great at first, but then . . ."

Lori frowned. "I don't get why you want to act like Jerry was evil."

"That's not what I mean." I wasn't explaining it right. "I just don't want you to get hurt."

"Well, I won't." Her voice was petulant.

We sat in awkward silence for a few moments, and then I looked at my phone. "I have to get to work."

Lori hugged me goodbye, but I could tell her mind was already somewhere else.

The air had cooled while I was inside. Cars were pulling into garages as people got home from work. Kids played outside, riding scooters and kicking balls.

The path I needed to take to get to Scoops was across the bridge and through the woods. It wasn't the safest place to ride my bike since the road was narrow, but I'd be late if I went the long way. I got on my bike and pedaled, passing from clean streets and even lawns to the bumpy asphalt back road, covered in fallen twigs and leaves.

As I pedaled, I thought about Lori and how we hadn't talked as much over the last year as we had before. I'd always thought it was my fault, pulling away because Jerry thought she was a "bad influence," whatever that meant. But maybe she'd been pulling away too. Maybe JD hadn't wanted her to talk too much about their relationship. Because no matter what Lori said, something didn't feel right.

My tires made a hollow sound as I rode over the bridge. There were no road sounds, no cars going by. Birds chirped and leaves crackled under my tires. The river meandered next to my bike. Dappled sunlight peeked through the trees that were slowly losing their leaves and dying little deaths.

Jerry, Ian, and I had spent a lot of time in those woods. It was the first time I'd been back to the woods since Jerry had died, and I hadn't realized how much I missed it.

As I had that thought, I approached the curve of road where Jerry had died and my palms broke out in sweat. We'd been coming from the other direction, on the wrong side of the road. His car had been going too fast, heading straight for the big oak tree.

If Brittany and Caleb hadn't come around the curve at just the right moment, we would have hit the tree head-on.

I was back in Jerry's car. Speeding toward the tree, Caleb's car. I couldn't stop it. I was going to die.

I blinked, and the flashback was over. It had only been seconds, but my body quaked and my mouth was dry. I stopped on the side of the road and tried to breathe.

I could still go the long way, avoid passing the curve that had changed my life and ended Jerry's. I could make up an excuse for my manager. I was never late, so it wasn't like I'd get fired.

But I'd come this far. And I couldn't avoid this road forever.

The trees were tall and thick. Although it was autumn, the branches crisscrossed in a way that left the woods in perpetual twilight even on the brightest days.

As I rounded the curve, my eyes went right to the healing scar on the tree trunk. Jerry's car had spun into it when we crashed. Beneath the tree were flowers, stuffed animals, and pictures.

The last time I'd stood there, I'd been covered in blood and safety glass. It didn't seem real that I'd survived. Sometimes it still didn't, like I'd actually died that day, and everything that came after was a dream.

I tore my gaze away and kept riding, forcing myself to pretend that I was just a normal girl, riding on an ordinary road, and everything was fine.

CHAPTER 9

After I got home from Scoops, I took my books out of my backpack and started to pile them on my desk, when one of them bumped my pen cup and almost knocked it over. I automatically grabbed the cupcake-shaped mug to put it back where it belonged, when my hand froze.

My things were out of place. I glanced around.

My desk chair wasn't tucked all the way under my desk. I looked at my bed, and the bedspread was rumpled in a spot, like someone had sat down after I'd made it.

My sewing table seemed untouched. Thread and notions were in jars, the way I'd left them. A half-finished shirt was folded next to my sewing machine.

My journal was in my nightstand drawer, where I always left it, but pages were wrinkled, like someone had paged through them roughly. I froze. Jerry read my journal. He saw what I'd written about him. What I'd written about Nate. He'd shake me and accuse me of not loving him.

Jerry was dead.

I forced myself to take a deep breath and focus on the present. He couldn't read my journal or check my phone anymore.

Unless he was a ghost.

The other morning, I'd convinced myself that I'd imagined that cold touch. But what if I hadn't? What if Jerry was haunting me? Could he have moved my things?

The page I'd written on the other day wasn't the only one with wrinkles, and I didn't remember wrinkling the other ones. It was possible I'd done it after writing about prom, that I'd paged through and had been careless. But I was always careful with my books. I flipped through it. Toward the back, a blank page had been ripped out.

Why would someone rip out a blank page? Could a ghost tear a page out?

I went through the rest of the journal more carefully in case someone had ripped out one of the pages I'd written on, but the rest of the pages were untouched.

Why would anyone other than Jerry want to read my journal? Who else would care who I talked to or what I thought?

I went downstairs. Mom and Dad were sitting in front of the TV, laptops open in front of them, probably still working. Dad looked up at me, then patted the couch next to him. "Want to watch something with us?"

I shook my head. "Did either of you go in my room today?"

They looked at one another and shook their heads. "No," Mom said. "Why?"

"Some of my things were moved." It sounded silly, and I wanted to take the words back the instant I said them.

His eyebrows lifted. "Moved?" Dad asked. "Like what?"

"My pen mug and desk chair. And my bedspread was rumpled."

Dad half smiled, like he thought I was joking. "Maybe Paisley did it."

"I'm serious. I always put my pen mug in the same place and it was moved. I always put my desk chair back under my desk, but it was out like someone had been sitting on it. And you know I always make my bed."

Dad narrowed his eyes and opened his mouth, then closed it again without speaking.

"There was also a blank page ripped out of my journal," I said. "I didn't do that." I'd never rip a page out of my journal. There were lots of things I didn't know about myself anymore, but I was sure of that.

"Don't you think that sounds a little paranoid?" Dad smiled like he was trying to soften the word, but it didn't work.

I hunched my shoulders. Maybe it did sound irrational.

"Maybe the journal was like that when you bought it," Dad said. "Someone was in the store and needed to make a note so they ripped the page out." He shrugged.

I frowned. When I bought the journal, I would have paged through it to make sure there were no folds or wrinkles, but would I have noticed a missing page? I couldn't be sure.

The dent on the bed was bigger than Paisley, and she didn't go in my room anymore. But I could have sat down for a minute this morning and forgotten to smooth the spread. I didn't remember doing it, but it was possible.

It was better than the idea of a ghost doing it anyway.

"Are you having nightmares again?" Dad asked.

"What does that have to do with anything?"

"I just wondered if you were stressed out, with school starting and the memorial last night. It's a lot. You've had a rough couple of months."

"Do you think I'm making it up?"

Dad shook his head. "Of course not. But . . . what do you think happened? Do you think your mom and I are lying?"

"You know we respect your privacy," Mom said.

"No." If they'd read my journal, they'd know about the things Jerry did, and there was no way they'd pretend they didn't. I hesitated. "Maybe someone broke in."

They exchanged a worried look. Mom frowned, put her laptop aside, then got up and went to the back door. We followed her through the kitchen as she checked the lock. It didn't look tampered with. She checked the emergency money in the box of ice pops in the freezer, then went upstairs and checked her jewelry box, but everything was there too. She shook her head, and my stomach dropped. "Nothing's missing."

I looked around their bedroom, but nothing seemed out of place.

I bit my lip. No one would break in just to mess with my things.

Mom spread her hands out in a placating way. "When people get stressed, sometimes they forget things. I'm always misplacing my reading glasses."

That explanation was completely reasonable except that it felt wrong. "You're probably right." I forced a smile.

Dad motioned me over to hug him. "You're a strong kid. We're so proud of how you've rebounded since the accident."

You're so strong, they always said. *We're proud of you.*

But I knew I wasn't really strong. I always felt like I was a breath away from breaking down. And every time they said it, I took one step further from telling them the truth. It was the same reason I'd never told them about Jerry. I didn't want them to know who I'd let myself become.

"I know."

Mom hugged me, then they both headed toward the stairs.

I stepped into my room, but stopped and turned. "Can I get a space heater for my room?"

Dad turned back to me and frowned. "Why?"

I shrugged. "It's freezing in there sometimes."

"Is the vent open?"

"Yep."

But even as I said that, my dad moved down the hallway and into my room. He looked up. "It's open. And it feels okay to me."

My room was warm at that moment. "Yeah, it's only cold sometimes."

He shrugged. "Your room is over the garage, which isn't insulated that well. You're probably getting a chill from that."

It made sense, but it didn't make me feel any better. But I kept my mouth shut as my parents went back downstairs.

It had been a while since the last time I'd seen that concerned look on my dad's face, but I remembered the first time perfectly. A month after Jerry died, we went grocery shopping. I was already freaked out about being in the car, but my dad had insisted it would be good for me. A car had cut him off, and he'd swerved. He told me later that we weren't in danger of crashing, but I'd suddenly been back in the car with Jerry. I'd screamed, "No, Jerry, don't!"

I didn't remember much of the hour or two after that, but I'd babbled about what I'd seen, and that's when they made the first appointment with Gemma. That hadn't been the last time I'd seen Jerry, but it was the worst.

You're a crazy bitch, Jerry's voice whispered. *I told you everyone would find out.*

I ignored the voice and put everything back where it belonged. Except my journal. I hated the idea of someone reading it. My room wasn't exactly huge, so there was no good place to hide it. I put it in the shoebox of period supplies I kept under the bathroom sink. That was the last place Jerry would have looked.

I tried to do my homework, but found myself staring off into space, trying to remember moving my own things. I'd thought the ghost of

Jerry was messing with my computer. Could a ghost also move my stuff? I shivered.

Nope. No. I was not being haunted by my dead boyfriend. I'd rather believe my parents were right about me just being stressed out. Anything was better than Jerry being back.

CHAPTER 10

It had been a while since Ian's family had last been over, so my parents invited them over for a barbecue. They lived two houses away, so our families often did things together. Dad fired up the grill, I baked an apple pie and a shoofly pie, and Mom made lemonade.

Jacqui, Ian's youngest sister, tackled me in a hug. Karen, his other younger sister, was absorbed in her handheld game. She waved, and a moment later, they ran off to play horseshoes.

Mr. Williamson grinned and enveloped me in a huge hug that smelled like the lemon candies he loved. Then Mrs. Williamson hugged me, surrounding me with the sweet scent of her perfume. The hugs made my throat tighten, like I wanted to cry. Ian's parents had always treated Jerry and me like part of the family.

"Terri's staying at college this weekend," Mrs. Williamson said, referring to Ian's oldest sister. She smiled. "It's been too long since you stopped by. How are you doing?"

"I'm okay."

"Are you?" Mrs. Williamson stroked her hand down my hair. "We miss you. Don't be a stranger."

"She took my phone again," Ian said, patting the pockets of his cargo shorts.

"Jacqueline!" Mrs. Williamson called. "Give your brother his phone back."

Jacqui ran over, giggling, and handed the phone to Ian.

"What did we say about taking his things?"

"I'm not supposed to?" Jacqui said, hiding a grin, then ran off.

Ian and I settled on the porch swing. "Younger sisters are the worst." But his half smile told me he didn't mean it.

He draped his arm along the back, and the swing creaked softly. Our dads were at the grill, and our moms were sitting at the picnic table, sipping drinks. Trees shaded the yard, casting soft light on the grass. My shoulders relaxed as I took in a scene I'd watched countless times before.

"I feel like I didn't see you all summer," Ian said.

"You were busy." I shrugged. "Basketball camp, vacation."

"I'm never too busy for you." Ian shifted to look at me. "You know you can tell me anything, right?"

"I know," I said automatically. I wondered how the conversation would go if I did try to tell Ian the truth about Jerry. I thought he'd believe me, but I didn't want to be responsible for how much it might hurt him.

"Brittany said she texted you a bunch of times. She thinks you're mad at her."

Was that why she'd glared at me at the memorial? "I'm not mad at her." I frowned.

"I told her I didn't think you were mad. Just that you were having a hard time."

"I kept meaning to text everyone back." I looked down at my hands. It wasn't much of an excuse.

Ian stared off at nothing. "I started to text Jerry a million times this summer. Every time anything happened, I wanted to tell him. And then I'd remember he was dead all over again. It's like part of me is missing."

"You guys were friends for a long time."

"I don't remember a time when we weren't," Ian said. "It was always the three of us. I know it must be as bad for you as it is for me. Worse, probably."

It was, but not for the reasons he thought. "After Jerry died, I kept replaying the accident. Not just in my head, but like it was actually happening. I got confused about what was real sometimes."

"Damn." Ian pulled me to him, hugging me. "Why didn't you tell me? I could have been around more. I didn't have to go to camp."

I shook my head. "There's nothing you could have done."

"I could have been here. You could have texted me."

"I know." I didn't know why it was so hard to confide in my friends. Maybe it was because I was used to keeping secrets. Maybe it was because Jerry always made me think I misremembered things.

"I'm in therapy," I said.

"I'm glad you have someone to talk to."

Muscles I hadn't realized were tense loosened. Ian wasn't judging me. "I don't even remember most of the summer. It's like I'm waking up from a long sleep. I don't know how else to explain it."

"I stayed busy so I wouldn't have to think about him," Ian said. "Every time I stopped doing something, I'd remember he was dead, and it would hurt all over again. It feels like someone hit me in the gut. Actually, a punch would hurt less."

"I guess you needed me as much as I needed you," I said, realizing it for the first time.

Ian looked at me for a long moment.

"I feel like there should be music," Ian said quietly. "In movies, doesn't the music always swell during these special bonding moments?" His lips twitched before he gave up and laughed.

"Jerk."

Ian ruffled my hair and I swatted his hand away, laughing.

"So what's the deal with you and Brittany?"

He grinned. "We're talking."

"I should probably tell her that I didn't mean to ignore her."

"She's had it rough. Lots of people like Caleb and they're pissed off that he'll never play football again." Ian shifted his gaze to the yard, where his sisters were playing horseshoes and laughing. "They're taking it out on her, giving her a hard time because she's not acting 'sad enough.' Whatever that even means."

"Everyone wants to tell you how to feel," I said.

Ian nodded. "I think that's why she wants to talk to you. She can't really talk to anyone else."

"She's talking to you."

"Yes, and I love sitting around discussing feelings, braiding hair, all that chick crap."

I nudged his shoulder with mine. "Sexist pig."

He grinned. "Nah, I'm into chick stuff. That's why girls like me. Remember all those tea parties you made me sit through?"

I laughed. "You looked good, all dressed up." He wore aprons or hats, though he drew the line at nail polish. "I think my mom has some pictures of those parties," I said.

"If you ever show them to anyone, I'll show everyone that picture of you taking a basketball to the face."

I smacked him in the arm. "You said you deleted that!"

"No, I didn't! You told me to delete it. I didn't answer you."

"I'm going to kill you!"

"You'll have to catch me first." When he launched himself off the porch swing, I didn't realize what he was doing until he was almost to the hose.

I sprinted after him, but I was too slow. The spray hit me in the chest. I tried to swerve out of the way, but I was laughing too hard. I tackled him, and we sprawled on the grass in a heap.

Ian laughed hysterically and didn't even try to defend himself. I grabbed the hose nozzle and sprayed him in the face.

Later, after we'd eaten burgers and potato salad until we were all ready to burst, Karen and Jacqui went inside to watch a movie, and Ian and I went back to the porch swing. The sun had set, and the yard was dark and quiet except for the chirping of crickets. "Today was fun," Ian said. "We haven't hung out like this in forever."

"Yeah. It was a good day." We sat in silence and swung back and forth.

"I know Sandy seemed mad at you at the memorial," Ian said, "but I think she's feeling abandoned."

"Abandoned? By me?"

"She misses you," Ian said. "She's never said it, but I can tell."

"Why would she miss me?" I asked. "We only hung out because of Jerry."

"Yeah, but you were always there and then you weren't." He shrugged. "She asks about Jerry's accident sometimes. I've told her what I know, but I wasn't there."

I couldn't look at him. "I can't . . . talk about that."

Ian nodded. "I don't think she wants the gory details. She just wants to hear from you. She needs someone."

She had Ian. She didn't need me.

Ian's phone chimed and he took it out of his pocket.

I didn't want to talk to Sandy, but I could talk to Ian. Jerry hadn't wanted me to hang out with Ian, so I hadn't. But today, it was like we'd picked up right where we left off.

Telling Lori about Jerry had been a relief. Like Gemma said, it felt better to let go of secrets.

I didn't have to tell him everything. If I told him about things in my room being moved, he could help me figure it out.

When he looked up from his phone, I opened my mouth, but he started talking before I could say anything. "A bunch of people are going to Scoops. Let's head over."

I frowned. "But it's my day off."

"It'll be fun. My treat."

A bunch of people . . . and then it clicked. "Is Brittany going to be there?"

He shot me a lopsided grin. "She will. But so will Gabe."

I wrinkled my nose. "I don't want to hang out with Gabe."

"Fine, so don't talk to Gabe. Come hang out with me and Brittany. Have a little fun."

"I've been having fun here with you. We could keep talking."

"You want to sit on the porch swing like we're eighty. Jerry died and it sucks, but you're not dead yet. Stop acting like it."

I flinched. "You're an asshole." Ian grabbed my arm when I got up to walk away, and I froze. It was dark enough that he didn't notice that all the blood drained from my face.

Jerry never let me walk away from him. Sometimes I tried, if an argument was going bad. He'd grab me, digging his fingers into my arm until I was bruised and sore. My breathing sped up and I braced myself.

"Charlie, wait, I'm sorry . . ." Ian pulled me into a hug, and as his strong arms enveloped me, I relaxed. It was Ian holding me, not Jerry. Ian's hand had been gentle. He rested his chin on the top of my head.

"That *was* an asshole thing say. I just miss you. Sometimes it feels like I lost both of you in the accident."

We were both quiet for a minute.

"I'm sorry," he said again.

My arms came up slowly and I hugged him back.

Even though I didn't want to, I agreed to go to Scoops. Maybe Ian was right. Maybe I needed to get out of my head for a while. I used to like hanging out with other people. Maybe it would be good for me.

CHAPTER 11

The drive to Scoops was only two miles, so it didn't take long, but even the short ride had me silently panicking. I curled my hand around the door handle and forced myself not to freak out. Ian was talking about something, but I barely heard him. By the time we got to Scoops, it was packed with what looked like the entire cheerleading squad and the basketball team. Brittany was there and so was Gabe, as predicted. Nate played basketball, so I scanned the room, searching for him.

My stomach jittered. It might be fun to hang out with Nate. But he wasn't there.

Brittany beamed when she spotted Ian. When she saw me beside him, she frowned a little but quickly smoothed out her expression. "Hey, I didn't know you were coming," she said to me.

"We were hanging out when you texted," Ian said.

"So you guys were hanging out today."

Her tone of voice said that he should have told her, but Ian didn't notice. "Yeah. So what can I get you ladies?"

We told him what we wanted and he went to get our ice cream while Brittany and I faced each other awkwardly.

I thought about what Ian said, that Brittany thought I was mad at her. "So . . . how are you doing?" I asked.

She shrugged. "Okay. My doctor finally cleared me to go back to cheer."

"That's good," I said.

I was looking at the ground and Brittany was looking past me. "Are you ever coming back to cheer?" she asked.

"I don't think so." I didn't care about anything I used to.

"Too bad. You and Lori were the best on the team. Other than me, I mean. With you guys gone, I don't have any competition. No one to keep me on my toes." She smiled, as if to soften her words.

"I'm glad the crash didn't ruin it for you."

Someone laughed behind me, and Brittany stiffened, her expression going blank. I turned to look, and old friends of mine from the cheer squad were looking our way as if we were the joke.

Brittany looked down, her face scarlet. "Yeah. It didn't ruin *that*. Just the rest of my life."

"I'm sorry I didn't text you back this summer. I was . . . my head was in a weird place."

"Weird," she echoed. "That's one way to put it."

I studied her. I'd always thought of Brittany as impervious, like nothing could get her down. Her auburn hair was always smooth in a ponytail during cheer, without the frizzies that plagued the rest of us. She had clear skin and wore her cheer uniform like it was made for her.

On the surface, she still looked perfect. But she kept smoothing her immaculate white T-shirt. Ian said that people were getting on her case because she wasn't sticking by Caleb. But the same people who were giving her a hard time probably hadn't even been to see him.

I hadn't answered her all summer and I didn't want her to think I was one of the people who was judging her for being with Ian. "It's cool that you and Ian are hanging out."

"Yeah? Lots of people don't think so."

"Lots of people are wrong," I said.

She turned her head and finally looked at me. "True." A small smile tugged at the corners of her mouth. Then it faded and she studied my face for a long moment. She looked away again before speaking. "Everyone hates me. What happened to Caleb . . . I mean, I feel horrible about it. But what was I supposed to do? It's Jerry's fault, not mine. And no one is mad at him."

People never got mad at Jerry. Everyone made excuses for guys like him. "They'd rather blame you," I said softly. So softly, I wasn't sure she heard me.

She kept going. "I'm just . . . furious. Like, okay, you're not supposed to speak ill of the dead or whatever, but what kind of asshole drinks and drives? Why isn't anyone talking about that?"

Her words knocked the breath out of me. I knew that Brittany was saying things about Jerry online, but I wasn't prepared for how it would feel to have someone else see one of the less than perfect sides of Jerry.

Not one person talked about Jerry drinking and driving or said that *he'd* ruined Caleb's life. And that was right there in the open. Even if I wanted to tell people what he did to me, no one would want to hear it.

I gripped my hands together in front of me, trying to keep them from shaking. I looked down and tried to think of what to say, but Brittany didn't wait for an answer.

"The school had a candlelight memorial for him and not one person, not even the principal, said anything about *why* he died. People leave him notes and flowers, like it wasn't his fault. Meanwhile, no one even visits Caleb, and I may as well have a red letter *A* tattooed on my forehead."

"No one wants to talk about it," I said. "That's not how they want to remember him."

Her eyes flashed. "Why didn't you stop him?" she demanded. "Why didn't you drive?"

"I don't have my license."

"Oh, right." But she didn't say it like she was agreeing with me. She said it sarcastically.

"It wasn't my fault." I wasn't sure how she'd gone from blaming Jerry to blaming me. I looked around to see if anyone was eavesdropping, but the shop was loud with chattering voices, and no one was paying attention.

"No one is blaming *you*. But you let him drive. You're as guilty as he is."

I recoiled as if she'd slapped me. Was there something else I could have done? "I didn't come here for this."

"Then why did you? I've texted you at least a dozen times but you've ignored me. Not even a single 'Hey, how are you?' And you just show up, acting like we're friends?"

"Ian said he thought you needed someone to talk to."

Her face went scarlet again. "Oh, *my boyfriend* told you that? Why were you two hanging out, anyway?"

"Because we're friends."

"Right. Friends."

I narrowed my eyes at that but ignored the implication. "Look, I'm sorry I didn't tex—"

"That's what you're apologizing for? Whatever. I don't care about that. If you hadn't let Jerry drive, none of this would have happened. All you had to do was take his keys."

She made it sound so easy, like I could have snatched the keys out of his hand and gone back into prom, like he wouldn't have hurt me if I tried to walk away. She made it sound like Jerry wasn't bigger, stronger, angrier than I was, like there was any way I could have won that fight. "You don't know what you're talking about."

"You're kidding yourself if you think you aren't responsible."

I touched the scar on my head. Maybe there was something else I could have done. Maybe I could have made Jerry listen to me if I were better or smarter or not so afraid of him.

My throat was hot and tight, and my vision started to narrow. I tried to speak but no words came out.

My breath started coming in sharp gasps and I couldn't get enough air. I had to get away.

I shoved past several people to get outside but I didn't care.

My heart was racing and I started to sweat.

Not now, I told the panic attack. *Please, not now.*

Maybe it wasn't a panic attack. Maybe this time, I was actually dying. Maybe I was supposed to have died in the car with Jerry, and death was coming for me. That's why I couldn't escape Jerry. I'd never escape.

I tried to force air into my lungs. My head swam.

I staggered through the parking lot and hid under a tree. My knees collapsed and I clutched my chest. I concentrated on taking slow breaths, trying to force air in and out of my lungs. When the panic attack eventually receded, I got up, dusting off my jeans. My head was still throbbing and I was exhausted. I looked toward Scoops, but no one seemed to be watching me.

On shaky legs, I started walking home. If I could get home, everything would be fine.

"Charlotte!" a guy's voice called after me.

I ignored him and sped up.

"Wait up." The guy caught up to me and then matched my pace. It was Gabe, the last person I wanted to talk to.

"I'm going home," I said.

"Cool. I'll walk with you. Are you okay?"

"I'm fine."

"Okay, so a bunch of us are playing Werewolf next weekend. Want to play?"

I kind of did, but I didn't want to encourage him. *Do you have to flirt with every guy you see?* Jerry's voice whispered. "I think I'm busy."

"Just text me when you know."

He was not taking a hint. "Okay, so can we talk later? No offense, but I kind of want to be alone."

"I'm not going to let a pretty girl walk home alone." His tone was cheerful, like I wasn't even making a dent. "What kind of guy would I be?"

"One who took no for an answer?"

Gabe looked like I'd slapped him. It just slipped out. I hadn't meant to say it, but I wasn't going to take it back.

"What? I wanted to make sure you were safe. I wasn't trying to . . . do anything."

I looked down at my hands. My nail polish was flaking, and I picked at it. I wasn't trying to be mean, but he wouldn't listen. I told him I wanted to be left alone, but he ignored me. I wanted to hit something. "I'm just . . . please just leave me alone."

Gabe took a step back. His face crumpled. "I thought we were friends. That you needed time to get over Jerry, and then—"

"Then what?" I interrupted. "Then we'd get back together?"

"I was a good boyfriend to you. You're the one who cheated on me."

I recoiled. "I didn't mean to. It just . . . happened." I winced at the apologetic tone of my voice and wondered what the old me would have said, before Jerry convinced me that everything was my fault.

"Oh, so it was an accident? You fell on his lips?" Gabe shook his head. "I thought you were different from other girls."

What was wrong with being like other girls? Was I supposed to think there was something wrong with being a girl? "I guess you were wrong," I said quietly.

"About a lot of things." He shook his head. He paused a moment, like he was waiting for me to say something else, but then strode away.

I stared after him, my stomach churning. Even if he left me alone now, it didn't feel like a victory.

Gabe wanted me to pay for a mistake I'd made a long time ago. And I'd been punishing myself for it too. But how long was I supposed to feel bad about it?

I was a mile down the road when Ian pulled up beside me. He rolled the window down and yelled, "Get in."

"Leave me alone." I knew I was being awful but I didn't care.

Ian kept driving at a crawl to keep pace with me. "You can't just disappear like that."

"Go away."

"Charlie, I swear if you don't get in this car, I will get out and put you in. Stop acting like a brat!"

I was sick of guys bossing me around. I stopped and put my hands on my hips. "What is your problem?"

He pulled over and jumped out. "What's wrong with you?"

"You're acting like a . . . a . . . curmudgeon!"

Ian opened his mouth to yell again, but stopped, looking confused. "I'm a grumpy old man?"

I burst out laughing. "I couldn't think of anything better."

"Good one." He smiled, then ran a hand through his hair. "What happened? Brittany is pissed. She said you just ran out."

I didn't want to put the idea in Ian's head that the accident was my fault. I couldn't stand it if he blamed me too. "I got a headache. Too many people, too much noise."

"Why didn't you tell me? I would have taken you home."

I shook my head. "You wanted to hang out with Brittany. I didn't want to make you leave." I forced a smile, hoping he'd think I was fine so I could go home and crawl into bed.

"I'm sorry I made you come out." He stepped toward me and put a hand on my shoulder. "C'mon, I'll take you home. Your shake is in the car."

"I'll take my shake," I said, even though the idea of chocolate and peanut butter was no longer remotely appealing. "But I can walk home. I want to clear my head. You should go back."

"I'd rather hang out with you."

If he hadn't insisted on going to the ice cream shop, we'd still be hanging out. "I think I'd rather be alone."

Hurt flashed across his face, but he didn't say whatever he was thinking. He got my shake out of the car and handed it to me. "You going to be okay?"

"Yep, I'm fine. Go have fun." I turned and walked away. After a moment, I heard his car start and the crunch of his tires as he pulled away.

Part of me had hoped he wouldn't leave, that he'd notice how not fine

I was. I couldn't even go for ice cream without it turning into a disaster.

Brittany blamed me, and maybe she was right. Maybe I could have done more to stop Jerry from driving. Caleb's life was ruined. Jerry was dead. Brittany had gone from being popular to being hated. Maybe there was something wrong with me and I ruined things.

After the accident, I thought maybe I'd be able to move past all of this, that maybe I was done letting Jerry hurt me. But it seemed like, even dead, he wouldn't let me go.

CHAPTER 12

Every autumn, this guy we knew had a bonfire party. He lived across the river, on a farm in the rural part of our school district. I wanted to stay home, but I thought about what Gemma and I had talked about, that I wanted to feel better. Maybe it would be good for me to start doing the things I used to enjoy.

Ian picked me up and we headed to Lori's. He grinned when he saw me. "Hey, you made a new shirt!"

I smiled back. It was a shirt Jerry had liked. It was periwinkle, with pin tucks and lace running down the front. I'd hated it, but rather than getting rid of it, I'd stitched multicolored flowers all over it, turning it into something that I actually liked. "Yeah, I wanted something fun."

"So . . . when are you getting your license so I don't need to drive you everywhere?" Ian smirked.

I tried to ignore the fact that Ian was driving too fast. I held on to the door handle as if it would help if we crashed. My shoulders were hunched, and I tried to relax them, but they wouldn't stay down. "Why would I want to drive when I have a perfectly good chauffeur?" My voice sounded casual, but the truth was that I didn't want to drive. What if I had a panic attack and killed someone? At least if I had a panic attack as a passenger, embarrassment wasn't fatal.

Lori was waiting outside when Ian pulled up. As soon as the car stopped, she hopped in the back and slammed the door. She scooted forward in the seat as Ian pulled away from the curb. "I've so been looking forward to this!"

"It's usually fun," I said. I tried to find my enthusiasm. "Except when Ian decides to scare people in the corn maze." One year, he and Jerry had dressed in all black and hidden in the corn maze, jumping out at people. It had been the year before Jerry and I started dating, when everything was still easy and fun.

"It was fun for me." Lori laughed. "Especially once we started spraying them with the water guns you brought."

"You two sprayed the hell out of us," Ian said. "I caught pneumonia and nearly died."

"So dramatic!" I chuckled.

"Yeah, well you'd be dramatic too if you were the one freezing their ass off for the rest of the night," Ian said.

"Oh, whatever." Lori shook her head. "So, I'm meeting Connor tonight. We've been texting."

I wondered if Connor was more exciting than Aiden. "And? How's it going?"

Lori slumped back in the seat and I watched her in the visor mirror. She shook herself and forced a smile. "He keeps telling me I'm gorgeous, and he seems to like me a lot, so that's something."

Lori leaned forward again. "I got some new lipstick if you want to try it. It's smudge-proof, so if you and Nate find yourself in the corn maze . . ." Lori puckered her lips and made a smacking air kiss.

"Wait. You and Nate?" Ian asked. He turned his head to glance at me.

"Watch the road. And we're just friends."

"For now," Lori said. "You and Jerry were just friends too."

I heard an annoyed note in her voice. Lori hated to be out of the loop on anything. "He's just fun to talk to." Heat rose to my cheeks.

"Jerry's only been gone for four months," Lori said. "A rebound fling never works. Even though it makes it hurt less for a little while."

"Four months." Ian sighed. "Sometimes it seems like years." He paused. "I still can't believe he's gone."

I hunched my shoulders some more. Ian missed him. Lori missed him. I wished it were that easy for me.

Lori thought I was moving on too quickly. Sandy thought I wasn't sad at all. And Ian wanted me to *join the land of the living*. It was like no matter what I did, I was wrong. Which way was the right way? "Like I said, we're just friends."

"Life is short. You should hang out with whoever you want to," Ian said quietly.

Ian slowed down as he drove up the long, gravel driveway. The sun was setting over the apple orchard that lined the road, and we rolled down the windows to enjoy the sweet smell. My mom and I used to pick bushels of them to make apple dumplings and apple butter when I was younger, but we hadn't done that in ages.

The old farmhouse had peeling white paint and a sagging porch. We parked in the field near a dozen other cars and crossed to where everyone was gathered. I poured some apple cider and wandered around while Ian greeted Brittany, and Lori went looking for Connor.

Stars shone brightly in the clear night sky, and smoke undulated from the crackling bonfire. The scents of burned marshmallows and wood smoke wafted through the crisp air. Music blasted through a portable speaker.

I scanned the people sitting around the fire. Alisha and I used to mess around with temporary dyes and hairstyles, but I didn't even know who'd helped her dye the tips of her hair blue. Before Jerry, Danny and I texted each other memes and talked about guys, but I didn't know the guy he was making out with now. When had he and Colin broken up? Paige and

I used to play this game where we texted one another random lyrics and had to guess the song without looking them up. I had no idea when the last time I'd gotten a text from her was.

I'd dropped out of my own life, and now that I wanted to start having a life again, I wasn't sure where I fit. I didn't think I could settle back into my old life, so that meant I'd have to make a new place for myself. It sounded exhausting, but also kind of exciting. Like I could remake myself, if I wanted.

Alisha and Paige spotted me. Alisha waved and forced a too-wide smile. "Hey! Charlotte. Hi."

I took a few steps toward them. "Hi."

"So . . . how *are* you?" Paige asked.

I shrugged. There was no good answer to that question.

"Paige and I were just talking about how much we miss Jerry. He was such a great guy." Alisha sighed. "Finding your soulmate, then losing him that way . . . I can't imagine what that must be like."

That seemed like a heartless thing to say. I suddenly remembered that Alisha had always been a little mean. "At least I'm still alive."

They didn't answer, and after a few moments of awkward silence, I said, "I'm going to go talk to Ian."

"Yeah, of course. We'll talk to you later!"

I turned to look for Ian. He and Brittany were tangled together. Brittany wore a short red tube dress, and her hair gleamed in the firelight.

"Can you believe her?" Alisha asked. She was watching Brittany.

I started walking away, not wanting any part in whatever they were about to say.

"She's got no shame," Paige said. Their voices were loud. Brittany's shoulders stiffened.

"That dress!" Alisha said. "She'd better not bend over or she'll be showing her ass."

"She likes to bend over," Paige said, and they both laughed.

I turned and scowled at them. Brittany was not my favorite person, but she didn't deserve people trashing her behind her back. Besides, she was hanging out with my best friend.

"Hi," I said to Brittany, wondering what she'd say with Ian standing right there.

"Hey," she said. Another burst of laughter came from Alisha and Paige, and Brittany's eyes drifted toward them.

Someone called Ian's name and he walked off, leaving me and Brittany standing together.

"Ignore them," I said. "They're just being stupid."

"That's because they are stupid," Brittany said. "Stupid bitches who don't know anything. I could ruin their lives if I wanted to. They should be nicer to me."

The venom in her voice startled me. "They're lucky you're a better person than they are."

"Damn right. When they least expect it, I'm going to tell everyone what I know. About them, about everybody who's been terrible to me, even about Jerry. I don't care if he's dead."

What? "What about Jerry?" I reached out and grabbed her arm.

She jerked away. "Get off me."

I realized what I was doing and let go. "What are you talking about?"

"Nothing. I'm just talking shit. Though I do know stuff about Alisha and Paige."

She wouldn't meet my eyes. I hadn't even known she and Jerry were friends, so I had no idea what she knew or if she was just making things up.

The hair on the back of my neck stood up, and I was suddenly sure that someone was watching me. I looked around, trying to seem casual. I didn't see anyone watching, but I couldn't see everyone's eyes. Especially with the shadows and flickering firelight.

I shivered.

Ian turned back to us. "You cold?" he asked, touching my back.

"I am," Brittany said, leaning against him.

He turned to smile at her. "No, you're not. You're hot. Smoking hot."

She giggled, and I rolled my eyes. "Let's dance," she said. "That'll warm me up."

"Me too," he said. Ian shot me a smile as Brittany led him away.

I stood there for a while longer, sipping my apple cider. Lori came up to me and wrapped her arm around my neck, then took a selfie of the two of us and posted it. She laughed, and I caught a whiff of liquor.

"Are you drinking?" I rubbed my scar.

She shrugged. "It's a party."

"But you don't drink." We never did.

Lori took another sip. "It's not a big deal."

"Jerry *died* because he was drinking." It wasn't the only reason, but it was one of them.

"Yeah, I know." Lori crossed her arms. "Everyone knows. But I'm not driving."

"That doesn't make it okay."

Lori's jaw clenched, and she took another gulp. "Not everyone is perfect, like you."

"What does that mean?"

Lori shook her head. Tears shone in her eyes.

"Did something happen with Connor?" I looked around for him, but I didn't seem him.

"What's the point?" Lori asked. "All he cares about is hooking up. All any of them care about is hooking up."

"I know you miss JD, but . . ."

"You don't know anything." She whirled around and stomped away.

Tears sprang to my eyes and I blinked them back. Lori was never like that. I looked around, wondering if anyone else had seen our fight.

Sandy was standing with a group of older kids at the edge of the fire. She was wearing too much makeup again, and it made her face look older and tired. She was laughing, and Penny passed Sandy a cigarette. Sandy took it and inhaled like she'd been smoking for a while.

Sandy was looking around the party, and when she spotted me, she scowled and flipped me off.

I turned away before she could do anything else. I wasn't up to another argument with her.

I retreated past the hay bales, toward the trees, where it was darker, and sat on the ground where I'd be hard to see. I just wanted a moment alone.

Someone was coming toward me. They were backlit, their face in shadows, and I couldn't tell who they were, except that it was a guy. My heart thumped instinctively. *Jerry?*

The guy stopped several feet away and crouched down. It was Nate, and he was smiling. "Hey, I thought that was you. Do you want to be alone, or can I join this party?"

My muscles unclenched. "I don't know if there's enough room." I gestured to the wide expanse of yard.

"I'll squeeze in somewhere," he said, sitting cross-legged next to me.

He was quiet, and so was I. Sitting with him like that was peaceful. I listened to the buzz of voices and the crackle of flames.

Then I spotted Gabe, watching me from near the fire. His face was tight with anger. I shifted my eyes away so that he wouldn't take it as an invitation to come over. I fidgeted, feeling his eyes lingering on me. "Do you want to take a walk?" I asked. "We could try the corn maze."

"Yeah, okay. But you should know that the only movie that ever scared me was *Children of the Corn*. I watched it when I was like eight. So if I start freaking out, don't say I didn't warn you."

I laughed. "I don't like horror movies," I said as we started walking down the path toward the maze. It was lit with torches, but they only made the shadows denser and creepier. I shivered. "Why would I want to be scared on purpose?" I was already scared in real life all the time.

"It's the thrill," Nate said. "Gets the blood moving. Makes you feel alive."

I made a show of checking the pulse in my neck. "Blood's moving. I'm alive."

He laughed and his arm bumped mine. "Horror movies are great. I'm always trying to predict what happens next, what the characters should do to survive or what I'd do if I were in that situation. Like, would I be stupid and run upstairs or would I run out the front door and call 911?"

From the outside, it was easy to believe you'd do the smart thing. But it was impossible to know how you'd react unless it happened to you. From the outside, you couldn't know how it felt to love and fear someone so much at the same time. I never thought I'd be *that* girl, the girl who stayed with a boyfriend who hurt her. Of course, we all wanted to believe we'd run out the front door, but sometimes you ran upstairs because that's what you always did.

Nate didn't seem to need me to respond. He just kept talking. "I'd like to think I'd be the hero, or die a really memorable death, but I'd probably break my neck falling down the stairs. Why doesn't that ever happen? And why does the blond girl always fall down and scream instead of getting back up?"

I laughed. Talking to Nate was always an adventure. It didn't even matter what we talked about. "Like I said, horror movies aren't my thing. But I guess everyone expects them to fall."

"That was the great thing about Buffy," he said. "She was the cute blond girl who wanted to look nice and had great clothes. But she also took no crap and could kick some serious butt."

"Buffy?"

Nate stopped and faced me, his face horrified. "Please tell me you didn't just act like you don't know what *Buffy the Vampire Slayer* is."

Him saying the full name triggered something in my brain. "I think my mom watched that show. Isn't it from the nineties?"

Nate shook his head. "Aren't you all 'girl power'? That show is all girl power, all the time."

"Yes to girl power, no to vampires. My friend Lori is into all that ghost and vampire stuff. I think what's dead should stay dead."

No one else was on the path and it was quiet inside the maze. We were far away enough from the bonfire and music that they didn't interrupt the stillness of the night. It was a quarter moon, and with the stalks towering over us, anything could be hiding in the shadows.

"Who came up with the idea for a corn maze?" I asked. "Doesn't it seem like a weird thing to do?"

"Aliens," Nate said.

We turned right. I had no idea where in the maze we were, and I didn't care. It was nice to just be. "Aliens? Did you know that you say the weirdest stuff?"

"I did know that. Think about it. Some alien had a little too much to drink one night, and boom! First corn maze."

"Don't you mean crop circles?"

"What makes you think they don't do both?"

Dead stalks crunched under our feet. We followed the maze, turning left or right at intersections. It got darker in the maze as we got closer to the center.

"How long do you think we'd have to be stuck in here before someone found us?" Nate asked.

"Days? Weeks?" Or in my case, maybe like five minutes before someone showed up to remind me that Jerry was a great guy.

"Centuries from now, someone will come upon our bodies sitting side by side at a dead end. That is an awesome shirt, by the way."

I grinned. "I like to remake things I find at thrift shops. This was an old shirt I didn't like anymore, so I made it into something I did. I love fall, but I miss summer flowers."

"That is such a cool thing to do."

I heard a crunch, just one. I listened, frowning, but if someone had been walking around, they stopped. "I . . . think I hear someone."

"It's about time. Hello?" Nate called. "Who's there?"

No one answered. Something seemed off to me, and my skin crawled. "Let's go."

Nate shrugged and followed me but I had no idea where we were going. I heard a crunch again.

"I think someone's following us," I whispered. Was it Ian, messing around again? He wouldn't do that now, knowing how scared I got and that I was in therapy . . . would he?

Nate looked at me, half smiling, like he wasn't sure if I was serious or if he was supposed to have a funny comeback.

I grabbed his arm. The softness of his sweater and the warmth of his arm distracted me for a moment. It was the first time I'd touched him, and even frightened, I wondered if he was thinking about that too. "Seriously. I think someone is following us."

"It's probably someone messing around. I'll take a look. Wait here," he said, then went back the way we'd come.

"No, don't," I whispered as he disappeared around a corner. I thought about following him, but if I got lost, I'd be wandering around by myself. What if he didn't come back? What would I do then?

My heartbeat sped up until it choked me. The stalks rustled like someone was nearby. "Nate?" I called out, but it came out as a whisper. What if someone was watching me? I backed up to the maze wall so I could see in both directions down the corridor.

If I couldn't get my breathing under control, I'd have a full-blown panic attack. I tried to close my eyes and calm down, but I couldn't stop my thoughts. *What if he's hurt? If he doesn't come back in another minute, I'm going to scream. Everyone will come.* I wouldn't think about how they were probably too far away to hear me.

My heart was trying to hammer its way out of my chest, and my head felt swimmy. *Nate will come back and I'll be freaking out and then he'll know I'm crazy and won't want to talk to me anymore or else he won't come back because someone's following us even though this isn't a horror movie and—*

My phone chimed. It jolted me out of my thoughts. I fumbled it out of my pocket and tightened my hand around it. I focused on the picture of Lori and me on the home screen and my panic leveled out a bit.

My mom had texted to ask what time I was coming home. I had a signal. I could text Lori or Ian and they'd come for us and get us out of the maze. Everything would be fine. They'd make fun of me for being stupid, but we'd be fine.

Something crackled behind me, and I whirled around. There was a white thing caught between the cornstalks. I pulled it out with shaking fingers. It was a crumpled piece of paper. I turned on my phone flashlight to see better and unfolded it slowly. It was lined paper, torn out of a book, printed in block letters.

JUST BECAUSE YOU FORGOT ME

DOESN'T MEAN I FORGOT YOU.

I'M WATCHING YOU.

I tried to peer through the cornstalks, but they were too thick to see through. My hands trembled harder, and my phone slipped out of my fingers. I picked it up and shined it through the tiny gaps in the stalks, but no one was there.

I held my flashlight up and swept it back and forth down the corn corridor.

"There's no one here," Nate said from behind me.

I screamed as I whirled around.

"Sorry!" He held his hands up. "I didn't mean to scare you. Are you okay?"

I pressed my fist to my chest, the note crushed in my hand. I willed my breathing to slow down.

"What's that?" Nate gestured.

I stuffed the paper into my pocket. "Nothing." Nate said no one else was in the maze, but he was wrong. "Let's go back to the fire."

Nate shot me a look that said he didn't believe me, but he just nodded. "Okay, let's go."

Nate tried to talk to me as we wandered our way out of the maze, but I couldn't focus on anything he said. Who would give me a note like that? Jerry would, but that was impossible. Unless he was a ghost.

I stopped that thought before it went any further. Ghosts didn't exist.

When we got back to the bonfire, Nate asked, "Do you want some cider?"

"Actually, I need to talk to Lori."

His face fell. "Okay. Well, I'll see you later, then."

"Yeah, see you later." I watched him go. I'd actually been having fun hanging out with him. So of course something had to ruin it.

Lori was talking to Shanice and Danny. They were laughing, but Lori was staring into her cup. Her expression reminded me of myself, how she looked like she wanted to fit in but had forgotten how.

She was going through a lot too, and I needed to be better about being there for her.

I tapped her on the shoulder. "Can I talk to you?"

She shrugged, but followed me.

We went inside to the kitchen, where it was quieter. It was decorated in country kitchen decor, with lots of cows and wood paneling. An embroidered sign saying BLESSED BE hung above the door.

Lori crossed her arms, leaned against the counter, and stared at me. Still mad, then.

"I'm sorry I gave you a hard time," I said. "What's wrong?"

"Do you actually care?" Lori asked. "Or are you just going to lecture me again?"

"I care," I said. "I'm sorry. I just . . . Drinking freaks me out."

"Yeah," Lori said.

She shook her head and tears gathered in her eyes. "I know this sounds crazy, but sometimes it feels like there's some force that wants me to be miserable. Like every time I try to be happy, something makes sure I can't be."

"That doesn't sound crazy," I said. "Sometimes I feel like I should have died in the crash with Jerry or something."

"I see other people being happy, and I think, 'Why can't that be me?'" Lori rubbed her forehead. "Drinking makes me feel better for a little while."

"It doesn't solve anything, though. I know things suck, but it just makes the problem worse."

"I know." Lori twisted a lock of hair around her finger. "But sometimes I just want to get away from myself for a little while. I swear I wouldn't even have a sip if I was driving. You don't know what it's like to feel like you're falling apart."

"Actually . . ." I took a deep breath. "I do. That panic attack you helped me with at the memorial . . . I have them all the time. I keep lying and saying I'm okay because my parents hate when I'm not, but then I always wonder why no one sees through it."

Lori looked at me and blinked. "You're not okay either?"

"I haven't been. Not for a long time."

We looked at each other for a long moment and I felt a weight leave my shoulders. I pulled her into a hug.

She returned the hug, and we stood there like that. For the first time in a long time, I felt like everything could be okay.

When we broke apart, Lori stepped back.

"You know what we need?" I asked. "A girls' night. Junk food, movies. And we can talk about everything."

Her eyes lit up. "That would be amazing. We haven't done that in forever!"

I missed hanging out with Lori. It was one of the many things that Jerry had taken from me.

"So, not to change the subject," I said slowly, "but did you see anyone follow Nate and me to the corn maze?"

She frowned and shook her head. "I don't think so. Why?"

I handed her the note. She frowned as she read it then looked up at me, obviously confused. "I don't get it."

"I thought I heard someone in the corn maze. Nate went to look, and then I found this note. Someone must have stuffed it through the stalks."

She looked down at the note again. "You didn't see who it was?"

I shook my head. "I looked, but I didn't see anyone."

"Weird. Who would write that?"

I hesitated. "I don't know."

"Is anyone mad at you?" she asked.

"Gabe saw Nate and I talking."

Lori shuddered. "Ugh. Creep."

"And Brittany's mad that I didn't text her back all summer. I guess she wanted to talk about the accident, but now she's decided that Jerry drinking and driving was my fault."

Lori pursed her lips. "She's such a bitch."

"Can't we hate her without calling her names?"

Lori just leveled me with a look. "Are you really lecturing me right now?"

"No. Sorry." Bad timing.

"You think you know something about the note, don't you?" She narrowed her eyes. "Spill it."

"I just keep thinking . . ." I took a deep breath. "Jerry. Jerry would write a note like that." Even thinking about it made me sick to my stomach. My knees went weak and I lowered myself into a chair.

"I guess he'd be pissed about you hanging out with Nate." Lori frowned and then sat next to me.

"Am I crazy to even think it could be him?"

Lori shrugged. "Do you think it's his ghost or something?"

I took a breath and reminded myself that thinking my dead boyfriend was sending me notes sounded a lot like paranoia. "Someone's pranking me, that's all."

Lori frowned. "I did notice Brittany disappear for like ten minutes."

"You didn't see where she went?"

"No. She and Ian were making out and then she got up and went somewhere. I assumed she was going into the bathroom. She got back to the fire right before you did."

I frowned. Maybe scaring me was Brittany's revenge for all the reasons she was mad at me.

The note was written in all block letters, so I couldn't even try to match her handwriting. "I could ask her if she wrote it."

Lori shook her head. "She wouldn't admit to it. If she wrote it, it's because she wants to scare you."

"Yeah," I said. "Well, it's working."

CHAPTER 13

I had tucked the note from the corn maze into my desk drawer, hoping to be able to ignore it, but the next day, I pulled it out again and reread it. It didn't make any sense.

I put the note aside and opened my journal to write about the panic attack in the corn maze, like the good little patient I was. I started writing when my hand stilled on the page. I stared at the mostly blank notebook paper for a long moment.

I looked back and forth between the note and my journal. The paper was the same. Like, exactly the same.

My breathing sped up.

I flipped through the journal to the back where the page had been torn out and I held the note up to it. My hand shook.

The edges matched perfectly. My stomach dropped

Someone had been in my room. Up until that moment, I'd been half convinced that my parents were right and I'd just forgotten moving things around. But now I knew for sure that someone else had done it. Someone who wanted to scare me.

The note said the person was watching me, that I'd forgotten them. What did that mean? And how were they getting in the house? We never left the doors unlocked. Ian's family had a key, but I trusted all of them.

I went downstairs. Dad was on his laptop in front of the TV. "Where's Mom?" I asked.

Dad pointed at the home office they shared. "On the phone. She's on call this week." He looked back at his laptop, but after a moment, looked back up at me, like he was surprised I was still there. "Everything okay?"

I took a deep breath. "Something weird happened at the bonfire."

"Weirder than the music you like?" he asked. "Because I was listening to the radio today and—"

"Dad, it has nothing to do with music."

His eyebrows drew together. "I'm listening."

"I was in the corn maze with a friend." I almost said that I thought we were being followed, but he'd think that was paranoid and I wanted him to take me seriously. "We got separated, and someone stuffed a note through the corn. It said, 'I'm watching you.' The paper was torn out of my journal."

"How do you know it was from your journal?" Dad asked.

"The edges match."

"The edges match?" he asked, half laughing like he thought I was joking.

"They match exactly! Someone was in my room!" I gestured wildly. "They moved my things and paged through my journal. I told you that."

"I remember," Dad said, his voice carefully neutral. "I also remember your mother and I checking the locks. Was the door locked when you got home from school today?"

"Yes."

"Have you lost your keys?"

"No. They're always in my backpack."

My mom walked in from the other room. There were dark circles under her eyes. "What's going on?" She looked back and forth between me and my dad, probably feeling the tension in the room.

Dad's lips pressed into a thin line. He looked at me and raised his eyebrows. After a moment, when I didn't say anything, he said, "Charlotte still thinks someone broke in the other day. That they tore a page out of her journal and wrote her a note, that they then left for her at the corn maze."

When he put it like that, it did seem ridiculous.

Both Mom's eyebrows went up and she opened her mouth to speak, then closed it and frowned.

Dad sighed. "The thing is, there are a lot of explanations that are much more reasonable. A creepy note in a corn maze was probably someone horsing around. 'I'm watching you' is so vague that it could have worked for anyone. We already talked about someone being in your room, that you might have forgotten you moved things."

"What about the page from my journal?" I asked.

"Just because it was similar paper and the edges looks like they match doesn't mean it's actually from your journal," Dad said. "Coincidences happen."

Jerry used to do this thing where he'd twist my words and convince me I'd said something completely different than I had. I couldn't help but notice how much talking to my parents made me feel the same way.

I stared at the floor and tried not to cry as all the things I wanted to say burned the tip of my tongue.

"When you hear hoofbeats, don't think zebras," Dad said.

I just nodded, willing my frustrated tears not to spill over.

"Are you . . . ?" Mom asked. "Have you talked to Gemma about this?"

"I haven't seen her since then," I said. "I'll tell her next time."

"Make sure you do. The insurance only gives us twelve sessions, kiddo," Dad said. "You're already halfway through."

He said it like I wasn't taking it seriously. Like I wasn't trying to get better. Of course I was, but I also wasn't convinced twelve sessions were enough to get over your boyfriend dying in the car right next to you.

"Charlotte, honey, I'm glad you're talking about this." Mom rubbed her temple. "We're always here for you, and it's important to check in to see if your thoughts sound rational. School is stressful, and stress could be making your condition worse."

My condition. Like I had a disease. I found myself nodding. Their explanations sounded logical. I sometimes had flashbacks of my dead boyfriend and heard his voice. Maybe I couldn't tell what was real and what wasn't anymore.

"You know," Mom said slowly, "maybe it would do you good to get out with friends more. Or join cheerleading again. Get some exercise and get those endorphins going."

"What?" Like hanging out with friends was going to fix everything.

"I just think"—she looked at Dad, and I realized they'd been discussing this, waiting for the right moment to talk about it—"that you spend a lot of time alone."

"I just went out with Ian and Lori last night, remember? Corn maze, note?"

"You don't have to get smart," Mom said.

I wanted to scream. They said they wanted me to talk to them but then dismissed everything I said. It was like they didn't hear me. I wondered what explanation they would have had for Jerry, if I had told them the truth about him. Maybe they would have said he needed to get his endorphins going. Maybe they would have said I should have tried harder not to make him mad. Or that I was imagining the things he did.

The phone rang, and my mom checked the screen. "I've got to take this." She answered the phone and said, "This is Patricia. Please hold a moment." She hit the mute button on her phone. "Look, I know things have been tough for you since Jerry died. I know you worry. But no one has been sneaking in. Your mind is playing tricks on you, but you can't let it win. Promise me you'll think about what I'm saying."

"Sure." Was my mom right? Could I not trust anything I thought anymore?

"You're a strong girl." Mom squeezed my hand before turning to leave. "I know you're going to get through this."

I went back to my room and tried to concentrate on homework, but my mind kept drifting. I tried to convince myself that no one was breaking into the house. That I wasn't being haunted.

When I finally fell asleep, I dreamed that I was sprinting through the corn maze. Stalks slapped me in the face and scratched my arms, but I didn't stop. Jerry was behind me, and if he caught up to me, he would kill me.

Heart racing, I ran and ran. I desperately wanted to turn around and see how close he was, but I knew if I did that, he'd get me.

A hand touched my shoulder, and I spun around, ready to fight.

It was Sandy behind me, her expression hateful. She had a knife.

The knife slashed at me.

And I screamed.

CHAPTER 14

I drifted through first period on Monday, barely paying attention. My brain was foggier than normal. What little sleep I'd gotten had been interrupted by nightmares. When I saw Nate standing outside my homeroom, my stomach dropped. I wasn't up to pretending to be okay. I was coming unraveled.

I'm the only one who'll ever love you, Jerry's voice echoed.

"Hey." Nate smiled. "You didn't text me back yesterday. Does that mean you got some sleep?"

I gave him a tight smile. "I have to go in."

He checked his phone. "Class doesn't start for a few more minutes. You okay?"

"I'm fine." I started to walk past him, but he put his hand on my arm to stop me.

The pressure from Nate's hand was light, but I jerked out of his grip. "Don't touch me!"

Nate's smile blinked off like a switch and he took a step back. He looked like I'd slapped him. I didn't look at him as I walked past him to my seat.

Whenever I'd tried to walk away from Jerry, his fingers would clamp down and leave bruises. If we were in public, his face never gave anything away. But if we were alone, his face would be red with fury, veins popping out along his forehead. The image of Jerry played over and over in my brain, blotting out images of Nate.

"What was that?" Lori whispered.

"Nothing," I choked out. In my head, all I could see was Jerry's furious face.

The bell rang and the morning announcements started. It was too much. I needed quiet.

I reached in my pocket and wrapped my hand around my phone. It was solid and the plastic was warm from my pocket. I ran my finger along the edge of the case.

"Are you okay?" Lori whispered.

My breathing had slowed down, and it was no longer Jerry's face I saw but Nate's devastated expression.

"Panic attack?" Lori leaned toward me. "Can I do something to help?"

I still felt a little out of breath, but I turned toward Lori. "I'm okay," I whispered back. But I wasn't sure that was true.

Nate would think I was a freak, and I couldn't blame him. He hadn't done anything wrong, but I'd yelled at him like he'd hurt me. He didn't deserve that.

All I could do was apologize.

Before I lost my nerve, I texted him.

8:33 AM

Me

I'm SO sorry I yelled at
you. I had a nightmare
last night and am
in a crappy mood.

Nate

I'm sorry you had a bad night.

```
I was so confused.
I couldn't figure
out what I did.
```

Me

```
              It wasn't anything you did.
              It was my messed-up brain.
```

```
Nate
I like your messed-up brain.
You can just tell me if
you're having a bad day.
```

Me

```
              I will next time. I promise.
```

I could barely concentrate the rest of the day. My mind was on how I'd reacted to Nate, how I'd confused him for Jerry, even though his hand was gentle. I felt out of control, like my body had a mind of its own. My cheeks burned every time the memory of Nate's shocked face played in my head.

At lunch, I looked up from my phone to see Lori tearing her sandwich into pieces but not eating. "Are you okay?" I asked.

Her normally perfect eye makeup was smudged and her hair was caught in a messy ponytail, rather than the careful waves she normally wore. Her shirt seemed baggy, like she'd lost some weight. I'd been so caught up in my own stuff all day that this was the first time I'd noticed how disheveled Lori looked.

"No, I'm not. Everything is terrible."

"What happened?" I asked.

"I can't afford college. I was going to live at home and do the community college thing, but all of a sudden, my mom says I have to pay rent." She threw a piece of sandwich on her tray. "How am I supposed to work full-time and study?"

"How can she expect that?" I asked.

"Right?" Lori jerked her head. "And the worst part is, I would have gotten a scholarship for cheer. I know I would have."

I looked down at my tray and rubbed my wrist. Lori was right. If she'd gone to nationals, she probably would have been offered a scholarship.

"What about field hockey?" I asked.

Lori's jaw tensed. "I sucked. It was pointless, so I quit."

"Oh, I'm s—"

Lori interrupted me. "I keep thinking about the accident. Going over it in my head. We had that routine down." Lori fidgeted with her necklace. "And I keep thinking: Was it my fault? Did someone drop me on purpose? Was someone's grip off?"

My stomach tightened, remembering the jolt of panic when I'd realized Lori was falling. She'd landed hard and had stayed so still that I thought she'd been knocked out.

She brought up a video on her phone. It was me, Brittany, and Angelica throwing Lori in a basket toss twist. It was the same move we'd been practicing when Lori had gotten hurt. "Look at this," she said. "It's perfect." She flew through the air, lithe and graceful, then landed in our perfect basket. "How could anyone mess up something that we had down like that?"

"My wrist hurt that day." I could barely squeeze the words out past the lump in my throat. "Maybe it was my fault." I should have just made up a story about why my wrist hurt so I could sit out. But the team had been counting on me. We had a competition the next day and needed to practice our routine.

Lori looked up at me, and for a second, it was almost as if she didn't see me. "What do you mean, your wrist hurt?"

"I mean . . ." I leaned closer to her and dropped my voice almost to a whisper. "Jerry pushed me the night before and I landed wrong. I iced it, and it wasn't broken or anything, but at practice, it hurt, and I . . . Maybe my grip was off."

Lori's jaw tightened. "Well, was it or wasn't it?"

"I don't know. Honestly, I just don't know. I keep thinking about it, and I'm not sure."

She looked back down at her phone. The video had stopped playing, but it was still there, frozen on the screen, ready to restart. "I wish you'd told me that before."

"I wish I knew for sure. I'm so sorry. If I'd known you were going to get hurt, I would have sat out."

Lori's eyes lost focus. "I've lost everything. My life would be totally different now if I'd never gotten hurt."

I was always hurting the people I cared about most. It might have been my fault Lori got hurt. It might have been my fault Jerry died. I opened my mouth to apologize again, but it wouldn't do any good. I couldn't take back what I'd done.

"I knew how my whole life was going to be," she said, sounding like she was talking to herself. "When I had JD and cheering, everything was perfect. But now . . . everything is terrible."

"Things will get better," I said, even though I knew they might not.

Things didn't get better just because you wanted them to.

Lori looked at me and cocked her head. "You don't get it. I mean, I know you said you're having panic attacks and that things suck for you too, but . . . you have your parents and Ian and Nate. I have no one."

"You have me," I said. "I know I wasn't there for you this summer. I pulled away from everyone. But I promise I won't do that again. I'll make it up to you."

"How? How could you ever make something like that up to me?"

I flinched away from her.

She put a hand up. "I'm sorry. I don't know what's wrong with me. I shouldn't have said that. I'm being a miserable bitch and taking it out on you."

"No, you're right." I looked down, blinking back tears. "It's true."

"I try to be happy and let things go. I try so hard. But I can't." Her voice cracked. She looked around the cafeteria.

"I'm so sorry," I said again. "I'm sorry that maybe I dropped you and I'm sorry for this summer and . . . I'm just sorry."

Lori's eyes glinted with tears. "It's okay. I know you didn't mean to hurt me." She took a deep breath and forced a smile. "I'll be okay."

As I was walking from my locker after school, Ian threw an arm around my shoulder. "Want a ride home?"

He steered me to his car. I stopped in front of the passenger door. It had been a long day, with me overreacting to Nate, then Lori feeling down and my guilt. I wasn't sure I was up to riding home with Ian. I sighed.

Ian had started to get in the driver's side and paused halfway in. I hadn't even opened my door yet. "What's up?" he asked.

"Just having a bad day."

"Want to tell me about it?"

I shook my head. I couldn't get into Jerry today, and Lori's problems weren't mine to talk about. "I'm mostly thinking how you drive like a lunatic."

Ian cracked a smile. "I've never been in an accident. Or gotten a speeding ticket."

"Because they can't catch you." But I got in the passenger seat. I couldn't let fear stop me from doing things.

His car was a black hatchback with faded paint outside and worn seats inside. The car was vacuumed and clean, as always. It smelled faintly of sweat and more strongly of Febreze. I'd spent a lot of time in that car before Jerry had started getting pissed off whenever I hung out with Ian.

Not long after Ian got his license, the four of us had gone to the Jersey Shore for the day. It was only a two-hour drive from where we lived in PA, so our parents had agreed to let us go. Jerry and I sat together in the back seat, and Lori rode shotgun. We'd bought way too many snacks at Wawa, and the sounds of bags crackling and us crunching competed with the rock Lori was playing.

"Do not get crumbs in my car," Ian ordered.

Jerry laughed. "Too late. I already crushed up a bag of chips and dumped them on the floor."

Lori turned around and grinned at him.

Ian glared into the rearview mirror. "I will drown you in the ocean. Do not play with me."

I tried not to laugh, but when Lori looked at me, I lost it. Ian pretended to be mad, narrowing his eyes at all of us, but his lips twitched.

As Ian started to drive, I put my head on Jerry's shoulder, sure that the four of us would always be friends.

I could almost smell the salt and sunscreen as Ian drove slowly out of the school parking lot. "The speed limit is ridiculous!" he said. "How do people get anywhere in a timely manner?"

I curled my hand around the door handle and tried to focus on something other than the trees and cars whizzing by outside. I wanted to tell him about the corn maze and things in my room being moved, but I was already freaked out enough just being in the car.

"So how's Brittany?" I asked, trying to keep my voice even.

"Meh, I've moved on."

"That was fast."

"Yeah, well. She's hot but has a one-track mind."

"Since when is that a problem?"

He laughed. "That's not the track. She's obsessed with those musical reality shows. Like, they're the only thing she ever talked about. I watch them sometimes with Jacqui and they have some good singers. But damn, girl. Change the channel once in a while."

I burst out laughing, and for a moment, forgot to be scared of being in the car.

"Even worse, sometimes she'd try to sing the songs. That girl cannot sing. She may have damaged my eardrums. I suggested she maybe reserve her singing for the shower and she lost it. No thank you. There are other girls who are less trouble."

Was he trying to piss me off? He had to know I couldn't let that go. "Trouble? That's a nice way to talk about a girlfriend."

"Oh, whatever."

"I don't care that you broke up with her. But looking for a girl who's 'less trouble' is so sexist."

"It's not like I lie to anyone," he said. "I make sure they know I just want to have a little fun."

"They probably think they can change you." I rolled my eyes but then stopped. I'd thought I could change Jerry if I tried hard enough. *If you didn't make me crazy*, Jerry's voice echoed, *I wouldn't get so mad.*

"Not happening," he said. "It's my senior year of high school. Next year, college girls. I'm not ready for 'till death do us part.'"

We were quiet for a while. It sounded so easy when Ian said it. That when a relationship wasn't working, when you realized you weren't happy, you just ended it. But that wouldn't have worked with Jerry. I hesitated, the question I wanted to ask sticking in my throat a little. "Did you notice Jerry acting . . . different in the months before he died?"

Ian pulled in front of my house and put the car in park. He stared out the windshield. "He started drinking a lot," he said quietly. "But I never thought he'd drink and drive with you in the car. He loved you so much."

Had he loved me, though? I couldn't imagine hurting someone I loved. I pushed the thought aside. "Did he drink and drive when I wasn't there?"

"Sometimes. I mean, we'd have a few beers, but no one really drove drunk. But then he started getting pissed off over nothing and he smelled like booze a lot." Ian tapped his fingers on the steering wheel. "I don't know. He always had a temper, so I didn't really think much of it."

Jerry was hard to get along with if things didn't go his way. Ian laughed when I beat him at *Mario Kart*. Jerry pouted and said that he'd been given the crappy controller or he'd been distracted. He'd gotten into fights, but because it was usually defending Ian or me, we'd been okay with it.

"One of the guys had a flask at prom, and we were all spiking our drinks. But if I had known he was going to leave then . . . I would have stopped him." Ian turned to look at me, his eyes haunted. "You have to believe me. I never thought he'd be so stupid."

"It wasn't your fault."

"I didn't know his drinking was a problem. I thought he could handle it." Ian shook his head. "And I don't even know why he was leaving early in the first place."

"I don't blame you. If anything, I should have stopped him. I knew Jerry was drunk when I got in the car."

"Why did you get in the car, Charlie? You were sober. You know better."

I shook my head. "I don't know what I was thinking." But that wasn't true. I knew exactly why Jerry left early. I knew exactly why I'd gotten in the car. And I was never going to tell anyone.

CHAPTER 15

It was my mom's turn to drive me to therapy, and she was using her Air-Pods to talk on the phone when I got in the car. I put mine in and listened to music while staring out the window, thinking about what I wanted to tell Gemma.

When I got to her office, I still wasn't sure what I wanted to say. "Can I ask you a question?" I said.

"You can ask me anything," Gemma said. "If I don't feel like I should answer it, I'll just tell you."

"What if I tell you something . . . something bad? Would you tell my parents?"

Gemma raised her eyebrows and leaned forward in her chair. "You might not remember this, but when you first started seeing me, I had your parents sign a contract saying that they understood that what we talk about is between you and me. The only way I would breach your confidentiality is if I needed to tell someone to help keep you or someone else safe. Otherwise, it stays between us until you're ready to tell them yourself."

That would be never.

I took a deep breath. Was I really going to do this? I gripped my shaking hands together. "Jerry . . ." It was all I could get out. The rest stuck in my throat.

After what seemed like hours, Gemma prompted gently, "Jerry?"

I couldn't catch my breath. My face burned and I couldn't stop the tears from spilling out.

"Charlotte, I want you to ground yourself. Concentrate on what your body is doing right now. Flatten your hands on your thighs."

My vision was narrowing, but I could still hear her. I pried my hands apart and flattened them.

"Good. Now I want you to concentrate on how your jeans feel under your hands. Are they cool or warm? Are they smooth or rough?"

Warm from my body heat. Smooth and comfortable. They were my favorite pair.

"I need you to take some deep breaths. In through the nose, feel your stomach expand. Hold it . . . and let it out to the count of four. Bring your stomach in."

Gemma kept coaxing me through the panic attack, and it started to recede. When it was finally over, I just wanted to hide my face and disappear. I felt better, but my stomach was still in knots. "I'm sorry."

"For what?" she asked.

"For . . ." I gestured.

"For having a panic attack?" Gemma's brows drew together, and her lips quirked up.

I nodded.

"First, that's the whole reason you're here. I *want* to help you. Second, you don't have to apologize for your emotions. You're allowed to feel however you feel. Now, if your emotions make you behave badly, then that's different. Emotions aren't good or bad. They're just human."

The knots in my stomach loosened.

"You wanted to tell me something about Jerry?" she asked.

I finally looked at her. Behind her glasses, her eyes were soft and brown and completely focused on me.

I wanted to lie. I wasn't ready yet.

But I wanted to be done with the nightmares and the panic attacks. And I was done hurting people I cared about. I'd been a bad friend to Lori and Ian. I'd snapped at Nate. I didn't want to feel this way anymore. Maybe I'd never be ready to talk about Jerry. But I had to try.

"He shoved me," I blurted out. "He used to grab me so hard I had bruises. And when I'd try to get away, he wouldn't let me go."

I couldn't look at Gemma. I wasn't ready to see her reaction, but the words kept spilling out. "He never hit me. It wasn't like that. And it was only sometimes when I did something stupid."

Gemma nudged the tissue box toward me, and I realized I'd started crying again. I grabbed a few tissues.

"I'm sorry," I said.

"Thank you for being honest with me," Gemma said.

My head whipped up and I looked at her. She was looking at me seriously, but she didn't seem surprised.

"It takes a lot of bravery to tell the truth," she said.

Tears leaked out of my eyes and I tried to blink them back. "You believe me?"

"Yes."

I covered my face with balled-up tissues and cried. I tried to stop. I didn't want to waste her time, but the tears just kept coming. When I finally uncovered my face, Gemma didn't seem impatient. "So, I'm curious. What's the difference between hitting and shoving?"

It seemed obvious to me. "When you hit someone, you might give them a black eye or a split lip. Jerry never did anything like that."

Gemma nodded. "Did he scare you?"

"Sometimes."

"What scared you?"

"I was scared he'd hurt me." I shook my head. "I don't know why I can't get him out of my head. I just want him to go away."

"Maybe you keep thinking about it because you're trying to figure it out."

"But . . . why do I still miss him? Even though he was like that? It makes me feel like I'm just making a big deal of nothing."

"You know what no one tells you?" Gemma asked. "No one tells you that when someone is terrible to you, the feelings you have for them don't just disappear. Love doesn't just go away because we want it to. Even when you know that what someone did to you was wrong, it's still hard to let go of the person you fell in love with."

"I don't want to be scared anymore. I don't want to freak out because a friend put his hand on my arm and it made me think of Jerry. I want to learn how to get creepy guys to leave me alone. I just want to . . . be okay."

"You took the first step today, telling me the truth about Jerry. Don't back away from that, as hard as it feels."

"Okay." I gripped my hands together in my lap. I felt like someone had rubbed my skin with sandpaper. Maybe secrets kept the wound from healing, but the truth hurt too.

Gemma glanced down at my hands, then back to my face. "You said that Jerry shoved you, that he scared you, and that he sometimes stopped you from leaving. It sounds like your PTSD isn't just from the accident, but from the abuse you suffered."

The word *abuse* made my mouth fall open. "But he always said he didn't mean it. He always apologized."

Gemma nodded. "They always do. But when someone apologizes, but then keeps doing the same thing, does that apology mean anything?"

"He really seemed like he meant it, though," I said in a small voice.

"He didn't just apologize. He did nice things to make it up to me. When he wasn't mad, he was really sweet."

"Okay, so he meant it. But not enough to change. He probably didn't know how, but that doesn't excuse it." She leaned forward. "Everyone gets angry. I do. I'm sure you do. But not everyone deals with their anger in a healthy way. Sometimes people lash out at others. That's usually because they have some deep wound inside that's festering. But no matter what was going on with him, that doesn't mean it was okay for him to lash out at you."

I shifted in my chair, trying to get comfortable. "I just feel like it was all my fault. The accident, how he was sometimes . . . I thought I could help him."

"When someone is hurting you, no matter how much you want to, you can't help them," Gemma said softly. "And the thing is, you can't help anyone who doesn't want it. You're responsible for you. If you want to change, you're the only one who can make it happen. I can sit here and listen and offer guidance, but it's up to you what you do with it."

CHAPTER 16

After therapy, my mom was craving Mexican food, so we went to our favorite place. The tables were scarred wood and it was dark inside. But the food was really good and the servers were always nice. As soon as we sat down and ordered, Mom pulled out her phone to check her work email. The restaurant was crammed full of people and the buzz of voices made it almost too loud for conversation.

I'd told Gemma and Lori about Jerry and things had been okay. Even though my eyes ached from crying, I felt better, lighter. I hadn't realized how heavy my secrets were.

I needed to text Nate. I felt like I owed him an explanation and hoped I hadn't scared him off.

5:01 PM

Me

About before . . . I had a
nightmare last night, and it was
still in my head when you
put your hand on my arm.
Sometimes I don't react
well when people touch me.

I typed *even though I really like you*, but deleted it. I wasn't sure I was ready to go there.

5:05 PM

Nate

I get it. We all have those nights.

And I won't try to touch you again

without asking.

I didn't want Nate to feel like he couldn't touch me, but I appreciated it. And if I was going to react like that, it was probably for the best.

5:07 PM

Me

I feel like I have more bad

nights than good ones. You know

about the accident, right?

Nate

Jerry crashed the car

on prom night.

Me

I still have nightmares about it.

Nate

Is that why you don't sleep?

Me

Yeah.

It was true, but not the whole truth.

5:12 PM

```
Nate
I don't know if you know,
but my mom died around
the same time as Jerry.


Nate
She had cancer. Toward
the end, she was home,
and she often woke up at
night with pain. She tried
to be quiet, but I'd still
hear her and my dad
moving around the
house or talking.


Nate
I haven't been able to get back
to a regular sleep schedule
since then. Part of me is still
listening for her voice.
```

My heart ached for him. I didn't know his mom died. We weren't friends last year, and if people had been talking about his mom around the time Jerry died, I wouldn't have heard them.

5:13 PM

                                        Me

        I'm sorry about your mom.

It felt like a stupid thing to say, but I was.

5:15 PM

Nate

Thanks. I just wanted to tell
you that so you know I
understand what it's like
to be messed up.

Nate

My dad won't talk about it.
My little sister Megan has
funerals for her dolls.

Nate

You can always talk to me.

                                        Me

        I just don't want to bother you.

Nate

Bother me anytime you want.
That's what I'm here for.

A smile spread across my face. Tension flowed out of my shoulders. I hadn't even realized I was hunched up. I had people who wanted to hear what I had to say. I didn't have to keep lying, and there was something freeing in that.

My mom slammed her phone down on the table, and I flinched. "You'd think adults could follow through on a simple task without constant reminders. It's like herding cats." She blew the hair out of her face. "Who are you texting?"

"Oh, um . . . a friend."

5:19 PM

                                        Me
          Got to go. At dinner with my mom.

Nate
K. I'll text you later.

"Did you tell Gemma about how you thought someone has been breaking in?" she asked.

I hadn't even thought about it. "No. I forgot."

"You forgot?" Mom's phone buzzed, and she glanced at the message and rolled her eyes before looking back at me. "How is she supposed to help with your anxiety if you don't tell her what's going on? What *did* you talk about?"

"I don't know. Other stuff."

"You don't know?" She made a face. "It seemed really important to you the other night. Maybe I should call her and tell her what's been going on."

"Mom, no." I shook my head.

"I just want you to feel better," Mom said. "I hate seeing you so scared of everything. I just wish I could do something."

"I'll tell her, I promise. Next session."

"You know," Mom said in an overly casual voice, "if you can't talk to Gemma, or you don't think she's helping, we could find you another therapist."

"No, she's helping." I broke a tortilla chip into tiny pieces. "I . . ."

"It's just . . . I know how much you loved Jerry, and I know you're grieving. You feel like he was your whole life, but that's not true. You have your whole life ahead of you. It's not betraying him to move on."

I couldn't talk to her. She only asked questions when she thought she knew the answer, and she didn't hear what I actually said. So I swallowed all the things I wanted to say and just said, "I like Gemma."

"Liking her doesn't make her a good therapist," Mom said. "I really hoped everything would be back to normal by now."

No matter how hard I tried, it was never enough.

The waiter delivered our dinners. As he set our plates in front of us, Mom smiled. "Well, this looks delicious!"

CHAPTER 17

When I got home, I fell on my bed. I had homework, but no motivation.
I was exhausted from crying and my stomach was full of enchiladas. My
phone pinged, pulling me from my stupor.

7:03 PM

Nate
Some people believe the Bermuda
Triangle is a time portal.
People lose or gain time there.

Me
The losing time part sounds
kind of like school.

Me
Why are you so interested
in all this weird stuff?

Nate
I like learning about things
there aren't real answers for.

Me
So are you going to be like
a paranormal investigator?

Nate

A veterinarian, probably.

How about you?

                                                    Me

                                    I don't know.

Nate

Didn't you hear? If

you don't have it

all figured out by

your junior year,

the world will explode.

                                                    Me

                            I did hear that somewhere.

Nate

Do you want to be

responsible for that?

                                                    Me

                                    I don't want to be

                                    responsible for

                                    anything.

I used to have goals, like selling upcycled clothes online, but now I was just trying to get through one day at a time.

7:10 PM

Nate

So you want to be a sloth?

Me

I was thinking raccoon.

They're adorable and up all night.

Plus they're all about the snacks.

Nate

I could seriously watch

videos of raccoons all day.

In fact, let's do that sometime.

Come over and we'll eat nachos

and Cheetos and Combos and

watch videos of raccoons.

Me

All the important food groups!

I'm in. Just tell me when and where.

I grinned as I pulled my books and notes out of my backpack and piled them on my desk. Beside my laptop was my locket.

I froze. My math notebook slid out of my hands and slapped the carpet. I jumped at the sound, but didn't take my eyes off the locket.

It had been months since I'd seen it. After Jerry died, I'd put things he'd given me in a cardboard box and taped it shut.

The locket was a gold heart on a long chain. If I opened it, there would be a picture of Jerry on one side and me on the other. Face-to-face, forever.

Jerry would be mad at me for taking it off. My heart pounded in my ears. My hands were squeezed into fists and my fingernails dug into my palms.

Jerry had given the locket to me early on, when a locket with our pictures still seemed romantic. It had been our one-month anniversary, and he'd been nervous when he handed me the box. "You're the best thing that's ever happened to me. You were made for me."

"I'll never take it off."

I hadn't kept my promise. They'd taken it off me at the hospital, and' I'd never put it back on.

I couldn't take my eyes off it. How had it gotten on my desk? Had I taken it out of the box in the middle of the night? Was I doing things I didn't remember? Collapsing into the chair, I reached out toward the locket with shaking fingers, but then stopped before I touched it.

My breath clogged in my throat as I looked around my room, searching for anything else that was out of place.

I bolted out of my chair and checked the window. It was locked. I fell to my knees in front of my closet, shoving shoes out of the way until I found the box at the back. It was still taped shut. I left it there and sat back on my heels, thinking.

I knew I'd put the locket in the box. Hadn't I? I squinted, trying to remember.

The day I'd gotten home from the hospital was a blur. I remembered grabbing a big box from the recycling pile and throwing everything of Jerry's I could find into it. Pictures, gifts, cards. The locket and my prom dress had been in a drawstring bag from the hospital, and I would have just dumped it in, wouldn't I?

The memory was muddy. I couldn't remember for sure if I'd put the locket in the box. But even if I'd put it in my jewelry box, how had it gotten to my desk?

I finally picked up the locket, using my thumbnail to pry it open. Jerry's picture was missing. My photo was on the other side, but my face was scribbled out so violently that the picture was torn.

My heart slammed in my chest. Someone hated me.

Jerry's voice echoed in my head. *I told you I'd never let you go. I'm the only one who'll ever love you.*

If anyone could find a way to stick around after death, it would be Jerry. Just to make sure I never got away.

I grabbed my phone and sent a text to Lori, and then one to Ian.

7:31 PM

Me

So . . . something
weird just happened.

Lori responded right away.

7:32 PM

Lori

Weird?

Me

I think someone broke in.

The locket Jerry gave me was in
this cardboard box in my
closet, and while I wasn't home,
someone moved it to my desk.

Lori
That is so creepy! WTH?

Lori
Do you think this has something
to do with that note?

Me
I think someone is messing
with me, but I don't know why.

Lori
OMG, I would be totally
freaking out! Are you okay?

Me
I don't know. What am I supposed
to do? My parents think I'm
making it up or something.

Lori
You don't think they'll
want to call the police?

Me

I've told them twice that

I think someone is breaking in,

but they don't believe me.

Unless there was something concrete I could show my parents to *prove* that someone was breaking in, there was no use in telling them about it. I went downstairs and checked the windows. I checked the back and front door locks again. When I got to the living room, where my parents were watching TV and working on their laptops, Paisley was curled up between them. I hated that she preferred them to me now. I tried to be subtle about checking the window locks in the living room, but my dad asked, "What are you doing?"

"Just . . . checking the locks."

"Why?" He frowned.

"You don't think someone broke in again, do you?" Mom asked, sounding concerned.

For a second, I thought about telling them. But I didn't want another lecture about taking therapy seriously.

"Um . . . it's part of my treatment. Reality testing. When I get worried about something, I check to see if it's real. So I'm just . . . checking the locks." It actually had been something Gemma and I talked about several sessions ago, and I was glad for the sudden memory.

Mom and Dad exchanged glances, like they weren't sure if they should be worried or glad. Eventually, Mom took a deep breath and said, "That's great. We're proud of you."

I got cleaning spray and started wiping down everything in my room. I was sure someone was breaking in, even if it made no sense. I wanted to wash my sheets and all the clothes in my drawers too. My skin crawled, imagining someone picking up my pens, opening my drawers, maybe lying on my bed.

I sat at my desk, turning the locket over in my hands, when my cell phone pinged.

8:10 PM

Ian

Sorry. Jacqui hid my phone again.

I didn't want to talk about it any more right now. I didn't even want to think about it.

8:11 PM

Me

Never mind. It was nothing.

Ian

Okay, but if you change your mind
and it's something, I'm here.

CHAPTER 18

I stared at Ian's message for a long time before putting my phone down. I put the locket on top of my desk, then dragged the box of Jerry's things out of the closet.

Opening the box was like ripping a seam. When I sewed something and got it wrong for whatever reason, I never wanted to pull out that first stitch and undo all my hard work. But if I didn't, the shirt would be unwearable until I corrected it. I had to open the seam completely in order to make it right.

It would be hard, but I had to pull the first stitch.

I cut the tape and looked inside. On top were pictures of Jerry and me. The one at the very top was a framed photo. I was wearing a shirt with clashing colors, which meant it was before things went bad. He'd beat me at some video game, and I was pretending to be mad at him, so he'd tickled me. My mom had snapped a photo when we were laughing, heads together.

In the beginning, it had been like that all the time. I'd blushed when Jerry had first started saying things like "You're beautiful." He had a way of making me feel like I was the most important person in his life. When he was around, he was the only person I could concentrate on. My body felt electrified the moment he walked into a room.

In the beginning.

I couldn't pinpoint when "You're beautiful" changed to "You'd be beautiful if you stopped wearing that weird shit," but I'd never forget the first time he shoved me.

I flipped the picture over so I wouldn't have to look at it and shuffled all the other photos into a pile without looking at them. Underneath the pictures was the hospital bag with my prom dress. It was crumpled up and stained with blood. When the ambulance arrived, the EMT had asked me a bunch of questions. I was too out of it to answer her but remembered looking down at myself in my bloody dress and thinking, *Jerry ruins everything.* I hadn't known he was dead until later.

There was a glass paperweight Jerry had given me for Christmas when we were kids, along with a stuffed leopard he'd won for me at a carnival. But the notes and cards he'd written to me were missing. Someone had let Jerry out of the box where I'd tried to put him.

I put the pictures on the bottom, intending to pile everything else on top when the locket fell off my desk, making a soft clink as it hit the carpet. I looked around for Paisley, but she wasn't there. The locket had fallen off the desk for no reason. Goose bumps popped up on my skin. My room had gotten cold. Really cold.

Dad had the heating system checked and said my room was fine, but I blew out a breath and expected to see a cloud of vapor.

Someone was watching me. I stood up and scanned every corner of my room. I dropped to my knees and looked under the bed. There was no one there. But my muscles screamed at me to run away.

When I picked up the locket, it was as chilly as if I'd just taken it out of the fridge.

The hairs on the back of my neck stood up. No one else filled a room like Jerry, and this felt like him.

The first bars of "You Were Made for Me" drifted from my laptop. I froze. I could almost hear Jerry singing it to me.

I hurried to my laptop, slamming it shut to make it stop.

When silence fell, it seemed too loud.

I clamped my jaw shut so my teeth wouldn't chatter. There were logical explanations for everything. Just because I couldn't think of them didn't mean they didn't exist.

"Ghosts aren't real," I said out loud.

I dropped the locket in the box and wiped my hand on my pants. My arms felt limp and rubbery. I stuffed everything back in the box.

The song wouldn't stop echoing in my head as I hurried downstairs and grabbed a roll of tape. I circled the entire box four times before shoving it back in my closet. My room had gone back to a normal temperature.

I put on my pajamas and curled up under the covers, hugging my old teddy bear.

But when I tried to close my eyes, I couldn't. I looked around my room. My walls were the same turquoise as always. My multicolored backpack was leaning against my desk, right where I'd left it. Everything was in its place. It all looked the same as it always did, but it felt different somehow. Like I wasn't safe in here anymore.

And if I wasn't safe in my room, then maybe I wasn't safe anywhere.

OCTOBER

CHAPTER 19

Nate fell in step beside me as I walked to homeroom. "Question. Why did you quit cheer?"

We'd gotten into the habit of him walking me to class and asking random questions. I could never tell what he was going to ask, but I liked that he was curious. It was like he was trying to learn everything about me. "After Lori got hurt and had to quit, I wasn't that into it anymore."

"You didn't want to go out for the team this year?"

"I got the job at Scoops this summer, so I'm too busy anyway. Why did you quit basketball?"

Nate shrugged. "I missed a lot of practice when my mom got sick. Coach was cool about it, but eventually I just stopped going. It wasn't important anymore." His excuses sounded as threadbare as mine.

Nate wasn't looking at me. He was staring over my head, his eyes unfocused. "My parents didn't come to every game, but they came to the big ones. When my mom was in the hospital, my dad came to a game alone. And when I looked at the crowd and saw him sitting there with an empty seat next to him, I realized that was how it was going to be from then on. That was my last game."

I wasn't sure if I should say anything. I always felt weird offering sympathy, but I had to do something.

I threw my arms around him and hugged him. He wrapped his arms around me and rested his chin on my head. Everything about Nate was different than Jerry. He smelled like mint and soap, not cologne.

The bell rang, and we sprang apart, red-faced and grinning. "I'd better go," he said.

I dropped my eyes, feeling suddenly shy. "I'll see you later."

I felt like I was floating as I walked into homeroom, and my cheeks still felt warm, but I didn't care if I was blushing. I sat next to Lori, who looked at me, puzzled. "What's up with you?" she whispered as morning announcements started.

"Just Nate," I whispered back.

"You like him."

"He's pretty great."

Our homeroom teacher clapped her hands. "Ladies! Pay attention!"

I kept thinking about that moment with Nate, how a hug from him was enough to make me happy. I barely concentrated on class that day, but for once, it wasn't because of anxiety.

When I got to chemistry, I was just hoping my lab partner, José, would pay better attention than me so that we wouldn't burn down the building. I was setting up the supplies we'd need when my phone buzzed.

I smiled, figuring Nate was sending me something silly. I checked my phone under the table, where Mrs. Perella wouldn't see.

10:24 AM

Jerry

Did you miss me?

Everything froze. My body, my breath, time.

I couldn't answer. I couldn't think. I couldn't move.

Jerry was back. He was texting me. But he was dead.

Wasn't he?

José nudged me. "Earth to Charlotte."

I screamed.

The room fell silent as everyone turned to look at me. Heat crept into my face as my heart began racing.

Mrs. Perella moved toward me, her long skirt swishing against her leather boots. The heels click-clacked on the tile. "Charlotte, are you all right?"

My throat was so dry I couldn't answer.

My phone buzzed in my hand but I didn't look down. Was my dead boyfriend really texting me?

"Do you need to go to the nurse?"

Someone giggled, but I didn't look.

"Yes. Nurse," I choked out. Before Mrs. Perella could say anything else, I fled, leaving my backpack behind.

I ran for the bathroom, but when I shoved the door open, I heard voices. I backed out, wanting to be alone. Gabe was in the hallway, staring at me. "Charlotte, are you . . . ?" But I kept moving, not waiting to hear what he was going to say.

When I peeked into the auditorium, it was dark inside. I ran up on the stage and hid behind the curtain.

10:29 AM

Jerry

Answer me! Or are
you too busy
texting your
new boyfriend?

I couldn't breathe. I started typing a response, trying to soothe, like always.

Me

You know there's no one

But then I stopped. *It can't be Jerry.* With shaking hands, I deleted what I wrote.

10:35 AM

Me

Who is this?

Jerry

I've been watching you. You and Nate

Jerry

What's wrong? Don't you want
people knowing that you've
already forgotten me, like
I didn't even matter?

Me

WHO IS THIS?

Jerry

You know who it is. And you didn't
answer my question

Autocorrect helped me, for once, since I kept hitting wrong letters.

10:42 AM

Me

Jerry's dead. Leave me alone!

The phone went silent for several seconds, half a minute, a minute. I tried to make myself breathe normally as I waited, fighting panic and hoping that there'd be no response or that the person on the other end would say it was a wrong number. It wouldn't make sense, but I hoped for it anyway.

But then my phone buzzed. I told myself not to look, to ignore it. But I couldn't.

10:45 AM

Jerry

I told you I'd never let you go

I threw my phone across the stage and leaned my head against the wall, gasping for breath. The air felt too thick.

The memory slammed into me. Jerry and me, in his living room. Him, standing in front of me, red-faced and angry. Spit had sprayed from his lips, but I didn't dare flinch. If I flinched, that made it worse. *He gripped my arm so tightly that he left finger-shaped bruises. "You're cheating on me. Admit it!"*

"No, I would never. I love you."

He'd jerked me toward him, and I couldn't control my reaction. I pulled away. His eyes went wild. "You are. You're a lying bitch! I will never let you go. Do you understand me? I. Will. Never. Let. You. Go."

Tears flooded my eyes. The panic attack sucked me down into it. My insides shook and my heart pounded in my chest. I tried to force myself to breathe evenly, to try to remember how Gemma would coax me through it, but nothing worked. I just had to ride it out.

Eventually, the panic attack released its grip, and I was back to myself again. My cheeks were wet with tears, and I was drenched with sweat. My muscles were shaky, like I'd just gotten done running drills. *It isn't real. He can't hurt me anymore.*

But maybe he could. If he could text me, he could hurt me. Someone had been in my room.

My phone buzzed as another text came through. Jerry got mad if I didn't answer. Accused me of talking to someone else. Text after text, demanding I answer.

My phone vibrated again.

Someone was messing with me. I got up and retrieved my phone. Taking a shaky breath, I sat in one of the auditorium seats and looked at my messages.

11:11 AM

Jerry

Other people might not
see what you're
really like, but I do

Jerry

I haven't forgotten what
you did to me. I'll never forget

My breath caught in my throat. There was only one thing I'd ever done to Jerry, and no one else knew about that.

Maybe he wasn't really dead. I couldn't say for sure. It had been a closed casket.

But he had to be dead. People didn't fake their deaths, not in real life.

CHAPTER 20

After I picked up my backpack from Mrs. Perella and arranged to make up the lab, Nate and I met in one of the library's meetings rooms. We were supposed to study for a history test together. As I walked down the hall toward the library, I kept looking around. The hair on the back of my neck stood up, like someone was watching me. But I didn't see anyone looking my way.

Nate was wearing a T-shirt that had a screen print of Earth with the words NASA on the top and NOT FLAT; WE CHECKED on the bottom. With everything that was going on, I just wanted to lay my head on his shoulder and close my eyes for a little while.

Instead, I sat down across from him.

"I'm thinking of joining the circus," Nate said. "I feel like a life as a trapeze artist would be better than taking this test."

I laughed. "And have you ever been on a trapeze before?"

"No . . . and I'm kind of afraid of heights. But Mr. Heller is so boring!" Nate threw his head back dramatically. "How can he make war boring?"

"I should record his lectures so I can actually fall asleep at night," I said.

"I know!" Nate said. "I'd just be afraid I'd dream of him. Can you imagine worse dreams than listening to him go on and on about the Great Depression?"

I'd been grinning, but the mention of dreams made me think of Jerry again, and the smile slid off my face.

"What's wrong?" Nate asked.

I shook my head. "It's nothing." I tried to force a smile, but it didn't work.

He studied me for a long moment, looking uncharacteristically serious. "I know you have a lot of secrets," he said quietly. "And I'd never push you to tell me anything you didn't want to. But you can talk to me, you know."

"I know." I looked down at my history notes and rubbed at a smudge with my finger.

"I just hate seeing you so unhappy," Nate said. "Not that I'm saying you have to be happy all the time or anything. But it makes me want to fix it. And I know I probably can't, but it doesn't stop me from wanting to try."

He couldn't fix it, but he could listen. And the messages mentioned that the person had been watching Nate too. So he deserved to know. I opened my mouth, wanting to tell him, but the words wouldn't come out. It was easier to take my phone out of my pocket and hand it to him.

Nate mouthed the words as he read, and it made me want to smile. But I was too jittery inside. I wiped my clammy palms on my jeans.

Finally, Nate looked up from the screen, his face scrunched up with confusion. "That is super weird. And this is me saying that, so . . ."

I looked back down at my history notes. "I'm scared. Who would even do that?"

"That's the question. Because what kind of creep pretends to be your dead boyfriend?" Nate looked down at my phone again, like he wanted to reread the messages, but my phone had gone dark.

"I don't know."

"It's just . . ." He looked up at me, studying my face. "Did the messages feel . . . threatening to you?"

"Yes." So he'd seen it too. Even without knowing about Jerry, he'd seen the threats implied. A knot loosened in my chest.

"Why would someone pretend to be Jerry and act like that? Why not just be . . . anonymous or something?"

Because the person had to know about me and Jerry.

My hands started to shake. I dug my fingers into my thighs, trying to make them stop, trying to make myself breathe normally. Someone had known how Jerry treated me, but hadn't done anything about it. And now they were using it against me.

"You okay?" Nate asked.

"I need . . . just . . . bathroom," I choked out.

I fled to the bathroom and took several deep breaths. I washed my face and took a moment to get myself under control. Was I really going to do this? Tell Nate about Jerry?

I tried to picture myself walking back into the study room and talking to Nate, but I couldn't. I didn't think I could force the words out through the lump in my throat.

I pulled out my phone.

4:28 PM

Me

I'm sorry. I want to tell you what's going on, but I don't think I can say it out loud.

Nate

So don't. Come back and we'll text.

Me

Won't that be weird?

Nate

Did you forget who you're talking to?

If anyone would be okay with being a little weird, it was Nate. Nate, with his government conspiracy theories, with his thoughts on aliens. Nate, who constantly surprised me with the bizarre things he said.

I went back to the room where we'd been working, and Nate glanced up at me, then flashed me a smile. Then he looked back down at his phone, like he was giving me space.

My shoulders relaxed. It was just easier when I didn't have to say it out loud. But there was something comforting about his being there with me.

4:31 PM

Me

Jerry was mean to me.

Like, really mean.

The stuff in the text

messages are things he

actually said to me,

and someone apparently

knows that.

Nate glanced up at me, his eyes wide. Then back down to his phone.

I rubbed my wrist as I waited for him to type a reply. Talking about Jerry was getting easier. Sort of.

4:33 PM

Nate

So it WAS a threat.

That thing about

"I'll never let you go."

Me

He used to say that to me
all the time. He said I
belonged to him.

Nate made a sound in his throat and took an audible deep breath. His fingers hovered over his phone like he didn't know what to type.

Gemma had said what Jerry did to me was abuse. She'd said it casually. Like the word was just a word and didn't redefine everything. I bit my lip, then sent a follow-up text.

4:34 PM

Me

My therapist said he was
abusive? I don't know. ☹

Nate rubbed his temple, then looked over at me. "I don't know what to say to that. I want to ask if you're okay, but that doesn't seem like the right thing. And I want to hug you or . . . do something. I just . . . I'm sorry that happened to you."

"You . . . believe me?" No questions? No justifications? He just believed me? I blinked back tears.

Nate leaned forward, reaching out like he wanted to hold my hand, but stopped himself just before he touched me and sat back. "Yeah. Of course I believe you. Why wouldn't I?"

My muscles vibrated with the need to run out the door and take a minute to get myself together. But maybe I didn't have to run away from my feelings every time they felt tangled up. Nate wasn't acting like he wanted me to calm down or pretend to be okay. So maybe I didn't have to be.

"No one knew," I said, looking down at my notes. "I didn't tell anyone. Not until recently."

"Thanks for trusting me," he said softly.

We sat in silence for several heartbeats. A single tear escaped, and I brushed it away. Gemma had believed me, but this was different. Nate was someone who knew both me and Jerry.

"What do you want to do about the messages?" Nate asked.

"Do?"

"Tell your parents? Try to figure out who wrote them?"

"I can't tell my parents," I said. "They won't believe me."

Nate frowned, like I wasn't making sense. But he didn't know everything. I took a breath. "This isn't the first weird thing that's happened. Someone was in my room, moved things around, and read my journal. They took this locket Jerry gave me out of a box hidden in my closet and left the locket on my desk. With my picture crossed out. And the night in the corn maze, someone stuffed a note through the stalks." I had a picture of the note stored on my phone and I showed it to him.

"And you told your parents all that?"

"Yeah, they don't believe someone broke in because nothing was stolen. They think I just forgot moving my own stuff and that the note was a prank. If I show them these messages, they'll just say it's no big deal, and I . . . I can't take any more of them not taking me seriously."

Nate nodded. "Okay. So option two. We figure it out ourselves."

We. He said "we." A ghost of smile touched my face. "Yeah."

"I just . . . I want you to know you can tell me anything. I'm on your side. I will always be on your side."

"I just got so used to trying to act normal, trying to be normal, that lying is easier."

Nate grinned, wide and easy. "Normal is overrated. You don't have to pretend with me. Ever."

His words made me feel like I'd just been hugged. I didn't have to figure it out alone.

"We need proof," I said. "But I don't even know where to start. I don't know who'd mess with me like that. I didn't think anyone was paying attention to me."

"I've been paying attention."

I dropped my eyes back to my notebook, but not before noticing that Nate's face had turned as red as mine felt.

Nate cleared his throat. "Okay. So. Um. Is anyone mad at you?"

"It seems like everyone is," I said. "Brittany, Jerry's sister. And Gabe isn't mad at me, but he's a huge creep who won't leave me alone."

"Why is Brittany mad at you?"

"She . . ." The words stuck in my throat, but I forced them out. "She blames me for the crash. She thinks I should have stopped Jerry from drinking and driving."

Nate looked at me, his eyes soft as he studied my face. "It wasn't that simple, was it?"

I shook my head.

Maybe he could tell I didn't want to talk about it, couldn't talk about it, because he moved on. "Why is Jerry's sister mad at you?"

"I think Jerry told her I was cheating on him. Before he died, he kept saying I was." I looked up at Nate quickly. "I wasn't, though."

"What a jerk." Nate pressed his lips together. "Can I see the messages again?"

I unlocked my phone and handed it over.

"What about this? 'I haven't forgotten what you did to me. I'll never forget.' Does that sound familiar?"

"No." No one knew about that. It couldn't have anything to do with this.

"Okay, but the messages are from someone pretending to be Jerry. The rest of it seems to be in character, but maybe that isn't. It could be a clue."

I tried to think about what I'd done to people, but my brain was stuck on that last night with Jerry. "I don't think I've done anything to anyone."

Nate shook his head. "It's not what you've actually done. It's what someone thinks you've done. Or maybe . . ." He looked past me, thinking. "Why are they pretending to be Jerry? Maybe it was something Jerry did, not something you did."

"Like how Brittany thinks the crash was my fault, that her getting hurt . . . that Caleb . . . it was my fault."

"You know it wasn't, right?" Nate asked. "Jerry made his choices."

"I know," I said quietly. But I didn't always believe it.

Nate blew out a breath. "I mean, Brittany is a huge snoop. She would definitely read your journal if she could. That's kind of her thing. Whenever she's at someone's house, she goes through their cabinets and stuff. And she does have a bad temper."

I narrowed my eyes. "How do you know so much about Brittany?"

"Um." Nate tapped his finger against my phone. "So we kinda went out."

"How do you 'kinda' go out with someone?"

He tapped the case twice more, then met my eyes. "We were together like a month. She'd be cool sometimes, but then she'd get pissed because I wanted to spend time with my mom instead of her."

"Did she know your mom was dying?"

"Yeah, but she doesn't like it when things aren't all about her."

"I'm sorry," I said. It just sucked when people around you made a bad situation worse. I never liked Brittany. She did seem pretty selfish, and she could be mean. But . . . "Do you really think she could be doing this?"

Nate shrugged. "I don't know how anyone could do this. It seems like someone knew you were abused, and now they're using it against you. It's just cruel."

"How could anyone know?" I asked. "Jerry was the perfect boyfriend in public, and I never told anyone."

Nate looked past me, like he was thinking. "His sister could have overheard something. But I don't know how anyone else would."

"I didn't think Jerry and Brittany hung out, but she said that she knows something about Jerry, so maybe they did. He and Gabe definitely didn't hang out. He hated Gabe."

"Yeah, I know. The team all hung out together sometimes, and

Jerry was always a jerk to Gabe. Always picking on him."

I nodded. "Yeah, he was mad about Gabe kissing me."

Nate shook his head. "No, it was before that. I don't know why Jerry hated him, but he definitely did."

Jerry had hidden his texts from me, and at the time, I wondered if he'd been cheating on me. One time, when I'd asked him about it, he accused me of not trusting him and shoved me. I'd broken a glass and cut my hand.

Brittany had said she knew something about Jerry. What if she and Jerry had been texting behind my back?

She *said* she was mad at him, but she blamed me. What if she blamed me for him dying?

"The texts are coming from Jerry's phone. Maybe they just know because they read our texts to each other."

"Maybe," Nate said. "And his sister's the most likely to have his phone."

I frowned, thinking. "But if someone was sneaking into my house, they could have snuck into Jerry's house too."

"We won't be able to get into his texts, but maybe his email?"

"I don't have his password."

Nate pulled his phone out. "If you know his email address, we can try to break in."

My eyes went wide. "You want to *hack* his email?"

"It's not hacking," he said. "We're just going to guess his password."

"If we guess wrong, we'll lock the account."

Nate shrugged. "So we'll make three guesses a day. I think that's what you get before it locks."

I didn't have any better ideas, so I agreed.

Nate flipped his notebook open to a blank page. "We just need to make a list of things he liked. People usually use things that are easy to remember, like their middle name or pets."

"Jerry didn't have any pets, but his middle name was Dean."

"Okay." Nate wrote it down. "So what did he like?"

I moved around the table to sit next to him so I could see the list better. "Basketball. And fast cars. He wanted to own a McLaren one day."

We made a list. Nate asked me about Jerry's favorite foods (meat lover's pizza) and teams (76ers). Talking about my dead boyfriend with another guy was weird, but after a few minutes, it wasn't any weirder than the other stuff we talked about.

When Nate was done, I brought up Jerry's email app and typed in his address. Nate and I discussed it and decided to start with Jerry's name. I didn't think he was stupid enough to use it as a password, but it made sense to try.

I typed in *Jerry* and pressed enter. Invalid password.

76Jerry. Invalid password.

Jerry76. Invalid password.

"Let's try a few more," I said.

"We'll get locked out," Nate responded. "Patience. We'll try every day. At least it's something."

"Yeah." I blew out a breath and smiled. "Thanks for doing this with me. I've been feeling so . . . helpless."

"That's the worst feeling. Sometimes when you're the one in the situation, it's hard to know where to start."

I looked at Nate, and the way he was looking at me made me feel seen. Our eyes locked, and I felt my heart start to race. We were so close that I suddenly realized our hips and arms were practically touching, and

I could feel the heat radiating off him. The room was quiet, cut off from everyone else, though it was lined with windows, and anyone could see us. I was so close that I'd just have to lean forward a little and . . .

I realized I was starting to lean toward him and I turned away quickly, looking back at my laptop. After a moment, Nate cleared his throat and said, "Um . . . so should we start? Studying, I mean. Studying for the test." He was staring down at his hands, his face as red as mine felt.

I moved to the other side of the table, where my backpack and books were sitting. I took a few moments to rearrange everything on my side of the table and let my racing heart slow back to normal. "Yeah," I said, looking down at the table. "Let's get started."

CHAPTER 21

When I woke up the next day, I realized that I could at least ask Jerry's parents what happened to his phone.

As I biked toward Jerry's house, I tried to figure out what to say. Neither of his parents ever liked me. But Jerry said they hated everyone, so it wasn't personal. His parents probably wouldn't tell me anything, but I was tired of doing nothing.

I left my bike on the lawn and rang the bell. After a moment, Sandy answered the door.

Her face was clean and bare, without the heavy makeup from last time I'd seen her, like she'd just woken up. I tried to say "hello," but the word stuck in my throat.

She stared at me like I was a ghost, but then a half smile flittered across her face. "What are you doing here?"

I hadn't expected to see her, so I just blurted out, "I wanted to ask your mom something."

The half smile blinked out, and her eyes went blank. "You want to ask my mom something?" she repeated.

"Is she around?"

Her jaw tightened, and she got a hard, mean look in her eyes that reminded me of Jerry. "Yeah, she's here. Where else would she be on a Saturday morning? You can wake her up if you want. She'll be *thrilled* to see you. Or come back later and enjoy the show. They'll be hungover and screaming at each other."

I didn't know what to say. They'd been like that ever since I could remember. Jerry and I used to take Sandy out with us when we could.

Ian told me that Sandy missed me, and I hadn't understood why. But maybe she didn't miss me so much as she missed having someone to help her escape. Though at that moment, she looked like she wanted to stab me, like she had in my nightmare.

If I asked for Jerry's phone, it could tip her off that I suspected her of stalking me. Even if it wasn't her, she probably wouldn't give it to me.

"I just had a question for her," I finally said.

Sandy made a face. "My mom says it's your fault. That you're the reason Jerry died. The only question she might answer is how you can fuck off and die."

I stumbled backward a step. Those couldn't be Sandy's words. She'd always been quiet and sweet. She had to be repeating what her mom said. "I didn't do anything to him."

"He drove that road every day." She held her arms across her stomach, like she was in pain. "He knew that curve. He couldn't have just . . . crashed."

It sounded like she didn't know he was drunk. But she had to know, didn't she? "He didn't crash because of me."

"He was a good driver! It doesn't make sense! Just tell me what happened." Tears glittered in her eyes.

"Fine." I ran my finger along the scar on my head. "He was drunk."

Sandy shook her head like she was trying to make my words go away. "Why do people keep saying that? He didn't drink."

So she knew but couldn't believe it. I understood that. "Yes he did," I said quietly. "He was drinking at prom and he shouldn't have been driving."

"You're lying," she yelled. "He promised me he'd never drink!"

I couldn't look at her directly. The pain on her face was too much. "I know. But he did."

"He wouldn't break his promise." Her voice cracked. "Not to me."

I'd lost count of the number of promises Jerry had broken. "I'm sorry, but . . . it's true."

"You're a liar!" Tears streamed down her face. "When he told me about you and Ian, I said it couldn't be true, that you wouldn't do that. But then he told me what you said about me and . . ."

I raised my chin. "I never said anything bad about you."

"Then why didn't you text me?" she choked out between sobs.

She was in so much pain that even though I was mad, I still wanted to comfort her. "Sandy . . ." I stepped forward.

She cringed away from my hand. "Don't touch me. Don't ever touch me." She started to close the door, but I stepped forward and put my hand against it, stopping her.

"I'm sorry I didn't text you. I . . ."

Sandy shook her head. "I don't even care anymore."

My feelings were a messy tangle of awful.

I'd come to the house to figure out what happened to Jerry's cell phone, not make everything more confusing. If this was how Sandy was acting, then there was no way Sandy's parents would talk to me. What did it matter if Sandy knew I suspected her? "What happened to Jerry's phone?"

Her face twisted in a grimace, and she tried to shove the door shut, but I was stronger than her. "Well?" I asked.

"Why do you want to know?" Sandy asked.

"I just do."

Sandy shook her head. "It's always about what you want. You don't care about anyone else! You were always getting him in trouble. Dad kicked his ass for sneaking out to meet you but he still did it."

"Sneaking out to meet me?" That didn't make sense. We hung out every day after school. "When did he do that?"

"In the middle of the night. Don't act like you don't know."

His other girlfriend. Suspecting was different from having it confirmed. It knocked the breath out of me. "He wasn't meeting *me*."

An expression I couldn't read crossed Sandy's face. She knew something.

"He was talking to someone else," I said, my voice sounding steadier than I felt.

"No." She wouldn't meet my eyes.

"Now look who's lying."

Sandy's face flushed. "You should have died and he should still be here!" With a burst of strength, she shoved me out of the way and slammed the door.

I raised my trembling hand, intending to jab the doorbell again, but then I let it fall without ringing it. There was no scenario I could think of where she'd tell me what I wanted to know. I rubbed my left wrist as I trudged down the driveway.

If Sandy was my stalker, would it be any surprise that she'd snapped after her brother died? After living alone with parents like hers?

I got on my bike and pedaled away, a knot in my stomach. Sandy and I had always gotten along, but Jerry had filled her head with lies. She loved her brother and blamed me for the crash. She'd never answered me about his phone and she knew something about his other girlfriend.

It all fit. Sandy wished I was dead. If she was my stalker, I knew what her endgame was now. But if I went to the police, it would be my word against hers. I needed proof.

CHAPTER 22

My parents went out for dinner, so Lori and I had the house to ourselves for a few hours. I was in sleepover mode, wearing my comfiest sweatpants with my hair in two braids. Lori slouched on the barstool while I added ingredients to the mixer.

I glanced at her. She was tracing circles in flour I'd spilled on the counter.

"What's wrong?" I asked.

Lori rolled her eyes. "My mom. It's always the same stuff with her. It's like she wants me to fail. No wonder my dad left."

"That sucks."

"Yeah, but it's not a surprise. She's the Queen Bitch. Distract me with something else. Anything. I just want to get out of my head for one freaking night."

"Well, this will definitely distract you. I've been getting text messages from someone who says he's Jerry."

She stood. "Shut up! When did this happen?"

I handed her my phone, and she read the messages, her face flushing. "Wow. Someone is really mad at you. Can you think of any reason why?"

"I don't know. I didn't do anything."

She shook her head. "You must have done something. Whoever wrote this thinks you did anyway. They're talking about you forgetting them again, like the note."

"I don't know. I ignored so many people this summer. And even before that, I stopped being a good friend to you and Ian."

"Yeah." She looked down again and spoke in a low voice. "When you and Jerry got together, it was like you . . . disappeared."

We'd pinkie promised the summer I turned thirteen that we wouldn't be those girls who ditched each other for a guy. Everything had been so different then. "Jerry didn't like when I spent time with you or Ian."

"He wanted you all to himself," she said.

"Yeah, but . . . I shouldn't have given in." He'd said if I loved him, I wouldn't need to spend time with other people. But I was pretty sure that's not how love worked.

"It's okay. Relationships can be . . . intense."

I sighed. "Tell me about it."

"I would have spent every second of every day with JD if I could have." Lori dusted the flour off her fingers, leaving white streaks on her black leggings, then reached up to toy with her heart necklace. She frowned. "Do you think the text messages could actually be from Jerry?"

"I don't think dead guys have phones." My tone didn't sound as light as I wanted it to. I put the brownies in the oven.

"Maybe not," she said doubtfully. "But it's as likely as him writing a note."

"I've been trying to figure out who's doing it. Nate and I were talking about Brittany, Sandy, and Gabe."

"You've been talking to Nate about this?"

"We went to the library to study yesterday and it came up." I said.

She pursed her lips and squinted. "Brittany's been posting all this stuff online about drunk driving. Like, 'If you let someone drive drunk and they kill someone, you should be charged with murder.' Anytime someone posts a meme about drinking, she has to jump in and be a bitch about it."

My stomach twisted. "Brittany blames me for the car accident. She said I let him drive drunk."

Lori shook her head. "I wasn't going to tell you, but she keeps tagging you. There was this one that looked like a street sign and said 'Drive Drunk' with arrows pointing to the 'morgue,' 'jail,' or the 'hospital.'"

I felt like I might throw up.

"Forget her. No one likes her anyway," Lori said. "What else did you and Nate come up with?"

"We can't be sure of who it is, so we thought we'd work backward. We're trying to get into Jerry's email to see if anyone sent him anything before he died that might show why they'd want to get revenge on me."

The doorbell rang. It was our pizza being delivered. As I brought it into the kitchen, my phone buzzed with a text.

7:28 PM

Ian

Lori's mom dropped her off,

now pizza delivery.

There are brownies, aren't there?

Me

It's girls' night. GIRLS.

Do not come over.

Ian

Cool, I'll be there

in five minutes.

I groaned.

"What?" Lori asked.

"Ian," I said. "He saw you and the pizza, so he knows there's brownies."

"Tell him to go away!" Lori said.

"I did."

Lori huffed out a breath. "Well, can you at least not tell him about the text messages tonight? He'll never leave if you tell him."

Lori was right. It wasn't lying to put it off for just a little while. I'd tell him soon.

Ian rang the bell and I opened it, scowling. He just kept smiling at me and went straight to the kitchen, grabbing a slice of pizza and shoving half of it in his mouth.

"Gross," Lori said.

"Starving," he said through a mouthful of cheese.

"It's girls' night," I said. "I'll save you brownies for tomorrow. Go home."

"They're better fresh. And anyway, you're just going to watch that stupid movie again."

"*Secrets We Keep* is not stupid." I crossed my arms over my chest.

"It's our favorite," Lori said. "It's got everything. Romance, thrills, jump scares."

"Yeah, and you've watched it how many times?" Ian grabbed another slice of pizza. "Eight thousand? You just like Jake Evans."

"Like you don't like watching hot girls?" Lori raised her eyebrows.

Ian grinned. "Sure, but I prefer to watch real girls. How about I stay and we watch something cool? That new superhero movie is streaming."

"Are you trying to be annoying?" I asked.

Ian draped his arms across both Lori's and my shoulders. "Yes."

"Go away!" Lori rolled her eyes.

Ian groaned. "Fine, I'll go. But you'd better save me brownies. I never get homemade baked goods anymore."

I practically shoved him out the door. Lori and I went to my room, piled a bunch of pillows on my bed, and sprawled together.

Neither of us had seen *Secrets We Keep* in a while, but we still could recite all the best lines. After it ended, we scooped ice cream onto the warm brownies.

"Why can't that be real life?" Lori sighed. "The hot, rich guy adores me and we live happily ever after."

"Because it's a movie," I said. "Everything's better in the movies."

"Seriously, though." Lori stared off into space for a minute. "You know, that's not even what I want. I just want JD back." She sniffled. "I miss him so much. It's my fault."

"How is it your fault?" I grabbed tissues and handed them to her.

"I knew he was talking to this other girl, so I kept bugging him about it. And he said I needed to stop pressuring him, but I wouldn't, so he shoved me against the wall, told me I was nothing, and that he never wanted to see me again."

"Lori, it doesn't sound like it was your fault. He shouldn't have shoved you like that."

"I shouldn't have pressured him," Lori said. "I should have appreciated him more."

"What?" I felt like we were having different conversations. "He shoved you. How is that okay?"

Lori's jaw got tight. "It wasn't like that! He told me to leave him alone and I wouldn't. He warned me."

"That doesn't make it right."

"What's your deal? He didn't hurt me."

"But he could have."

Lori rolled her eyes. "This is why I never told you. I knew you'd make a big deal out of it."

I opened my mouth to tell her she was totally wrong, but I stopped, realizing something I should have understood before. In the beginning, I'd never told anyone about Jerry because I didn't want them to make a big deal out of it. I didn't want anyone to hate Jerry because he was so good to me most of the time. Did every girl do this? Could we only see how wrong it was when it happened to someone else?

Lori was teary-eyed, her jaw tense. "Maybe I should just go home."

"No," I said, grabbing her hand. "I'm sorry. I was just thinking about Jerry, and about how I used to cover for him, so I get it."

"No you don't," Lori said. "You want to act like the worst things he did were the real him. You want me to think about JD like that."

I had a million good memories of Jerry, games we played as kids, of times he made me laugh. But all that didn't make me forget the times he'd hurt me.

"No," I said slowly, thinking it through as I said it, "I just want you to see what he did clearly."

"I do see it clearly." Lori sighed. "And anyway, he . . . blocked me and I can't get him back, so it doesn't matter. I just wish . . ." Lori trailed off, suddenly shivering and rubbing her arms. "It's freezing in here!"

Goose bumps popped up on my skin. I tried to act casual even as my heart started racing. "Yeah. The thermostat does this sometimes."

"Weird." She wrapped a blanket around herself and stared off into space.

Lori started talking about something, but I was only half paying attention to her. I looked around, trying to be subtle. Nothing had moved. Because it was just a faulty thermostat. Like I said.

"You Were Made for Me" started playing from my laptop. I froze. Papers blew off my desk. A jar of beads on my sewing table tipped over and scattered across the table. A handful rolled onto the floor.

I swiveled my head, looking everywhere at once. Lori's hand tightened around mine.

"What's happening?" she whispered.

"Turn it off."

Lori was closer to my laptop than I was. She didn't move.

"Please, turn it off." I whispered.

Her hand trembled as she reached out and slapped my laptop shut.

As the sound of that terrible song cut off, the room went still.

"What was that?" Lori's voice shook.

"I don't know." I could barely breathe. It had to be Jerry. I couldn't deny it anymore. He was back for me.

My room was a mess. I needed to clean it up. I needed to put everything back where it belonged. But I couldn't move. My muscles wouldn't obey me. My eyes darted everywhere.

"Was that . . . was it a ghost?" Lori asked.

"I think . . . maybe it was Jerry," I gasped.

"Charlotte!" Lori shrieked.

I turned to look. There, in the corner, something moved. It was a person-shaped shadow. I screamed and scrambled backward on the bed. The shadow wavered, and when I blinked, it disappeared.

CHAPTER 23

"Oh. My. God. That was amazing!" Lori tried to look everywhere at once. "You saw that, right?"

"What did you see?" I asked. My voice sounded strange, like I was hearing it from a distance. My head swam.

"A shadow! It looked like a person. Do you think it was him?" Lori's eyes glimmered with excitement.

"No. It couldn't be." My voice sounded pleading.

Lori walked around the room while I sat on my bed and forced myself to breathe slowly, fighting the panic attack that was creeping up on me.

When Lori got to my sewing table, she gasped.

The sound broke my paralysis, and I hurried to the table. Lori hadn't moved and was staring at the table, wide-eyed. Beads spelled out LIAR.

"No," I whispered. My knees gave out, and I sank to the floor. Lori said something but I couldn't hear her through the ringing in my ears. My vision narrowed.

I clamped my eyes shut, my hands flat against the floor. After a few moments, I felt Lori's hand on my back.

We stood, clinging together like marooned survivors. Lori had cleaned up the beads.

"Please tell me that didn't say what I think it did," I said. "Please say it was random or I was seeing things."

"It said 'liar,'" Lori replied. "I took a picture before I put them away."

I collapsed on the edge of my bed. "Why is he here? Why is he doing this to me?"

There was a knock at my door and my mom poked her head in. "Hey, we're home and headed to bed. Time to quiet down." She paused. "Everything okay?"

Lori flashed her a smile. "Yep, everything is great."

Mom nodded and left.

I turned on my bedside lamp so we wouldn't have to sleep in the dark. Lori took my bed and I lay down on the air mattress. I pulled the blankets up to my chin. We were silent for a while as I flinched at every creak in the house, every noise outside.

"It's so romantic," Lori whispered. "He's trying to tell you he's still around."

"He just accused me of lying. That's not romantic," I said.

"What do you think he meant?"

I blew out a breath. "He always said I was lying when I tried to talk to him about the times he hurt me. He said no one would believe me."

"Yeah, but it's obvious he loves you," she said. "He came back from the dead for you."

A shiver raced down my spine and I shuddered. It didn't feel like love. It felt like Jerry texting me thirty-seven times when I didn't answer because I was in the shower. It felt like Jerry asking me to take a selfie to prove I was just out shopping with my mom.

"But I don't want him to," I said. "I want him to leave me alone."

Lori rolled over to look at me. "I guess I just don't understand how you wouldn't want someone who loved you so much."

"Because he . . . abused me." My tongue tripped over the word. "And anyway, I think he was cheating on me before he died."

"Cheating on you?" Lori's face disappeared as she turned onto her back. "Why would you think that?"

"He was always texting someone. And he wouldn't let me see his phone. One time, I picked up his phone to play a song, and he shoved me. That was the night before . . . before your accident, actually."

"Oh," she said softly, a note in her voice I couldn't decipher. "And you don't have any idea who it was?"

I shook my head. "Brittany, maybe. She said she knew his secrets, so it would make sense."

"He wasn't desperate," Lori said in a venomous voice.

We went quiet. Lori's breathing slowed, so I knew she'd fallen asleep. I stared at the ceiling, willing my brain to rest. I pulled my phone out and texted Nate. He didn't answer. After a few minutes, I slid it back under my pillow and closed my eyes.

Loneliness wasn't a stranger to me; it went hand in hand with the middle of the night. Somehow, it felt sharper now that I expected someone to be there.

I could wake Lori up and try to continue our conversation, but that would be selfish. I didn't want her to lose any sleep just because I hated being awake and alone. When we were kids, I was usually the first one asleep. Lori would be talking, and I'd murmur responses, trying to stay awake. I'd always thought that magical things must happen in the middle of the night and that if I could only stay awake, I'd discover them. But the only thing I discovered was that there was no one there. Everyone disappeared.

CHAPTER 24

Lori had to work the next day, so she left just after breakfast, but we made plans for another sleepover soon. Hopefully without Jerry.

My phone was almost dead. I grabbed a different charger from the junk drawer and as soon as I plugged it in, my phone chimed.

10:13 AM

Nate

Do you want to hang out today?

I smiled and told him where to meet me. There was a wooded park near our houses. The trails got crowded with families and older people on weekends, but it was also somewhere our parents weren't. I got dressed, and it wasn't until I was checking myself out in the mirror that I realized I hadn't had a huge existential crisis over what to wear. I'd picked out a fuchsia shirt and braided my hair. My reflection and I smiled at one another.

The house was quiet. Mom had gone out with friends and Dad was in the garage. I grabbed my tan peacoat from the closet and went out to tell him I was leaving.

"Is your homework done?" he asked.

"Mostly," I admitted. "I just have one more thing to read."

"Okay, have fun," he said. I thought we were done, so I turned to leave, but he started talking again. "I'm glad you're hanging out with friends and getting back to normal."

It was hard not to roll my eyes, but I managed. "Yeah. See you later," I said as I left the garage.

It was chillier than I thought it would be, and I wished I'd brought a hat. I looked cute in hats and I wanted to look cute for Nate.

Thinking about Nate that way made me nervous. We were just friends.

We messaged every night, so he probably liked me. But maybe he just enjoyed having someone to talk to. Our insomnia gave us something in common, but that didn't mean he wanted to date me. When we'd hung out at the bonfire, he hadn't even tried to hold my hand or anything. Maybe he wasn't into me.

Sometimes I hated my brain.

My phone pinged with another text.

11:58 AM

Gabe

I'm sorry about what I said the
other day. I'm such a jerk
sometimes. Let me make it
up to you. Let's hang out.
No expectations, just friends.

Me

After everything, I don't
think I'm ready to try
being friends again.

Gabe

Like, ever?

Me

I don't know. Can I just

have some space?

Gabe

I said I was sorry.

What do you want from me?

Me

Space. I literally just said that.

Gabe

You want to pretend I don't exist

Me

That's not it. I

I stopped typing mid-explanation and realized it didn't matter what he thought. There was no point in arguing with him.

I deleted my last message without sending it.

I was so deep in thought that I didn't see Nate come up next to me. "I hope I'm not the one who pissed you off," Nate said, startling me.

I jumped back, heart racing. The shock wore off quickly and then it beat fast for other reasons. "No! Definitely not."

"It looked like you were thinking about something annoying."

I half smiled as I looked at him. A breeze ruffled his hair, and he was turned toward me, the grin on his face lopsided. One of his incisors was crooked. It was all so adorable, so Nate.

He looked confused. "What? Is something wrong?"

I shook my head and looked away, my face heating up. I said the first thing I could think of. "It's just a nice day."

The sun was bright but didn't offer any warmth, and the breeze was already cutting through my jacket, making me wish I'd worn another layer. My hands were starting to get chilly, so I stuffed them in my pockets. Even though it was freezing, there were lots of other people walking the trails or playing Frisbee, trying to enjoy the sun before winter trapped us all inside.

"It is a beautiful day," Nate agreed. I glanced at him, and he was looking at me.

I blushed and looked away.

We got off the busy, flat path as soon as we could, diverting to the one that was rockier and had fewer people. Trees with dying leaves clinging to the branches stretched up around the path, patterning the blue sky overhead. We stayed quiet. Our arms bumped as we walked side by side, and I took my hand out of my pocket, hoping he'd reach over and grab it. After a few minutes when he didn't, I tucked it back in my pocket, debating with myself again if we were just friends or something else.

Was I even ready to think about this?

We ambled along, and most of the other walkers on the path outpaced us. The buzz of their conversations faded, and then we were alone and quiet. The breeze swept dead leaves across the path and they crackled under our feet.

"Did you know that sometimes, when an amusement park closes down, they just leave everything?" Nate asked. "There's this one called Storyland with old fairy-tale stuff, and another one called Williams Grove."

I was used to his randomness by now, so a smile spread across my face as I listened.

"I saw pictures. Grass and vines grown up over the roller coasters and the Tilt-A-Whirl. It's like a glimpse of a postapocalyptic world."

That made me shiver. "That sounds super creepy." An uneven spot in the path made me stumble, and Nate steadied me before quickly removing his hand.

"Yeah," he said. "But it's also really cool. Like, people just abandoned it. I guess they could have torn it down when it closed, but I like knowing that it's still there. That it left a mark."

I pictured what Nate was talking about, an abandoned Ferris wheel sitting still in the middle of a field, vines growing over it as the vibrant colors faded. It seemed depressing. "Have you ever seen one in person?"

"No," Nate said. "I'd love to, but it's kind of trespassing."

"I didn't think something like that would stop you." I looked over at him and grinned.

He laughed. "Nah, I'm a law-abiding citizen. And if you've heard anything different, I'll just say that I was only seven when I broke into that abandoned house. But in my defense, someone told me there was a dragon inside."

We followed a curve in the path, and a cluster of boulders off to one side towered over us. Nate veered over and started climbing. He put a hand out for me. "It's a great view."

I grabbed his hand and my heart gave a little leap. It was warmer than mine. He helped me up, and I didn't want to let go. But then he dropped my hand and it just felt cold again. He dug in his jacket pocket and drew out gloves. "I think you need these," he said, handing them to me. They were too big, but soft and warm.

At the top, we stood, looking around. A creek ran near the path, and a small waterfall burbled over rocks. When we sat, because of the angle, we were mostly hidden from the path. The cold from the rock seeped through my jeans, but I didn't care.

"I was wondering if you're going to the dance next month," Nate said, looking intently at the waterfall.

Butterflies danced in my stomach. "It could be fun."

"Would you like to go with me?"

"Yeah, I would."

Then he looked at me, and the crooked smile was back on his face. He was going to kiss me. I could tell. And I almost couldn't breathe with anticipation. His face inched closer to mine, and his smile faded. He reached up with his hand and brushed my hair out of my face. "Is this okay?"

Some kids shrieked on the path, and I flinched, jerking away from Nate without meaning to.

He frowned and moved away from me. "Sorry."

My face flamed. "It wasn't you. The kids startled me." But the mood was ruined. Before Jerry, before my PTSD, I wasn't so easily startled.

Jerry was suddenly looming between us. It didn't matter if he was a real ghost, or only a memory. He was there as surely as if he'd been there in person. We were still side by side, but the space between Nate and me seemed much wider than before.

We were both quiet, like neither of us knew what to say. It felt like I should apologize, even though I hadn't done anything wrong. The silence between us was awkward for the first time that day.

I tried to come up with something to break it, and realized I hadn't told Nate what happened to Lori and me. "What do you know about ghosts?"

"Like Nearly Headless Nick?"

I laughed. "No, like real ghosts."

"Nearly Headless Nick isn't real?"

I shook my head. "I'm sorry to be the one to tell you, but no."

"I swore I was going to get a letter to Hogwarts. My mom kept trying to convince me it was just a story, but I wanted to believe it."

"Of course you did," I said.

He flashed me a sheepish grin. "I sat by the mailbox every day for the month before my birthday. Every time I saw a bird, I swore it was an owl. It drove my mom nuts." His smile dimmed a little when he mentioned his mom, like the memory was bittersweet now. "She was the one who first read them to me when I was little. She said they were her favorite books when she was younger." He shook off the mood and met my eyes again. "Ghosts tend to hang around when they have unfinished business."

"Well, I might have one." I meant to sound light, but my voice sounded flat.

"Really?"

I told him about all the weird things that had happened in my room recently. About my laptop, the beads, and the person-shaped shadow that Lori and I saw.

Nate frowned. "You think it was Jerry?"

"I don't want to think about Jerry haunting me, but yeah. But . . . ghosts can't text, can they? And the stuff with my laptop could have been a glitch, right?"

"Ghosts can probably text. They're always taking over electronics in anime."

Could Jerry really be texting me? I shivered.

"Cold?" Nate asked.

I shook my head. "But do you think a ghost would go through my stuff? Read my journal? Take a locket out of a box?"

"Probably not." He nodded. "So maybe they're two separate things. Jerry's ghost and someone stalking you."

I pulled my knees up to my chest and put my head down on them. "Lucky me."

"They could be connected. Did any weird stuff happen before someone started messing with you?"

I thought back. "My room was freezing sometimes over the summer, but I just figured the air conditioner was set too high. And Paisley stopped coming into my room."

"Maybe Jerry is getting stronger because of the stalker. The stalker is pretending to be him, and if I remember correctly, ghosts can get stronger when you pay attention to them."

I thought back. The times my room had gotten cold or something had fallen was when I was talking about Jerry or when I was handling the locket. "So I should ignore him?" Jerry didn't like being ignored. "If that doesn't work, how do I get rid of him? An exorcism?" I was half joking.

Nate was silent for a moment, and then he shook his head. "Exorcisms are for demons. As far as I know, you can't get rid of ghosts. At least, not until they've done what they came to do."

My breath caught in my throat. I didn't want to believe he was haunting me, but Lori had seen it too. I couldn't pretend it wasn't happening. Not anymore.

CHAPTER 25

I had to tell someone about the almost-kiss before I exploded. I texted Lori, and she was home from work, so I biked over. When I got to her house, I noticed I had a text from Gabe.

3:35 PM

Gabe

You've been hanging out with another guy

And that just breaks my heart.

I've loved you for two years, that's no lie

But we were over before the start.

Give me a chance, take me back

Let me show you how I feel.

Without you, my heart feels black

My love for you is real.

Had he seen me hanging out with Nate, or did he mean in general? He'd seen us at the bonfire, but the fact that Nate and I had just gotten done hanging out made me wonder if he'd been watching us.

Gabe was creepy, but how creepy? Break-into-my-room-and-read-my-journal creepy?

I wiped my clammy hands on my pants and looked around me. No Gabe. At least, not that I could see.

I ducked my head and hurried the rest of the way to Lori's, fighting the urge to keep looking behind me to see if Gabe was there.

When I got to Lori's, we went into the kitchen and she got out hot chocolate mix.

"I've had the weirdest day," I said.

"Weird good or weird bad?"

"Both." I handed her my phone so she could read Gabe's poem.

She wrinkled her nose. "He's literally the worst."

"Do you think he was watching me?"

"Maybe? You didn't see him?" She put the mug of milk in the micro-wave.

"No, but I wasn't looking for him. I was . . . busy." My face heated up.

"Oh really?" Lori smirked and raised an eyebrow. "Busy how?"

"I was just at the park with Nate and I thought he was going to kiss me."

"Shut up!" Her eyes glimmered.

"He is so adorable." A smile spread across my face. "We were talk-ing and then he got quiet. Then he leaned toward me and asked, 'Is this okay?' I was freaking out."

"What did you say?"

"Nothing!" I threw my hands up in the air, too agitated to sit. "Some kids screamed and I flinched. I couldn't believe it." I shook my head. "I hate when I do stuff like that."

"Did he say anything about it?"

"No, but when I flinched, it made me think of Jerry. And then it just felt weird after that." All the excitement drained out of me.

Lori fell silent as she turned away and ripped open a mix packet. The microwave still had twenty seconds to go, but she watched it count down, then took the mug out and dumped the hot chocolate mix in. "Yeah, I was always thinking about JD when I was kissing Aiden or Connor. It's like I wasn't even there with them."

"It wasn't like that." I took the mug from her and set it on the counter.

"It just . . . doesn't sound like you're over him." She turned away to put her mug in the microwave.

"I wouldn't want to be with him anymore." I watched the milk turn brown as I stirred my drink and thought of what Gemma said about feelings not just going away. "I can't help that we have history and he's in my head."

"Maybe if you have to work so hard to keep him out, you're not over him. Maybe that's what that means."

Lori's mom walked in before I could respond. "Hey, Charlotte, nice to see you. How you been doing?"

"Hi, Mrs. Wells. I'm fine, thanks."

Mrs. Wells went to get a mug out of the cabinet and paused, her hand in the air. "So, we just throw trash on the counter now?"

"No, Mom." Lori huffed. "I was going to clean up as soon as I was done making mine."

"Because walking two steps to the trash can is so difficult?"

"Sorry." Lori swiped the packet off the counter, then threw it away. She rolled her eyes at me.

Mrs. Wells poured cold coffee from the pot into a mug and set it in the microwave. "You still cheering, Charlotte?" she asked.

"No, ma'am." I looked toward Lori, but she was looking down at her mug as she blew on her drink.

Mrs. Wells turned toward me and leaned against the counter. "It's for the best. You kids don't think about how dangerous anything is. I hurt

my back ten years ago, and I'm still on meds for pain and anxiety." She
pointed at Lori. "That's why I made her quit. She bitches about a scholarship, but if she bashes her head in again, she won't have to worry about
college."

"Okay, Mom," Lori said. "We get it, cheering is dangerous. Neither of
us are doing it anymore, so can we please not talk about it?"

Mrs. Wells chuckled. "It's good you're coming around again. This
one"—she gestured with a jerk of her head toward Lori—"gets all
broody. Maybe you can snap her out of it."

"We're going to my room." Lori grabbed my arm and pulled me out
of the kitchen. Once we were in her room, she slammed the door. I sat
on her bed and she thumped her mug down on her desk.

"Ugh, she brings up cheerleading every five minutes." Lori took a
shaky breath.

"Are you okay?" I asked.

Lori blinked. Her eyes shone with unshed tears. "I miss it so much.
I've lost everything that meant anything to me."

"I'm sorry," I said, not knowing what else to say.

"I have these nightmares. The cheer accident happens all over again,
but then you guys stand over me, laughing about how you did it on purpose because you hate me. And then when I wake up, it still feels real,
like that's how it happened. I have to tell myself it was a nightmare." She
massaged her temples. "It just feels like everyone's life is going on while
mine is over."

Lori's words triggered a gnawing in my gut. I struggled to find the
right words. "Your life isn't over."

She looked away from me, her eyes unfocused. "My dad forgot all
about me. Then JD broke up with me. Why am I so easy to abandon?"

"I'm here," I said. "You're wonderful. You're smart and fun. Loyal and beautiful." I shook my head. "If they abandoned you, it's because they're terrible, not you."

"JD wasn't terrible." Lori's jaw set in a stubborn line. "Maybe the problem is that I didn't try hard enough."

"What?"

"What if I can get him back? What if I prove I'm the one who loves him most?"

"I thought he blocked you."

"Yeah, but I might know a way to contact him."

"Lori, I don't think . . ."

"Just listen. I've been miserable for months because I pushed JD away. But what if I prove to him how much I regret it? Maybe we can be together again."

That seemed all kinds of wrong to me, but Lori's eyes were bright, and she was so animated and excited that it was hard for me to argue. "I don't think you should have to do that."

"Why not?" she asked. "It's easy for you. You and Jerry were friends, and then he fell for you. You weren't even looking for Nate, and now the two of you are into each other. Gabe is a creepshow, but even he won't give up on you. Nothing comes easy for me. I have to fight for everything, so why wouldn't I fight for JD?"

"He shoved you and said you were nothing to him. That's . . ."

Lori huffed out an impatient breath. "Our fights were always intense. But it was because love can make you so crazy. Maybe when he broke up with me, he didn't mean it. Maybe he expected me to try harder."

"Lori . . ." The more she told me, the more wrong it felt. I wished that I'd paid more attention when they were dating, but it had been hard for

me to see anything but Jerry. I wanted to keep pushing, to make her see
how wrong it was. But I worried she'd get upset if I said too much. "I just
want you to be happy."

"JD made me happy."

I tried to think back to when Lori and JD had been together. I hadn't
seen her outside of school often, even though we'd texted and hung out
at lunch and cheer. Had she seemed happier then? Lori had always been
a glass-half-empty kind of girl.

I'd just have to pay close attention to her. If she and JD did get back
together, I'd have to meet him and see how they were together. Maybe
then I could make her listen.

"Trying to get JD back is something I need to do. Can't you understand that?" Lori looked down into her mug and traced the lip with her
finger.

"I don't understand," I said. "But I'm here for you."

CHAPTER 26

I didn't really want to go back into my room, but I couldn't avoid it forever. I had to change into my work uniform, but I hesitated outside the door, trying to feel if the air was unusually cold or not.

I stood in the hallway and put just my hand inside my room. My hand trembled, but I held it up, then walked slowly forward. It didn't feel any different from the temperature in the hallway.

Still, I grabbed my work clothes and took them into the bathroom to change. If it *was* the ghost of Jerry, I didn't want him watching.

At work that night, Nate and Ian showed up within minutes of each other. Even with everything going on, just seeing them both made me smile.

They got their desserts and sat at a high top. Scoops was busy but not crowded, with only a few empty tables. The shop had a fifties vibe, with bubblegum-pink booths and a checkerboard floor. I looked over at Nate and Ian. They were leaning toward each other like they were deep in discussion. I frowned, but moved to help the next customer in line, trying to keep an eye on them.

Nate knew things Ian didn't. I kept making excuses not to tell Ian about Jerry because I didn't want to hurt him, didn't want to ruin the image he had of his best friend. But wasn't keeping secrets more hurtful?

If I was being honest, I'd gotten out of the habit of talking to Ian even before Jerry died. Jerry used to pick apart every interaction. If I looked at Ian too long, I obviously wanted him. If Ian touched my shoulder, it meant we were hooking up. Not talking to Ian was just easier.

Nate came over to say goodbye before waving to Ian as he left. Ian didn't look at me as he wiped the table with his napkin and got up. After he threw his trash away, he turned toward me and met my eyes. He looked furious, and I flinched. When Jerry got that look on his face, it meant I'd be sorry. I couldn't breathe. What did it mean that Ian was looking at me like that?

Ian scanned the room. Most people had left and it had gotten slow. Trevor, my manager, was sweeping up in the back.

Ian stalked toward the counter and I automatically took a step back. He leaned over the counter and said, in a low voice, "Take your break."

My breath caught in my throat at the anger in his voice. "I already took it."

"Take. A. Break."

I told Trevor I needed to go outside for a few minutes. Trevor rolled his eyes. "Fine, whatever. But I'm taking an extra break next time we work together."

"Done," I said.

I followed Ian to his car, my hands balled up in my apron. I hesitated for only a moment before getting into the passenger seat.

Ian turned toward me, but I stayed sitting straight in my seat, looking out the windshield.

"What is going on?" he demanded.

"What did Nate tell you?" I wasn't sure if I should be mad at him or myself.

"He told me *something* was going on. He assumed I already knew since *I'm supposed to be* your best friend."

I closed my eyes. "I'm sorry. I know I shouldn't be keeping secrets from you. I just . . ."

"I don't even care about that. Nate says you're in danger. Just . . . tell me."

"The other day, I got these text messages from someone pretending to be Jerry." I handed him my phone, and he scrolled through them, his expression getting darker and graver. He handed my phone back to me.

"That's not everything." I paused, trying to collect my racing thoughts so that I made sense. There was so much to tell. "Someone snuck in my room and moved things around. I had all Jerry's stuff packed away, and someone put the locket Jerry gave me . . . you know the one?"

"Yeah," he said quietly, his voice gruff.

"Someone put it on my desk, but took his picture out and scribbled all over mine. And shoved a note through the corn at the bonfire. Weird stuff like that."

Ian's jaw clenched. "Why didn't you just tell me? Why do you think you have to do everything alone?"

"I'm sorry."

"Did I do something wrong?" Ian swallowed. "Is that why you won't talk to me?"

"Ian, no." I wondered how long he'd thought he was the problem. He wasn't really mad at me. He just wanted me to let him in. "If you did something, I'd just tell you."

"I hope so. I thought we were the kind of friends who can call each other on their bullshit."

I took a breath. I needed to tell him the truth about Jerry. The whole truth, not just pieces. "It's . . . complicated."

I checked the time. Trevor's patience probably wouldn't last much longer. "I have a lot to tell you, but I have to go back in. Can you pick me up tonight and I'll tell you everything? We'll be done with cleanup by ten fifteen."

"I'll be here."

* * *

The rest of the night was slow, and we got everything cleaned up early. I texted Ian, but he didn't text back. Trevor locked up.

"My ride isn't supposed to be here until ten fifteen. Can you wait a few minutes?" I asked.

Trevor grimaced. "I can't. I already told my girlfriend I was on my way." Without waiting for me to respond, he got in his car and took off.

It was exactly ten, and Ian still hadn't texted back.

I buttoned my jacket and put on my hat. My breath fogged out in the frigid night. Hopefully Ian would see my text and show up soon. I scanned the shadows, feeling exposed.

I went around to the back of the store and grabbed my bike, which was chained up by the dumpsters. When I started to wheel it around the front, I noticed it felt wrong. One of my tires was flat.

I bent down to look closer. There was a big gash in the front tire. It had been slashed.

My hands went clammy. I didn't see anyone in the parking lot, but there were deep pockets of shadow where no light reached.

Lots of places for someone to hide.

I hurried to the front of the store and fumbled my phone out of my pocket.

10:02 PM

Me

Where are you? Are you coming?

I was hyperventilating, and the lack of air made my head swim.

Ian would arrive in thirteen minutes no matter what. Nate lived fifteen minutes away, so even if I texted him, he wouldn't get to the store before Ian. There was no way Lori's mom would let her borrow the car at this time of night.

My parents were probably asleep, and they didn't take their phones into the bedroom. They didn't wait up for me because I was *so responsible*.

I was depending on Ian.

What if he forgot or fell asleep?

With shaking fingers, I texted him again.

10:04 PM

Me

I got out early.

Please hurry.

I'm scared.

Eleven minutes. I only had to make it for eleven minutes at the most.

I stood with my back to the front of the store and scanned the parking lot again.

There was a residential neighborhood just a block away. And across the street, shops were closed or in the process of closing. Deja Brew, the coffee shop on the corner, was open for another half hour. If I needed to run, I could go there.

It was so quiet. And isolated. A few cars glided by on the road in front of me, but aside from that, I was completely alone. Wind raked its cold fingers across my neck.

My phone buzzed, and my heart jolted.

10:07 PM

Jerry

What happened to your bike?

My breathing hitched and my eyes darted around, examining every dark shape in the shadows.

Eight minutes. Ian would get me in eight minutes.

Please see my text. Please come early.

My breath sounded loud in the silent night. No cars drove by. I spun around, making sure no one was sneaking up on me.

Was Jerry nearby? Would he come up to me, slide an arm around my waist, and ask, "Did you miss me?"

Ian had forgotten me. I was alone. My mouth was so dry, I wouldn't be able to scream if I needed to. My heart raced. I fought the creeping panic attack. *If I panic, I'll be helpless.*

My phone buzzed again.

10:08 PM

Jerry

It's a looooong walk home,

isn't it?

"Leave me alone," I whispered. I'd call Nate. If my stalker showed up, Nate could call the police.

Where was Ian? Why wouldn't he text me back?

Six minutes.

I went to my favorites to call Nate when an unfamiliar SUV pulled into the parking lot. I froze, then inched backward around the side of the store, hoping the shadows would hide me.

I couldn't see who was driving. Nothing was open. Why was anyone here?

My heart pounded so hard it hurt. I gasped for air.

The SUV parked in a swath of darkness and turned off its lights. No one got out.

When my phone buzzed again, I whimpered.

10:10 PM

Jerry

You know I hate when

you braid your hair

I abandoned my bike and took off running. If someone wanted to hurt me, they'd have to catch me. I'd always been fast, but now I didn't feel fast enough. *Are those footsteps behind me? They could be footsteps.*

The coffee shop was open. I fled into the street. A car honked and slammed on its brakes.

I crossed the lanes and sprinted into the parking lot. Headlights followed me.

It was him. It was Jerry. I fought tears and kept running. Almost there.

The car honked. I flinched and my foot hit loose asphalt. I stumbled but didn't fall. The car was beside me.

"Charlotte!"

Just a little further. Faster. Please. My lungs burned. Footsteps pounded behind me. Too close. Right behind me.

"Charlie!

A hand grabbed my arm, and I stopped and spun. I hit and kicked. I had no breath to scream.

Strong arms enveloped me, pinning my arms. I kicked the person holding me and he grunted.

"Charlie, stop! It's me." Ian's voice finally penetrated my panic.

The fight left me all at once, and my legs collapsed. Ian caught me and maneuvered me to sit on the curb. I let out a strangled sob and covered my face with my hands.

"What's going on? Did someone hurt you?" he asked.

I didn't answer, and he wrapped his arms around me. I couldn't stop crying.

Dimly, I heard a bell ring and someone ask, "Is she okay?"

Ian answered, "I'll take care of her."

The man came into my line of view. He was an older man, and he bent over to look at me. "Is this guy bothering you?"

I shook my head, and through tears, managed, "He's my friend."

The man nodded and went back into Deja Brew.

When the tears dried up, Ian scooted away to look at me. "What happened?"

"I need tissues."

He nodded, then went to his car and pulled a bunch of napkins out of the glove compartment. I took a shaky breath and wiped my face.

Ian sat back down beside me and stretched out his long legs. "Are you okay? Just tell me that."

I wasn't sure I'd ever be okay again. But that's not what he meant. "I'm not hurt."

"What happened?"

I told him about my bike tire, the texts, the car in the parking lot. Even before I was finished, he started getting up.

"Go inside and wait for me. I'll go see who's in the car."

"I'll go with you."

"The hell you will. Just wait for me. I'll be back in a few minutes."

I couldn't let Ian go alone. If it was my stalker and they were dangerous, they could hurt him. I got in the passenger seat of Ian's car and buckled myself in. After a few moments, he got in behind the steering wheel. "Stubborn brat."

"Sexist pig."

The side of his mouth lifted in a partial smile. He drove across the street and into the parking lot. The SUV was still there.

We parked in front of the ice cream shop, right under the light. "How about you stay in the car?"

"How about you stop saying stupid things?" I took my phone out, ready to call 911 if necessary.

Ian grumbled and got out of the car. I followed him to the SUV.

Ian pounded on the window, then stepped back. The interior light went on and the window rolled down.

I gripped my phone so hard that I was surprised the screen didn't crack.

Trevor blinked at us. His hair was messed up. "What? Didn't you get a ride home yet?"

I moved toward the SUV and saw a girl in the passenger seat. They'd come to a deserted parking lot for a make-out session.

"Trevor, you asshat," I said, stepping toward him, my fear turning to anger. "Didn't you see me standing in front of the store when you got here?"

He glanced toward the front of the store like I'd still be there.

"That's not your car," I said. "Where's your car?"

"It's Kylie's," he said, gesturing to the girl.

Ian reached his hand out to Trevor. "Let me see your phone."

Trevor looked at him, confused. "What?"

"It's not him, Ian."

Ian didn't even look at me. "I want to see your phone."

"What's your problem?" Trevor ran a hand through his hair.

"Call the phone, Charlie."

I took my phone out and called the number that had been sending me text messages. Trevor started to speak, and Ian motioned for him to be silent. When I got the message that the voicemail box had not been set up, I hung up.

Ian stared at Trevor for a few more moments, and Trevor shrank back.

"How sure are you that it's not him?" Ian asked.

"Like 99.9 percent."

"You can see my phone," Trevor said. Without taking his eyes off Ian, he reached over and unlocked it. Ian took it from him and scanned the text messages. After a moment, he handed the phone back.

"What's going on?" Trevor asked.

"Charlotte has been getting threatening texts," Ian said. "Then you pulled into the lot while she was getting the messages, so you can see why I was concerned." He smiled at Trevor and smacked him on the shoulder in a friendly way. "No harm, right?"

"Yeah. No. It's all good." Trevor didn't look like it was all good. He looked like Ian had scared him half to death.

We went back to Ian's car. Ian threw my bike in the trunk, got in, and started driving.

"I texted you," I said, "when I realized we were getting out early."

He shook his head. "Freaking Jacqui hid my phone again, and my parents didn't want to wake her up to figure out where she put it. I should have just come early."

I read him the text messages from Jerry, and his lips tightened.

His brows drew together. "Why'd they say that thing about your hair?"

It was time to tell him the truth. I hated what I was about to do. I took a deep breath. "Jerry didn't like when I braided my hair. He said it looked better and was 'more feminine' down. So he used to pull my hair if he caught me wearing it in a braid. Not like, in a playful way. To punish me."

We pulled into his driveway, and Ian shut his car off. Then he turned toward me. He looked like I'd just told him the world was flat. "He what?"

"He pulled my hair," I repeated. "He used to grab me." The words gushed out of me in a flood. "He left bruises on my arms, and I had to start wearing long sleeves. He shoved me sometimes, and I hit my head once. I told everyone I slipped. I had a cut and a bump on my head. Jerry drove me to urgent care and then teased me for weeks about being clumsy."

"I remember that," Ian said quietly. "We all teased you."

"He said if I told you, you wouldn't believe me. That your loyalty was to him." I couldn't look directly at Ian as I talked, but out of the corner of my eye, I saw that he was rigidly still.

Ian's hands clenched into fists. We were so close that it would be easy for him to reach out and touch me. To grab me. I was trapped. I forced myself to take a deep breath. It was Ian in the car, not Jerry.

But I'd never seen Ian look as angry as he did then. "If he were alive, I would kill him," he said. "I'm not exaggerating. He would be dead."

My eyes went wide. "He was your best friend."

"My friends don't hurt girls." He put his hand out, and I flinched. His face fell, and he shifted back against the car door, giving me more space. "I'd never hurt you."

My cheeks burned. I hadn't meant to flinch. Ian wouldn't hurt me. Even though my head knew it, my body remembered what it felt like to be hurt by someone I trusted.

But Ian. If I couldn't trust Ian, then I couldn't trust anyone. I leaned toward him, and he shifted slightly, not quite pressed against the door anymore. I put my arms out and then he moved toward me, hugging me gently. His arms were loose, like I could pull out of them anytime.

I breathed in and told myself that everything would be okay.

Ian walked me to my door. He kept my bike and was going to put a new tire on. But we agreed that he'd take me to and from work.

When Nate got online, I debated whether to tell him about what happened. I wanted a Nate conversation. Just for one night, I wanted to pretend that I was just a girl talking to a guy she liked, and that there was nothing more than that.

11:40 PM

                                        Me
               Will you do something for me?

       Nate
       Probably.

                                        Me
               I'm going to tell you something,
                   but I don't want to talk

about it tonight. I want
to talk about other stuff
that's not this.

Me

But I don't want to keep
secrets from you.

Nate

Okay, you're freaking me out.

Are you okay?

Did something else happen?

I sent him screenshots of all the text messages. I told him about the tire and running into Ian.

11:44 PM

Nate

You can't go home from work by
yourself anymore. I'll pick you up.

I smiled a little. It was out of his way, but really nice that he offered.

11:45 PM

Me

Ian already volunteered.
Plus, isn't that
past your curfew?

He didn't answer for a long time. I saw the dots on-screen that signaled he was typing a message, but in the end, he just said:

11:51 PM

Nate

You're right.

Okay.

I puzzled over it, wondering what he typed that he'd deleted. His next message came through a moment later.

11:52 PM

Nate

Just promise me you won't take any chances.

I know you don't want to, but maybe it's time to talk to your parents and go to the police.

My stomach sank. Then the lights blinked on and off several times, as if someone had hit the switch. Was it Jerry? Why was he bothering me? I did a quick internet search for "how to get rid of a ghost," but all the articles I skimmed had things about crystals and dream catchers, nothing that would help me immediately. Nate, my expert on the weird, had said he didn't think you could get rid of a ghost. The only thing I could do right now was ignore Jerry, unless I wanted to sleep in the guest room. I had no idea if Jerry would follow me. If my parents found me sleeping there, they'd ask questions. It was easy to imagine what they'd say if I told them I thought I was being haunted.

I focused back on Nate.

11:55 PM

Me

I want to get proof
before I go to them.
Otherwise they'll just find
another excuse why
it can't be real.

Nate

I just don't want anything
bad to happen to you.

The lights blinked again. I wrapped a blanket around my shoulders to keep the chill off me. Then I turned off the lights and waited to see if anything else happened.

11:56 PM

Me

I'll be careful. We'll figure
out who it is before anything
really bad happens.

I hoped it was true.

11:58 PM

Nate

As long as you're safe,

that's all I care about.

Nate

Now, you asked for a favor.

So, here goes . . .

did you ever notice that

Halloween and jalapeño are

spelled nothing alike but

sound similar?

CHAPTER 27

On Monday morning, Ian parked in my driveway. I slid in beside him, and he started driving toward school.

He didn't talk at first, which was weird because he almost always had something to say. His hands clenched on the wheel, and I prepared myself for a lecture.

"I have to tell you something," he said. "Two somethings, actually." He took a deep breath. "First off, I should have known something was going on with you and Jerry. I did know, actually. I just didn't trust my gut."

"You knew he was hurting me?" I asked. That was worse than no one paying attention, if Ian had known and did nothing. "Why didn't you do anything?" I said, my voice rising. "Why—"

"No!" he interrupted. "I swear I didn't know anything specific. I just . . . got a weird vibe from the two of you sometimes. And I didn't ask and didn't trust my gut because . . . I was jealous."

I hoped he wasn't telling me what I thought he was telling me.

"Not romantically jealous," he clarified. "Just . . . you and I used to hang out. Then you and Jerry got together and you and I never hung out without Jerry anymore. So, I thought the weird vibe was me. And I didn't ask. I'm sorry."

I blinked back tears. "I'm sorry I didn't tell you. I'm sorry I stopped hanging out."

"I get it now," he said. "But for a long time it was the three of us. Then it was the two of you and . . ." He shrugged. "I missed how things used to be."

"I wish things had stayed that way," I said.

"Me too."

"Part of me wanted you to figure it out," I said. "I wanted you to know without me having to tell you."

He started to say something, but I talked over him. "I know that's not fair. I know it's stupid to want you to read my mind. But I didn't know how to tell you."

"Why is it so hard to talk about things?" He blew out a breath. "Okay, that was the first thing. The second thing was that I didn't break up with Brittany because she was a crappy singer." He half smiled. "I don't care what a girl sounds like, if you know what I mean."

I jabbed him in the shoulder, and he laughed. "So why did you?"

"Because she punched me in the face."

I almost laughed at the idea of tiny, cute Brittany hitting tall, muscular Ian. It couldn't have hurt him. But it wasn't funny. It was wrong, even though Ian was a guy. Getting hit was never funny or okay, even if she was smaller and couldn't do any real damage. It wasn't about the physical pain. "That's terrible."

His jaw clenched. "It's a double standard, like she thought it was okay. You know that she was actually shocked when I told her we were done?" He shook his head. "I'm not going to stay with someone who thinks it's okay to hit me."

"Why . . ."

"And it's not like I did anything to deserve it. Like if a guy puts moves on a girl, and she says to stop, but he doesn't, then obviously he deserves to get hit. Hell, I'll be happy to hold him while she hits him." He smacked the steering wheel. "But that's not what went down."

Now I was curious. "What did happen?"

Ian sighed. It was obvious he didn't want to tell me. "She was super jealous of you. Told me she didn't want me hanging out with you anymore because guys and girls can't be friends. That we'd . . . I don't know . . . start hooking up." He laughed. "As if that would ever be a thing."

"Why would anyone think that?" I asked.

"I know, right? Like, why can't we just be friends? I told her that's how it was and I wasn't going to let her bad-mouth you. So she just hauled off and punched me."

"I'm sorry," I said, feeling guilty and not sure why.

"It's not your fault. She's the one with the problem. I'm only telling you this because I get it. Jerry hurt you. You trusted him and he betrayed you."

"I just kept wondering how someone I loved could do something like that to me. On purpose."

"I've been asking myself that since Saturday night, and the only thing I can come up with is that he couldn't have really loved you. Or maybe he hated himself so much that it spilled out on you. I don't know."

A knot in my chest loosened, and I nodded. "The first time he grabbed me was because he was mad that you gave me a ride home."

Ian's shoulders slumped. "He hurt you . . . because of me?"

"You didn't make him grab me. I don't know why he got so jealous, but he grabbed me and shook me. His face got all red, and he screamed at me. I don't even remember most of what he said. When he finally let go, I had red marks in the shape of his fingers. He said he was sorry, that he loved me so much it made him crazy sometimes. He begged me to forgive him, swore it would never happen again. So I did."

Ian blinked a few times, like he was having a hard time processing it all. "How did I not know he was like that? Whenever he talked about you, it was like you were the only thing that mattered."

"Half the time I didn't believe it either. It was like a bad dream," I said.

"I always thought he was such a good guy. When we were kids, he talked about how awful his parents were, swore he'd never be like them. I never thought he'd hurt someone he loved."

We both fell silent then. I stared out the window, watching the trees go by, thinking that you could never really know someone, not all the way. I'd believed Jerry loved me, even up until the end. But the farther I got from that time, the more I wondered how much of what I believed about Jerry was real and how much was just a story I told myself.

CHAPTER 28

A couple days later, I was walking out to catch the bus when Ian swung his arm around my shoulders. "I'll give you a ride home."

We got in the car and he pulled out of the parking lot but didn't turn toward our neighborhood. "Where are we going?" I asked

"We're going to meet Lori and Nate at his house. We're going to brainstorm about your stalker."

My face flushed. "Wait, have you all been discussing this without me?"

"We're getting together so we can discuss it *with* you. And we wouldn't have had to do it this way if you weren't so secretive."

"Whose idea was it?"

"Mine."

I opened my mouth to tell him that I didn't like being tricked. But I couldn't figure this out on my own. And they were just concerned about me, the way I was about Lori. "Thanks. It was a good idea."

His eyebrows arched up. "Who are you and what have you done with Charlotte?"

I rolled my eyes at him. "Next time, let me know what you're planning. I don't like the alpha-male, 'I'm in charge' thing."

"Noted."

"So why is Lori riding with Nate?"

"Because I figured you'd be pissed and didn't want you to take it out on anyone else." Ian glanced over at me. "I had this whole speech ready about how I didn't care if you were mad and how I told you I'd always protect you."

"I mean, I can pretend to be mad if you want to give the speech."

He laughed. "Nah."

We drove across the river into the more rural part of town, where the houses were spread farther apart and not everyone had fences. We pulled up in front of a two-story brick house. There was a large, bare tree in front, along with weeds and dead flowers in a circle around the tree. Nate's car was in the driveway. Ian pulled in behind it. I had a moment of panic, wondering if I was going to meet Nate's dad and if Nate had told him anything about me. I flipped down the visor and checked my reflection, then ran a brush through my hair and dabbed on some lip gloss.

Ian laughed. "Why do girls do that? You look fine."

"Fine?" I made a disgusted face at him. "Why do girls like you?"

"Because I'm so charming and funny."

I tried not to roll my eyes at him a second time. "Whoever told you that you're charming and funny lied."

A dog barked as we got out of the car and approached the house. Nate opened the door and Galileo, the black Lab from Nate's pictures, wagged his tail as he stood next to Nate.

Nate's smile looked like a grimace. "I hope you're not mad."

"You were just trying to help."

He mimed wiping sweat off his brow.

Lori was already sitting on an armchair in the living room. I sank into the brown, overstuffed couch. Galileo jumped up and put his head in my lap. I stroked his soft fur. There were photos on the wall, of Nate and his little sister, Megan, of his parents. His mom was pretty and looked young in the pictures. Nate and his mom had the same grin and the same mischievous light in their eyes.

"Megan is at a friend's house until I go get her, and my dad has a meeting Wednesday nights. So it's just us," Nate said. He gestured toward a whiteboard easel he had set up. "I thought we could all brainstorm ideas for finding out who your stalker is, and I'll write them down. Unless you changed your mind and want to call the cops?"

"Not until we have proof."

Nate sighed. "A slashed bike tire is proof."

"It's proof that someone slashed her tire," Lori said. "Not that someone is stalking her."

"She's right, Nate." Ian made an apologetic face.

"I'm more worried about how someone is getting in the house." My palms went clammy. "There's no sign anyone is breaking in, and we always lock the doors."

"Did your keys ever go missing?" Nate asked.

"No, never."

"We have copies of your house key, but they're in the laundry room with all our other spare keys," Ian said.

"I don't think someone would have broken into your house to get Charlotte's key," Lori said. "That seems overly complicated."

Ian frowned in thought.

We all fell silent, then Nate typed something into his phone. "Listen to this! You can copy a key using a flattened soda can." He sounded horrified. He turned the screen toward us. "All you have to do is trace it on the metal and then you have a model for a blank." He met my eyes. "Someone only would have needed to get your key for a few minutes."

My stomach lurched. "I keep them in my backpack. Someone could have gotten to them in gym or the library." I took a deep breath. "I have to make my parents change the locks."

Nate looked at Lori and Ian. "Charlotte and I have been trying to get into Jerry's email. Do either of you happen to know the password?"

Lori and Ian both shook their heads.

"We've been trying different combinations, but we still haven't cracked it," Nate said.

"We think there's a chance that whoever is stalking me might have emailed Jerry at some point," I explained. "Since we don't know where his phone is, it's our next best option."

"Couldn't the stalker just reset the email password if they have Jerry's phone?" Ian asked.

I grimaced. "Hopefully the stalker won't think of that. We'll keep trying anyway."

Nate wrote down *Gabe*, *Brittany*, and *Sandy* on the whiteboard. His handwriting was slanted, but mostly legible, a blend of print and cursive. It was unique, just like Nate.

Ian glanced at the board and then did a double take. "Sandy?" Ian turned toward me. "Why is she on the list? She's only thirteen."

Nate and I traded a look. "I've tried talking to her a few times," I said, "and she won't listen. She pretty much said she hopes I die. And she was there when I got the note in the corn maze. She'd have access to Jerry's phone."

Ian shook his head. "Come on. It's not her."

"Jerry had secrets." Lori leaned forward. "Things the rest of us didn't know. We all thought we knew him. So why couldn't Sandy have secrets too?"

Ian swallowed. "Can't we just . . . We haven't ruled out Brittany or Gabe. Let's focus on them."

"We can't just ignore her as a suspect," Lori said.

"She's like my little sister," Ian said, his voice rising.

"And Jerry was like your brother," I said quietly. "I'm sorry, Ian, but we have to consider her. She hates me."

"She's grieving." Ian spread his hands like he was trying to placate me. "She's a kid who lost her brother. You've met her parents. She's way more normal than she should be."

I exchanged glances with Lori and Nate. Ian had a blind spot with Sandy.

"And Sandy wouldn't have had access to your keys," Ian said. "So it can't be her."

"You have my keys at your house," I said. "Has she visited?"

Ian made a face but didn't answer. "Let's talk about the others," Ian said. "Gabe could be a stalker. We already know he's obsessed with you. And mad you chose Jerry over him."

I wrinkled my nose. "Maybe I should talk to him. See if I can find anything out."

"We could try to trace the phone," Ian said.

Lori bit her lip. "I think you have to have an app installed."

We all went to our phones to search for how to trace a phone.

"Apparently you can get apps that clone a phone number," Nate said, looking up at us. "So the person might not even have Jerry's phone."

"Seriously?" Lori asked.

"Yeah, it doesn't even seem that hard to do." Nate glanced at his phone again.

My shoulders slumped. My stalker was always a step ahead. It seemed impossible.

But we had to try. "Well, we can't do anything if the phone number is cloned. But we can still try to find the phone."

"We could search their backpacks to see if anyone has it," Lori suggested.

I nodded. "Brittany never used a lock on her gym locker while she was at practice."

"I can check Gabe's during basketball," Ian said.

"How can we get to Sandy's backpack?" I asked.

Ian closed his eyes. "Seriously. Can you not?"

"What if it's her?" I turned toward him, trying to make him meet my gaze. "Would you want me to just pretend she wasn't doing all this?"

"It's not her!"

"Are you going to help or not?"

"With anything except messing with Sandy. I won't do that."

He meant it. Ian was the most loyal person I knew. No matter what I said, I wouldn't budge him. But Sandy was our best suspect, so I couldn't just let it go. "I need to get inside Jerry's house, look in his room and hers."

"Then make up with her and get her to let you in."

"You could help me get in," I said.

"Hard pass." Ian shook his head. "Any other ideas?"

"What about Jerry?" Lori asked.

Ian and Nate exchanged a look. I didn't know what she meant either. "What about him?"

"His ghost is trying to communicate with Charlotte." Lori gestured. "We should try to see what he has to say. What if we had a séance?"

"What are you even talking about?" Ian asked.

"Weird stuff has been happening," I said. "It's been getting ridiculously cold in my room. Things move without me touching them. And . . . Lori and I saw something when she slept over."

Ian smirked. "There's no such thing as ghosts."

"You weren't there," Lori snapped. "We both saw it. It knocked over some beads and spelled out 'liar' with them. It was a ghost, wasn't it, Charlotte?"

"It was pretty scary," I said. "I don't know what else it could be."

"Literally anything else," Ian said.

I narrowed my eyes at him. "So you're the only one who's allowed to have input? First you want us to take Sandy off the list and now you're just dismissing what Lori and I saw!"

"You're wrong about Sandy. And the beads probably lined up randomly."

Lori turned toward him, eyes flashing. "It wasn't random." She showed him the picture on her phone.

He shrugged. "I'm sure there's a logical explanation."

"You're being the opposite of helpful," I said.

Ian scowled, then sighed. "I believe you. I just don't think you're right."

I glared at him.

Lori hurried on. "A séance is perfect, then. We can prove it."

"So . . . what? We'll light candles and sit around a dark room, intoning the spirits to speak to us?" Ian asked.

"No." Lori shot him a dirty look. "I have a Ouija board. We can use it to ask Jerry questions."

Nate shook his head. "A Ouija board isn't a toy."

"That's funny." Ian smacked Nate on the shoulder. When Nate didn't react, Ian's brows drew together, as if he wasn't sure if Nate was being serious. "C'mon, you don't believe in that stuff, do you?"

I realized that most people didn't know the side of Nate I did. Late-night Nate, Connoisseur of the Weird, with his conspiracy theories and alien obsession. Knowing Nate in a different way than most people was the best kind of secret.

"We don't know that the ghost is Jerry." Nate shook his head. "None of us know what we're doing with a Ouija board. Charlotte already has enough going on without us messing with the occult. The ghost didn't slash her tire."

"How do you know that?" Lori asked.

"Because Charlotte is being haunted, not her bike," Nate said. "Ghosts latch on to places that were significant to them, but can't just do whatever they feel like."

She glared at Nate as if he'd betrayed her. "Fine, so Jerry didn't slash her tire. But still, any information is helpful, and if you guys don't want to help us, we'll use the board to talk to Jerry without you. Won't we?" She looked at me, her face clearly telling me I had to agree with her.

The idea of communicating with Jerry made me uneasy. But I was just ready for this to be over so I wasn't going to turn down any idea. And if it gave us answers, it might be worth it. "I guess so."

"It's going to work," Lori said. "You'll see."

CHAPTER 29

When I got home from Nate's, I took off my jacket and started to open the closet door. I paused, hearing angry voices coming from the kitchen. It was rare that my parents got home before I did, but I'd texted them from Nate's and let them know I'd be late. I didn't mean to eavesdrop, but they were too loud to ignore.

"Oh, and my job isn't important?" Mom demanded. "I'm up for a promotion!"

I hated when they argued. Even though it never got physical, I couldn't hear yelling without tensing up.

"It's an important meeting, Patty!"

"We agreed on this. We take turns driving her to therapy!"

My heart sank. They were arguing about me. Because I needed therapy.

"How do we even know she's making progress?" Shoes slapped the tile like my dad was pacing. "Gemma refuses to give us any updates. It's ridiculous. If I were working on a project and refused to give updates, I'd be fired."

I stifled a gasp. They'd called Gemma?

"She's not a project! Charlotte said she likes Gemma and she feels she's making progress."

I was surprised to hear Mom defending me. I didn't think she'd been listening to me when we talked at the restaurant.

"Look," Dad said, quieter. I edged closer to the kitchen to make sure

I could hear him. "All I'm saying is that sometimes talking about things makes them worse. Whenever I think about what happened to Jerry, I start thinking about what might have happened to Charlotte and . . ." His voice cracked and he cleared his throat. "Those thoughts don't do anyone any good. Maybe she'd feel better if she stopped dwelling on everything. Maybe it's time to see how she does without therapy."

"Yeah, that's a fantastic idea," Mom said flatly. "Maybe she'll learn from your family and start drinking her feelings."

"Like your family is any better?" Dad's voice got louder. "Your mom—"

"Leave my mother out of this!"

I felt like I was going to throw up.

"All I'm saying is that maybe therapy isn't the answer." Dad's voice was soft and reasonable, even though his words felt like poison. "We put her in therapy because we thought it would help. I would do anything. Anything. To make her better. But I don't think she is."

"You know what? I'll take her to therapy tomorrow, Ken," Mom said. "You just go to that stupid meeting that's more important than your daughter."

"You know it's not like that," he said.

"Do I?"

I heard a chair scrape against the floor and scrambled upstairs as quietly as I could.

Later, I smelled popcorn, so I went downstairs. My parents were watching some old movie on TV. My shoulders were tight as I walked into the living room, but at least they weren't fighting.

My mom smiled and held out the bowl. "Want some?"

I grabbed a handful and munched, thinking maybe I should let them watch their movie and talk about the locks another day. But Dad paused the movie. "If you don't have much homework tonight, you could watch with us. We can start it over."

I couldn't sit here and watch a movie with them without replaying their argument. And thinking about how they'd called Gemma and talked to her behind my back. They hadn't even asked me. I made my voice neutral. "I need to finish a paper tonight."

"A paper on what?" Dad asked.

"English." I made a face. *Romeo and Juliet.*

"You didn't like it?" Mom asked. "I thought it was better than *Hamlet.*"

I shrugged. "They were stupid."

"They were in love," Mom said with a dreamy smile. "Love can make people do stupid things."

Like stay in a relationship where someone was hurting you. I looked at her. I still wasn't ready to look at my dad. "Maybe that's why I don't like it. Maybe I don't want to see people doing stupid things for love."

"Very wise," Dad said. "Very mature."

Mom glared at him. "But not very romantic."

Neither of them had phones or laptops out, which was unusual. "You're not working tonight?" I asked.

"I needed the night off," Mom said. "I've been so stressed lately that I'm starting to become difficult to live with."

"Yeah, you and me both," Dad said. They exchanged a look.

They seemed to be over their argument from earlier. I didn't want to make them fight again, but I was sure someone was breaking in. It couldn't wait.

I took a deep breath and sat down on the couch next to them. "I need to tell you something."

Mom blinked at me a few times, the smile melting from her face at my serious tone. Dad raised an eyebrow.

"Um . . ." I looked down at my jeans and picked at a thin spot. "The other night at work, someone slashed my bike tire."

"They what?" Dad asked.

"Slashed my bike tire," I repeated. "I think it's my stalker."

"What stalker?" Dad leaned toward me and frowned.

"The person who was messing with my things. They've been text—"

"We talked about this. No one has been messing with your things," Dad said.

"Fine, then you tell me what's happening." I lifted my chin. "Am I lying? Am I crazy?"

Dad sighed and dropped his head in his hands. His hair was grayer than I remembered. It used to be dark brown, but now it was threaded with silver. He didn't speak for what felt like a long time.

When he looked back up, his forehead was wrinkly, and his face seemed to droop. "I think you're looking for answers. And because you're afraid, you're . . . misinterpreting real things. It's like when you're home alone, watching a scary movie, and you hear a sound. You get scared, even if you know it's just the cat."

It was so reasonable that I had to think about the reasons why it wasn't true. The text messages. I wasn't making those up.

"Okay, but I have proof."

He made a face. "The note? With the matching edges?"

My jaw tightened. He wasn't listening. It didn't matter what I said. He already had his mind made up. "I heard you," I said, forcing myself to meet his eyes. "When I came home, you were arguing. So I know what you really think of me."

"Oh, honey." Dad ran a hand through his hair. "I don't know what you think you heard, but . . ."

"Don't do that." I put up a hand to stop him. "I know what I heard. It's just like how you keep trying to tell me I don't know what's going on. You said I'm not making progress. You called my therapist and you didn't even talk to me about it."

Dad sighed. "I'm sorry. Maybe we shouldn't have done that. But listen to yourself. Someone slashed your bike tire, snuck into your room to move things around, and tore a page out of your journal? Why would anyone do that?" His voice sounded almost pleading. "I just don't want you constantly worrying that someone is out to get you."

I looked over at Mom, wondering whose side she was on, but she stayed silent, eyes going back and forth between us with a serious expression.

I didn't know how to make him believe me. I sighed. I only needed one thing from them. "Fine. But I want you to change the locks."

Dad held his hands up. "Hold on. How did we get from a slashed bike tire to changing the locks?"

"I told you I think someone was in the house. I know you think it didn't happen, but it did."

"No one could be getting in the house," Mom said. "We checked the locks, and none of our keys have gone missing."

"I looked it up," I said. "Someone would only have needed to get my key for like five minutes. You can make a copy using a soda can, then take it anywhere to have an actual key made."

"Let's say we change the locks," Mom said. "What's to stop someone from getting your keys for five minutes again and making a new copy?"

"I'll keep my keys in my pocket when I'm at school. Just . . . please."

"I'm worried that if we do this, if we feed your paranoia, it will make you worse." Dad shook his head.

"How would it make things worse if I feel safer? And anyway, what if I'm right? Am I still paranoid if I'm right?"

Mom looked at me for a long moment. "We'll change the locks," she finally said.

"Patty," Dad said. "Maybe we should talk about this privately."

Mom put her hand on Dad's arm. "Just change them."

My dad fell silent, then after a long moment, he said, "If that's what you think is best."

Mom studied me as if she was really seeing me. "I don't know what's going on. But Charlotte has never given us a reason not to trust her. If this is what she needs to feel safe, it's what we'll do."

CHAPTER 30

My mom seemed distracted when she picked me up from school. As I got out of the car to go into Gemma's office, my mom said, "Your dad is really stressed out right now. He didn't mean what he said."

I paused, my hand on the car door. "It still hurts that he said it." I looked out the car window. Speckles of rain darkened the sidewalk. "I just wish you would believe me."

"Honey . . ."

I shook my head. "I'm going to be late."

I didn't have an umbrella, so when I got into Gemma's office, my hair was damp.

I settled in the big armchair across from her.

"How have you been doing since I saw you last?" she asked.

"I don't even know." I looked past her to the snake plant she had in the corner of the room. Sometimes it was easier to say things if I didn't look at her.

"Your mom emailed me," she said. "She wanted to let me know she's worried about how fearful you've been. She's concerned that it's excessive, though hypervigilance—being on high alert—is just part of your PTSD."

My jaw went tight and I looked at her, waiting to see if she'd scold me for not getting better, like my parents did.

"I just wanted to let you know she contacted me. We don't need to talk about that if you don't want to."

"I heard them arguing about it. They said you wouldn't talk to them."

She shook her head. "No, as I said before, I wouldn't betray your confidence that way. Jerry can't harm you anymore, so there's no safety concern."

That might not be true, but I wasn't sure where Gemma stood on ghosts. "I wanted to ask you about what you said last time, about me being abused." The word felt fake in my mouth, like I was making things up. But I kept going. "Is that really what . . . what you would call it?"

"It is. People in abusive relationships feel lonely and helpless, scared of doing anything to make their abuser mad. They often make excuses for them. Feel guilty for everything."

My hands started to shake, so I folded them in my lap. She'd just described my life. "I didn't think I'd ever be *that* girl."

"What girl?"

"Just . . . I didn't think this could ever happen to me, that I would ever *let* it happen to me. I didn't think I'd ever be the girl who stays when she should leave."

Gemma nodded. "No one plans to get into an abusive relationship. No one wants to be hurt. But abusive relationships often start off with someone who's charming and seems like the perfect romantic partner. And then as time goes on, they get angry with you for things, and you try to re-create the way it was in the beginning."

"That's what I wanted. Just for him to be the person he used to be." The Jerry who was my friend, the guy who made me laugh and made me feel safe.

Gemma leaned back in her chair. "Have you ever heard of the cycle of violence?"

I shook my head.

"It's the typical way abusers interact with the people they hurt. There's the honeymoon, the tension building, and the explosion. The explosion is what most people think of as abuse: hitting, insults . . ."

"Hair pulling?"

"All that. The tension building is like walking on eggshells. You know the explosion is coming, but you don't know when."

I could always tell when things were about to get bad because Jerry started drinking more and I couldn't do anything right.

"The honeymoon phase, that's the reason you stay. They apologize, make promises, do nice things for you. You stay because they insist that they'll change and you want to believe it."

I picked at the hem of my shirt. "When he was alive, it felt like if I could just do the right things or say the right things, he'd stop getting so mad."

Gemma shook her head. "He would have found an excuse to hurt you anyway. No matter what you did."

"But why?" It was the question I most wanted answered. And was most afraid of. "Why did he want to hurt me?"

Gemma pursed her lips. "I didn't know Jerry, and I can't speak for him. But what I can tell you is that most people who abuse others were abused themselves. A lot of abusers have drug or alcohol problems. And almost all of them are deeply unhappy people."

I nodded. Jerry's dad smacked and punched him. Jerry drank too much. But unhappy? "He got good grades and played basketball. He didn't seem unhappy." Had I missed something?

"Do you think people know you have PTSD?" Gemma asked.

"No, I . . . oh."

"One of the hardest and bravest things a person can do is admit they need help," Gemma said. "It's hard to be vulnerable, to admit weakness."

"Why didn't he tell me he was unhappy?"

"Maybe he didn't know what was wrong. For some people, unhappiness looks like anger. It looks like substance abuse and headaches. It can look like reckless behavior or problems sleeping. If he didn't tell you, maybe it's because he didn't know how. Not everyone does."

"If I'd known, maybe I could have stopped him." I thought back, wondering if I could have changed anything.

Gemma cocked her head. "Stopped him from what?"

"Oh . . . um . . . from dying. The accident."

"No," Gemma said firmly, leaning forward. "You're only responsible for your choices. You're not responsible for his."

I shifted uncomfortably and couldn't look her in the eye. Would she still think that if she knew the truth?

CHAPTER 31

The next day, we decided to search Brittany's backpack during cheer practice. Lori and I went into the girls' locker room while Nate monitored the hallway and Ian watched the practice.

There were no assigned lockers. People brought their own locks if they wanted one, but mostly everyone just shoved their stuff inside, and other than some pranks like putting fake cockroaches in someone's bag, it was fine.

Brittany's backpack was gray and white striped. We tried the locker she usually used first, and her backpack was in there.

I went through the backpack while Lori checked Brittany's clothes. Brittany's backpack was a mess of crumpled papers and broken pencils, along with her notebook and books. I found her phone in a front pocket, and it was the one I'd always seen her use, in a white pearlescent case.

"Anything?" Lori whispered.

"Just her phone."

Lori took the phone out of my hand and touched the screen. It was locked, of course.

I called Jerry's phone and waited, listening to see if anything vibrated in her backpack. I held my breath, but I didn't hear anything. "Try her birthday for her password," I said. "It's May thirteenth." Two days before Jerry died.

"That's not it," Lori said.

"Try it backward."

"Nope and nope."

I sent a text to Jerry.

3:56 PM

Me

Hey there.

If Jerry texted me back while Brittany was at practice, we'd know for sure it wasn't her.

My phone buzzed with an incoming text. But it wasn't Jerry. It was Nate.

3:58 PM

Nate

Someone's coming!

Lori shoved Brittany's phone into her backpack and I put it back in the locker. We'd just closed the door when Alisha walked in.

She stopped and frowned. "What are you guys doing?"

"I thought I dropped something when I was getting ready for gym today," I said.

Her eyes shifted between Brittany's locker and me but I couldn't tell from her expression if she believed me or not. Then she shrugged and put her backpack in an empty locker.

Lori and I went out to where Nate was waiting. "Did she catch you?"

"I don't think so," I said.

"She wouldn't care even if she had," Lori said.

* * *

With nothing to show for snooping in Brittany's backpack, I texted Gabe. Nate and I agreed that I should meet him in a public place, so I asked Gabe if he'd meet me at Molten Java in an hour. He sent me an excited emoji and I grimaced. I wasn't trying to lead him on. I just needed answers. But I cringed when I realized the message asking him to meet me was the first thing I'd sent him since he'd sent me the poem. It was days ago, but he was still probably reading too much into it.

I rubbed my sweaty palms on my jeans.

"You okay?" Nate asked. He didn't take his eyes off the road, but he reached out, like he was going to take my hand, but then stopped and put it on the gearshift.

My heart sped up, wishing Nate had taken my hand. But I couldn't focus on that. "I think Gabe thinks I want to get together. I didn't mean to lead him on. I . . ."

"Lead him on?" Nate asked. "How? By not answering his texts? By telling him you want space?"

The knot in my stomach loosened a little. "I know. But maybe I should have been clearer when I asked him to meet me."

"You're not responsible for what he thinks. Could you have been clearer? Maybe. But you've told him you're not interested."

Nate pulled up in front of Molten Java and I got out. "I'll be over by the taco place." He pointed. "Text me if you need me."

I ordered hot chocolate and sat outside. It was a gray day and looked like it might start raining at any moment. My puffy jacket, hat, and gloves protected me from the worst of the cold. Everyone else was inside, where it was warm. If Gabe got too dramatic, I could just leave.

Gabe showed up a few minutes early, and when he saw me sitting there already, his smile faltered. He took a step toward the door, but then stopped and wavered, like he couldn't decide if he should go inside and order or greet me. He finally settled on sitting down across from me and the smile spread back across his face.

"I would have gotten your hot chocolate for you," he said.

"I got here early and ordered. I'll wait if you want to get something."

"Nah. So what's up? I thought you hated me."

"I don't hate you," I said. "I just don't want to go out with you."

Gabe's face morphed from happy to confused. I looked away from him.

"Then why am I even here?"

"You said something to me once when I was dating Jerry, that I didn't seem happy, and that you'd treat me better. Remember?"

"Of course," he said. "I was just trying to make you smile, but Jerry picked a fight with me over it."

"No. He hit you because you kissed me." I looked up at him and tried to keep my voice steady. "I told you not to. You knew he and I were together."

He shrugged. "Yeah, and you were dating me when he kissed you. I figured if it worked for him, it might work for me."

I wanted to look away again but I made myself continue meeting his eyes. Jerry's voice whispered, *Do you have to flirt with every guy you see?* "What made you think I wasn't happy?"

"Because you weren't. Your smile looked weird. You stopped wearing bright colors. You were crying a lot."

Gabe had noticed all of that, even though I'd managed to hide it from everyone else. But he couldn't grasp that I wasn't interested in him. He wasn't stupid. If he wasn't hearing me, it was because he didn't want to.

But then my brain caught up with what he said and my shoulders tensed. I curled my hands around my cup. "When did you see me cry? I never cried in public. Not once."

He froze. Then words burst from him in a torrent. "I wasn't watching you or anything creepy like that, I swear. You know I run. I live in the neighborhood next to yours, so I ran by your house sometimes. I saw you crying a couple times. I was worried about you." He reached out and grabbed my hand.

I yanked it away and wiped it on my jeans. He'd just admitted to watching me when I was in my room. My room was on the second floor, partly blocked by a tree, so it's not like he could have seen in with a casual glance. He'd have to stand on the street at just the right angle. That was a stalker-y thing to do.

And what was even worse, he'd just admitted to watching me and was acting like it was no big deal. He wouldn't get a clue that I wasn't interested. It had been almost two years since he and I had gone out and he was still hung up on me, so he was patient. Patient enough to be the one doing all this.

Gabe's eyes widened and he put his hands out, like he was trying to calm me down. "I just wanted to be there if you needed me. Jerry wasn't treating you right, so I was watching over you."

I had to get out of here. I looked around, but we were alone. Because it was cold, everyone else was inside. I hadn't thought about what I'd do if Gabe admitted to stalking me. Nate had parked so that Gabe wouldn't see him, but now he felt too far away to help.

"Is that why you've been texting me? To remind me how terrible Jerry was?"

"What is this?" he asked. "Why are you interrogating me?"

"Have you been stalking me?"

"You're such a tease! Why do girls only want assholes like Jerry? What is it? Maybe if I shoved you, you'd like me better." Gabe was suddenly on his feet, towering over me, and I stood so quickly that my chair tipped over and crashed on the cement.

He put his hands up. "I wasn't going to do anything. I'm not like that. Geez."

I could throw my hot chocolate in his face if I needed to. It should be hot enough to distract him. "How do you know he used to shove me? How often were you spying on me?"

"I wasn't spying!" he said. "And it was lucky I was there, anyway. Once, when I walked by his house, I saw him yelling and shaking you. I called 911. You should be grateful I was looking out for you."

We'd thought it was the neighbors who called. But we should have known better. The neighbors would be used to screaming coming from Jerry's house.

"I'm leaving," I said, taking a few steps backward. My skin was crawling and I desperately wanted a shower.

"Don't be like that," he said. "Guys are supposed to protect the people they love."

"You don't love me," I said. "You don't even know me."

"I know you better than you think," he said.

I couldn't stand to hear him say one more thing. I ran toward the door, my feet slapping the concrete. Gabe said something to me as I fled, but it just sounded like white noise. Once I'd locked myself in the bathroom, I texted Nate to come get me.

When Nate got there, he texted me and I ran out. As soon as I was in the passenger seat, I pressed the door lock button. I looked around but didn't see Gabe anywhere.

"Are you okay?" Nate asked. "Your hands are shaking. Is it him?"

"I think so." My words tripped over each other as I told him every detail of our conversation as well as I remembered it.

"Damn." Nate put the car in gear but stopped and stared through the windshield. "I can't even . . ." He turned toward me. "Are you okay?" he asked again.

"I don't even know. I'm freaked out and mad. He acted like . . . like I should be grateful that he was looking out for me. He said that."

Nate tapped his fist on the steering wheel twice. "Tell me what you want me to do."

"I just want to go home," I said.

He hesitated, like he was about to say something, but then he just took a breath and backed out of the space. "It could definitely be him, but it sounds like he didn't say anything that proves it."

"When you guys go through his backpack, if you find the phone, that's proof. I just want this to be over."

"Me too," he said.

"He acted like everything he said was totally normal."

"I mean, going past someone's house when you like them is a thing everyone does. But peeking in the window is over the line. And if he knew about Jerry, he should have said something. To someone." Nate's hands were curled around the steering wheel and his knuckles were white. His face was bright red and his jaw looked tight. I was so used to looking for signs of anger in Jerry that it was easy to recognize them in other people. Nate was furious, but his tone was even.

"You're not going to meet him alone again, right?" Nate asked as he parked in my driveway. "We don't know what he's capable of."

"I don't ever want to see him again."

Nate walked me to the door. "Do you want me to come in?"

"I kinda want to be alone, but . . . I . . . Can you come in to make sure no one is inside?"

I felt silly asking the question, but Nate didn't even hesitate. "Yeah, definitely."

My parents weren't home yet, so we walked around turning on lights, making sure windows and doors were locked, then checking all the rooms. He opened every closet and pushed back the shower curtain in the bathroom. He even checked under my bed.

Nate acted like it wasn't weird, and when we were done, we walked back downstairs. "Text me if you need anything, okay?" he said. Then he hesitated in the doorway, like he wanted to say something else. For a long moment, he just watched me, and then slowly, so slowly that I had plenty of time to back away, pulled me into a hug. His arms circled me and I put my head against his chest. I could hear his heartbeat, which, like mine, was going faster than normal. He rested his head on top of mine for a moment before he pulled away, sooner than I wanted.

He said goodbye, and I watched him walk to his car. My stomach fluttered, but this time it was for a good reason.

After Nate was gone, I picked up Paisley and cuddled her, trying not to think of my awful conversation with Gabe.

My phone pinged with a text.

                              5:47 PM

        Gabe

        I'm sorry if I upset you.

        Don't be mad

It took every ounce of self-control I had not to throw my phone across the room.

CHAPTER 32

That weekend, my dad replaced the locks on the front and back doors. When he was done, he and Mom called me into the living room. Dad held out the new key, and when I went to take it, he said, "We'd like to talk to you."

I wasn't sure what they wanted but knew it wasn't the truth. "Okay."

They traded glances. "We understand that you're scared of something," Mom said. "We read that it's not uncommon for people who experience a trauma to be . . . sensitive. Maybe worry about things when there's nothing to worry about."

"Yes, I have anxiety. Yes, I worry. But that doesn't mean I'm wrong. I can be anxious and hypervigilant and still know when something is actually happening." It was always about facts, something they'd been told, something they read. Never me.

"We're trying to figure out how to help you," Dad said.

"Then listen to me when I tell you something!" My face got warm. "You say you want me to talk to you, but every time I do, you just tell me all the ways I'm wrong."

Dad shook his head. "It's not like that. We're—"

Heat flashed through my whole body and I made a sharp gesture. "You're not listening! You act like you're trying to be supportive, but you're just trying to prove me wrong!" Tears burned my throat, but I refused to cry.

"That's not what we're doing, sweetie," Mom said. She sounded like she was on the verge of tears.

"Just because it didn't happen to you doesn't mean I'm imagining it. Whenever I try to tell you things, you make me feel stupid. Why would I tell you anything?"

I was going to cry. I couldn't hold it in anymore. I turned and fled to my room.

"Charlotte!" Dad said.

They weren't going to listen, no matter what I said. I slammed the door behind me and threw myself on my bed. I grabbed my phone and started a new group chat.

1:11 PM

Me

My dad changed the locks

but still thinks

I'm imagining things.

Nate

That sucks. You okay?

Lori

Why don't parents listen?

Ian

At least they changed the locks.

You'll be safer now.

Nate texted me separately.

1:18 PM

Nate

Seriously . . . are you okay?

Me

I haven't gotten any creepy texts
today so I guess I'm fine? I'm just
so sick of my parents not believing
me. If you guys didn't believe me,
I don't know what I'd do.

Nate

I will always believe you.

Me

I noticed. I'm glad to know
I can count on you.

Nate

I wish I could be there to
give you a hug right now.

Me

Just knowing that makes everything
a little better.

CHAPTER 33

A few days after our disastrous conversation, my parents called me downstairs and I braced for another lecture. "We were thinking about going to visit Aunt June," Mom said.

I wrinkled my nose before I could stop myself. Aunt June just had her third son and her house was always full of screaming boys. "When?"

"Next weekend. I know you don't want to come with us, so maybe you and Lori can have a sleepover at her house, or if she's not available, I'll ask the Williamsons."

"Yes, please," I said. Weight dropped off my shoulders. Not only did I not have to spend the weekend avoiding the Lego obstacle course, but we could do the séance at my house, like Lori wanted.

My mom huffed out a breath and I thought she was going to say something else, but she just started putting our tacos on plates.

The silence was too loud and I wanted to say something but had no idea what.

After a moment, Mom said, "Honey, you're doing okay, right? No more weird stuff has happened since the locks were changed?"

I looked between her and Dad. He was watching me with a neutral expression. For a second, I considered telling them everything. Maybe they'd listen to me tell them about the text messages this time. But then she continued, "I know it's been hard. Jerry was such a sweet boy."

I forced myself not to cringe. And just like that, the moment passed.

"Everything's fine," I said.

* * *

On the Friday night my parents went to Aunt June's, I went to Lori's. We took snacks up to her room and sprawled across her bed.

"I'm so excited about the séance." Lori sat up and pulled her laptop over to her lap. "I've been reading stuff online and watching videos. Has Jerry come around again since I slept over?"

"Just lights blinking."

"I read that ghosts manifest more strongly when they're feeling strong emotion. I wonder what makes him show up."

I nodded. "If we figure that out, we can figure out how to get rid of him."

"That's not what I . . ." She shook her head. "I meant in case we have trouble getting him to cooperate. Anyway, when we're doing the actual séance, only one person should talk. And I think it should be you and me using the planchette. The guys can just observe."

"I don't want to talk to him," I said.

"I will." She smiled. "Let me know what questions you want to ask, and I'll make a list. That way I don't forget anything."

"The only thing I want to know is if he's seen who's been sneaking into my room."

Lori wrinkled her nose. "He's communicating with you from beyond the grave! You have to be more interested than that."

"I just want this to be over."

"But having Jerry come back and try to communicate with you is amazing. We know there's something after death now. I want to ask him if he's doing okay and why he's still here. I want to know what he misses most. What it's like."

Lori's eyes were shining. She didn't understand how much I hated the idea of Jerry communicating with me. She was imagining we had some fairy-tale love story and didn't understand how it felt in real life.

Lori and I met Nate and Ian at my house the following day, near dusk. The house seemed eerily quiet. We went up to my room. Before I'd left, I made sure anything embarrassing was hidden. Nate's gaze lingered on a half-finished shirt on my sewing machine, on the beach poster on my ceiling, on the photos of Lori and Ian tacked up on my wall.

It made me wonder what his room looked like. I pictured posters of aliens and models of space shuttles. Maybe he even had glow-in-the-dark stars on the ceiling.

"No extra phone in Gabe's backpack," Ian said. "I kept Gabe talking during practice while Nate checked it out."

I sighed. "I knew it wouldn't be that easy."

Lori and I had brought the Ouija board and candles from her house. Lori set the candles around my room. Nate had an incense stick and a holder. "I'm going to smoke cleanse the room," he explained. "My mom used to do it all the time to clear out negative energy. This one is lavender and peppermint for calming and protection. I figure it can't hurt, right?" He walked around the room, waving the smoke into every corner, and when he was done, left it burning on top of my dresser.

Lori and I sat cross-legged on the floor, knees touching, Ouija board balanced in our laps. Ian turned off the light. Candlelight flickered, sending shadows dancing on the wall. I kept seeing motion out of the corner of my eye, and it made me jumpy. The smell of incense smoke perfumed the air. *This isn't a big deal. Just relax.*

Nate sat on one side of us, ready to take notes on his phone. Ian leaned against the wall, arms across his chest, his smile faintly mocking.

Lori and I rested our fingertips on the planchette. "Relax and clear your mind of negative thoughts," she said.

I glanced over at Nate. He smiled and whispered, "It's okay."

"Concentrate on Jerry." Lori paused. Every sound seemed too loud. Someone shifted. A candle flame popped. My neck prickled.

Then Lori spoke again, and I flinched. "Jerry, are you there? Move the planchette if you're there."

Nothing happened. My heart pounded, filling my ears.

"This is stupid," Ian said under his breath.

I don't know if Lori heard him, because she didn't say anything. Nate frowned at him and shook his head slightly.

Time dragged out as we continued to sit quietly. No traffic noise came from outside. I had the bizarre thought that the world had stopped.

"Jerry, we know you've been visiting Charlotte. We want to talk to you. Charlotte wants to talk to you."

Goose bumps stood up on my skin. The temperature of the room was dropping. My stomach churned. Lori gasped, and her eyes went wide. Nate looked grim. Ian scowled and looked around, as if he was trying to find the source of the cold.

"Is that you, Jerry?" Lori asked.

The planchette began moving, and I almost jerked my hands away. My hands shook, but I kept my fingers glued to the planchette. My breath came too fast.

The planchette stopped at YES.

It felt like someone had punched me in the stomach, and I couldn't catch my breath. Jerry was here. He was dead but not gone. It was like a nightmare. It didn't feel real. I wanted to escape, but I couldn't move. Lori started talking again.

"Why have you stayed?" Lori asked.

The planchette began moving again. Nate copied the letters, but after the first three, I think we all knew what it was spelling. C-H-A-R-L-O-T-T-E

"You're here for Charlotte?"

YES

"What do you miss most?"

I looked at her sharply. *Who cares what he misses? I want to know if he knows who's stalking me.* But I didn't say anything, because both Nate and Lori had cautioned me that only one person should speak.

L-I-F-E

I laughed nervously. It was either that or run screaming from the room. Lori glared at me. I guess ghosts were literal-minded.

"Did you know that Charlotte is getting text messages from someone saying he's you?" Lori asked.

YES

"Is it you doing it?"

NO

A knot in my chest loosened. A ghost was not texting me. Though he'd lied to me when he was alive. Could he still be lying?

"Do you know who's texting her?" Lori asked.

NO

Disappointment overwhelmed me. I had hoped being dead would grant him some special insight into what was happening. But if it wasn't him and he didn't know who was doing it, this had all been a waste of time.

I wanted to quit, but Lori was already asking another question. "Is there anything you want to tell us?"

S-O-R-R-Y

Tears pricked my eyes, but I blinked them back. Like Gemma said, apologies didn't mean anything when the behavior didn't change, but he didn't have anything to gain by apologizing now. Could he be sticking around just to apologize to me?

"Do you have any regrets?"

P-R-O-M

I gasped. That could mean so many things.

The planchette was moving again. What else could he have to say?

W-H-Y-I-S-N-A-T-E-H-E-R-E

I frowned and looked at Nate. He was grim-faced.

Lori gave me a questioning look, and I shrugged. "He's our friend," she said.

C-H-E-A-T-I-N-G-B-I-T-C-H

I froze. "What the . . . ?"

Lori shushed me.

"For the record," I said, "I never cheated on you."

L-I-A-R

Ian had stepped forward, as if to get a better view of the planchette moving. "What is happening?"

"He's not helping us. I'm done," I said.

I started to pull my hands away, but Lori grabbed them and put them back on the planchette. "Please don't stop."

D-O-N-T-T-R-U-S-T-H-E-R

"What the hell?" Ian said. He was looking around the room as if he expected to see Jerry somewhere.

Jerry had always pushed me around, and I'd always let him. Before,

I tried to lie and deal with him alone. But I wasn't doing that anymore. My voice shook. "That's what you're sticking around to say? Go to hell, Jerry."

M-I-N-E

"She doesn't belong to anyone," Ian said.

"Guys, stop," Lori said, tearful. "Only one person is supposed to talk!"

"Let's end this," Nate said.

The planchette broke free from our fingers and moved across the board. Lori flinched and I struggled not to scramble away.

C-H-E-A-T-I-N-G-W-I-T-H-I-A-N-A-N-D-N-A-T-E

"What the . . . ?" Ian stepped forward again.

"You're delusional!" I yelled.

A-L-L-G-I-R-L-S-L-I-E

"I didn't lie to you."

C-H-E-A-T-A-N-D-L-I-E-C-H-E-A-T-A-N-D-L

I stood, and the board and planchette fell to the floor. It stopped moving and lay there like nothing had happened.

Lori looked shaken. "Charlotte, come back."

"No. I don't have to put up with this anymore."

The temperature had plummeted even further. The candle flames flickered, as if a breeze had just blown through the room. Papers on my desk rustled and then flew off. Pictures I had taped to the wall fluttered and several of them fell.

The book on my nightstand flew off and hit Nate in the stomach. "Oof!"

Ian looked around, tense and watchful like he was waiting for something to fly at him.

I stood, frozen. Jerry was here and he could hurt us. He would hurt my friends and then he'd hurt me.

Nate grabbed a fresh incense stick out of his backpack. He fumbled to light it.

My lamp fell over and almost hit Lori. She jumped out of the way with a shriek.

I finally broke my paralysis and stepped forward. "Stop it!"

Nate got the incense lit and started walking around, filling my room with fragrant smoke.

The air started to pick up speed and blew the fallen pictures and papers into a tiny whirlwind at the center of my room. The air pulled tendrils of hair loose from my braid and blew them into my face as the pictures continued to swirl. Enough was enough.

"Get out!" I yelled.

Air rushed out of my bedroom, and the door slammed shut. The candles went out and the room plunged into darkness. The pictures had stopped swirling, leaving us in sudden silence. None of us spoke or moved as the echo of my slamming door still rung in my ears.

CHAPTER 34

I stood in the darkness, breathing hard and trembling. No one moved at first, and then someone turned on the light. Ian grabbed me. "Holy . . . crap. Are you okay?"

"I'm fine." My teeth chattered, and shivers wracked my body. Nate wrapped me in his arms. He was much warmer than I was, and the ice in my bones thawed.

"She's freezing," Nate said.

Ian threw a blanket over my shoulders and Nate tucked it around me.

Between the blanket and Nate, I warmed up and the shaking slowed down. Lori had already started packing up the Ouija board.

"I don't know how he did that." Nate clenched his jaw. "Ghosts can't usually move stuff around like that, unless we invite them to, like the planchette. I don't think it's safe for you to stay here anymore, Charlotte."

"I live here. Where am I supposed to go?"

"You'll have to tell your parents . . ."

"What? That my dead ex-boyfriend is haunting me? And that I have a real stalker too?" I didn't want to yell at him, but couldn't stop.

"I was here and I barely believe it," Ian said quietly.

Nate raked a hand through his hair. "What if we all talked to them together?"

I shook my head. "They'll call it a 'group hallucination' or whatever they need to so they won't have to deal with it."

"I don't know what to think about what just happened," Ian said. "I don't believe in ghosts. But I was here. And that happened."

Lori was sitting on my bed with the Ouija board box in her lap. She was staring down at the carpet, one hand touching her necklace.

I looked at my friends. Jerry had made me feel like no one would believe me, like he was the only one who would ever care about me. But my friends had proved him wrong so many times already. And I couldn't keep hiding things from them. I was finally ready to let go of my last secret, the thing I never thought I'd be able to tell anyone.

"There's something I should tell you. About prom night." My stomach churned. Lori, Nate, and Ian all looked at me.

"Ian, do you remember when you asked me why I got in the car with Jerry even though I knew he'd been drinking?"

"Yeah, and you never really answered me."

I kept my eyes on the floor, not wanting to look at anyone while I told the story. "Prom night was good at first. Jerry started off in a good mood, but then it all went bad."

"Was it when I asked you to dance with me?" Ian asked, his voice sounding choked. "I remember he asked me if I was flirting with you or something and I didn't think anything of it. I thought he was joking."

I just nodded. I hadn't told the hard part yet, but I already had to force words out through the lump in my throat. "He dragged me out of prom, around the side of the parking lot where no one could see us. When we got to the parking lot, he stopped, and . . . he . . . he said I was cheating on him and he should just kill himself."

Lori gasped.

"He what?" Ian took a step forward, hands clenched into fists.

Tears had choked me then. The same way they were squeezing my throat now. "Of course I told him I didn't want him to kill himself. But he wouldn't listen. He just kept going on about how his life revolved around me and I was his everything."

I looked up from the carpet, into Ian's eyes. They only held understanding. I kept talking as if he were the only person in the room. "He started walking toward his car. And I thought, just for a second, that if I went back inside prom, you'd take me home and it would be over between Jerry and me. And that maybe it would be okay."

My stomach clenched, mirroring the reaction I'd had that night. As I told the story, it was like it was happening again.

He'd threatened to kill himself before, but I'd always been able to talk him down. If he hurt himself, and I could have stopped him, I'd never forgive myself. So I followed him through the parking lot.

Spatters of wetness hit my arms, and I looked up at the raindrops sparkling in the streetlights. My dress was speckled with rain, and the parking lot was slippery. Jerry was almost at the car, and I couldn't run in heels. I pulled off my shoes and followed him.

Jerry yanked open the car door as I stumbled to a stop beside him. "Just go back inside," he said. "You don't care about me."

I couldn't keep doing this. He'd just keep saying the same things over and over, and I could never convince him. He'd never change. Not ever. No matter what I did. "If you feel that way," I said, "maybe we should break up."

His eyes went wide. "You're breaking up with me? On prom night?" His voice thickened. "You really don't love me."

"I do love you," I insisted. "But you're not happy with me. You're always accusing me of cheating. So maybe you'd be happier with someone else." Saying the words out loud felt like a huge weight lifted off my chest. We'd go our separate ways and both be happier. Maybe we could even be friends again.

"*I can't believe this,*" *he said. Tears streamed down his cheeks.* "*You don't love me.*"

Seeing Jerry cry terrified me. I'd never seen him cry before, not when he'd broken his ankle in sixth grade. Not when he had bruises all over his back. Not when his grandma died.

I took a step toward him. "*No! I'm sorry. We don't have to break up . . . I just thought . . .*"

"*Go back inside, Charlotte,*" *he said quietly. He slid into the driver's seat, not looking at me.* "*I'm going to do it. I'll drive into a tree and hope I die. I'll do us both a favor.*"

I had a moment, just the tiniest sliver of time, where I didn't care. If he died, he couldn't hurt me anymore. But then it passed, and I was ashamed for even thinking it. He was still one of my best friends. "*No, let's talk. Don't do that.*"

"*If you want to talk to me, get in.*" *He nudged me out of the way and slammed the door. I knocked on the window, but he didn't look at me. The locks engaged, but I tried opening his door anyway.*

Again, I looked back toward the castle, my mind racing and my stomach churning. When Jerry started the car, I hurried to the passenger side and yanked on the handle. The door was locked. "*Let me in!*" *I wouldn't have enough time to get help.*

The locks disengaged, and I got in the car. He backed out of the space without looking behind him while I fumbled for my seat belt. He took a flask out of his jacket pocket and took a long drink.

"*Jerry, buckle your seat belt. Maybe you shouldn't be driving.*"

He smacked the steering wheel. "*You can't tell me what to do anymore! You just broke up with me, remember? I know you've been cheating on me. That's why you're doing this. Why won't you just admit it?*"

"*Why do you think I cheated on you?*"

"*Because some people tell the truth!*"

"*Someone told you I was cheating on you?*"

"*Yeah, and I trust them. More than I trust you. You're always going to play with my feelings like this. Always.*"

"*They're lying.*"

He didn't answer. He took the first curve too fast, and I grabbed the door handle. I tried to find the right words to calm him down, but my mind was blank.

He gained speed on the straightaway, and I scanned both sides of the road, hoping that a deer wouldn't jump in front of us.

"*I love you, Charlotte,*" *he said, his voice thick.* "*I can't stand the thought of you with someone else.*"

"*There isn't anyone else, I swear.*" *I blinked back tears.* "*We're together all the time. You check my phone and my email. You know there's no one else.*"

Jerry pounded the steering wheel. "*Liar! Liar! You're a fucking liar!*"

He turned to look at me, and I braced my hands and feet. "*Watch the road!*"

He looked at me for a long time, tears shining in his eyes.

My heart felt like it would pound its way out of my chest. I couldn't catch my breath.

"*I have to do it,*" *he said.* "*You're not giving me a choice.*"

There was a curve in the road ahead. Trees loomed up at us from either side, and there were no other drivers as he drifted across the centerline. "*Pay attention to the road, Jerry, please.*" *Tears streamed down my face.*

"*If we die together, we'll be together forever.*" *He reached out and touched my face gently.* "*I won't let anything come between us.*"

"*Just pull over. Please!*"

"*You were made for me.*" *He turned back toward the road and gripped the steering wheel with both hands, his knuckles turning white. He sped up.*

Just beyond the curve was a large tree. We were going too fast to make the turn. He was aiming for the tree. Dread knotted my stomach. "No, Jerry!"

"I'm the only one who'll ever love you," he said, his voice calm.

I spotted Caleb's car too late to do anything. There was a crash. And the world went black.

CHAPTER 35

Ian touched my arm. My cheeks were wet with tears, but the knots in my stomach had loosened and I took a deep, shuddering breath. I finally let myself look at Nate. He was staring into space, arms crossed and frowning.

"I had no idea. And all this time, you've been dealing with that alone." Ian shook his head.

"It wasn't your fault," I said. "You didn't know how he was."

"None of it was your fault," Ian said quietly. "You know that, right?"

I mostly did. But hearing someone who knew him say it made another one of the knots in my stomach unravel.

"I don't understand why he killed himself," Lori said, her face pale and her eyes too wide. "Because you broke up with him? But . . ."

I hesitated. "I just wanted him to stop accusing me of lying and cheating. I didn't know what else to do."

"You couldn't have known," Ian said.

"Maybe I should have," I said softly. "Like I said, it wasn't the first time he'd threatened to do it."

"He made his choices." Ian shook his head. "We need to worry about now. Who told him you were cheating? That could be your stalker."

"Maybe," I agreed. It made my stomach hurt, thinking that someone other than Jerry had wanted to hurt me, even back then.

"Someone who wanted you and Jerry to break up," Ian said. "That's obvious."

"Like Gabe?" Lori asked.

"That's really twisted," Ian said.

"Or Brittany, if they were hooking up," I said. "But if Sandy had told him I was cheating, he would have believed her. But . . . I didn't think she hated me before he died."

"She didn't," Ian said. "She still doesn't. If you made up with her, you'd see it's not her."

I didn't answer.

This whole time, Nate had been quiet, which was unusual. I looked over at him, and he was frowning at the floor. I wanted him to say something, but he didn't look up at me. Hearing my dead boyfriend had tried to kill me was probably a lot.

Maybe this was too much for him. Maybe *I* was too much for him. That thought made my stomach hurt even worse. It was all too much for me, but I didn't have a choice. I'd known that I liked Nate, really liked him, but until that moment, I hadn't realized how important he'd become.

I dragged my eyes away from Nate and tried to concentrate. "It could still be anyone," I said.

Nate looked up at us. In a quiet voice, he said, "It's not just anyone. We're missing something. I feel it, but I don't know what it is. I just hope we figure it out before it's too late."

Lori and I had to get back to her house, so we said goodbye to Nate and Ian. Lori was quiet for the rest of the evening. After we'd shut the lights off and were trying to sleep, she said, "That was intense."

"Yeah. But that's how Jerry was with me. Fine one minute and out of control the next."

"What about that thing he said about dying together and being together? Do you think he really meant it? That he meant to die?" Lori asked.

"He looked so determined and . . . resigned. Like he just wanted to get it over with. Yeah, I think he meant to die and take me with him." I shivered.

Lori got quiet then, like she didn't know what to say. I didn't either. Eventually I heard her breathing slow. I didn't realize how tired I was until I felt myself sink into the most restful sleep I'd had in longer than I could remember.

When I got home on Sunday, my room was a mess. I picked up papers and pictures off the floor. One was a picture of Ian and me. It had originally had Jerry in it too, but I'd cut him out after he died. Another was of Lori and me, wearing funny hats and making silly faces at the camera. I tried to put them back on the wall, but they wouldn't stick. I put them in a stack on my desk.

I took my pajamas to the bathroom, intending to take a quick shower. But once I got under the hot spray, it felt so good that I stayed in way too long, enjoying the feeling of being completely warm.

The bathroom was steamy when I finally got out of the shower, and I started drying off. Then I spotted it, on the bathroom mirror, like someone had drawn the letters with a fingertip.

SORRY

NOVEMBER

CHAPTER 36

Lori and I always got ready for dances together, so she came over to do my makeup and hair. I'd made her a lacy black wrap to go with her coral sheath dress. My dress was a thrift shop find. It was emerald and had been too big on me, but I'd shortened the skirt and cut triangular panels, adding flowered teal material to make the skirt flare. I'd also added big teal buttons down the front for decoration. I loved everything about it. It was bright and cheerful, and I smiled at my reflection so much that my cheeks hurt.

Lori arrived, carrying her dress and her makeup bag. A curling wand peeked out one side. "That dress is gorgeous. You look so amazing," she said.

I hugged her. "I feel amazing! It's going to be such a good night."

She grinned. "You're going to have so much fun with Nate!" But then her smile faded.

"What's wrong?" I asked.

She turned away from me and started digging through her purse. "I'm happy for you, I am, I just . . . I wish JD would come."

My heart plopped into my stomach. "Have you guys been texting?"

"Not really. I've been trying to get him to talk to me, but he won't."

"Lori . . ."

"I'm just going to show him how I look tonight. So he knows what he's missing."

"Are you going to ask him to come to the dance?"

Lori sighed. "He won't come." She turned back to me and was smiling again, but I could see that it was forced. "Let's get you ready."

I could do the basics, like mascara and eyeliner, but Lori had all the brushes and creams and powders. I sat, and she lined them up on my desk. There was so much makeup there that she probably could have turned me into Gamora if she wanted. "I'm still going to look like me when you're done, right?"

Lori laughed. "Of course you are. I'm just going to bring out your eyes a little more, cover up the dark circles under your eyes, stuff like that. Trust me."

She covered up the zits I had forming, but it looked totally natural. She made my eyes look bigger and bluer. She curled my hair so it looked smooth and shiny. When she was done, she stepped back from me, smiling. I turned left and right, admiring my reflection in the mirror. A grin spread across my face.

I wrapped Lori in a hug. "You're the best!"

While Lori did her makeup, I paced and took deep breaths. Tonight I was going to tell Nate how I felt about him.

The doorbell rang. It was Nate, exactly on time. His voice drifted upstairs, and then I heard my parents talking to him.

Lori put a hand to her temple. "Ugh, I have a headache. Will your parents mind if I lie down for a little while? Then I'll get ready."

"They won't care. Text me when you're on your way, okay?"

"I will." Lori nodded and sat on my bed.

I gripped the handrail as I walked downstairs.

Nate was standing awkwardly by the front door, and he forced a laugh at something my dad said. His eyes went wide when he saw me. "You look gorgeous."

I felt incandescent.

He looked wonderful too, in a purple-and-black-striped button-down shirt tucked into jeans. His glasses had fogged up when he walked into the house, so he had them resting on top of his head. His hair was neater than usual, like he'd combed it aggressively, but it was starting to stick up on the sides. I liked it better messy. My mom made us take a picture. He started to wrap an arm around me but paused, like he wasn't sure where to put his hand. My face got warm as I wrapped my arm around him, and he let his hand hover, not quite touching my waist. The smile on my face felt wide and happy.

We got in the car and he started driving. I smoothed my dress while butterflies fluttered around my stomach. The last dance I'd been to had been prom, with Jerry. That night had started out like a dream and ended like a nightmare.

Tonight won't be like that. I fidgeted with the big button on my dress like a worry stone. Usually the silence between Nate and me was fine, but I wanted to fill it, tell him how I felt about him. But the words wouldn't come.

And maybe he didn't like me like that anyway. After he put his hand on my arm and I yelled at him, and the time he tried to kiss me and I jerked away, who could blame him?

When we pulled up at the school, Nate put the car in park but let the engine idle. He turned the music down. He was facing forward, and my heart pounded.

When the song ended, he shifted so he was facing me. He took a deep breath. "I'm sure you've already figured this out, but I think you're amazing. Hanging out with you, texting you is the best part of my day."

I cleared my throat, hoping my voice wouldn't squeak. "You're the best part of my day too."

"I've, uh . . ." He rubbed his palms against his jeans. "I've liked you for a while. I'm not trying to rush you into anything. I just wanted you to know."

"I've liked you for a while too," I said. "I've never known anyone else like you."

Nate grinned. "Uh-oh. I'm not sure that's a good thing."

"It's definitely a good thing. You're one of my favorite people."

"Yeah?" Nate's grin faded, and he looked like he wasn't sure what to do next.

"I don't feel rushed," I said. And then I shifted in my seat, leaning toward him. He moved slowly so that I'd have time to say no if I wanted to.

He touched the side of my face, and together, we closed that last inch. His lips were warm and soft, and the butterflies in my stomach took flight.

He kissed me as if he wasn't thinking of anything but me. He kissed me as if we were the only two people who had ever existed. It felt dangerous and real and too good to be true. There wasn't enough air in the car, but I didn't need to breathe ever again. I was so warm, I might burst into flames.

When we broke the kiss and sat back slightly, Nate was grinning like an idiot, and it felt like the same grin was on my face. "This is the best dance ever." He laughed.

It was contagious, and before I knew it, I was laughing until my stomach hurt and tears gathered at the corners of my eyes. When we finally stopped, my lips felt tender and swollen. I pulled down the mirror to check my makeup. The smudge-proof lipstick Lori used had done its job, but it was probably going to be obvious to everyone that we had been making out in the car. I didn't care.

"Should we . . ." I began, but as I spoke, Nate leaned over and gently kissed my neck.

I turned toward him. We started kissing again, as if, now that our lips knew what they'd been missing all this time, we couldn't stop.

When we finally got out of the car, several songs later, I was light-headed. The crisp air stung my cheeks. I buttoned up my yellow coat and stuffed my hands in my pockets. Nate put his arm around me, blocking some of the chilly wind.

We walked into the hall outside the gym, where kids stood around talking or drinking sodas from the concession stand. The air was stuffy. I stripped out of my coat and draped it over my arm, then linked my fingers with Nate's. Tonight, I could just be me. I didn't have to watch what I said or did. I could just enjoy myself.

Brittany walked by with some big guy from the football team. Were people bugging him because he was with Brittany, or had that all died down? When Brittany spotted us, her eyes flickered to our entwined hands, then back to my face. She stopped in front of us. "I wonder if people are going to treat you like shit now that you're not acting like the widow anymore."

Is that what she wanted? "That's not what I was doing," I said.

"Whatever. Did you know Caleb is in speech therapy? And he actually took a few steps the other day, no thanks to you."

The football player shifted and looked away. Nate squeezed my hand.

I leaned toward her. "I know you want to blame me for this, but it isn't my fault. I didn't *let* him drive. I did everything I could to stop him."

"You got in the car! That means you were okay with it!"

Heads turned toward us. A teacher chaperone took a step toward us like he was going to intervene, but I flashed him a smile to signal that everything was okay.

"You don't know what you're talking about," Nate said quietly. "And why do you want to blame her and not Jerry?"

"I *do* blame Jerry! But he's dead, so I'm pretty sure he paid for what he did."

"So you want me dead?" I asked.

Brittany scowled, her jaw set. "I want you to admit you're to blame."

"I'm not responsible for Jerry's actions," I said. "Jerry was drunk and angry. We were fighting. I thought if I got in the car with him, I could calm him down. I didn't know what would happen."

"You didn't know that you shouldn't let a drunk guy drive?" Brittany pointed at me like she was going to jab me in the chest. "You didn't know he was going to hurt someone? A kindergartner could have told you that. You were sober, so what's your excuse?"

"Let's go," the football player said. He tugged on her hand, and after a moment, Brittany let him guide her away but kept glaring at me.

I rubbed the scar at my hairline. Brittany knew where to ram the knife.

"Ignore her," Nate said.

I sighed. "She's not wrong, though."

"You were in a bad situation, and you did the best you could."

"That's what my therapist said."

"Smart lady." Then Nate gave me the kind of hug that made me feel like I could survive anything and be okay.

We went into the gym. It was dimly lit, the edges of the room in deep shadows. The DJ had big speakers set up at the end of the gym, and bass pounded in my chest. I looked for Ian but didn't see him. Lori had texted me while Nate and I were in the car, but I didn't see her yet.

Nate and I threw our coats onto the pile on the bleachers. We started dancing to a fast song. Nate showed off and acted silly, but he was fun to watch.

Lori texted me and I told her where we were. She joined us and we danced together for a while. Then Ian and a senior girl came over and started dancing with us. Ian motioned to Nate and gave me a thumbs-up.

When a slow song came on, I rested my head on Nate's chest. His arms made me feel safe. It was too warm in the gym, but I didn't care. Being close to Nate already made me feel like I was on fire, and if this was what it felt like to burn, then I'd surrender gladly.

I spotted Gabe sitting on the bleachers, watching us, wearing a grim expression. I closed my eyes and blocked out the world.

When we took a break, Lori dragged me to the bathroom. "Are you finally official?"

"Yep. When we got here, he was like, 'You're amazing' and kissed me."

"Wow." She sighed. "Was it great?"

"It was great. Are you feeling better?"

"What? Oh, yeah . . . I'm fine. The headache is all gone." Lori leaned forward to check her mascara in the mirror.

Lori stared at herself like she didn't recognize her own face.

"Did you send JD a picture? Did he respond?"

"He's still ignoring me," she said, her voice flat.

"I'm sorry." Part of me wanted JD to respond to her because it would make her happy. But I didn't want her getting back into a bad relationship. If JD was ignoring her, she was safe from him.

"I told him how much I still love him, and that there's no one but him.

I told him no one else will ever love him the way I do. And nothing."

"Maybe you should let him go."

"I don't think I can." She braced her hands on the sides of the sink and hung her head.

I opened my mouth to speak when Lori straightened up, looked at me, then forced a smile. "What is wrong with me? Go hang out with Nate. This is a special night for you. Don't let me ruin it."

I did want to hang out with Nate, but I wasn't going to desert Lori if she wasn't okay. "I'm not ditching you for a guy this time."

The side of Lori's mouth quirked up. "I appreciate it, but I'm fine. Go. I'll catch up with you in a little while."

I hesitated, but she seemed okay now, like whatever mood she'd had had passed. Stepping carefully on the slick tile floors, I pushed open the bathroom door. A crowd of girls came in, and I ended up holding the door for them. As I walked out, I spotted Gabe leaning up against a wall. As if he'd been waiting for me. I froze, then straightened my shoulders and strode past him.

"So are you and Nate together?"

I kept walking. "Leave me alone." There were other people in the hallway, but it felt like it was just the two of us.

"He'll cheat on you," Gabe said. "Like Jerry did."

I stopped and turned to look at him. "How do you know Jerry cheated on me?"

Gabe ignored my question. "You don't know what guys are really like. But I'm different. I wouldn't do that."

I took a step toward him. "It's really important that I find out who else Jerry was hanging out with."

"I guess it's fitting. You know? You cheated on me. He cheated on you. I guess I'm the only one who thinks relationships mean something."

Gabe acted like I owed him something, and the only reason I was still talking to him was that I felt guilty, like I *did* owe him something. It wasn't right for me to kiss Jerry while I was still dating Gabe. I'd made a mistake. But it was two years ago. And I'd apologized.

I didn't need to beat myself up about it anymore. I was done.

"Whatever." I shook my head and walked away.

Nate was waiting for me by the concession stand. He touched my chin. "You look sad."

I forced myself to smile. "I'm not really. Tonight has been the happiest I've been in a long time."

"Me too." Nate blushed. "I've maybe been thinking about kissing you for a long time."

"Maybe I've been thinking about the same thing."

We grinned at one another. Why had I ever thought this thing with Nate and me wouldn't work?

Nate leaned down and kissed me. He tasted like soda and happiness.

I wrapped my arms around him, forgetting for a moment that we were in a public place. I wasn't thinking about Brittany or Gabe anymore. My phone buzzed with a text message, but I ignored it. For that moment, there was no one and nothing else that mattered.

At the end of the night, Nate gathered his coat from the pile. Mine wasn't there, so we went searching. Luckily, I'd been smart enough to give Nate my house keys, so even if we didn't find it, I could still get in without waking my parents. Nate found the coat, bunched up in a corner of the gym. He picked it up, and then wrinkled his nose. "It's wet."

Someone had probably spilled soda on it, then dumped it in the corner. It was too wet to wear, so I started folding it, but my hand went through a gap in the fabric that shouldn't have been there. There were huge slices. All over the coat.

It was completely shredded. There was no way it was an accident.

Brittany could have done it after we talked. Or Gabe could have done it anytime. Nate touched one of the cuts in my jacket. "Your stalker carried a knife to the dance?"

Anger flooded my veins. I stuffed the coat in the trash and stormed out of the gym. Nate caught up to me and draped his coat around my shoulders.

On the way home, I checked my text messages.

10:31 PM

Jerry

If I don't get a happily

ever after, neither do you

CHAPTER 37

After Nate dropped me off at home, I took a shower to clear my head. As I brushed my hair, I thought about what happened at the dance, trying to find clues, trying to figure out what the text meant. My stalker could still be anyone. But maybe if I talked to them, they'd reveal something by mistake.

11:22 PM

Me

You need a life if you're
that obsessed with what I do.

Jerry

You stole my life!

Me

You're not Jerry.
He's dead.

Jerry

You of all people should know
that the dead can speak to you.
I told you I would never
let you go. Some of us
keep our promises

> Me
>
> Fine, then prove it.
> Tell me something that
> only Jerry would know.

There was a long pause.

> 11:28 PM
>
> Jerry
> Your password for
> everything is
> "P3mb3rl3y"

I gasped. While it was no secret that I loved *Pride and Prejudice*, that was too specific to be a guess.

Jerry had been the only one who'd known that. He'd insisted I give him all my passwords. That if I didn't, it meant I was hiding something.

How would anyone else know that?

Maybe he wrote it down. Or put it in his phone.

But what if Jerry's ghost was texting me? Nate had said maybe they could, so I looked online. I found stories of people who said they'd gotten texts from ghosts, but nothing like this. All those stories were about texts received once or twice, not repeated extended conversations.

I immediately changed my passwords.

> 11:33 PM
>
> Me
>
> How did you know that?

Jerry

Because I know

everything

about you

Jerry

You couldn't even wait

for me to be cold in

my grave before you

replaced me, could you?

                                        Me

                          Just stop. You're

                          not Jerry and that's

                          not how it happened.

Jerry

Then how did it happen?

One boyfriend is the

same as another to you?

                                        Me

                          You don't even know what

                              you're talking about.

My hands trembled. Ghost Jerry or a stalker? Either option was
terrible.

11:37 PM

Jerry

I saw what you wrote about me.

You're such a liar

Me

No, I'm finally telling

the truth about you.

Jerry

You have no idea what

the truth is. You even

lie to yourself

Me

Then tell me the truth!

Who are you?

Jerry

I'm the person who's

going to make you pay

for what you did

I went cold all over. My stalker definitely wanted to hurt me. That was the endgame.

If I showed my parents that text message, would they take it seriously?

Probably not. It was vague, and "make you pay" could mean a lot of things. If I could get him to make a real threat, I could tell my parents and we could go to the police.

I rubbed my wrist.

11:44 PM

Me

Is that a threat?

Jerry

Do you want me to

threaten you?

Me

I just want to know who you are

and why you're doing this.

Jerry

Don't worry. You'll find

out soon enough

I wasn't going to get the last word, so I put my phone down. It was almost out of battery again anyway.

To distract myself, I opened my laptop and cued up a playlist I liked. I opened a book, wanting to get lost in someone else's head.

Jerry's voice registered in my ears before the words did. "What are you doing?"

I froze. My heart pounded.

He laughed. "You're taking video?"

I heard my own voice. "Tell me something good."

My head swiveled to the computer, and I saw that a video was playing. It was a video that currently resided on the thumb drive in my desk.

I'd taken that video on one of our good days.

Jerry's smiling face filled the screen. "Something good? What is there, other than you?" The phone backed up a few steps, then Jerry rushed at me and tackled me. The phone thunked on the ground and I shrieked with giggles.

Moments later, the phone switched to selfie mode, and there we were, our cheeks pressed together. He turned his head and kissed my cheek. "Good things? The sound of your laugh." Kiss. "The fact that you love me even though I'm an asshole." Kiss. "I love you forever. You were made for me."

Then he turned my face toward him and we kissed.

Tears streamed down my cheeks as I got up and hit stop. "Is this your idea of an apology?"

The photos taped to the wall fluttered and several of them fell down.

Icy fingers brushed my arm and I gasped. The hair on the back of my neck stood up.

My book fell off the bed with a thud that made me jump. I was suddenly very aware that the last time this happened, I had Lori, Ian, and Nate with me. This time I was alone. I fought the urge to run out of the room.

But it was my room, damn it. I shouldn't have to run.

"You know what? I'm done." I hadn't known fear could turn to anger until that moment. "Get out of my room!"

On my desk, the pages of my notebook fluttered, like Jerry was perusing it.

I spun around in a slow circle, fists clenched at my sides. "You aren't welcome here. Get. Out."

The air rushed out of the room and my ears popped.

I tried to slow my breathing and after a moment, my mom's voice cut through the silence.

"Charlotte?" Mom knocked on the door. "Are you okay? Did you yell?"

I opened the door and forced a smile. "Sorry. I was watching something and yelled at my laptop."

She frowned and tried to peer around me, but then met my eyes. "Oh." She didn't look convinced. "Well . . . you should probably get some sleep."

"Yeah, okay," I said.

Mom lingered at the door a moment, like she wanted to say more. After a moment, she looked away and said, "Don't stay up too late."

I watched her go. What had she wanted to say? Maybe she never knew what to say either.

We weren't a family that talked about what hurt. Maybe it wasn't that she didn't want to. Maybe she just didn't know how.

Jerry wasn't going to just go away. No one had rescued me from him when he was alive. Nate, Ian, and Lori would help me as much as they could, but it was *me* he was haunting. If I wanted him to go, I had to figure out how to *make* him leave.

CHAPTER 38

The next morning, I texted Ian, and when he said he was home, I headed over there.

The street was deserted. There was a dusting of snow on the ground, but Ian was shooting hoops in the driveway. In shorts. He was that guy.

"So, what's up?" Ian asked, lining up to make a shot.

"Last night, at the dance, someone cut up my coat."

He paused, then threw the ball right through the sweet spot. "Damn. But that means it couldn't have been Sandy."

He passed me the ball and I lined up a shot. "I guess not. Unless one of her friends did it. Renee or Penny?"

Ian groaned. "And Renee was at the dance last night. Damn it."

"I need to talk to her."

"I told you before, if you want to talk to her, make up with her. I'm not going to treat her like a suspect."

"Why not?"

"Because I get it. She needs to blame someone. She's just a kid. First she lost Jerry and then you. I know you don't think you mattered to her, but it's not like she has a lot of people she can count on."

I concentrated on taking my shot so I wouldn't have to look at Ian. If Sandy was my stalker, would things be different if I'd texted her? "Do you ever blame me?" I asked in a small voice.

Ian caught the ball on the rebound and bounced it a few times. "Before I knew what really happened with Jerry, I blamed you for checking out. I wanted to grieve with you, talk about him with someone who understood. But you wouldn't talk to me. I get why, now. But Sandy doesn't know that. She needs all the friends she can get. I try to get her out of that house as much as I can."

Jerry and I used to do that. We spent many afternoons playing board games at Deja Brew.

"She's different now," Ian said. "I can't imagine what it's like for her."

There was one day that stood out as especially vivid in my memory. It had been raining, and Jerry and I had been at my house, snuggled up in front of the TV, half watching a movie. Sandy had texted him. When we got to his house, she'd been standing in the rain, looking bedraggled in her soaked T-shirt and jeans. She'd gotten in Jerry's car, and he turned the heat all the way up to help her dry off.

I gave her napkins out of the glove compartment, and it was only then I realized that it wasn't just rain on her face. Tears were still streaking down her cheeks, but she was crying so silently, I wouldn't have known if I hadn't been watching her.

I'd turned toward the front of the car, thinking that I wanted to give her privacy. But now I wondered if me turning away like that was really for her benefit, or for mine. Even in the memory, her pain was so great that it hurt me to watch.

Jerry had been Sandy's safe space, where she had run when she needed comfort. All this time, I'd been thinking that I was the one Jerry had hurt the most, but was that true?

After a while, I'd expected him to hurt me. So when he tried to kill me, it had seemed inevitable.

But how did you feel when the person who always kept you safe drank and drove and died? At least she didn't know that he'd killed himself.

"So how do I make up with her?" I asked. I could be there for her and also find out if she was my stalker. If she wasn't, no harm done. But it left a sick feeling in my stomach. It felt like a secret I shouldn't keep.

"Just be honest," Ian said.

When I got home, I spent a long time staring at my phone before I typed anything.

2:44 PM

Me

Hey, Sandy. I'm really sorry
that I wasn't there for you,
and I feel like we should talk.
Can I take you for coffee?

Sandy
Why?

Me

You had questions about how
Jerry died. Maybe I can answer
some of them for you.

Sandy
Why now, all of a sudden?

Me

Because I'm trying to stop
hiding from hard conversations.

Sandy

You don't have to act

like you care about me.

I don't care what you do.

Me

Please give me a

chance to apologize.

Sandy took a long time to respond. I figured she'd end up telling me she hoped I died again, but eventually, she texted back.

3:06 PM

Sandy

Okay.

Sandy was already waiting outside of Deja Brew when I got there, dwarfed by one of Jerry's old winter coats. The feeling of déjà vu washed over me. She was wearing dark eye makeup and lipstick. The scent of Jerry's cologne, probably still clinging to the jacket, wafted to me. My stomach churned, and I wrinkled my nose.

Adding to the weirdness, we'd never hung out alone before. I felt Jerry's absence, so she probably did too.

She followed me inside, and the stifling warmth made it hard to breathe. Sandy's glasses steamed up and she waved in front of her face to defog them.

"My treat," I said. "What do you want?"

"Espresso."

Jerry had always gotten espresso, but Sandy used to drink those super-sweet blended coffee drinks. "Aren't you a little young for that?"

She shot me a glare. "I'm too young for a lot of things."

The silence hung between us like something poisonous. I went to the counter and ordered.

She put two sugars in her espresso, just like Jerry used to. She was wearing Jerry's coat and drinking what he liked. My stalker was pretending to be Jerry. It could be coincidence, just her dealing with the loss of her brother, but it still made me sick to my stomach.

There were only a few other people in the shop, and music played in the background. We sank into comfy armchairs under a painting of trees covered in snow. Sandy stirred her drink and didn't look at me. I shifted around in my seat, not sure what to say.

"So, what do you want?" she asked.

"I know I wasn't around for a while, and I know you're mad at me. I just wanted to see if there was anything I could do."

"Can you bring my brother back?" she asked.

My mouth went dry, so I took a sip of hot chocolate. "You know I can't."

"Yeah, well, that's all I want. I want him back."

"I wish—" I began, but Sandy cut me off.

"What happened that night? He was so excited to pick you up. I was watching him, and he turned around to wave at me before he got in the car . . . And that was the last time I saw him." Her voice cracked.

I took a deep breath. "He'd been drinking, and he lost control of the car."

She made a face. "Why didn't you drive?"

"I don't have my license," I said. "I thought if I rode with him, I could make sure he'd be okay."

"Were you guys arguing?"

There were some things she deserved to know, but telling her the truth about Jerry seemed cruel. "No. We had a great night."

"Then why was he drinking?" Her voice got louder with each word. "And why did you leave early?"

"I—"

She leaned toward me. "You're still lying." Her eyes glittered like she was fighting tears, but her voice was firm. "I can tell. You still aren't telling me the truth. Why did you ask me to meet you if you were just going to lie?"

"I'm not—" I tightened my grip on my cup until it dented. "It's hard to talk about." That was true, at least.

Sandy laughed, but it wasn't a happy sound. "Yeah, it's been hard to live with too. I'm so stupid. I thought we were friends. Jerry said you thought you were better than us, because your parents weren't mean drunks, but I defended you. You didn't deserve him." She stood up.

I grabbed her arm. "Sandy, wait. I'm sorry. But after Jerry died, I couldn't deal. I couldn't think about anyone else."

"I still miss him every second of every day. But you have a new boyfriend. And it's like . . . Jerry never even existed. You don't care that he died. It should have been you!"

Sandy stormed out of the shop, and I watched her go, unable to move. I thought I'd been braced for her to say it, but it turned out I never got used to being hurt.

My hot chocolate tasted sour. I threw it away and left. I unchained my bike and got on, but then just sat there.

I had to make peace with her. It was the only way I'd get to the truth. I'd have to try harder. I still needed proof.

I gripped the handlebars. I didn't want her to be my stalker. Maybe she wasn't. Maybe she *was* just an angry kid dealing with the death of her brother.

I crossed the parking lot and pedaled to catch up. Sandy was a block away, fingers flying over her phone. I pulled up beside her. "Sandy . . ."

"Go to hell," she said without looking at me.

I didn't want her to hate me. Not just because she might be my stalker, but because I really did care about her. I didn't want to hurt her with the truth, but I didn't want to take the blame either. I hopped off the bike and fell in step beside her. "Your brother and I were fighting. Someone told him I was cheating on him, even though I wasn't. I loved him. I'm so sorry I didn't text you before this, but I've been messed up with everything that happened. I've been going to therapy and trying to get better."

She faced me, scowling. "Why would someone say you were cheating if you weren't?"

"To break us up? I don't know."

Sandy searched my face, like she was trying to decipher something. "Was he really drinking?"

I forced the word out. "Yes."

Sandy crossed her arms over her stomach and hugged herself. "He promised."

I tightened my grip on my bike. "I don't think he meant to break his promise, but he was angry a lot. Maybe he was just trying to get out of his head."

"But he wasn't stupid. Why would he drive?"

"Sometimes people do stupid things when they're upset."

"Was it because of me?" she asked in a small voice.

"Was what because of you?"

"I try not to make Dad mad, but sometimes I can't help it. Whenever Dad got mad at me, Jerry would stop him, and then Dad would hit him instead. So was it because of me?"

Tears sprang to my eyes. Jerry had never said anything about it, but he wouldn't. The Jerry I'd loved wouldn't have hesitated to take a punch for someone. He'd refused to talk about his bruises. "Jerry loved you. It wasn't because of you."

"Then why?" Tears streamed down her face.

I wasn't sure if she was asking why he drank or why he drove or why he died. But my answer was the same. "I don't know. None of it makes sense."

"It's not fair."

I touched my scar.

"Ian said you were having a hard time dealing, and that you stopped texting him too."

"I couldn't be there for anyone. I was just trying to survive."

She dropped her eyes to the sidewalk and shuffled her feet. "Are you really in therapy?"

"Yeah." I hesitated. If she was my stalker, I didn't want to give her anything to use against me. But if it was her, and I made her understand, maybe she'd stop. "I have nightmares and flashbacks about the crash. Everything reminds me of Jerry. I'm still pretty messed up."

Sandy shivered, and I put my arm around her, giving her a half hug. She didn't push me away, which was something.

"The park's right there." I gestured. "Want to go sit?"

We brushed snow off the swings, then sat and swayed.

"I have nightmares too." She scuffed her feet in the mulch.

"About what?"

"About the crash. In my nightmares, he begs for me to help him, for me to call for help. But I can't move." She dropped her head into her hands. "I'm useless."

I put my arms around her and let her cry it out. When she was done, I let her go and faced forward, looking at anything but her. "I hit my head and blacked out . . ." My throat was closing up, but I forced the words out. "They told me he died instantly, that he didn't suffer. Brittany was conscious the whole time and called 911 right away."

Sandy leaned against the swing chain and didn't speak for a long time. I wanted to go home, crawl under my covers, and pretend to sleep.

"Why did you want to know about Jerry's phone?" she asked.

It was such a sudden change of subject that it took me a moment to figure out how to respond. "Someone's been texting me from his number." I studied her face, searching for some sign that she already knew.

She cocked her head. "Who would do that?"

"Someone who's mad at me for Jerry dying."

"Lots of people loved Jerry," she said. "He was the best."

"Lots of people loved him," I agreed.

"Well, what's the person saying? The one texting you."

"Awful things," I said. "The person is pretending to be Jerry, threatening me, blaming me for his death."

She looked down at her hands. "Could you have stopped him from dying?" she asked softly.

I hesitated. "I tried." Even if I'd gone back into prom to get a teacher or Ian, Jerry would have already pulled away. Maybe he wouldn't have killed himself if I hadn't been in the car, but I couldn't know that.

Sandy nodded. She swiped at her eyes before turning back to face me. Her eyeliner had run and I handed her some makeup wipes from my purse.

"My mom didn't change anything in his room after he died, so I can look to see if the phone is there," she said. "Would that help?"

My stomach jumped, but I kept the excitement out of my voice. "That would definitely help. But I was hoping I could look through his room. I think he was talking to another girl. If he was, maybe she's the one stalking me."

Sandy flushed, and I wasn't sure if it was from embarrassment or anger. "Um . . . well . . . my parents are home today. You could come over Monday before they get home."

Something seemed off about her response. "What about after they're asleep?" I asked. Sometimes Jerry had snuck me in once they passed out.

"It's not a good idea," Sandy said, her voice firm. "Come over Monday after school."

Was she delaying me so she could hide something? I hated that I'd tipped her off, but at least she was letting me search Jerry's room. "Sure. Monday."

After Sandy left, I sat on the swing for a little while longer and swayed.

Everyone knew that Sandy's parents drank and fought. Sandy and Jerry had both been good students, involved in extracurricular activities. Jerry had a lot of friends and had seemed like he was doing fine. You just could never tell about anyone or anything from the outside. From the outside, our relationship had been perfect.

Sandy seemed like she'd forgiven me, but she could be pretending.

Jerry had been a good actor, so maybe she was too.

My stomach ached. Was it safe to trust anyone?

My thoughts kept circling as I biked home.

Sandy texted me later that night. The phone was not in Jerry's room.

But that's what she would say if she were my stalker. She wouldn't admit she had it.

My stalker knew a lot about both Jerry and me. Almost like it was someone close to us.

Anxiety choked me and wouldn't let go. It couldn't be . . . but what if it was? I had to be sure it wasn't someone I trusted.

I could set a trap for my stalker. Something had happened at both the bonfire and the dance, where lots of people had gathered. Angelica was having a party next week, so my stalker would probably do something.

I wouldn't tell anyone about my plan. The thought of keeping something from Lori and Ian and Nate almost made me sick to my stomach. But the anxiety was stronger. Before Jerry had betrayed me, I wasn't like this.

I was tired of secrets. I didn't want to hide things or lie anymore.

But I had to. I just hoped when I explained what I'd done that everyone would understand.

CHAPTER 39

On Monday, Nate asked to start driving me home after school so we could do homework and hang out. We could hang out most days I didn't work or have therapy, except on Wednesdays, when he had to watch Megan because his dad went to grief group.

Nate dropped me off a few blocks away from Sandy's house. Knowing about Nate wasn't the same as me showing up with him. I didn't want to upset her if I could help it.

"Text me if you need me," Nate said.

I walked the last couple of blocks, wondering what I'd find. Would I find a picture of Brittany stashed somewhere with something cutesy written on the back? Maybe I'd find a Post-it note with his email password. We were still trying different combinations and hadn't broken in yet.

When Sandy opened the door, she looked around and waved me in like she was worried someone would see me. She was wearing that heavy makeup and a black outfit, but her face wasn't as closed off.

She led me to Jerry's room. The door was closed, and as she opened it, I braced myself, wondering if his ghost would visit me here.

The faint scent of his cologne still hung in the air. His desk and shelves were heavy with dust, as if no one had been in the room for a while. Everything was exactly the way I remembered it. His sheets were rumpled because he never made the bed. His scarred wooden desk was against the wall. A foam ball lay underneath the basketball hoop attached to the closet door.

Clothes were heaped on the floor, including the shirt he'd worn to school the day before prom. It was a yellow-and-gray-striped T-shirt, and seeing it reminded me how that last day at school, he'd thrown his arm around me and told me I was smart and gorgeous and he didn't deserve me.

"I looked for his phone but didn't find it," Sandy said, breaking into my thoughts. "What do you think happened to it?"

"I think my stalker took it," I said.

Sandy was silent for a moment, probably remembering him, like I was. He'd been so alive, it was hard to imagine he could ever die.

"We should start looking," I said.

"What are we looking for?" Sandy asked.

"Anything that might help me figure out why someone is stalking me. Anything that'll show me who he was talking to."

Sandy went through the desk, and I started with his closet, sticking my hand in his shoes and pockets in case he'd hidden something. When I didn't find anything, I pulled his desk chair over and balanced on it, peering at the shelf above. There was a shoebox on top, and I took it down, then sat on his bed to open it.

On top was the one-year anniversary card I'd made for him. I'd sewn scraps together to make a quilted pattern with hearts and lined it with stiff interfacing so it would keep a card shape. In fabric marker, I'd written inside, "You mean more to me than I can say. Love you!"

Underneath that card were other cards and notes I'd given him. One was just a doodle of a heart with our initials that I didn't even remember. I turned it over, and on the back, he'd written the date. I'd drawn it when I was ten.

I wasn't sure how that made me feel. If he'd liked me enough to keep something I drew when I was ten, why had he waited until I was fifteen to kiss me?

As I continued looking through the box, I found valentines, the paper kind kids gave to each other in elementary school. It looked like he'd kept every valentine he'd gotten. Was he really that desperate for love?

He hadn't kept the heart because he'd liked me; he'd kept it because I had liked him.

Something twisted in my stomach, but I couldn't name the emotion that went with it. I just wished I'd understood Jerry better when he'd been alive.

"Did you find anything?" Sandy asked.

I jolted and dropped the stack of cards back into the box. "Just a bunch of old valentines."

"I'm going to get a soda. Do you want anything?"

"Sure. A soda would be great."

She walked out, and I went back to looking at the box. When I'd dropped the cards, they shifted to reveal a card on the bottom.

It was a store-bought card, and I knew right away it wasn't from me. It had a cartoon peanut-butter-and-jelly sandwich on the front. On the inside, it said, "Meant for each other." It was signed, "Yours forever XOXO," and below that, the date. It was from while Jerry and I were together.

I wanted to shred the card and burn the pieces, but I made myself put it back in the shoebox. I could be upset later. Anyway, what did it matter? Cheating on me hadn't even been the worst thing he'd done.

It occurred to me that while Sandy was downstairs, I could peek in her room. Even though she'd agreed to let me look in Jerry's room, there was still a possibility that she was my stalker. I wouldn't have another opportunity.

I listened. Ice cubes rattled downstairs. I didn't have long. Maybe another minute or two.

I inched her door open, trying to be quiet.

I didn't think I'd ever been in Sandy's room before, and it surprised me. In contrast to her dark, goth-like appearance, her room had prints of animals everywhere. She had cats and dogs but also llamas and hedgehogs. All the eyes watching would freak me out.

I dialed Jerry's number but didn't hear a phone vibrate. I heard something scrape downstairs, so I had another few moments.

I stepped into the room, intending just to take a quick scan in case she had left out my house key or a stalker checklist. But then I spotted Jerry's laptop. I knew for sure it was his because of the stickers on the case. It was vertical, leaning against the desk in a way that meant I wouldn't have seen it if I hadn't gone in.

Sandy could be texting me from Jerry's laptop. I put it on Sandy's desk and listened for her as I turned it on. I didn't hear anything, but I couldn't stop now.

The laptop finished booting up.

It required a password.

I let out a groan of frustration.

"What are you doing?" Sandy demanded. She was holding two cups, and her expression was furious.

"I was just . . ."

"Did you come here to *spy* on me?"

I averted my eyes, but when I looked at the laptop, I flushed. "Why didn't you tell me you had his laptop?"

"I let you into his room!"

"I'm just trying to find out who's stalking me!"

Sandy's jaw tightened. "And what . . . you thought it was me? Is that why you texted me in the first place? The whole reason you're even being nice to me?"

"No, of course not." But it was partly true.

"Get out!" She put the cups down on her desk, grabbed my arm, and yanked me out of her room.

She was surprisingly strong for her size, but I was still able to pull my arm out of her grip. "You said you hoped I'd die! What was I supposed to think?"

"I don't care what you think!" She shoved me toward the door.

Sandy all but pushed me through the front door, and when I got out to the street, she slammed the door so hard that the front windows rattled. I flinched at the sound.

I walked back to Nate's car on autopilot, and he got out to greet me. "You okay?" he asked.

I put my arms around him. "Just hold on to me for a minute."

He wrapped his arms around me so I was enveloped in his warmth. "As long as you want."

CHAPTER 40

On Saturday, I borrowed my parents' GoPro. Well, technically, I hadn't asked them if I could use it. But they wouldn't even notice it was gone.

When Nate picked me up for Angelica's party, I already had everything set up. I'd secured the GoPro in my purse with Velcro strips. When I got to Angelica's, I was going to walk around with the purse for a half hour or so, then leave it somewhere with my sweater on top. If someone messed with my sweater or my purse, the GoPro would record it.

". . . so what do you think?" Nate asked.

"What?" I hadn't heard anything he said. "Sorry. I wasn't paying attention."

"Are you okay?" Nate asked. "You seem . . . weird tonight."

"I'm fine." I wiped my sweaty palms on my skirt. Anticipation fluttered in my stomach. After tonight, I might know the truth.

It was already crowded when we got to Angelica's. Music blared in the living room, and the sliding glass door to the backyard stood open. People gathered around the firepit. Nate and I found the last empty lawn chair and shared it. We tried to squeeze together, but after a lot of awkward shifting that left us both blushing, I was half sitting on his lap.

Voices droned around us, pierced with an occasional laugh. The fire crackled. Sparks and smoke drifted upward. The sky was clear, and the stars shone brightly. It was a perfect moment, and I wanted to press pause on my life and just stay like that.

"Look at that," Nate said, pointing at the sky. "What were people smoking when they came up with constellation names? Do you think that looks like a dog?"

I looked where he was pointing, but they just looked like stars to me. "It looks like an alien," I said.

He squinted. "Gray or reptilian?"

"Um . . . just a regular alien."

"You probably mean the grays, then. But just so you know, five types have visited Earth. So it's important to be specific."

"You're so weird." I rolled my eyes.

He laughed.

"Good thing I like weird," I said.

He stopped laughing and his face turned soft. "I like that you just let me be me."

"I like that you say things I wouldn't think of and that sometimes I'm not sure if you're serious or not," I said. "I like that you understand me without me having to explain and that you're okay with how broken I am."

"There's nothing wrong with you," he said. "Everyone's got something. You're like kintsugi. All your broken parts are repaired with gold. Maybe you still show the cracks, but it just makes you more beautiful."

Tears pricked my eyes. "You always say the right thing."

He kissed my nose and laughed. "Trust me when I say that I do not always say the right thing. It's just the right thing to say to you. Just like you always seem to know the right thing to say to me."

"I'm so glad I found you."

The hairs on the back of my neck stood up, and I felt eyes on me. I looked around, trying to see if anyone was looking my way, but it was impossible to tell with the flickering firelight. I shivered.

"Are you cold?" Nate murmured in my ear.

I wasn't, but it reminded me why I was there. I needed to go back inside so I could be seen with my bag. I needed to talk to people and make
sure that if my stalker was there, whoever it was saw me. "Yeah, let's go
inside."

The warm air inside felt oppressive. The living room was large and
expensive-looking, with a sleek black stereo and matching speakers on
stands. People had drinks sweating on polished wood end tables and the
ornate kitchen table. Angelica had parties all the time, so her parents
probably didn't care. But I never understood people who didn't take care
of nice things.

I scanned the room to see who was there. Brittany was flirting with
some guy I didn't recognize. Ian was dancing with a pretty senior girl.
When he saw Nate and me, they moved over toward us. "Hey, this is
Jessica."

I waved.

A fast song was playing, but Ian grabbed me and twirled me around
in a waltz. I laughed.

He kissed my cheek, then went back to Jessica.

I turned and saw Gabe. He was talking to Shanice, but she wasn't looking at him. It was clear she wasn't interested in whatever he was saying.

Gabe stopped talking when he noticed me watching him. His eyes
shifted to Nate, and his lips tightened.

Renee and Penny were on the couch talking, heads together. Sandy
wasn't with them, and I scanned the crowded room but didn't see her.

Nate went to talk to someone he knew, so I made my way over to
where Lori was talking to Alisha.

"Hey!" Alisha said, grinning. "I was just telling Lori that our team is really awesome this year. Obviously we miss both of you, but I think we can get to nationals. I'm so psyched!"

Lori's smile was forced and rigid. "It's so great!" she said, too brightly. "Charlotte, isn't that great?"

"Yep," I said. "I'm happy for you." I didn't really care one way or the other, but Lori did. "Time to dance?"

"Yes!" Lori gripped my hand tightly enough to crush bone. "We'll see you later, though, okay?" Lori was already turning away before Alisha answered.

"Sure."

When we were out of earshot, Lori said, "I should be with them." Her voice was thick with tears.

I bit back the apology that was on the tip of my tongue. Apologizing wouldn't get Lori to nationals. "You should." It was the only thing I could think to say.

She glared over at Alisha, then took a deep breath and turned back to me. "Let's just go dance before I go back and hit her."

"Let me put my purse down."

Lori steered me to a bedroom down a hall, just off the bathroom, where people were dumping their stuff. I put my purse down and draped my sweater half over it, like I'd practiced. The camera was hidden but would still catch anyone leaning over my bag.

My heart pounding, we went back to the living room and danced. Nate and his friend were still talking on the side of the room. Ian and Jessica joined Lori and me, and we danced together. My mind wasn't on dancing, and my eyes kept drifting to the hallway. I watched for Sandy. I watched her friends to see if they looked up at me like they were in on it.

No one seemed to notice how distracted I was. Ian and Jessica went to talk to other friends. Lori and I danced for a while longer. When a slow song came on, I looked for Nate, but he'd disappeared. Lori and I headed to the kitchen for drinks.

We leaned against the counter with our sodas. My eyes drifted toward the hallway. I jolted when Lori slammed her cup down, splashing soda on the counter.

"Can you believe her rubbing my face in it? Nationals! And do you know who took over as flyer? Brittany. That trashy whore took my place. She's probably the one who dropped me. I'll bet she did it on purpose."

"I don't think she'd do it on purpose." I didn't think Lori would appreciate a "lecture" right now about not using slut-shamey names.

"Why are you defending her? You don't know what she'd do."

I opened my mouth to argue but realized I couldn't. I didn't know Brittany. She might be the one stalking me. "You're right. People do terrible things sometimes."

Lori picked her soda up and drained it. "I'm going outside to the bonfire for a little while. You coming?"

"I'm just going to hang out in here."

She went outside and my eyes drifted to the hallway. Had my stalker already done something to my bag? And where was Nate?

I looked around, but Ian and Jessica were gone. I didn't see Gabe or Brittany or Renee or Penny, but the room was crowded.

It seemed like a good time to text my stalker.

9:24 PM

Me

Hi there. Having fun?

After I hit send, I scanned the room. Lots of people already had their phones out. If one of them was my stalker, they might react to a text from me, glancing my way. No one did.

I didn't think he'd respond, but I finally got a text back.

9:29 PM

Jerry

Did you miss me? You're

such an attention whore

I kept my face impassive as I scanned the room. I casually walked around as I typed, peeking at phone screens when I could. No one reacted.

9:30 PM

Me

I'm here. You're here.

Let's talk face-to-face.

Jerry

How do you keep scamming

guys into thinking you're

not the worst?

First Jerry, now Nate

Me

Are you done pretending

to be Jerry?

Jerry

Enjoy things with Nate
while you can. Hopefully
he figures out you destroy
people before it's too late.

I frowned. Was my stalker threatening Nate? Or just trying to get in my head?

9:32 PM

Me

Unlike Jerry, Nate isn't a
pathetic loser who hits girls.

Jerry

There you go again,
making shit up

If he hadn't already messed with my purse, maybe texting him would make him mad enough to do something. Or better yet, maybe he'd finally confront me. I kept walking around the room, creeping on people's phone screens. I glanced around again. Where was Nate, anyway?

9:34 PM

Me

He abused me.

Jerry

Did he? Well, you have
your version of the
story, I have mine

                                              Me

                         What's your version?

                                              Me

                          Well? I'm waiting.

Fake Jerry stopped responding. I finished my drink.

Nate came walking down the hallway just as I was about to start searching for him. He leaned over and kissed me. "Hey, there you are."

"Where were you?" I asked, a sinking feeling in the pit of my stomach. Him coming in right after Fake Jerry stopped texting was just a coincidence. Of course he wasn't my stalker. It was ridiculous to even think it.

"Oh, I was out front talking to Bill. He wanted to show me his car. He finally got it running."

A minute later, Brittany came from down the hallway. Her eyes scanned the room and met mine. She frowned and quickly looked away. It formed an uneasy knot in my stomach.

"Did you run into anyone else when you were looking for me?" I asked.

He hesitated, and an expression I'd never seen before crossed his face. "I didn't see Lori or Ian, if that's what you mean. Where are they? I was watching you and Lori dancing before I went outside. I waved when I left, but I don't think you saw me."

"I didn't."

Nate frowned. "What's wrong?"

"No . . . just . . . Brittany came down the hallway right after you."

Nate didn't meet my eyes. "Yeah, I saw her, but I didn't know you were looking for her."

I thought Nate was acting weird, but I was freaked out, so maybe it was just me. "Was she texting anyone?"

He shrugged. "I don't know."

The room felt too small and too warm. People crowded me from all sides. I didn't want to be there anymore. I should stay longer, give my stalker more time with my things, but I just wanted to leave. "I'm not feeling well. Can we go?"

Nate instantly looked concerned. "Are you sick?"

Lying made me feel sick to my stomach. I shouldn't have started keeping secrets again. How had I done it for so long? "I have a headache."

He rubbed my neck. "Want me to get your stuff?"

"No, I'll do it."

I walked down the hallway and into the bedroom. My stomach churned. My stalker might be on video. I wanted to know, but what would it cost me?

My purse and sweater were right where I left them. They seemed okay when I took a quick look at them.

Nate tried to talk to me on the car ride home, but I was having a hard time concentrating. Anyone could be my stalker.

When I got home, I checked my purse and sweater again, more carefully. They seemed untouched.

I brought the video up on my computer and watched it on fast-forward. People came in and out of the room. The lights went on and off.

My phone buzzed with several text messages at once. I paused the video. The first message was from Ian.

11:21 PM

Ian

Are you home? Can I come over?

Why wasn't Ian still at the party, hanging out with Jessica? We could sit in the backyard and not bug my parents. But it was kind of cold, and I was in pajamas.

Before I answered, I checked the next message.

11:21 PM

Nate

I'm sure Ian's already texted you,
but I swear I didn't do anything.

Dread pooled in the pit of my stomach.

I'm the only one who'll ever love you, Jerry's voice echoed.

No, you're not, I told the echo.

11:22 PM

Me

Texted me about what?

Nate

That Brittany and I hooked
up at the party. We didn't.

CHAPTER 41

My parents were asleep, so I tiptoed down the stairs and out the kitchen door. My stomach was in knots and I fought tears. Ian met me in the backyard. I sat on the porch swing and shivered. Ian stood in front of me, shifting from foot to foot. A chilly wind ruffled my hair, and Ian stuck his hands in his jacket pockets. "I was hanging out with Jessica when her friend texted her. She said that she heard from someone that Nate and Brittany hooked up at the party tonight."

This couldn't be happening. I'd trusted him. I'd even felt bad about lying to him and suspecting him.

"I don't know anyone who actually saw them," Ian said. "I texted with Nate and he denied it."

Why would someone say it if it wasn't true, though?

I didn't want to believe it. It just didn't feel like something Nate would do. "Do you think it's true?" My voice was hoarse.

Ian hesitated. "I don't know. He seems like a good guy. But so did Jerry. And that kind of rumor doesn't just start."

It didn't. And what had Nate and Brittany been doing in the hallway together? There were only bedrooms and a bathroom down that way. It could have been a coincidence. Brittany could have been in the bathroom while Nate was looking for me. But Brittany had given me a strange look when she walked past me and Nate. And Nate had acted weird and guilty when I'd asked him about it.

Jerry's words echoed in my head again. *I'm the only one who'll ever love you.*

"What are you going to do?" Ian asked.

"I don't know."

Ian sat down next to me. "I can't believe all this crazy stuff keeps happening to you. You have the worst luck. Jerry, the stalker, now this."

Ian's words started an itch in my brain. What if my stalker had started the rumor to hurt me? If my stalker was the one who'd told Jerry I was cheating, then they'd done it before.

"I can text some people, see if we can figure out who started it," Ian said. "I just didn't want to spread it around by asking everyone."

"What if . . . my stalker started the rumor?"

Ian paused, a thoughtful expression on his face. "It would make sense."

"I was texting my stalker from the party tonight." I showed him the texts. "He talked about Nate."

Ian rubbed his hands over his face. "Honestly, I don't know what to think anymore."

We sat in silence for a while. It made sense that my stalker started the rumor, but maybe I just wanted to believe that. The same way I'd wanted to believe Jerry would never hurt me again.

Nate denied it, and no one Ian knew had seen them together like that. Nate and I were good together. Was I really going to toss that away based on *a rumor*? "It's just a rumor," I said finally. "Even if my stalker didn't start it, that doesn't mean it's true."

Ian nodded. "Yeah, people like to talk. The juicier, the better."

I shivered, the cold leeching through my jacket. "I should go in."

Ian wrapped me in a hug and kissed the top of my head. "You good?" He held me at arm's length and studied my face, raising one eyebrow in an exaggerated way.

I laughed. "I'm okay."

"Let me know if you need me. Anything. You know that." Ian patted me on the shoulder, and I went back inside.

Nate and Lori had both texted me. I checked Lori's messages first. She had heard the rumors too and texted to let me know. I shot her a quick text back.

11:41 PM

Me

I heard. I was thinking maybe my stalker started the rumor.

Lori

Maybe. But sometimes things happen between exes

Me

Ugh, true. I'll text you later.

Lori

Be careful. You never know who'll hurt you

Nate had texted me a couple of times, asking if I believed him and swearing he didn't do anything. But I wasn't ready to talk to him yet. I wanted to believe him. I didn't like feeling suspicious of him. But Brittany *had* looked at me weird. And Nate *was* acting strangely.

I dropped my head in my hands.

Maybe I could get my stalker to admit it. I'd pretend that I was positive it was him and see what he said.

11:49 PM

Me

I heard your pathetic rumor.

You couldn't do better?

Jerry

What rumor?

Me

The one about Nate and Brittany.

Jerry

Oh yeah, I heard that.

At least you didn't have to

kill this one to get rid of him

Me

I know it was you, so you

can stop pretending.

Jerry

I didn't start any rumors. Don't

be naive. You know she puts out.

You don't think Nate misses that?

The suggestion made me feel sick to my stomach. I wasn't sure how far Nate and Brittany had gone. Maybe Nate did miss her.

But it wasn't like Nate was trying to pressure me into anything. Not like Jerry. If he wanted to be with Brittany, he'd be with her.

11:55 PM

                                                              Me

                              You don't know any of us
                         as well as you think you do.

Jerry

Lol. If you say so . . .

I put my phone down. I would not respond to any more messages from Fake Jerry. He was just making me doubt myself even more. I put his notifications on do not disturb.

Nate had finally stopped texting me. I couldn't make up my mind about what I thought. I wanted to believe him, but my anxiety kept telling me I was wrong about him, just like I'd been about Jerry.

I went back to watching the GoPro video on high speed. It was kind of funny watching the lights turning on and off, people going in and out of the room. A couple came into the room and made out. I wrinkled my nose and was glad when they moved out of view. If I caught Nate and Brittany making out, it would break my heart. But at least I'd know for sure.

When Brittany came on-screen, my heart leaped. But she didn't even look at my purse. She was looking at her phone. I turned the volume up and slowed it to normal speed.

"Caleb, hi!" she said. I could tell she was forcing herself to sound bright and happy.

She listened for a moment, then said, "At a party."

Silence. Then, "Angelica probably didn't think you'd want to come. You've been pretty sick and . . . Well, yeah, I'm here with someone."

Tears glistened in her eyes and she blinked them back. "Caleb, I . . ."

Then she took the phone away from her ear and looked at it for a few moments. He'd hung up on her.

She put her phone into her pocket and leaned her head against the wall. I wanted to stop watching, but I couldn't. Tears trailed down her face as she cried. I fidgeted in my chair.

Nate walked in, and I stiffened.

"Oh, sorry. I was looking for Charlotte."

"She's not here," Brittany snapped.

"Yeah. Sorry." Nate turned to leave, then hesitated.

Brittany swiped her fingers under her eyes, trying to erase the signs of tears.

"Are you okay?" Nate asked.

Brittany's face crumpled, and she threw her arms around him, sobbing. I couldn't see Nate's face, but his posture was rigid. Then he raised one arm and patted her back awkwardly. She cried for several minutes before pulling back from him.

"Do you want me to get you some tissues?" Nate asked.

"No, I . . ." Brittany fumbled in her purse and then drew out a pack of tissues. "I have some." She wiped under her eyes and blew her nose quietly.

"Are you okay?" Nate asked, fidgeting. "Sorry. I already asked that. But are you?"

"Caleb called me." Brittany sat on the bed and looked at the floor. "He wanted to know why he wasn't invited to the party and he was mad that I'm here with Josh." Brittany shook her head. "Everyone hates me. Even Caleb hates me. Why am I the bad guy?"

"I think it's just easier for them," he said. "But I don't hate you."

"Thanks," Brittany said quietly. She got a mirror out of her purse and fixed her makeup. "You should go," she said.

"Are you sure you're okay?" Nate asked.

She met his eyes. "I'm fine."

It was clear Nate wanted to say something else, but after a moment, he left.

Nothing had happened, but I felt betrayed. Why had he lied?

Maybe my stalker hadn't started the rumor. Maybe someone had seen them in the bedroom together and assumed they'd hooked up.

Damn it, he should have told me.

1:20 AM

Me

Hey. Are you still up?

Nate

You have to believe me.

I'd never do something like that.

Me

I do. But you were acting

weird. Is there anything

you need to tell me?

```
Nate

•  •  •
```

The three dots stayed on-screen for a long time, and I waited. If he just told me about what happened with Brittany, it would be okay.

```
                        1:26 AM

Nate

I didn't hook up with Brittany.

I told you what she was like. She and I

never connected the way you and I do.

Can't you trust me?
```

I watched the video again. Nate was acting concerned, like a good person. But why wouldn't he just tell me?

I wanted to let it go, but I wasn't sure I could.

I paused on Nate holding Brittany while she cried. I knew people were giving her a hard time about Caleb, but I'd thought that she was handling it, that it didn't bother her *that* much.

If it hadn't been for Jerry, she wouldn't have been crying about Caleb and people wouldn't be picking on her. It made total sense that she'd blame me.

Then I realized that Brittany was on video at the time my stalker was texting me. She'd talked on the phone and talked to Nate, but she hadn't been texting.

Brittany couldn't be my stalker.

It had to be Sandy or Gabe.

CHAPTER 42

It took me hours to fall asleep that night, the image of Nate holding Brittany burned in my mind. In the morning, I decided I needed to tell everyone about what I'd learned, come clean about the GoPro. But I wanted to see Nate first, so I texted him to see if he wanted to meet up.

When I got in the car, he had music playing. I leaned over to kiss his cheek, but he didn't respond. He pulled away from the curb and started driving. Dread churned in my stomach.

"What do you want to do?" he asked, his tone flat.

"I don't know." I twisted the hem of my shirt. "Do you have any ideas?"

He shrugged.

My skin felt too tight. I wanted to ask him why he lied, but there was something wrong between us, and it tied me into knots inside.

"Let's just go to the park," I said.

He nodded but didn't answer.

I twisted my fingers together in my lap. "Are you mad at me?"

"Why would I be mad at you?" he asked. "I'm not Jerry. I don't get mad for no reason." His knuckles were white on the steering wheel.

I knew what mad sounded like, and Nate definitely sounded mad. "Are you okay?" I asked.

"I'm fine," he said.

I turned away and looked out the window.

We drove in silence for several minutes when "You Were Made for Me" started playing. Panic rose in my throat and threatened to choke me.

I turned back toward Nate. "Can you skip this song?" My voice sounded tight.

Nate glanced over at me. "Yeah, of course." He skipped to the next one.

I let out a breath.

"You okay?" he asked.

"Yeah. Sorry. I just can't listen to that song."

"Why not?" But then he continued before I could answer. "Jerry, right?"

I nodded.

"It's always Jerry." The tone of his voice was uncharacteristically bitter. He scowled and stared straight ahead again.

Nate pulled in at the park but left the car running, and neither of us got out. "What does that mean?" I asked.

"You hassle me about Brittany, but I never talk about her. I don't think about her. I don't even look at her. She's in my past, but you bring her into my present."

"What are you talking about? I mentioned her one time. At the party, because you were acting weird. It's not my fault someone started a rumor."

"Yeah, but you believed it."

My jaw got tight. "Yeah. Well, you lied to me. You didn't tell me you were in the bedroom with her."

Nate's eyes went wide. "How do you know about that?"

"You lied to me," I repeated.

"We were in the same place at the same time for like five minutes. Nothing happened. You're being paranoid."

"I'm not paranoid if I'm right."

"Yes, I talked to my ex-girlfriend. So what? Jerry is always here with us. He's in the car right now." Nate slammed his hand on the steering wheel. "I don't want to share you."

My stomach churned. "What does that mean?"

Nate shook his head. "You know what it means."

"You're breaking up with me?" I asked, my voice squeaky.

"I can't compete with a dead guy."

"You're not. What are you even talking about? It's called PTSD, Nate. I can't control it." He looked over at me, like he was going to interrupt, but I was yelling, and if he said anything, I couldn't hear him. "Do you think I like being jumpy? Do you think I like freaking out when a stupid song comes on? Do you think it's helping that some creep is reminding me of Jerry every other day? You think that just because you have trouble sleeping, you know what it's like? You don't know anything!"

Nate wasn't scowling anymore. "I didn't mean . . ." He reached for my arm.

I flinched away from his hand. "Don't."

"I wouldn't hurt you," he said, his tone wounded.

"Whatever," I said, and shoved the car door open, barely missing the car in the space next to us.

"Charlotte, wait!" Nate yelled, but I'd already slammed the car door.

He started to get out of the car, but I put my hand out. "*Don't* follow me. I don't want to talk to you right now."

"But—"

"Leave me alone," I said, carefully enunciating every word.

"Fine." His jaw tightened and he nodded. I turned and stormed away.

CHAPTER 43

I'm the only one who'll ever love you.

I'm the only one who'll ever love you.

Jerry's voice played on repeat my head. I couldn't make it stop. I kicked a tree, but it just made my toe hurt. I kept walking, just wanting to put as much space between Nate and me as possible.

By the time I got to Lori's house, my eyes were red and swollen from crying.

I texted Lori to let her know I was there, and we went to her room. "What happened?" she asked.

But I couldn't answer. I sprawled facedown on her bed and sobbed into her comforter. She put a tissue box beside me, then sat next to me and rubbed my back. When I ran out of tears, my eyes and body ached, like I'd been sick for weeks.

"Jerry's and my song came on and I asked Nate to skip it. He went off about how he can't compete with a dead guy." I burst into tears again.

"Wow."

"And then . . ." I said between sobs, "I just yelled at him that I have PTSD and that I can't help it. He tried to say something but I screamed at him and left. I hate him."

"Me too," Lori said. "Who says something like that?"

"Right!"

Lori left for a few minutes and came back with hot chocolate and a pack of cookies. "What kind of a jerk gets mad about your dead boyfriend?" she asked, handing me a cookie. "He's not good enough for you."

I took the cookie, but then just stared at it. "I thought he understood."

Lori used her finger to trace patterns in the bedspread. "Do you think something happened with him and Brittany?"

My stomach lurched when I thought about Nate and Brittany. Brittany was gorgeous and skinny. And I was pretty sure something had happened with her and Jerry. "Do you really think he kissed her?" I asked.

"I don't know. I hope not," she said. But she wouldn't meet my eyes.

"I thought you liked him," I said in a small voice.

"I did. I do." She sighed. "I don't know. If he hooked up with Brittany, I hate him."

I sniffled and sipped my hot chocolate.

"I didn't know you had PTSD. Why didn't you tell me?" Lori ran her finger along the top of her mug. "It's like you had a whole other life I didn't know about."

I looked down into my drink like there were answers in the foam. "After Jerry died, I couldn't think about anything other than him. Sometimes I thought it was my fault he died, and sometimes I was so mad at him that I was glad he was dead. I had nightmares every night and couldn't sleep. Food tasted like nothing. It's not that I didn't want to talk to you. It's just, I felt like nothing mattered."

"That's how I feel without JD," Lori said. "It's why I need to get him back."

I didn't know what to say to that.

Lori's eyes glistened with unshed tears. "I thought maybe I did something that made you not want to hang out anymore."

"It wasn't you. It was like I fell into a black hole and nothing else existed. I didn't think about talking to you or Ian. Therapy helps, just knowing I'm not the first person to feel like that."

"Why could Nate help you, but I couldn't?" she asked.

Even hearing Nate's name hurt. "Being awake when everyone is asleep is so lonely. When we started talking, it was like we weren't even in the real world. And then I found out his mom died, and he understood some of what I was going through."

"I understand about being lonely," Lori said softly. "I just wish you'd talked to me."

"Me too."

She took my hand and squeezed it.

Nate didn't stop by Scoops that night. I didn't expect him to, but every minute that passed made the stone in my stomach feel heavier. I didn't even know if we were still together anymore.

It was a long Sunday. Minutes stretched into hours. Lori and Ian texted me. I wasted time online and stayed up too late. I did homework and cleaned my room.

I thought about texting Nate and apologizing. I even started writing a bunch of texts. But I kept thinking about him lying to me, what I'd seen on the video. I'd been wrong about Jerry, so maybe I was wrong about Nate too. I deleted all the texts without sending them.

I always had to be the one to apologize to Jerry. I knew Nate wasn't Jerry, but for once, I wanted someone else to smooth things over.

I kept my phone plugged in so it wouldn't run out of battery. I checked my phone a million times to make sure it was on, make sure it was receiving messages. I tried to ignore my phone, hoping if I could pretend I wasn't desperate for him to text me, a message would pop up and everything would be okay again.

It didn't.

By the end of the day, my head and eyes ached from too much crying.

When my phone pinged with a text, I hoped it would be Nate.

It wasn't.

10:11 PM

Gabe

Hey, I heard about
Nate and Brittany.
You okay?

I put my phone back down without answering. It pinged again.

10:15 PM

Gabe

I just wanted to
check up on you

I groaned. Why wouldn't he just stop?

10:20 PM

Gabe

Even though you don't want

to be friends with me,

I still care about you

Sometimes he wasn't the worst.

10:23 PM

Me

I'm okay. Thanks.

Gabe

Look, I know you don't owe

me anything, okay? Not your

time, not an explanation.

But I really liked you.

Can you just tell me what

I did wrong?

I understood wanting to know why. Maybe if I explained, he could move on and leave me alone. I kept trying to be nice, and maybe that was a mistake.

10:25 PM

Me

I didn't break up with

you because of anything

you did. I'd had

a crush on Jerry for

like my whole life.

Gabe

Okay, but you said we
could be friends but then
you completely shut me out

                                                    Me

                            We can't be friends because
                            you keep trying to date me
                            when I told you I don't want
                            that. Remember when you kissed
                            me at that party, even though
                            I said "please don't"?

Gabe

You told me Jerry just kissed
you and that's how you
started going out. I thought
that's what you were into

                                                    Me

                            The difference between those
                            situations is the word "no."
                            And Jerry turned out to be an
                            asshole, so maybe you don't
                            want to take lessons from him.

Gabe

He got the girl and I didn't

                                  Me

                       I'm not a prize.

Gabe

I'm saying this wrong. You were the
first girl I really connected with,
and I liked being your friend.
I don't want to give that up

                                  Me

             I get that. But it's become
             very clear that you can't just
          be my friend. You stand too close
          to me and guilt-trip me about
          something I did two years ago.
          That I apologized for. I just
          want you to leave me alone.

Gabe

I just don't get why you
like assholes like Nate
and Jerry, but not me

                                  Me

          Because when Nate and I were
              just friends, he was
            actually a good friend.
              He was there for me.

Thinking of Nate made everything hurt inside.

10:33 PM

Gabe

I'm here for you! I'm right here

Gabe

You know, guys like Nate
and Jerry seem nice, but
then they hook up with girls
like Brittany and you see
what they're really like

Girls like Brittany. I hated that playing-girls-against-each-other thing, like he could win me over by putting Brittany down.

10:35 PM

Gabe

I'm not like that. I'm only
interested in girls like you

He was never going to stop. No matter what I said, he didn't hear me. If I ignored him, if I was honest and direct, it didn't matter. All he cared about was getting what he wanted.

10:39 PM

Gabe

I just don't get why you don't like

```
me. I'm nice to you.
Nicer than Jerry or Nate
ever were. Why won't you
just give me a chance?
```

```
                                        Me
              I can't keep doing this with you.
```

I saw the three dots showing he was typing another message. I was done.

Heart pounding, I blocked his number.

It felt good. I stared at my phone. I wouldn't get another message from Gabe unless I unblocked him, and that wasn't happening. He'd finally have to leave me alone.

A few minutes after I blocked him, another message came through. This time, from Jerry's number. The timing of it, with the messages from the stalker texting right after I blocked Gabe's number, seemed a little suspicious. Like if he couldn't contact me one way, he'd contact me another.

```
                  10:43 PM

    Jerry
    Guess he got over you fast
```

Below it was a picture of Nate and Brittany at the park. Brittany was leaning toward Nate with her hand on his arm, and he wasn't leaning away. My stomach plummeted. All the relief I felt from finally blocking Gabe's number vanished.

I told you I'm the only one who'll ever love you, Jerry's voice echoed. I was too exhausted to shut it out.

Nate had broken up with me because of Jerry, and now I was alone again. He was back with Brittany, who didn't have a screwed-up ghost haunting her. As long as Jerry was around, my life would always be horrible. He was my stalker, my ghost, the voice in my head. I had to get rid of him or I'd never have anything good.

But over text, I could pretend. I wouldn't let my stalker see they hurt me.

11:12 PM

Me

Apparently I'm not the only
one you're spying on now.

Jerry

You just can't trust
anyone, can you?

Me

Let's meet. Tonight.
I want this over.

Jerry

It's all about you and what you
want, isn't it? What about me?

Me

Tell me what you want!

Jerry

If you were paying attention, you'd
know who I am by now, you selfish
bitch. You ruin everything.

                                              Me

                              I am paying attention.
                              I know it's you, Gabe.

Jerry

He didn't deserve what you did
to him. True love never dies

                                              Me

                              You have no idea who
                              Jerry really was. Tell
                              me who you are or this
                              conversation is over.

Jerry

I'm the person who's going to
make sure you get what you deserve

I looked at the picture of Nate and Brittany again. Pain radiated from
the hollow center of my chest. Was my stalker right? Did I ruin everything?

CHAPTER 44

Monday morning came, and I got into the car next to Ian. He narrowed his eyes. "Do I need to kick his ass?" Ian asked.

"Whose?"

"Nate's. You look like death warmed over."

"Thanks, jerkface." I pulled down the visor and looked in the mirror. My makeup looked okay, and I'd done a decent job of covering the dark circles under my eyes. I wasn't sure if Ian was joking about the ass-kicking or not.

Ian pulled away from the curb and drove toward school. "So I guess you decided to break up?"

My head whipped around to look at him. "Who told you that? Did Nate say we broke up?"

"I heard it from Jessica, who heard it from someone. Isn't it true?"

My stomach knotted. "I didn't know it was official. I guess it is if Nate is telling everyone." He and Brittany would probably be wrapped around each other at school. The thought of it made me want to vomit.

Ian took a hand off the wheel and squeezed my hand. "What happened? Did you get some proof or something?"

I teared up just thinking about it, so I shook my head and tried not to cry. Forcing myself to take several deep breaths, I finally calmed down a little. "We just had a fight. It was stupid. It wasn't even really about that. And it doesn't even matter."

"Why not?"

I didn't want to say it out loud, but I made myself. "I think he and Brittany got back together."

"No way," Ian said. "He's not an idiot."

"My stalker sent me a picture of Brittany and Nate at the park together."

Ian was quiet for a moment, then he said in a much kinder tone than he usually used, "Charlie, you're not thinking straight. I could believe he hooked up with her, like a spur-of-the-moment thing. But breaking up with you for her? No way. I wouldn't believe anything your stalker says. It could be an old picture. There might be a good explanation."

I wanted to believe it. But my stalker hadn't sent me video of Brittany and Nate in the bedroom together. My stalker hadn't made Nate lie. "Maybe I shouldn't be with anyone anyway."

Ian was silent for a moment. "You take everything way too seriously. With Nate, you lightened up a little. You're good for each other."

"What are you saying?"

Ian shrugged. "Jerry lied to us both, but not everyone will. Don't make Nate pay for what Jerry did."

"I'm not," I said. But was I?

It felt like everyone at school was whispering about me and Nate. People looked away when I caught them staring. They knew that Nate and I had broken up, and now I was some kind of sideshow. I kept my head down as I trudged to class.

When I walked into history, Nate didn't even look up. I sneaked looks at him, and he didn't look at me once. He doodled in his notebook, and when another guy talked to him, Nate's smile seemed forced. He wasn't acting like a guy who'd moved on to a new girlfriend.

When the bell rang, he was the first one out the door, like he was avoiding me.

I told myself that it wasn't the end of the world. Couples broke up all the time. When I sat at our lunch table, I kept my head bent and stared at my sandwich.

Lori touched my arm. "You okay?"

I looked up at her and blinked. I didn't want to cry in the middle of the cafeteria. "Nate must be telling everyone we broke up. I only told you."

Lori winced. "I didn't know I wasn't supposed to tell anyone. Alisha and I were texting. She said what a cute couple you guys were, and then I told her."

"Oh, no." I dropped my head in my hands. "He probably thinks it was me. This is such a mess." Maybe Ian was right, that there was a different explanation for the picture of Nate and Brittany. I shoved my tray away. "How do I fix it?"

"Are you sure you want to? What about Brittany?"

"I don't know." That's what my head said, but my heart didn't agree.

"At least the slut is getting what she deserves," Lori said.

"I hate that word, Lori. Please, find a different word."

Lori rolled her eyes. "Fine. At least the boyfriend-stealing young lady who definitely isn't a trampy-tramp because we don't define women by their choices about sex, at least she's getting what she deserves."

I huffed out an irritated breath but let it go. I didn't have the energy to argue about it. "What she deserves? What are you talking about?"

"Everyone is pissed that she hooked up with Nate. If she thought people were talking trash about her before, it's like a billion times worse now."

"That's not fair," I said. Anger tried to gnaw through the numbness. "No one even knows what really happened."

Lori shrugged. "Just because we can't prove it doesn't mean it's not true."

I thought about that for a second. Nate would never be able to prove he didn't cheat on me. I had to decide to believe him or not. It seemed like everyone had already convicted Brittany. "I bet no one is harassing Nate about this." Even saying his name shot a bolt of pain through my heart.

"No, why would they?"

"It takes two to cheat. It's not fair that the girl always gets blamed."

"She probably did something. You know what she's like."

I didn't really know what Brittany was like. I knew people talked about her and made assumptions. She could be mean sometimes, but she mostly stayed out of other people's business. She didn't deserve people to be up in hers.

I thought about the night of the party, sitting in the lounge chair with Nate, that perfect moment when he said, "Trust me, I don't always say the right thing."

I had to talk to him and figure things out.

I didn't need him to prove that he wasn't like Jerry; he'd already proven that countless times.

3:47 PM

Me

Can we talk?

Nate

Yes. Can I drive you home?

Me

`I'll meet you at your car.`

Nate was standing by his car, waiting for me and scuffing his feet. When we got in the car, neither of us spoke. He didn't turn any music on, and the silence pressed down on me.

When we got to my house, we went inside and sat at the kitchen table. I offered him a glass of iced tea. There was so much going through my head that I wasn't sure how to start.

"I'm so sorry about what I said, Charlotte," Nate said. "I know you can't help it when things get to you, and I know you don't want to keep remembering Jerry like that."

The anxiety that had been squeezing me all day loosened. "Then why did you say it?"

He looked away, like he was thinking, then shook his head. "I was mad at him and took it out on you. I can't believe I was such an asshat. I'm so sorry."

I traced my finger along the wood grain pattern of the table. "I don't know when I'm going to stop freaking out about Jerry." I didn't want to finish my thought, but I forced myself to say it. "I don't know if I ever will."

"You will," he said.

I wanted to believe him, but he couldn't know that. "But you said it yourself: Jerry is always there. We'll be having a good time, hanging out and then something happens that reminds me."

Nate reached over and took my hand. But tentatively, like he wasn't sure if I'd yank it away. "We could talk about him. You could tell me what might remind you of him, so then I wouldn't be so surprised next time it happens."

My heart jumped. He said *next time*. "I don't know," I said. "Like, our song, obviously. He used to sing it to me. But sometimes something reminds me, and it completely surprises me too. What happens the next time it surprises you?"

Nate's knee started to bounce, and he looked away. "There's something I didn't tell you."

My stomach flipped. He took his phone out and scrolled, then handed it to me.

It was text messages from the morning after the party between him and a phone number that wasn't in his contacts.

Saturday 10:10 AM

Unknown number

Charlotte doesn't love you

Nate

Who is this?

Unknown number

She would never have even
looked at you if I were
still around. She will always
love me more than she loves you

Nate

Oh, you're the creep
who's stalking her.
You're a coward!

Unknown number
You can say what you want,
but we both know that
when you two are together,
she's thinking of me

                                    Nate
                That's because you're stalking
                    her. Leave her alone, and
                        she'll forget you.

Unknown number
I'm sure you want to
believe that. Just go
back to Brittany. She'll
make you feel better

                                    Nate
                        Who are you?

"I stopped answering because it was such crap," Nate said. "But it got in my head and I was thinking about it. So then when the song came on, I just . . . snapped."

I knew what it was like for things to get in your head. "I wish you had told me."

"I know, I'm sorry. But honestly, I didn't even know this was why I was so mad until I sat around and thought about it all weekend." He looked down at our hands. "I'm such a jerk."

It was such a relief to get this all out in the open, but there was one more thing we needed to talk about. I needed to tell him about the GoPro, and I needed to understand why he'd lied. "There's something I need to tell you too." I took a deep breath. "At the party, I put my GoPro in my purse to catch my stalker if he tried to mess with my stuff, since he's messed with me every time we've gone somewhere."

"That's smart. Why didn't you tell me?" I could see the moment he understood. "Oh. You thought I was your stalker."

"No. I just started feeling like it was someone close to me. And I was feeling so anxious about it that I just . . . had to be sure."

He pursed his lips and huffed out a breath. "I get it." He paused and then went scarlet. "That's how you knew about me and Brittany in the bedroom."

"So I know nothing happened, but you lied about it."

"Yeah." He looked away from me for a second, then met my eyes. "I'm sorry. But Brittany would hate for anyone to see her like that. I felt bad for her and telling you would have felt like gossip. I could have told you I ran into her, but . . . I would have done that for anyone."

I nodded. "Okay, I understand." And I did. Nate was a stand-up guy. The fact that it had been Brittany in that bedroom had been irrelevant to him.

"Do you actually believe any of what the stalker texted you?" I asked.

"Not really," Nate said. "But I kept thinking about it and couldn't let it go. It kept replaying in my head. I was in a crappy mood because of the Brittany thing already."

"I mostly believed you. It's just, I think Jerry was cheating on me . . ."

"So, since Jerry was, you thought I was too. You have no idea how much I hate that."

"I can't just erase my past, Nate. I have trouble trusting people now. I trusted Jerry, and look how that turned out."

"I would never hurt you," Nate said.

"I don't think you would," I said. "But I don't know if I can trust my judgment. I trusted Jerry. And maybe you wouldn't hit me, but you hurt my feelings when you said what you did." I took a deep breath. My hands shook, but I was determined to say the next part. "I'm afraid you'll think I'm insane. That one day, it'll be too much. I feel crazy sometimes, and the way you treated me the other day, it was like my worst fear coming true."

He scooted his chair closer, leaned forward, and hugged me. "I'm so sorry. Really. I'd never think that. I just . . . I've never felt this way about anyone before. And it's hard to know that I can't do anything about the guy who hurt you. That and this stalker thing . . . It's making me nuts."

"That's another reason why we shouldn't be together. Bad things keep happening to me. I don't want anything to happen to you."

"Bad things can happen to anyone," he said. "I just want to be with you. I hate that I can't protect you." He pulled back. "Did you see the text from Sunday?"

I shook my head, so he handed me his phone again.

```
Sunday 3:32 PM

Unknown number

You want to know who I am?
```

```
Unknown number

Meet me at the park,

under the oak tree,

in 35 minutes. Come

alone or I'll disappear
```

"I went to meet him and there was Brittany. She said she'd gotten a text from Jerry's phone but wouldn't tell me anything else."

I pulled my phone out and showed him the photo my stalker had sent.

He sighed. "Fantastic. Your stalker was that close, and I missed him." He frowned. "Why do you think Brittany showed up?"

"Brittany said she knows something about Jerry. I think they might've been hooking up. Maybe my stalker knows that. If my stalker threatened to tell, with the way everyone has been treating her, even before this whole thing with you, she wouldn't want it to get out."

Nate put his arms around me and I wanted to stay like that forever. Eventually, I pulled away so I could look at him. "I didn't tell people we broke up. I told Lori what happened, and she told someone."

"When I heard everyone saying we broke up, I thought that you were sending me a message."

Tendrils of hair had come loose from my braid, and Nate reached up to brush my hair away from my face.

"I didn't want it to be over," I said. I took a deep breath and met his gaze. He was watching me with that Nate patience and kindness I was used to. "I love you."

Nate closed his eyes for a moment, like he was relieved. Then he opened them and grinned. "You don't know how much I needed to hear that." He reached for me, wrapping me in a warm hug, resting his chin on my head. "I love you too."

Later that night, my stalker texted me.

8:38 PM

Jerry

He'll never love you the way I did.

It's good you broke up

Me

You're right; he'll never

love me the way Jerry did.

CHAPTER 45

"My boyfriend and I got into a fight over the weekend," I said.

Gemma cocked her head. "What happened?"

"There was a rumor that he cheated on me, and I didn't really believe it. But then a song came on, and it's one that triggers me because it reminds me of Jerry. Nate got upset and said he can't compete with a dead guy. And everything I thought I wasn't mad about came to the surface."

"That happens," Gemma said. "When we try to deny our feelings, they usually come out in other ways."

"Like Jerry," I said. "Instead of dealing with things, he drank and he took it out on me."

"Exactly. That's one of the reasons it's important to deal with your feelings instead of trying to pretend they don't exist."

"He didn't pretend anger didn't exist, and anger's a feeling."

"True," Gemma said. "But anger gives people the illusion of control. Many people feel safer being angry than admitting they're hurt or scared."

I blew out a breath. "I'm mad at him. Sometimes I still feel guilty about him dying. And I . . . Sometimes I miss him. He was a good friend before . . . well, before he started hurting me."

Gemma nodded. "Feelings are complicated. You can feel more than one thing at a time, even when those feelings contradict each other."

"I just wish I'd done more. I wish I told someone about his drinking. Or that I ran inside to get someone instead of getting in the car. I wish I'd done it differently." A tear slid down my cheek.

Gemma leaned forward. "Of course you do. You've had lots of time to think about it. In the moment, though, did you make the best decisions you could, based on the information you had?"

"I don't know. When I got in the car, it all happened so fast. And the drinking . . . I didn't know it was a problem. But I should have."

"You're putting a lot of responsibility on yourself. What about Jerry? What were his responsibilities?"

I looked down at the crumpled tissue in my hand and thought about what she was saying. "He shouldn't have driven drunk and he shouldn't have hurt me."

Gemma nodded.

"And he should have asked for help?"

"It's complicated. Maybe he didn't even know he needed help. Or maybe he didn't know how to get help. But he was responsible for his life. Just like you're responsible for yours."

"I wish I could stop thinking about him all the time." I touched my scar.

"It's natural you'd think about him often. When someone you love dies, even if they aren't abusive, you see reminders everywhere. When you've been abused, those reminders can be more intense."

"Am I going to be like this forever?"

Gemma sat silently for a moment. "Do you remember what it was like for you when you started coming to therapy?"

I thought back to July. I'd been having frequent panic attacks and flashbacks. I was barely sleeping, and when I did, I woke up screaming from nightmares. "I was a lot worse."

Gemma nodded. "Don't ignore the progress you've already made. I know you want to be past this, but it takes time."

"I just don't want him in my head anymore."

"What's that like? Him being in your head?"

"I hear him say things he used to say, criticizing my clothes or saying, 'I told you I'd never let you go.'"

"And how does it make you feel?"

"I don't know." I shrugged. "Scared. Mad. Mostly mad."

"How have you tried to get rid of him?"

"By not thinking about him."

"Do me a quick favor," Gemma said. "Don't think of an elephant."

A picture of an elephant, huge and gray, popped into my head. I smiled.

"You thought of an elephant, didn't you?" Gemma wagged her finger. I nodded.

"By trying not to think about him, you're focusing on him. Accept that you're doing the best you can now, and that you did the best you could at the time. Stop judging yourself."

CHAPTER 46

When I got home, I took a trash bag up to my room. I didn't know why I'd been holding on to a ruined prom dress and pictures I never looked at, but I didn't want them anymore.

I pulled the box out of the closet and started transferring things from the box to the bag.

Jerry's face smiled up at me from the trash bag, but it didn't fill me with cold or dread. He was just some guy I used to love.

I threw the paperweight in the trash bag, then started to drop my locket in the trash but paused.

The temperature in the room was falling. It wasn't the air conditioner, and I knew that. I'd always known.

The trash bag rustled, as if a breeze had blown it. It toppled over, as if he'd given it a shove. The photos and other stuff spilled out onto the floor. I waited for the fear to come, but it didn't. I felt like I was finally letting him go.

I had so much I wished I'd told him when he was alive. But I could tell him now.

"You know, I used to think I didn't deserve you. When you kissed me that first time, I thought I was the luckiest girl in the world."

There were two sharp raps, as if someone had knocked on my desk.

"Then you started hurting me, and I just thought . . . because you loved me, that made it all okay. But it wasn't." I raised my voice a little, but not so much that my parents would hear me over the TV. "It wasn't okay."

My pictures on the wall fluttered. I braced myself but kept going. I was going to have my say.

"I didn't deserve the way you treated me. The names you called me. All the times you shoved me. I didn't deserve bruises or to feel like it was all my fault."

The paperback on my nightstand fell off. He didn't have to like what I was saying. I just wanted to say it to him, whether he heard me or not.

"When you first died, part of me was glad. It felt like the only way I could get away from you. I felt like a horrible person, like everything you said about me was true. But I'm not glad you're dead anymore. There were people who would have helped me, but I couldn't see it. Not then."

The room had gone still, like he was finally listening.

"I wish you'd gotten help. I wish you hadn't killed yourself. I wish you were still alive so maybe you could change, if you wanted. We wouldn't be friends, but I'd still care. But your dying was your choice, not mine. You hear me?"

I turned in a circle, looking for him.

"I'm not responsible for your death."

One of the photos of Jerry and me fluttered out of the trash bag. It moved closer to me, as if a breeze had pushed it. I picked it up and ripped it to shreds, then let the pieces fall on the rug.

"You have to leave. I don't want you here anymore."

The room started warming up. I wasn't sure if he'd left because I told him to or because he could only stick around so long, but it felt like a victory.

I put all the stuff he'd spilled back in the bag. When I picked up the paperweight, I paused. He'd given it to me when we were kids, and I'd always loved it. I cupped it in my palm and tried to figure out how it made me feel.

It made me remember happy times, when Jerry had been someone I could count on. When we'd played video games and basketball with Ian. We'd ridden our bikes to the ice cream shop. It hadn't been complicated.

He was an abuser. But once upon a time, he'd also been a good friend. It didn't make his abuse okay or worth it. But his friendship was part of what made me who I was, and I didn't want to pretend it had never happened.

I set the paperweight on my desk and texted Nate.

10:03 PM

                                                                    Me

                                        Can you take me somewhere
                                           after school tomorrow?

Nate

Sure. I'm thinking Reynisfjara.

                                                                    Me

                                              Where is that?

Nate

Iceland. It's a volcanic
beach. It looks like
another world.

I Googled it. It was a black beach, and it did have an otherworldly look.

                          10:05 PM

                                                Me
                    As long as we have time to get
                        there and back by Friday.
                              I have a calc test.

    Nate
    Might be tough.
    What's your second choice?

                                                Me
                        I've always wanted to see
                    New Zealand, but that's pretty
                    far away too. Since New Zealand
                          and Iceland are out this
                        week, will you take me to
                    Jerry's memorial tree tomorrow?

    Nate
    That's the third choice?
    What comes after that?
    A fun house with a psychotic
    clown holding a chain saw?

CHAPTER 47

After school the next day, we headed toward Jerry's memorial tree. As Nate drove, I concentrated on controlling my breathing. I hadn't been down that road in a car since Jerry died, and I couldn't help but remember that night. It wasn't a flashback, just a vivid memory.

The tree where Jerry had crashed and died was still stacked up with memorial gifts for Jerry, and though Nate was driving at a reasonable speed, it seemed to be rocketing toward us.

My hands clenched into fists on my legs, and Nate put a hand on top of one of mine. "This is the weirdest date I've ever been on," he said.

I smiled, though I wasn't quite up to laughing. I tried to relax a little. "You like weird. This should be perfect for you."

"I'm glad you asked me to come with you," he said, pulling off the road.

I smiled over at him and he squeezed my hand.

We got out of the car. It had only been a month since I'd last been past the memorial, but most of the cards and pictures were gone. There was a bouquet of fake flowers that probably hadn't been there long, as the colors weren't faded.

A plaque that said BELOVED SON had been placed next to the flowers. The way Jerry had talked about his parents, it was like they hated him. But they'd been devastated at the funeral and had put a plaque here.

I kept being struck, over and over, by all the different people Jerry was. Were any of them real? Were all of them real?

I turned to Nate. "It's been hard for me to let go of Jerry because my feelings were so complicated. I loved him and hated him. I didn't want to admit this to anyone, but for a long time, I was glad he died."

"Of course you felt that way," Nate said. "After what he did to you, who wouldn't?"

A knot in my chest unraveled. "I'm on my way back to who I was before, but maybe a better version. You helped me get there. You and Lori and Ian. Without the three of you, I'd still be hiding, keeping secrets."

"Maybe you weren't hiding. Maybe you were healing. It takes time, you know."

Healing, not hiding. Maybe Nate was right.

No matter what happened, I was going to be okay. If I could survive Jerry, I could survive anything.

I took the locket out of my pocket. I'd brought a garden spade, and I dug a small hole at the base of the tree, then dropped the locket inside. I'd held on to the things Jerry gave me because it felt like letting them go was erasing him. But erasing the past was impossible and things were just things. Sometimes you had to let go of old things to make room for what was new and better.

I stared at it for a long time, remembering how it had made me feel. But the girl who'd treasured it was gone. Letting go of Jerry meant letting go of who I was before. But that was okay. I liked who I was becoming. I covered the locket with dirt.

I turned to Nate and smiled. "I'm ready to go to the police."

His eyes widened. "Really?" He grinned. "What made you change your mind?"

"I can't make my parents believe me and I have no idea if the police will believe me or not, but it doesn't matter. I'm going to do everything I can to end this. I want to move on with my life."

"Great, let's call them now."

I shook my head. "The four of us should meet so we can go over everything that's happened, write it down, and put it in order. We'll get everything together: the bike tire, the texts on our phones, the note. The more organized I am, the better chance I have that people will believe me. Whether they do or not, I have to try."

I texted Lori and Ian, and we set the meeting for Thursday, at my house.

"I feel really good about this," Nate said. "Like maybe we're close to the end."

"Yeah." I smiled and let out a breath. "Me too. Maybe we can finally find out what it's like to be together without all this hanging over our heads."

Nate pulled me into his arms. "For the record, I don't regret one second of any of this as long as I get to be with you."

I turned my face up to kiss him. "Same."

When I got home, I went to my bedroom and found a T-shirt laid out on the bed. It hadn't been there when I'd left. In fact, I'd just finished making it, and I remembered hanging it in the closet. It was placed perfectly flat, with no wrinkles. It was teal, and on the front I'd stitched in cursive: *i belong to myself.*

DECEMBER

CHAPTER 48

On Wednesday, I was supposed to be working on a paper, but I was talking to Nate instead. "I'm just saying that the English curriculum is kind
of boring," he said. "*Dune* is classic literature that explores the meaning
of life, international relations, all kinds of things that are actually rel-
evant."

"You just don't want to read *Heart of Darkness*," I said. "It's . . . not
that bad."

"No, it's just mind-numbingly boring. If I have to hear one more
description of the jungle, I'll—" He stopped talking midsentence. A moment later, Galileo started barking.

"What's going on?"

"I heard something outside. And Galileo is losing his mind." Nate's
voice got a little farther away, like he wasn't talking into the phone. "Hey
boy, it's okay."

Galileo fell silent. A moment later, I heard a car alarm wailing, and
Galileo started barking again. "That's my car," Nate said. "All this noise
better not wake Megan."

I heard his footsteps pounding downstairs, and then the jingle of keys.
He was going outside to shut off the alarm, and I suddenly felt uneasy.
"Nate, maybe you shouldn't—"

"Hang on. I can't hear you over the racket."

My muscles were tense as I listened to him moving around. After a
few seconds, I heard the car alarm fall silent. "I wonder what made the

alarm go off," he said. "There's no one out here. I don't see any damage or anything."

"Nate, maybe you should go back inside," I said. Dread pooled in my stomach. "What if it's my stalker?"

Nate sounded distracted. "Your stalker is a coward and has only gone after you. It was probably kids. Or maybe a . . . What the hell?"

"What?" My heart jumped into my throat. Nate had sounded freaked out.

"The lights in my house just went out. The neighbors' are still on, though. Weird. Maybe it's the breaker."

"Please go back inside," I said. I gripped my phone so tightly I thought it might crack.

"It's probably just kids messing around or something."

"You're not listening to me!" My voice was too loud, but I couldn't help it. Panic threatened to choke me. "It's my stalker. You have to go inside!"

I heard the crunch of footsteps. "I just need to flip the breaker and I'll—" Something thumped on the other end of the phone. I heard a sharp sound, like he'd dropped the phone.

"Nate? Are you okay?"

There was just silence. I looked at my phone. The call had disconnected.

I called back, and he silenced it after one ring.

10:39 PM

Me

What's going on? Is everything okay?

Nate

Yeah, sorry. I'm fine

Me

What happened?

Nate

I dropped the phone

Me

Why didn't you answer

when I called?

Nate

I'm just listening to see

if I can hear those kids

It seemed reasonable, but fear still sat like a stone in my stomach. Something was wrong.

10:41 PM

Me

Just go back inside. I have

a bad feeling about this.

Nate

You don't have to worry about me

Me

Of course I do. That's what
you do when you love someone.

Nate

Is it? And here I just
thought you made them
kill themselves

Everything inside me froze. My brain stopped working. My heart
stopped beating.

10:43 PM

Nate

Just kidding

Me

You're not Nate.

Nate

What? Of course I am

Me

Prove it.

Nate

I'm not in the mood
for your games tonight,
Charlotte. It's me

Nate would never say that. I was positive of that. But if I called the police, would they listen? *"I heard a noise, officer, and then my boyfriend hung up on me, and now he's acting weird."*

I could not let something happen to Nate. I wouldn't. I dashed downstairs.

My dad looked up from his laptop. "Where's the fire?"

"I need you to take me to Nate's," I said, breathless.

"What are you talking about? It's late."

"My stalker did something to Nate. I need to go check on him."

"You're not making sense. Calm down and explain to me what's going on."

I didn't have time to argue with my dad. If something bad happened to Nate, I'd never forgive myself.

If I was wrong and he was fine, I'd rather get in trouble and look crazy than take the risk Nate needed help.

I sprinted out the front door and texted Ian.

10:49 PM

Me

911, need help now!

Ian

Where are you?

My bare feet slipped on twigs and other debris. Something jabbed my heel but I kept going, ignoring the pain. I pounded on Ian's front door.

"Charlotte!" My dad was standing on the sidewalk in front of the neighbor's house, breathing hard. His face was bright red. "Get back inside right now!"

Ian flung the door open. He was dressed in sweatpants and a ratty T-shirt. "What's going on?"

"I need you to take me to Nate's right now. I'll explain on the way."

Ian looked from me to my dad, hesitating for a second.

"Ian, please!"

He nodded and grabbed his keys off the hook. I ran to his car and got in. My dad stepped toward me, like he was going to pull me out of the car, but he stopped at the end of Ian's driveway. "Charlotte, if you don't come back right this second, you're in serious trouble."

I didn't hesitate and neither did Ian. For once, I was glad for his lead foot. He peeled out of the driveway. I explained as best as I could on the ride over, but I wasn't making much sense.

We made the fifteen-minute drive to Nate's house in less than ten. I saw a crumpled figure on the driveway in front of Nate's house, and I sprang out of the car before Ian even completely stopped.

I hurried to the crumpled figure, and it was Nate. He was on his stomach, his head turned to the side. Something red was smeared on the driveway. No. My breath caught in my throat. It wasn't blood. It couldn't be.

I dropped to my knees. Nate was so pale, his eyes closed. I watched his chest, holding my breath until I saw it move. He was breathing. I huffed out the breath I'd been holding and fought the urge to sob.

I wanted to cradle him in my lap, but I thought I remembered that you shouldn't move someone who was unconscious. I curled my hands into fists, feeling helpless.

I heard Ian talking to someone, giving the address and explaining

Nate was unconscious, but his voice sounded far away.

My hand shook as I brushed my fingertips across Nate's forehead, pushing his hair out of his face. "Nate?" I whispered. "Wake up. You have to wake up."

Nate groaned, and his eyes fluttered. "Charlotte?"

"Oh, thank goodness." I grabbed his hand. It was cold. He'd come outside wearing only sweatpants and a T-shirt. I was just in my pajamas too, and I suddenly realized how cold the sidewalk was. I rubbed his hand between mine, trying to warm it.

"What happened?" he asked, his voice tired and strained. "I came outside to check the alarm, and then . . ." He reached up and touched the back of his head. Blood coated his fingers. "Oh."

"You're okay," I said. "An ambulance is on its way."

"My head hurts," he said.

He started to try to sit up, but I pressed a hand to his back. "I don't think you should move."

Sirens screeched, and the ambulance pulled up in front of Nate's house. Paramedics asked me to move, and I stood, stepping back toward Ian, my eyes never leaving Nate's face.

One of the paramedics knelt in front of Nate and started asking him questions, shining a light in his eyes. Another paramedic brought a gurney over.

Police arrived a moment later. After Ian and I explained what happened, they went inside and checked the house. Nothing was disturbed, and Megan was still sleeping. The breaker had been thrown, just like Nate thought. They turned it back on, and the house flooded with light.

Nate was being loaded into the ambulance when the cops came back out. They asked me to tell them what happened again, starting from when Nate and I were on the phone earlier. "I have to go back before that. Someone's been stalking me for a couple months now . . ." I wished we'd made the list so my thoughts were more organized, but I told them everything I could think of. I didn't mention the ghost, though I would have if I thought that would help.

Officer Bly, a short cop with a beer belly, said he remembered Jerry's accident, but I didn't recognize him. Officer Nevins took a bunch of notes. I couldn't tell if they believed me or not.

When Nate's dad got home, he pulled into the driveway and sprang out of the car, not even shutting the door. "What's going on?" he asked, approaching us, panic in his eyes. "Charlotte? What's going on? Where's Nate?"

I couldn't look at him. It was my fault. I should have gone to the police when Nate wanted me to.

I listened to Officer Nevins explain what had happened. And then Nate's dad called someone to stay with Megan while he went to the hospital.

Officer Nevins turned to me while Nate's dad was on the phone. "We're going to give you a ride home."

"I can ride with Ian," I said. "He brought me here."

The cop nodded. "We might need to ask you more questions later, so we want to talk to your parents."

My stomach flipped. I had to sit in the back of the police car, which was not someplace I ever thought I'd be. Even though I hadn't done anything wrong, I still felt weird and guilty. I replayed what I'd told the police and wondered if I'd said too much. Or left anything out. Maybe I hadn't explained things right and they wouldn't understand.

Was Nate going to be okay? *Please let him be okay.* If we'd stayed broken up, maybe my stalker wouldn't have hurt him. Was it my fault he'd gotten hurt?

My parents must have been watching, because as soon as the officers and I pulled up, my dad threw the front door open. Dad must have woken Mom up because the side of her face was creased and her hair was a mess. Mom shoved in front of him. "What's going on? Is she okay?"

"She's fine, ma'am," Officer Nevins said, introducing himself and the other officer. "May we come in?"

My parents ushered everyone to the kitchen table. My mom took a blanket from the couch and put it around my shoulders. I hadn't even realized I'd been shivering.

My dad stood, leaning against the island, his arms crossed over his chest. A vein pulsed in his temple.

Officer Nevins explained what happened, and my mom gasped. "Will he be okay?" she asked.

"The hospital staff will take good care of him," Officer Bly answered. Which wasn't an answer.

"You told us you're being stalked," Officer Nevins said, turning toward me. "When did that start?"

I hesitated. "I don't know for sure. At least since September."

Paisley jumped up in my lap. I cuddled her as the officers interrogated me.

Officer Nevins asked me to remember times and places. My parents looked more and more upset as I talked, and I fought the urge to edit the story. I worried that they'd look at the cops, shake their heads the way they did, and say, "Our daughter is crazy." But it didn't matter what they thought; it didn't matter what anyone thought of me anymore. I had no idea how hurt Nate was, and for him, I could brave anything.

When I was done talking, Officer Nevins asked to see my phone. He scrolled through the messages for a moment, then handed it off to Officer Bly. "How did you know it wasn't Nate?" he asked.

"Nate would never say that about me making Jerry kill himself or that he wasn't in the mood for my games. He's not like that. And he knows about the stalker."

Office Bly nodded. "I see."

"Do you have any idea who'd want to stalk you or harm Nate?" Officer Nevins asked.

I hesitated for half a second. If Sandy had been the one to hurt Nate, I couldn't protect her. "Jerry's sister, maybe. Or Gabe Bortz, this creepy guy from school."

"We're going to need to take her phone for evidence," Officer Nevins said, looking at my parents.

"Whatever you need," my dad said in a gruff voice.

Officer Nevins turned back toward me. "Why didn't you call the police before this?"

I looked at my mom, but she wouldn't meet my eyes. My dad raised an eyebrow at me as if he had no idea, even though he'd been the one to keep shutting me down. "I didn't think anyone would believe me," I said. "My parents kept telling me I was imagining things. So my friends and I were trying to get proof."

CHAPTER 49

After the officers left, my mom made us all chamomile tea. "Sit down, Charlotte," she said. She gripped her mug with both hands.

I hesitated, and then sat.

"You need to tell us what's going on. The truth. Everything."

"I just told you everything," I said.

"Fine. Now tell us again. Start at the beginning."

It was such a huge relief to have the police doing the work now. They'd catch Sandy or Gabe and they'd get help. My parents would have to believe me.

I'd only told the officers about the stalker, and that's what I'd intended to repeat to my parents. But all my history with Jerry came spilling out. Once I started talking, I couldn't stop. I didn't want to. It was like a huge infection that had built up in my system was being released. I told them how Jerry had treated me, that his "accident" was actually suicide, and that he'd been trying to kill me. I told them about the notes from my stalker. I told them about everything except Ghost Jerry.

My mom looked down into her mug. "Why didn't you tell us that he hurt you?" she asked quietly. "That he tried to kill you?"

"You guys don't really like when I tell you things."

Mom's expression twisted and she looked away from me.

"It's not that we don't like it." Dad shook his head. "But you don't always like what we have to say. You should have told us about this."

"How am I supposed to know what I can and can't talk about when you dismiss what I say?"

"Sometimes I try to clarify, ask questions, and you get upset!" Dad jabbed a finger at the table for emphasis.

"Because it feels like an interrogation," I said.

"But I'm just trying to figure it out!" He threw his hands in the air.

"Stop. Both of you." Mom sighed and turned to me. "You don't talk to us much and I try to respect that. I know we're busy and . . . I'm sorry I didn't take you seriously when you came to us about this. I was so worried about your mental health that I didn't think about your safety."

My mom had never said anything like that before, and something inside me unfurled. "I know I keep things to myself when I shouldn't," I said. "I've been working on it."

Mom waved me over like she used to do when I was little, and wrapped me in a hug.

"Can we go to the hospital and check on Nate?"

"I'll take you," Mom said.

I got dressed, then got in the car. We pulled out of the driveway in silence. "We have such high expectations of you." She tapped her fingers on the steering wheel. "I know it's a lot of pressure, but it's the way my parents were with me. I never wanted you to think you couldn't talk to us, though. I wish you'd told us that Jerry was hurting you. He was such a nice, polite boy. I never imagined."

"No one did. I felt so alone. I didn't think anyone would believe me."

Mom made a face. "I knew you were quieter, you changed the way you dressed and wore your hair, and you always seemed to have something on your mind. I just assumed you were growing up." Mom shook her head. "And then we didn't believe you about the stalker. We thought you were being paranoid." She spit out the word *paranoid* like it had a bad taste.

"I tried to be strong." Tears burned in my eyes but I blinked them back. "I didn't want to disappoint you."

She pulled into a space in the hospital parking lot and turned toward me. "Charlotte, no." She ran a hand through her hair, pulling strands out of place. "You didn't. I—"

I interrupted her, the words spilling out. "I feel like I never do anything right. I am getting better, but you don't see it."

"I guess I just want you to be okay so much that I'm not paying attention to your progress." She touched my cheek. "I don't understand you. I always thought that if I had a daughter, we'd be more alike." She tucked a stray lock behind my ear. "That doesn't mean I'm not proud of you."

Tears flooded my eyes, but I blinked them back. If I started crying now, I wouldn't stop. "I thought you guys thought I was crazy."

"No, sweetie. I never thought that. I was so stuck on my vision of what you needed that I forgot to ask you." She shook her head. "I can't make you any promises about the future. But I'm listening now." She took my hand. "If we won't listen, *make* us listen. It's your life. You have to demand what you need. Even from us."

When we got up to the hospital waiting room, Nate's dad was sitting with his head in his hands. My mouth went dry. What if Nate wasn't okay?

My mom went up to him and introduced herself.

Nate's dad looked up and met my eyes. "He'll be okay," he said. "They're running tests, but they seem optimistic that he'll be fine."

Relief flooded my body in a wave. He was going to be okay.

Nate's dad got up, crossed the room, and wrapped me in a hug. "Thank you for coming to his rescue," he said.

The tears I'd been holding in all night broke free, and I sobbed in his arms. "I was so scared."

We had to find my stalker before he hurt anyone else I loved.

CHAPTER 50

My mom had a security system installed. When we got home, we had sixty seconds to enter the code or the system would call the police. There was also a panic button on it so that if we needed police immediately, all we had to do was press the button.

It made me feel better to know that even if someone got the house key, they couldn't sneak in.

The police returned my phone. Detective Garcia questioned me again, asking the same questions the officers had asked. He gave me his card and told me to contact him right away if the stalker did anything else. Nate and I were both staying up later online again. He didn't tell me if he was having nightmares, but I was. I wasn't dreaming of Jerry anymore. Now all my dreams were of me being too late to save Nate and a faceless figure laughing at me from the shadows.

I was on edge in the weeks leading up to winter break, but my stalker was silent. I didn't get any more text messages and nothing strange happened. Even Ghost Jerry didn't show up. Detective Garcia stopped by and let us know that he'd questioned Gabe, Sandy, and Sandy's parents, but there wasn't enough evidence to charge anyone.

Nate came over on Christmas Eve so we could exchange gifts. I gave him a navy-blue T-shirt on which I'd sewn stars in the shape of an alien head, one of the grays.

"This is so cool," he said. "You finally made me a cool shirt." He handed me a present wrapped in paper with little aliens in Santa hats. I slit the tape, careful not to tear the wrapping paper. Inside was a shoebox full of sewing notions. Weird buttons and interesting pieces of lace. There were large beads and other decorative items. My heart melted.

"Where did you find all this?"

"Online. I just searched for stuff I thought you'd like."

"I love it. And I love you." I threw my arms around him and kissed him. The present was great, but the best part about it was that not only did he get me, he liked me enough to want me to be me.

After we traded gifts, Nate told me there was a meteor shower happening. We took a couple blankets out and lay on the ground in my backyard. It was freezing, but we snuggled together, and there was nowhere else I wanted to be.

I saw a light streak across the sky, and I pointed, "Did you see it?"

"Make a wish," he said.

I closed my eyes, running through all the things I could wish for, but there was only one thing I really wanted. And I wasn't sure a wish would take care of that.

Nate pointed out the next one. "What are you going to wish for?" I asked.

"If I tell you, it won't come true."

I laughed. A dozen wishes streaked through the sky. I didn't really believe in wishing on a star, but it made me realize that I couldn't wait for this stalker thing to be over. I'd put my life on hold after Jerry and stopped wanting things, stopped believing in myself. It was time to figure out what I'd wish for and make it happen. As I was thinking about it, Nate sighed.

"I don't want to be a veterinarian," he said.

I had no idea what he was talking about at first, but then I remembered a conversation we had a long time ago when he'd told me he did. It didn't seem like a big deal to me, but his tone of voice said it was. "Why not?"

"I liked animals when I was a kid. I mean, I still like animals. But being a veterinarian is one of those things little kids want to be because they like dogs. I hate biology. I hated dissecting the frog."

"Okay." I wanted to encourage him to keep talking, but I still wasn't sure what we were really talking about. I squeezed his hand and waited.

"My mom got stuck on it. She loved the idea of me being a doctor, any kind of doctor." His voice got tight. "If I change my mind now, she'll never know."

"Would she want you to be something you didn't want to be?" I asked softly.

An owl hooted and a breeze rattled the trees. "That's not the point," he said. "When she was dying, she talked about it a lot. I couldn't tell her it wasn't what I wanted. If I don't do it, I'll lose one more connection to her." His voice cracked. "Like you. I wish she'd gotten to meet you. Even just once."

My heart ached for him, and I wanted to say something to make it better. But I didn't know what. There was nothing I could say to comfort him because he was right. Though it felt nice that he wished I could have met her. "Do you know what you want to do?"

"Not exactly. I'm interested in astrophysics, dark matter, that kind of thing."

"If you decide to do something with astrophysics or dark matter, you can't get closer to her than the stars." As I said it, as if agreeing with me, a particularly bright meteor flashed through the sky, leaving a trail of light in its wake.

"Do you think she would know somehow?" he asked.

I wasn't sure. I hadn't given much thought to religion or what I believed. But if I could believe that Jerry's jealousy and anger survived death, then why wouldn't love? "If there's any way to watch over you, I'm sure she is."

CHAPTER 51

Two days after Christmas, Ian texted and asked me to come over. I headed that way, thinking we'd play video games.

He'd left the door unlocked so I walked right in. I heard video game music, but otherwise the house was quiet, like the rest of his family was gone.

As soon as I stepped into the living room, I spotted Sandy sitting on the couch with a game controller in her hand. My muscles tensed and I considered turning around and leaving.

Sandy dropped her controller, looking shocked and betrayed. "What's she doing here?" She stood. She was wearing one of Jerry's T-shirts, and it dwarfed her. Between that and the lack of dark makeup, she looked so much younger than thirteen.

"You need to talk to each other," Ian said, his hands spread wide in a placating gesture. "You both have reasons to be mad, and that's fine. But this needs to stop."

"She might as well have killed my brother. I don't have anything to say to her." Sandy crossed her arms. Her voice cracked. "I hate her."

"Jerry was driving," Ian said. "You can't blame Charlotte for what happened."

"She didn't stop him! She didn't stop him from driving!"

I flinched. Even though I didn't believe it was my fault anymore, it still hurt to hear.

"Then it's my fault too." Ian ran a hand over his hair. "I knew he'd been drinking. I could have stopped him from drinking. I could have taken his keys."

"What?" Sandy went pale.

"But see, I'm not psychic. I didn't know that he was going to drive while he was drunk. And Charlotte didn't know how much he'd had to drink."

"It's not *your* fault," Sandy said. "It's hers. She thought she was too good for us."

Part of me wanted to walk out. But with her standing in front of me, looking so young and devastated, it was hard to believe she was the one stalking me.

"I never thought that," I said, cutting off whatever Ian was about to say. "And I tried to stop him from driving. But you know how stubborn he was. Do you think I could have stopped him from doing something if he really wanted to?"

"He would have listened to you. You just didn't try hard enough. If you really cared about him, you would've tried harder."

I couldn't tell her the truth of who her brother was to me. He was obviously someone different for her, and I didn't want to hurt her more than she already had been. But I could tell her enough. "I tried to make him listen, but our relationship wasn't great at the end. He was mad at me all the time and was hanging out with another girl. If there was something I could have done to save him, I would have."

"You lied to me! You spied on me!"

"I shouldn't have done that. I'm sorry." I picked at my nail polish. "I was scared. Someone's been stalking me, and I just wanted to find out who it was."

"I just . . . I want . . . I want my brother back!" Sandy burst into tears.

Ian grabbed her in a hug, and I went over to both of them and wrapped my arms around them.

She sobbed in our arms. When she was done, Ian went for the tissue box while I sat next to her on the couch. "You okay?" I asked.

"I guess," Sandy said. "Do you hate me?"

"No. I understand why you've been so mad. I would be too."

Ian handed the tissues to Sandy and then left the room again, probably to give us space.

"Jerry was the only person who ever cared about me," she said, wiping her nose.

"Ian cares about you." I wrapped my arms around her. "I do too. I've just been wrapped up in my own stuff."

Sandy hung on to me like she was drowning. After a minute, she pulled back to look at me. "Why did you think I was stalking you?"

"Because you were so mad at me. And my stalker blames me for Jerry's death."

"I didn't really want you to die," she mumbled.

"I'm sorry I suspected you." I finally understood why Ian hadn't been willing to consider her a suspect. Sandy was so mad, but she kept forgiving me when I messed up. She just wanted someone to love her, and no matter how much Ian cared about her, he'd never replace Jerry.

"Jerry took care of me. He never let Dad hit me. He always got between us or did something so Dad would pay attention to him and not me."

I remembered the bruises Jerry tried to hide from me. He never wanted to talk about it, even though I knew what was going on. Did Sandy have those terrible purple bruises now? "Does your dad hit you now that Jerry's gone?" I asked softly.

She shrugged. "He doesn't hit me in the face."

It was all the more horrifying that she said it in such a matter-of-fact tone. What kind of person was I, that I'd never thought about Sandy? I was so worried about the past and my stalker that I never even wondered whether she was in the line of fire now that her protector was gone.

"We have to report it," I said. "We have to tell someone about you getting hit. It's not okay."

Her eyes went wide. "No, I'm fine. It's okay."

Jerry had always said the same thing. But he clearly hadn't been fine. And I couldn't help but wonder who he would have turned into if some-one had helped him. No, I couldn't leave Sandy in a house where she was getting hit. Not now that I knew.

"Listen." I touched her arm. "Jerry protected you because he didn't want you hurt. Ian and I can't go in your house and stop your dad from hitting you. Telling someone is the only way for us to help you. I have this card from the detective who's looking for my stalker. We can call him. He'll know who to tell."

Tears shone in her eyes. "I don't want my dad to go to jail. He'll lose his job and it'll be my fault."

"No it won't," I said. "It's not your fault. Do you think Jerry would want you to keep getting hit?"

Sandy wiped her eyes. "He never wanted to tell anyone before."

"That's because he was afraid you'd be split up. I'm positive he'd want you to be safe."

She looked at her feet and then back to me. "I didn't tell you about the laptop because I knew he was messaging someone. I just wanted to protect him."

"It's okay," I said. "It doesn't matter."

"If you want, I can give it to the police when you call the detective to find out what to do."

I hugged her tight. I couldn't save Jerry, but I could help Sandy.

I vowed that I'd never again get so wrapped up in myself that I didn't help my friends.

CHAPTER 52

The next day, I called Detective Garcia and let him know about my conversation with Sandy. He helped me make a report to Child Protective Services and said he'd stop by for the laptop. But he didn't have any updates for me. They still had no idea who my stalker was.

I put the phone down on my desk and looked at it. All along, everyone had wanted me to call the police, but they still didn't know any more than I did.

I wrote everything down, trying to see if there was some clue I'd missed. There was nothing. But reading over Nate's notes from the séance, I wondered if Jerry could help us.

3:45 PM

Me

I was looking at Nate's
notes from the séance.
I think we asked Jerry
the wrong questions.

Me

We should have asked
if he knew who was breaking
in my room. That's where
he's hanging out, so
that's what he'd see.

Nate

Tell me you're not thinking
we should have another séance.

> Me
>
> I'm thinking we should
> have another séance.

Ian

Or we could let the
police handle it.

> Me
>
> They haven't made any
> progress. At least maybe
> Jerry can tell us something.

Ian

Remember that time we had a séance,
and Jerry started acting like an
asshole? What makes you think this
time will be different?

> Me
>
> He answered our questions, though.
> Let's just try it. My parents
> always go out on New Year's Eve,
> so we can do it then.

Ian

No, Charlotte, don't be silly!
Of course I didn't have plans!

                                        Me

                Whatever. You don't have to come.

Ian

Whatever. Like I'd let you
do it without me.

Nate

This is not what I had in mind
when I said I wanted to hang out
on New Year's Eve.

                                        Me

                Lori, what do you think?

Lori

We'll have our own little party.
Charlotte and I can make some
snacks. And if we start at like 7,
you can still go out afterward

Ian

Brownies?

```
Lori
Actually, I've been
craving a milkshake


                                    Me
                  I'll get ice cream from
                  Scoops. And Ian, I'll make
                  brownies for you. Okay?


Ian
Fine. I'll be there.
```

My parents wanted to break tradition and stay home on New Year's, but I convinced them to go out. I stayed at Lori's house, and we told Lori's mom we were going to a party. Lori and I got ready as if we were going somewhere fun.

Lori slipped a cute amethyst dress over her head. "Did the police get anything off the laptop?"

"Not that they told me," I said, buttoning my jade green top. I'd embellished it with some of the lace and flower beads Nate had gotten me.

"Have you heard from Sandy?"

"Yeah, we've been texting every day. She's in a foster home not too far away. She says it's weird but it doesn't suck."

Lori pulled out a mirror to put on her makeup. "Hey, can you go into my mom's medicine cabinet and get me some aspirin? I have a headache."

"Sure." I headed to her mom's bathroom and opened the cabinet. It was cluttered with prescription bottles, so it took me a minute to find the aspirin. I brought Lori two of them.

Lori borrowed her mom's car and drove to my house. She was quiet, like she was deep in thought.

"Last New Year's, if you'd asked me what I thought this year would be like, I wouldn't have guessed this."

Lori looked over at me like she was surprised I was there. After a moment, she grinned. "Me either. I thought my mom would murder us when she caught us sneaking back in." Lori and I had sneaked out to meet Jerry.

I smiled a little. "It was worth it, though. It was a great night." I was looking out the window, but I didn't see the view. I saw the three of us sprawled on a huge fleece blanket Jerry had brought. We were all bundled up in jackets and sweaters, and it was too overcast to see many stars last New Year's Eve. But we'd lain on our backs and talked quietly.

"When I'm a pilot," Jerry had said, "I'm going to go everywhere. See everything. The beautiful, the ugly, and everything in between. Nothing will tie me down."

"Not even Charlotte?" Lori had asked.

Jerry had put his arm around me. "She's going to be a flight attendant and go with me. Charlotte is my home."

My stomach sank. He'd been talking about being a pilot for years, but that was the first time he'd said that he expected me to be a flight attendant. I didn't know exactly what I wanted to do, but I was pretty sure it wasn't that.

"That sounds amazing!" Lori said. "I'd love to travel around the world. I was thinking maybe I'd like to be a physical therapist. Or teach gymnastics. After being a professional cheerleader for a few years, of course."

"Of course," Jerry had said, laughter in his voice.

No one had asked me what I wanted, what my dreams were. Jerry just assumed they lined up with his, since I'd always gone along with what he wanted.

Lori hit the turn signal, and it snapped me back to the present. She sighed. "That was the best night."

"I never wanted to be a flight attendant," I said.

Lori frowned. "You didn't?"

"Jerry never asked me what I wanted."

"I guess I always just assumed you wanted what he wanted," she said.

We got to my house, and Nate and Ian showed up just a few minutes later. "I'm starving!" Ian tore into the snacks.

"I know you just ate dinner," I said.

"My parents have this new thing where we all take turns cooking. To-night was Karen's turn." He wrinkled his nose. "I don't know how she manages to screw it up with my mom helping, but she does."

"I'll get started on the shakes," Lori said.

"Do you want help?" I asked.

Lori shook her head. "You guys go upstairs. I'll bring them up when they're ready."

We headed up to my room to set up the Ouija board on the floor. Ian took the chair at my desk, and Nate and I sat side by side on the floor next to my bed.

"You going somewhere after this tonight, Ian?" Nate asked.

"Nope." Ian shrugged. "This time next year, I'm going to be partying with college girls. But this year, I'm hanging out with my favorite people."

"Last year, I was watching *The Philadelphia Story* with my parents." Nate was looking at my wall, as if he could see the scene from last year.

"Megan had fallen asleep on the floor. It's not even a New Year's Eve movie or anything, but we knew my mom was sick, and it was her favorite movie, so we watched it."

I squeezed Nate's hand.

My phone pinged. Lori texted me to come down and help her carry the shakes.

When I got downstairs, she was wiping off the counter and biting her lip. She'd been happier lately, but tonight, she seemed stressed again. "You okay?"

She jumped, like she'd been deep in thought. "I'm fine." She toyed with the necklace JD had given her and sighed.

"Are you sure?" I asked, searching her face.

She took a deep breath, then forced herself to smile. "Yeah, don't worry about me. Here." She handed me two shakes. "These are for the guys."

"Okay." I took them from her and started to walk away, but I stopped. "You know I'm here for you, right?"

She blinked a few times, then looked away from me. "I know."

I walked upstairs and Lori followed. I handed the shakes off to Nate and Ian.

"Finally!" Ian said. He took a long drink of his shake.

I took my shake from Lori, then settled on the floor next to Nate and took a sip. It was chocolatey and good. I took a second sip and thought there was a slightly bitter aftertaste. I frowned. Was the ice cream freezer burned? I tried it again, and it tasted fine.

Lori sat on the other side of the Ouija board, nearest to the door. She'd been excited about the last séance, but this time she didn't seem to care.

"So, does anyone have any resolutions?" Nate asked, putting down his half-empty shake.

"I just want to enjoy every moment," Ian said. "I know Jerry didn't turn out to be . . . I mean he . . ." Ian paused. He looked unsure, and he never looked unsure. "I guess I'm just saying that I want to make sure I appreciate my life, my family, my friends." He looked at me and half smiled.

"Yeah." Nate nodded. "I think I should spend more time with Megan. Like maybe take her to the zoo or skating or whatever."

I took a deep breath. "I want to alter shirts and sell them online. The kind I make for myself, but also maybe I can get commissions for customized ones."

"That's a great idea," Nate said.

"You should make business cards and give them to all of us to hand out," Ian said.

I laughed and waved my hands. "Slow down. I haven't even made any shirts yet." But I felt warm all over.

We turned to Lori when she didn't say anything. "Any resolutions?" I asked.

"I guess it's not my thing." She shrugged. "We should get started."

I finished my milkshake and set the glass on my nightstand. "I'm ready."

Nate lit candles while Lori and I sat together on the floor so our knees touched. The board was balanced on our laps.

"Jerry, are you there?" Lori asked, her voice quiet.

Like last time, we sat and waited in silence. Candle flames popped. Fabric rustled as someone shifted.

"Come on, Jerry, we don't have all night!" I said. I wanted to start so we could be done. If we asked the right questions, we might actually get answers about who my stalker was. It could be over soon.

Lori scowled at me, but didn't tell me not to talk.

The temperature started dropping. On the Ouija board, the planchette went in a single circle, then stopped.

"Who's there?" Lori asked.

J-E-R-R-Y

Lori looked up and half smiled. "Hi, Jerry," she said softly.

L-I-A-R

I rolled my eyes.

Ian yawned. "Great. This again."

The planchette moved to NO.

"Jerry, did you know someone has been stalking Charlotte?" Lori asked.

YES

"Do you—" she began.

Nate cut Lori off. "Something's wrong."

I turned to look at him, and my vision blurred. I blinked a few times to get him back into focus. He was pale and breathing hard.

"I don't feel well," he mumbled.

I stayed sitting but shuffled toward him. I put my hand to my head, like that would make the room stop moving. "What's wrong?"

He shook his head but didn't answer. His eyes drooped.

"Nate?" I touched his face. He slumped forward. "Nate!"

He opened his eyes and looked at me. He blinked, like he was having a hard time focusing. He mumbled something I didn't understand.

My eyes felt heavy, but I forced them to stay open. What was wrong with me? What was wrong with Nate?

I twisted to look at Ian, and as I watched, he fell forward out of my desk chair and lay sprawled on the floor. "Someone call 911!" My heart raced. I tried to crawl over to Ian but it felt like I was moving underwater. My stalker had poisoned us. I didn't know how, but somehow they'd done it.

I turned to Lori. She was watching me with a solemn expression, the Ouija board still balanced on her knees. On the board, the planchette was moving wildly around the surface.

"Are you okay?" I asked, my voice thick.

"I haven't been okay for a long time," she said.

Her response didn't make sense. I frowned.

"I think my stalker poisoned us," I said. My voice didn't sound right, but I was pretty sure my words made sense. "Call 911."

Lori didn't move.

I fumbled my phone out of my pocket. My fingers felt clumsy and I had to concentrate to hold it steady while I unlocked it.

Lori set the Ouija board aside carefully. The planchette kept moving to NO, then circling the board again. It was like I was hypnotized by it, because for several seconds, I forgot that I was trying to make a call and just watched it keep going back to NO.

"You still haven't figured it out, have you?" Lori stayed sitting, but shifted closer to me.

Some warning was blaring in my head but I couldn't make sense of it. "Figured out what?" I spotted Ian sprawled on the floor. He'd fallen. I'd forgotten that. My head felt so weird. "We have to help Ian."

Lori sat cross-legged, facing me. My vision swam in and out. "Technically, I didn't poison them," she said casually. "I drugged them. But maybe that doesn't matter to you because they're still going to die."

Adrenaline shot through my system and cleared some of the fog out of my brain, but I couldn't make sense of what she said. I tried to think of a way to make it not true, but my thoughts were spinning and there was only one conclusion I could come to. "You're my stalker." I had to force the words out and they hurt my throat. "JD was Jerry. Jerry Dean."

Lori did a slow clap and said, "Well, you're not a complete idiot, after all."

"But . . . why? Why would you want to hurt us? What's wrong with you?"

Her expression went thunderous. "What's wrong with me? What's wrong with you? You have ruined everything good in my life."

"What are you talking about?"

"You took everything from me. Cheering, then Jerry. He should have been mine, but now he's dead. You killed him!" She jabbed her finger at me.

I put my hands against the sides of my head, trying to make the spinning stop. "He killed himself!"

"Because you made him!"

"No I didn't! I tried to . . . I . . ." My brain felt mushy and I couldn't remember what I was saying.

"You took him from me and you broke his heart."

On my end table, the milkshake glass rattled, then moved an inch, toward the edge of the table.

Lori grabbed my arms and shook me. "Admit it!"

I tried to push her away, but she was too strong. "Admit what?"

She put her face close to mine. "Admit that it's all your fault. Everything. That you killed Jerry. That you ruined my life."

My mind raced. She'd drugged us. I didn't know how long we had before we died, but I had to figure a way out.

Lori liked drama. She loved to be the center of attention. If I could get her talking, maybe I'd be able to get us out of this.

But time was not our friend. I didn't know how sick we were. Or how long I had until I passed out too.

"You told him I was cheating on him, didn't you?" I asked. Like it even mattered anymore.

Lori nodded. "If you'd made him happy, I would have let him go. But you didn't."

"No one could make him happy." I shook my head slowly.

Lori shoved me, and I fell backward, against the edge of my bed.

"You never understood him," she said. "I was the only one he could trust. I understood what he was going through."

"You lied to him," I said, blinking to clear the blurriness from my eyes.

Tears streamed down Lori's cheeks but she didn't brush them away. "I thought, once he realized we belonged together, he'd break up with you."

"He was never going to let me go." I looked past her, to the Ouija board. "But it wasn't love. It was . . ." I paused, eyeing her before I said the word. "Obsession."

Lori grabbed my arm, and her fingers dug into my bicep, but I barely felt it. "You don't know what love is. If you did, you would have died with Jerry. He's all alone. Being alone is . . ." Her voice cracked. "Unbearable."

I fought the fog in my head. "Lots of people hurt, Lori. But you know what they don't do? They don't kill their friends!"

She slammed her fist on the floor, and I jumped. "You don't know anything!"

Nate groaned. He was slumped forward. I grabbed his hand. "Nate? Wake up. Please." I'd dropped my phone. I picked it up, but my fingers were uncooperative. If I could just dial 911, they could trace the call.

Lori watched me fumble with the phone for a moment, then snatched it out of my hands. "Can't let you call anyone until after they're dead."

Until *they're* dead. "I'm not dying?"

"Nope." Lori smiled. "Just them. Look at them." She shoved at Ian with her foot. "They're already halfway gone. And you . . . you get to watch."

Panic burst through me. She meant for them to die with me right here with them but not able to do anything. "You don't have to do this. Let me call someone. Please."

"You killed the person I loved, so I'm killing the people you love."

"Lori, please. I'm sorry for everything. You're right, it's all my fault. Just please, don't do this!"

Lori patted my cheek. "It's done. I already did it. Now the only thing that's left is for me to take my drugs so I can be with Jerry." She reached in her pocket and showed me a handful of pills.

I blinked rapidly. "You're going to kill yourself?"

"I thought about killing you." She grabbed my hair roughly, making me meet her eyes. It should have hurt, but it didn't. I tried to shove her hand away, but I was so weak that she didn't even react. "Because it's what Jerry wanted. But you don't appreciate him. You don't love him. He deserves better. He said he regretted prom night. He was trying to tell me he regretted breaking up with me. He saw that I'm the one who's always loved him. Now we can be together. Forever."

The room was freezing. I glanced over at the Ouija board and saw that the planchette was still circling rapidly. As I looked to the board, the planchette went to NO. I didn't know if Jerry was saying no to me or to Lori.

I didn't know if this would work, but in the past couple of months, I'd realized that Jerry had hated himself more than he ever hated me. What I was about to do was a gamble, but I didn't have a lot of choices.

"Jerry, do you want Lori to kill Nate and Ian and herself?"

Lori froze, then turned slowly toward the Ouija board.

The planchette circled the board and moved to NO.

"Do you want Lori to be with you forever?"

NO

For a second, I thought I'd gotten through to her. But then Lori's face contorted with rage. She twisted, grabbed the Ouija board, and threw it against the wall.

While her back was turned, I lunged for the phone. I'd hit 9 when Lori seized the phone from my hand and threw it across the room.

She slapped me, once, twice, three times.

I fell, banging my head against the floor. My stomach lurched. "Do something, Jerry! Help me! You *owe* me!"

Lori looked frozen, staring at me.

Neither of us moved.

But nothing happened.

Lori laughed. "Just give up. When you wake up, it'll all be over."

The adrenaline was wearing off and I tried to get it back, but waves of sleepiness sucked me under.

Tears trickled out beneath my closed eyelids. I'd failed. I'd failed us all.

I didn't know how long I was unconscious, but I woke to freezing pressure on my arm as someone shook me. The pressure hurt, and it cleared some of the fuzziness out of my head. I looked at who was gripping me. It was Jerry. My vision was blurry, and I couldn't see my bedroom well, but he was sharp and clear. His lips moved like he was yelling, but I didn't hear a sound. Then I understood what he was trying to say. *Wake up!*

I held on to the bed to steady myself as I got to my knees. I tried to push myself up to stand, but the room rolled, and I collapsed. Nate and Ian were still lying where they'd been.

Lori was slumped on the floor, blocking my bedroom door.

I checked my pockets, looking for my phone, but then I remembered Lori had thrown it. It wasn't where it had landed.

Nate was sprawled beside me. On my hands and knees, I crawled closer to him. When I lifted my hand to check his pockets for a phone, I toppled over, slumping half on top of him. With a trembling hand, I pressed my fingers to his neck, and after several seconds, found a pulse. It was too slow, but it was there. I checked his pockets. No phone.

I crawled to Ian. He also had a slow pulse, but no phone. Lori had taken them. She could have put them anywhere.

I didn't know where to look, or how much time Ian and Nate had left. I had to get to the neighbor's house, have them call 911.

I crawled to my bedroom door and shoved Lori out of the way. She was heavy, deadweight, and I was sweaty and breathless by the time I'd moved her enough to squeeze out.

The hallway seemed longer than I remembered, and sleepiness dragged at me. But then Jerry appeared beside me and grabbed my arm. It jolted me awake.

I crawled toward the steps, but the hallway seemed distorted. It seemed to grow and shrink. Staying upright, even crawling, was a struggle. Jerry had disappeared.

Halfway to the stairs, I remembered the alarm and the panic button.

I stopped and almost collapsed. I leaned against the wall for just a moment, then turned around and crawled back toward the alarm. It was far above my head. I'd have to stand.

I got to my knees and swayed. Then Jerry appeared in front of me. He put his hands out for me to grip. I looked at him for a moment, but then put my hands in his. He was solid and cold, but didn't have enough strength to pull me up. I used his hands for balance and struggled to my feet. The world spun and my vision wavered. Inch by inch, I forced myself upward. And then I was standing.

The alarm panel was closed. It took me three tries to slide it open, and there was the button. The beautiful panic button.

I pressed it. Nothing happened.

Then the button pulsed red.

I slumped against the wall and looked at Jerry. "This doesn't make us even."

He nodded. And then he started fading, becoming harder to see. He reached a hand toward me like he was going to touch my face, but then stopped, dropped his hand, and stepped back.

I blinked, and he was gone.

My knees went out from under me. I sank to the ground and everything went dark.

NEW YEAR'S EVE . . .
ONE YEAR LATER

CHAPTER 53

Mom straightened the stack of paper plates and fiddled with the napkins. "You're sure you're going to be okay?"

"I'll be fine! You'll be literally two houses down. And anyway, no one's tried to kill me for a year now."

Nate barked out a laugh, but my mom frowned. She didn't find it funny when Nate and I joked about stalkers and poison, but we both used humor to cope.

"She'll be fine," Dad echoed. When my mom's back was turned, he winked.

It took us another few minutes, but we eventually got them to leave and head down to the Williamsons'. Mom had wanted to break her tradition and stay home with me on New Year's Eve, but I wanted to celebrate with friends. After lots of negotiating, she and Dad were celebrating with Ian's family, and I was having a party. "Text me every hour to check in," Mom said on her way out the door.

"Alone at last." Nate turned to me, his eyes sparkling as he leaned in to kiss me. "You look amazing." I was wearing a strapless sage-colored dress with appliqued violet flowers. I'd just finished it earlier in the day.

"So do you." He was wearing a royal-purple T-shirt with jeans. I put my arms around him. He was still too skinny from the weight he'd lost early in the year, but he was finally starting to recover it. His hair was a little too long, and I brushed it away from his glasses.

A few minutes later, Ian and Sandy showed up. She came in and then twirled around in her dress so Nate could see it. It was black and teal, vintage inspired.

"You look great," he said, giving her a hug. "Is that the one you guys made?"

"She made it. I barely had to help her with this one," I said, nudging Sandy's arm.

She laughed.

After Sandy was removed by Child Protective Services, she'd spent a month in foster care before Ian's parents qualified for kinship care so Sandy could live with them.

Sandy didn't wear that dark makeup anymore, just a little lip gloss so her lips were pink and shiny. She'd gotten cute glasses that didn't hide half her face. She didn't look like the same girl from a year ago.

After Ian and Sandy arrived, people started streaming in. Nate's friends Bill and Kevin along with their girlfriends. My friend Danny and his boyfriend, Dylan. Tammy, a girl who'd started working at Scoops a few months ago.

Brittany showed up alone an hour before midnight. I smiled when I answered the door.

"It's good to see you," I said. "I didn't think you'd come."

Brittany shrugged. "I figured why not." She smoothed her skirt.

"Come in," I said, leading her to the kitchen. "We have pizza and snacks."

Brittany had apologized to Ian for hitting him and had apparently gone to counseling. She was alone, and I'd never seen her without a boyfriend before. She picked up a bottle of water and fiddled with the lid. Music blared from a portable speaker hooked up to my phone.

Brittany leaned against the counter. "Caleb texted me and said you invited him."

I nodded. "I would have liked to see him."

"He appreciated it," she said. "But he's not up to parties yet."

"I just wanted to make sure he knew he was welcome."

Silence hung between us, but it was a good silence, like something had shifted. Then Brittany flashed me a tiny smile, like she felt it too, and she walked off to dance with Danny and Dylan.

Ian came over and grabbed a handful of chips. "Tammy's pretty cute."

"Already hit on all the girls at college?"

"Nah, I'm working my way through the freshmen before I start on the upperclassmen."

I shook my head and smiled. "It's weird knowing you're not just down the street anymore."

"Yeah, well, I feel like my life has been pretty weird for the last couple years." His smile faded, and I knew he was thinking of Jerry.

"I miss him too," I said.

Ian frowned. "You miss him? I don't."

"Ian . . ." I sighed.

"Why do you think he did it?" Ian asked. "I can't figure out why he came back and helped us."

"Maybe he was trying to apologize. Or trying to make up for what he did."

Ian cut me off. "He can't."

"Obviously." I touched my scar. "He abused me. He tried to *kill* me. Nothing could make up for that. Even if he was trying to make amends, that doesn't mean I have to accept it. I'm grateful for his help.

I'm grateful we aren't dead. But that doesn't mean we're even."

"You sound like a therapist," Ian said, shaking his head.

I shrugged. "I've been in therapy for like a year and a half. It was bound to rub off."

"I'd hate to think you were making excuses for him."

I shook my head. "Never again. I did that for way too long. But understanding doesn't mean excusing. And I just . . . don't want to be mad at him anymore."

Ian's jaw got tight. "It sounds like you're letting him off the hook."

"No, what he did was his fault. If he were alive, I wouldn't want him anywhere near me. But I wouldn't want anything bad to happen to him either. If I could get him help, I would."

"Help." Ian huffed out a breath. "He knew what he was doing."

"Maybe," I said. "But I think he was always really angry and didn't know how to handle it. We know his dad hit him, and he took beatings for Sandy. That doesn't sound like someone who's a villain. Maybe if he'd gotten help, he . . ."

Ian shook his head. "You can't go there. You can't make excuses for him. Lots of people are abused and don't hurt other people."

"Yeah, and some do. I'm not saying it was right. I'm just saying he was a complicated person and maybe, if he'd gotten help, he wouldn't have turned out the way he did. If he'd lived, maybe he could have changed. That's all."

"I still think he deserved to be punished."

I didn't think Ian and I would ever agree. One of the best things about him was his sense of right and wrong. But it was too rigid and didn't fit me.

"I'm not saying he didn't deserve punishment. I'm not absolving him. But I don't want to be angry anymore. I want to be completely free of him, and for me, that means letting go. Of him, of my anger. It happened, and I can't change it. I just want to move on with my life. I'm not telling you what to do. Gemma's helping me figure out what's right for me."

"I wish you'd asked someone for help," Ian said.

I shook my head. "It's like being trapped in a dark room, and you know there's a door somewhere, but you have no idea where it might be. I didn't know where to start." We were both silent a moment. "Well, if I ever meet another guy like Jerry, I'll run like hell in the other direction."

Ian chuckled. "I don't think that's going to be an issue for a while." Ian looked toward Nate, who said something that made Sandy laugh.

I smiled. "Nate is the best."

Ian took my hand and squeezed it. "Sometimes something reminds me of Jerry and I forget that I hate him."

"You don't have to hate him if you don't want to," I said. "He was a lot of things. He really was a good friend, especially to you, and I won't be mad if you remember that."

"Some days I'm so pissed off that I could put my hand through the wall," Ian said. "At Jerry, Lori, everything."

Thinking about Lori made my stomach hurt. I loved her and hated her and felt sad about where she'd ended up. On nights like tonight, I missed her so much that my chest ached. But it was okay to feel all those things. "She's not doing well," I said. "She—"

"I don't care," Ian said. "I hope she rots in jail."

I made a face at him.

"What?" Ian asked. "Being angry with her and Jerry suits me just fine."

"I am angry with them. But I also miss them. I have a lot of feelings. It's a process."

Ian grabbed a soda. "I can't drink milkshakes. And sometimes if I see a girl with long brown hair like hers, for a second, it all rushes back to me."

"Nate and I were both making progress for a while," I said. "But I don't know. Maybe it's the anniversary, but we're back to not drinking anything someone else poured." I gestured to the drinks. "That's why everything's in a sealed container."

Ian frowned. "I'm glad he's at least eating again." For the first couple months of the year, Nate didn't eat much of anything. It still hurt me to remember how skinny and hollow-cheeked he'd gotten. I didn't want anything bad to happen to Lori, but there were some things I didn't think I'd ever be able to let go of.

Ian put an arm around me. "It's never really over, is it?"

"No, not really. But that's what life is, right? All the good and bad stuff that happens to us. It's up to us what we get out of it."

Ian pulled back and looked at me. "When did you get all philosophical?"

I shrugged. "I figured out what I want to major in. I want to be a social worker so I can help other people who've been abused." It never should have happened to me, just like it shouldn't happen to anyone. But it did, and since I knew what it felt like to be *that* girl, I could help others who'd been her too.

Nate and Sandy approached us. Sandy's face was flushed from dancing, but she was smiling. She grabbed a soda and guzzled some. "What are you guys talking about?"

Ian and I traded a look. "The last year," I said. "How different everything is."

Nate leaned next to me and put his head on my shoulder.

"Did you guys make any resolutions?" Sandy asked.

"I think I just want to take things as they come," I said.

"Just keep spending time with the people I love." Nate looked at me meaningfully. "And tell them as much as possible."

Sandy cocked her head. "That's so sweet! I think . . . I want to try out for the play," she said shyly, like she thought we'd make fun of her.

"That's great," I said.

"She's been practicing singing," Ian said.

"Ian!" Sandy's tone was annoyed, like she hadn't wanted anyone to know.

"What?" he asked. "You have a good voice."

"I resolve to finish my college applications," Nate said.

"I should start those," I said.

Nate's and my song came on, and Nate grinned. He took my hand and pulled me out into the living room, where other couples were dancing.

The road's been long, the journey hard.

I put my arms around him and we swayed.

But we didn't give up, even though we're scarred.

"This party is way better than the one you threw last year," he said.

"Well, so far," I said. "There's still time for someone to try to kill us."

There've been hazards behind, but more ahead.

Troubles aren't over, but we're not dead.

"Poison is so last year, though," Nate said.

"Agreed. I'm thinking a guillotine is the way to go."

"How are you doing tonight?" Nate asked. "Seriously."

"Seriously?" I repeated, and took a moment to breathe. "I'm great tonight. I'm surrounded by my favorite people and having a good time. Tomorrow, though? Who knows, right?"

"We just take it day by day," Nate said.

"Or hour by hour," I added.

"Or minute by minute." Nate leaned down to kiss me. "But yeah, tonight is great."

It was a year since Lori poisoned us, over a year and a half since Jerry died, and my life was different in ways I couldn't have imagined.

There were things I couldn't control. I still flinched sometimes when someone moved too quickly near me, and "You Were Made for Me" still made my heart pound. I had nightmares and sometimes couldn't sleep.

But when I woke up from nightmares and needed someone, I texted Nate or Ian. Gemma was helping me get better. If I was alone these days, it was because I wanted to be.

I bought clothes from the thrift store and remade ugly, flawed clothes into things that fit me perfectly. I'd do the same with all the experiences that made up my life. And if it didn't work out the first time, I'd just rip out the stitches and try again.

"It's almost midnight!" Ian shouted. He and Sandy passed out silly hats and glasses.

Nate grabbed a tiara and I took green oversize glasses.

I grabbed my phone and took video of the room as everyone counted down.

"Happy New Year!"

We popped mini confetti cannons and cheered. Nate and I kissed for luck in the New Year.

"Did you know more people die from flying champagne corks than bites from venomous spiders?" Nate asked quietly.

I grabbed a bottle of the sparkling cider I'd set out for toasting. "So I should add champagne to my list of beverages that want to kill me?"

"What wants to kill you?" Ian asked, coming up to us and kissing me on the cheek.

"Absolutely nothing," I said, grabbing the two of them in a hug.

AUTHOR'S NOTE

Abuse is always wrong. Full stop.

If you're in an abusive relationship, there are resources to help you. I know it isn't easy, but you will never heal while you're trapped in one. And if you're staying because you want to help your abuser, you can't do that while they're hurting you. You need to get out of the relationship, especially if you're living with them.

Like many victims, Charlotte stayed because she wanted to help Jerry. She thought that if she loved him enough and tried to be the person he wanted, he would stop hurting her. But it doesn't work that way. People who abuse others need professional help. Everyone deserves to feel worthy of love, but love alone can't heal the wounds that allow people to harm others.

Many abusers apologize and say they want to change, but that's part of the cycle of violence. It's a predictable pattern of behavior. Anyone can say they're sorry and want to change. What matters is what they do. If you really want to help an abuser, help yourself first. When you're in an unhealthy place, you can't help someone else. Even if we understand the reasons someone abuses, even if the reasons are heartbreaking and real, no one is helped by staying in an abusive relationship. The victim is in great danger, and the abuser won't change.

Some people will tell you anger is a "negative" or "bad" emotion, but I don't believe that. Anger can be useful. It can be protective. Anger is a problem when it's used as a weapon. But when it's a shield or a tool, it can be positive and energizing. It's when you feel angry all the time that it might be a problem.

Some people will tell you that you can't move on unless you forgive. Forgiveness is great. It can have health benefits and a positive impact on emotional well-being. But it isn't the only way to heal.

We are all different people, made up of different life experiences. We have different levels of support and different coping skills. There is no one-size-fits-all pattern for how to heal from trauma. The important thing is that you get out, protect yourself and get healthy, and that you don't harm others during your process.

There were a lot of reasons I wrote this book. There are many wonderful books out there about mental health. But the best ones are usually about the recovery and treatment process. The problem is that most people struggling with anxiety or depression or trauma don't just pause their lives and get treatment. They have to continue to live and work, to go to school and deal with dysfunctional families. I wanted to write a book about that.

If you're the victim of abuse, or you know someone who's being abused, please talk to someone about it. You can start with an adult, like a teacher or a guidance counselor. But I want to be honest with you; sometimes even the people who are supposed to listen, don't. If that happens to you, don't keep secrets and think that your voice shouldn't be heard. Never keep a secret that makes you feel bad inside. Keep talking about it until someone listens.

Demand what you need.

You're worth it.

RESOURCES

National Domestic Violence Hotline
   TheHotline.org
   1-800-799-SAFE (7233)
   Text START to 88788

The Trevor Project
   TheTrevorProject.org/Get-Help
   1-866-488-7386
   Text START to 678-678

Teen Line
   TeenLine.org
   1-800-852-8336
   Text TEEN to 839863

988 Suicide & Crisis Lifeline
   988Lifeline.org
   988 or 1-800-273-8255 (Call or text)

National Child Abuse Hotline
   ChildHelp.org/hotline
   1-800-4-A-CHILD (1-800-422-4453) (Call or text)